Unbearable

Book Three of the Port Fare Series

Sherry Gammon

Praises for the Port Fare Series:

~ *Unbearable* ~

I've been a fan of all of Sherry's writing. She knows how to tug the heartstrings. Every one of her books has affected me emotionally. I didn't think she could get me any more than she did with Not So Easy . . . but then came *Unbearable*. I promise, this is one book you won't want to miss ~ Cindy C Bennett, author of *The End of Feeling*

A heart-wrenching tale of fear, friendship, and breaking down walls. Once again, the whole crew unites as Gammon seamlessly combines action and romance, tension and angst, love and loathing. A well-written, touching conclusion to one of my all-time favorite series ~ Jamie Canosa, Author of *Falling to Pieces*

Unbearable has the perfect mix of romance, suspense, intrigue, and drama. The story is both heartbreaking and inspiring as Booker and Tess fight to be free of the past and find happiness. I laughed. I cried. I cheered. I would highly recommend the entire Port Fare series ~ Cami Checketts, author of *Fourth of July*

Gammon doesn't disappoint with swoon-worthy Booker in this finale. Unbearable is a romance that will have you crying, cheering, and falling in love with your Port Fare friends all over again ~Juli Caldwell, author of *Arms Wide Open*

While reading the Port Fare series, you can feel your heartbeat racing, excitement building with the suspense of each story, never truly knowing where Sherry Gammon is going but highly anticipating her next moves ~ Keelie of Kiki Reads Hear

~ Unbelievable ~

For 24 hours my life consisted of nothing but this book. The twists and surprises kept me on the edge of my seat with this one ~ Erin of Wrathqueens Books

Just when you think the series can't get any better...it does!!! I totally loved the story of Lilah and Cole...Not to mention catching up with the rest of the gang...The way these books are written really draw you in and keep you there till the end -in my case 4am in the morning ~ KiwiBooknerd of Goodreads

~ Unlovable ~

It's next to impossible to find the words to express what a phenomenal book this was. It was so beautifully written. The author was able to realistically portray a story of abuse, love, co-dependency, romance, and triumph in a way that is far beyond most books I've read ~ Mollie of Tough Critic Book Reviews

Real, raw, undeniable emotions run through the pages of this amazing book. It's an eye opener and while writing this review, with a heart doubled in size, I'm experiencing a whirlwind of emotions just by reminiscing what I've read. If you aren't touched by this novel at all, you are definitely a rock. Really, I want to give a virtual standing ovation to Sherry Gammon for this novel that I cannot express into words how much I loved it ~ Giselle of Xpressoreads

DEDICATION

This book is dedicated to:

Booker Fans Everywhere
Thank you for your patience

CHAPTER 1
BOOKER

"Pink, Lilah?" I snatched the silky dress from her hands, my shoulders drooping and mouth pinched tight. "You know green's my favorite color"

"Sorry, Crookshanks." Lilah smiled sweetly. Since becoming part of our makeshift family, she too adopted the cat jokes that Seth's wife Maggie—or Magpie as I called her—loved so well. Why they couldn't just call me Booker like everyone else amused me more than it should. "The thrift store was all out of green chiffon. You're stuck with pink." She waved and shut the bathroom door.

I fisted the bright, 1980's looking prom dress in my hand and groaned. "Okay, buddy. Man up and put on the dress." I glanced into the oval mirror above the sink, and pointed at my reflection. "You made the deal. Now it's time to pay."

Lilah had exploded on Port Fare in June to avenge her brothers' deaths. Her three *drug dealing* brothers. Her sicko father tricked her into thinking my best friend Seth and I were responsible. Of course, technically we were. At the time, Seth and I were undercover agents for the MET, the Mobile Enforcement Team, a division of the DEA, and the Dreser brothers were part of our caseload.

I *knew* Lilah was in on her father's plan to kill all of us, despite her insistence that she was merely an innocent pawn in the scheme. After I did my best to make her life miserable, she struck a deal with me that if she were telling the truth, I'd have to apologize to our group of friends, and hand wax her car . . . in a dress.

Well, not only was I wrong, she went and married my good friend Cole. Now I stood in their bathroom, cowering at the sight of the gaudy dress in my hand, about to keep my word. I always kept my word.

I stripped off my t-shirt and jeans, setting them on the counter as I wrangled my way into the dress's many layers. The thing hung on me like a tent. I tugged the tag from the collar forward and glanced at the size.

"3X. Really?" I yelled through the door. Both Lilah and Magpie laughed.

I turned back to the mirror, running my fingers through my dark brown hair, smoothing it back into place. I was right, the color washed out my face. And the fact I even recognized that was disturbing on so many levels.

Fingering the skinny shoulder straps, I thought about Maggie and Seth in their bulky sweaters, and Cole and Lilah wrapped in thick wool jackets. "I'm gonna freeze." Only mid-October and the temperature had already dipped into the thirties. Welcome to Upstate New York.

I had no one to blame but myself for the rotten timing. If I hadn't been so busy setting up my law practice, I'd have waxed the car sooner, but today was the first Saturday I had any free time since quitting the MET. I also had some healing to do after the run-in with Lilah's father's hitman this past summer. I touched my still somewhat tender nose. Thankfully, with my law practice I'd have no more violent encounters to deal with. I could now live a quiet, peaceful life.

At least the skinny shoulder straps showcased my biceps. I flexed in the mirror. I'd like to say my devotion to the gym did that . . . but sadly, it was more my lackluster love life. What else was I supposed to do with my spare time?

"Enough with the pity party, Gatto. You chose to live a monk-like existence." However, working side by side with Tess Bennett, setting up my office for the past two months, had weakened my resolve to abstain from the fairer sex.

She used to work in the hospital's ER department until Cole asked me to find her a job after she fainted on a patient covered in blood. The girl didn't do blood, at all. I needed a secretary, and with his assurance that she was good, I hired her. Smart move. Tess knew how to work, putting in countless hours of overtime helping me setup and organizing my filing system. One on one, Tess was much more open, and she actually spoke, something she rarely did when she worked at the hospital. It took a couple of weeks, but eventually she smiled directly at me, instead of at the ground like she'd done for the past four years since I'd met her. "She has a great smile," I murmured, turning sideways to the mirror.

Whoever wore the dress before me had an impressive bust line. I bounced the excess material, grinning as an idea hit me. If I had to eat crow, I might as well have some fun with it. I grabbed my t-shirt before jamming my feet into the hideous bedazzled sandals Lilah set out for me. Thankfully, they weren't high heels.

Waves of laughter and wolf whistles filled the living room as I entered. Seth stepped over and poked my voluptuous bust line. "Did you get a boob job, too?" He peeked down my dress. "What's in there?"

"My t-shirt," I beamed, slapping his hand away. "I was going to add my jeans, but didn't want to look too Dolly Parton-ish."

"Hey, Booker!" A flash of light greeted me as I turned to Lilah.

"I better not see that on Instagram," I warned, pointing at her camera and blinking out the spots in my eyes. I cleared my throat. Time to pay the piper. "I believe part of the deal was that I had to apologize in front of everyone."

"No, you don't have to. I understand." Lilah waved both hands, her curly brown hair bouncing as she shook her head.

"I made a promise, and I always keep my promises." I took her hand in mine, bowed dramatically, and kissed it. "I apologize for being a complete a . . . a . . ." I turned to Magpie and grinned. "A complete pain in the rear-end."

I'd asked Mags to help me curb my swearing. She taped a label to an old jar that read *Curse Jar*, and cut a slot in the lid.

Whenever I slipped up, I had to add a quarter to the jar. It sat on my desk at work. Most times it had several quarters in it. I was truly a work in progress.

I squared my shoulders. "In all seriousness, I do apologize, Lilah."

She wrapped her arms around me. "Thank you for caring so much about Ducky," she said softly. It was her new nickname for Cole since she learned his given name was Duckworth Grimshad at their wedding a couple of months ago. Poor guy.

"Okay, enough sloppy emotions. Time to freeze my buns off and wax this orange VW bug of yours." I turned for the door.

"Now, Booker. Do you honestly think I'd allow you to freeze in those spaghetti straps?" Seth failed to hide his smirk. *Oh, no. Now what?* "I got you a coat." Seth reached into a brown bag and pulled out a hideous, fluffy white coat.

"He picked it out all by himself." Magpie beamed as I slipped it on. It fell to just below my artificial bust line. "It's a crop jacket," she explained as I tugged on the bottom.

"Thanks, *bro*." I sneered at Seth. "However, I don't feel comfortable wearing dead animal skin." I started to remove the coat when Seth stopped me.

"Booker, Booker." He shook his head. "You know me better than that. This is fake fur." Maggie and Lilah laughed. Cole had the decency to pinch his lips together to hide his grin.

"Where's Sofia?" I asked, looking around. Lilah learned only two months ago that the child she thought dead was in fact alive. Sofia was the spitting image of her mother, down to her audacious personality.

"She's napping," Lilah assured me.

"Good." The last thing I wanted was for her to see me dressed like a woman. She'd won my heart from the start and I didn't want to disillusion her. She thought I walked on water and I enjoyed having one female on the planet that believed the façade.

I headed out the door, my entourage in tow. I tromped over to Lilah's car after she handed me a green can of car wax and a yellow shammy. A nasty north wind shot up my dress, nipping at my assets . . . *Man, never thought I'd say something like that, not even in my head.*

"We can wait 'til spring, Book," Lilah said. "In fact, let's call it good now."

"No way. A deal's a deal." As a second rush of icy air shot up my dress, I rubbed a scoop of wax on the fender. "This is just wrong," I grumbled to myself, shoving the dress back down over my legs. How did women do this?

"How the man-parts doing?" Seth chuckled. My glare only added fuel to his amusement.

"You should've shaved your legs." Cole grimaced dramatically.

"You don't care for the European look?" I tugged the chiffon up a few inches.

"European is one thing. That's more like the woolly mammoth look." Cole, a walking accident if there ever was one, pressed at a loose bandage on his wrist.

I buffed off the wax on the rear fender while singing the words, "Workin' at the car wash."

"I'd still like to fix you up with the girl from my interior design class, Book. She's nice. And she's cute," Magpie said. Ever since she and Seth got married in June she'd been trying to fix me up.

"I've given you a list. Does she meet my criteria?" I asked.

"She's tall and has red hair," she offered.

"What about the rest of the list?"

"Get real, Book," she said, hands planted on her petite hips.

"Those things are extremely important to me, Mags. She has to know how to handle a gun. I don't want some sissy girl for a wife." I loved yanking Mags' chain. She hated guns and was a lousy shot.

"I'm not a sissy, Garfield," she complained. That was an understatement. She was anything but. Mags was strong, determined, a fighter. Living with an emotionally abusive, alcoholic mother for eighteen years did that to her.

"I also said she had to have AB Negative blood," I reminded her, rubbing at a stubborn spot on the passenger door.

"You're not serious about that, are you? That's an impossible list," she grumbled. "*You're* impossible." She shook her head. "Your boobs are hanging out, by the way." She pointed to the t-shirt that had worked its way up. I shoved it back into the dress and now cheerfully whistled the "Car Wash" song. I needed to finish this job and get the stupid dress off.

"Mommy, why is Uncle Booker dressed like a girl?" Sofia's voice cut through my whistling. I spun to face the little angel as she stood next to her mother, rubbing her sleepy eyes.

"Halloween's coming, remember? Booker is showing us his costume," Lilah said without missing a beat. She picked up Sofia, who was dressed head to toe in pink, and propped her on her hip.

"He looks funny," Sofia assured everyone. "Why is he washing your car?"

Before anyone could answer, a battered Honda Civic pulled up, coughing and hissing in front of Cole's yellow Cape Cod. Out stepped Tess in jeans and a blue sweater, looking fantastic. Of course, she'd look fantastic even if she wore a plastic bag. She opened the trunk and locked her purse inside before walking toward the house.

"Hi, Booker," Tess offered a shy smile as she passed. "Nice . . . dress."

I did love that smile of hers. She dipped her head and hid her eyes under thick lashes. Painfully shy would be how others described her. Unless I missed my guess, I'd say more like scared. She kept her hair dyed black and wore dark contacts. I'd been a cop long enough to spot a disguise.

"I made a promise and I'm following through," I explained, quickly moving to the other fender. The punishment needed to end before anyone else showed up.

"Hi, Tess," Lilah said. "He looks pretty good in a dress, don't ya think?"

Tess dropped her gaze to my artificial boobs. "Well, he certainly fills out a dress better than I do," she said.

Oh crap. I'd forgotten about the fake boobs. But at the same time I was impressed Tess made a joke.

"Funny one, Tess," I laughed, tugging the jacket around me to hide the stuffed bodice.

"I'm sorry," Tess blushed. "I guess that was a little uncalled for. I shouldn't have—"

"Tess, you have nothing to be sorry for," Magpie assured her. "I was thinking the same thing about myself." Magpie and Lilah fist bumped. Tess smiled behind her hand.

"I'm sorry to come over without calling, but I couldn't remember the restaurant you wanted to meet at." Tess didn't own a cell phone. I offered to get her one at the business' expense, but she adamantly refused. Since Tess was never adamant about anything, I didn't push it.

"Lilah and I wanted to talk about that anyway," Magpie said. "Let's go inside while Book finishes. It's freezing out here. You're a vegan, right?"

"Lazy vegetarian," Tess corrected as the three women headed toward the house with Sofia still in Lilah's arms.

"What's that?" Magpie asked.

"I eat poultry and dairy, but no red meat or pork. I try to avoid processed food, too, but I do love a good chocolate chip cookie." A guilty look hung on her face before she shut the door, as if eating a cookie was a sin.

I was painfully aware of Tess' vegetarian ways. She usually ate salads whenever we went out. Not wanting to look like the carnivore that I was, I too ate salads. What I wouldn't give for a full rack of ribs from Sticky Lips Barbeque right about now.

"She's a beauty." Seth interrupted my thoughts of animal flesh. "It's nice to know she can speak in complete sentences." Seth leaned against the fender I'd just waxed. "Are you two still dating?"

"They're dating?" Cole asked.

"He brought her to my wedding," Seth said. "And Maggie said the two of them went to a movie a couple weeks ago."

"The movie thing wasn't a date. She commented that she was going to see the new *Star Trek* movie, and I wanted to see it, so we went together is all." I finished the car and put the lid on the wax.

"So tell me, how many times have you been to dinner with her over the past, say, six weeks?" Cole pressed.

"I don't know." I rubbed my neck. I didn't want to talk about it right now. "Maybe twenty times, but they were working dinners." Both of their eyes popped wide open. "We've been setting up the office and we had to eat, right? I mean, she's nice and all, but . . ."

"I like her, don't you?" Cole took the wax and shammy from me, dropping the shammy. We hit heads bending to pick it up. "I mean, what's not to like?" Cole said, rubbing his head. "She's a sweet person, kind, hardworking."

"And she laughs at my jokes, which is nice." I tugged on the hideous dress. The straps cut into my shoulders. "She talks more now since she started working for me. Did you know she used to play lacrosse in high school?" Cole shook his head. "And she was a ballerina. Anyway, when I'm around her there's this calming feeling, you know? Peaceful. I don't have to put on an act. I can be myself. Well, except for the whole eating meat thing, but I think that's my hang-up, not hers." I glanced at my friends, realizing how much like a lovesick puppy that sounded. Dropping my head in defeat, I admitted, "Yeah, I like her, a lot. More than I want to." I scrubbed my hand over my jaw.

"Sorry, but I don't get it. Why does that bother you?" Cole dropped the shammy again. I let him pick it up this time.

"Doc, have you not noticed she's in disguise? Who is she hiding from? And why does she even need to hide?" I asked. "She could be a criminal mastermind hiding from the mafia." Seth rolled his head back. "Okay, she's not a criminal, though I'm not discounting the mafia idea. Maybe her ex-boyfriend . . ." Seth planted his face in his hand this time. "Alright, I'm grasping. The fact is I don't want any more chaos in my life. That's why I left the MET. It was clouding my judgment. Taking over my life. Don't you remember the way I treated Lilah before you got married?"

Cole patted my back. "I do, Booker, but you're overreacting about Tess. You said you had a calm feeling around her. Maybe you should trust that."

"Maybe it's the calm before the storm," I insisted. "Look, since changing jobs, I've not had a single panic attack. My life's normal again, and I like it." I slipped off the shoes. The stupid rhinestones dug into my toes. "Besides, Tess told me the other day that she viewed marriage as a prison."

"She actually said that? She's so passive I can't believe she'd make a bold statement like that." Seth poked my fake boobs again.

"Hands off the merchandise." I folded my arms over my chest. "I've been working with her on being more assertive after a near disaster with a sales rep last month. She was beside herself when he wouldn't take no for an answer. I came back to the office after running an errand and found her in a panic. I kicked the guy out and had a long talk with her about not letting people walk all over her. She's actually doing better."

"I, for one, don't think you should discount her until you learn the truth," Seth said as we walked to the porch. "Maybe she's just super shy."

"Whatever. You two think everyone should get married and live happily ever after. You forget I've already done the whole marriage thing." I shook my head against the memory of Nikkolynn. I never wanted to repeat that disaster. "Not everyone's so lucky."

"You just have to find the right person, Book, not rush into a relationship. You knew Nikkolynn less than three weeks before you married her," Seth pointed out unnecessarily.

"Maybe. Or maybe I'm too much for one woman. Maybe I need to spread Booker around a little," I teased.

Seth slipped backward off the porch as he laughed. "Is anyone truly shocked you're not married?" He stood, brushing the dirt from his jeans.

"All kidding aside, I'm in no hurry to rush into marriage again. Lesson learned."

A nasty wind shot up my dress again as the girls came back outside. Poor Tess groaned softly as it tossed her hair. She hated the cold.

"We're heading to lunch," Magpie said, giving Seth a kiss as he walked up the steps.

"Cole, will you make Sofia a sandwich? We'll only be an hour or so." Lilah stretched to kiss Cole. There had to be a ten-inch difference between them.

"I'd love to, m'lady." He bowed to Sofia and she jumped into his arms.

"I want bologna, please, Daddy." She wasn't his biologically, but she was his daughter in his heart. I handled the adoption for them. Her weasel birth father wanted nothing to do with Sofia, which made the paperwork less complicated.

I pointed to Lilah's waxed car.

"Thank you. You're a good man, Book, no matter what everyone else says. Well, I think you're a man." She poked my faux chest.

"Is that all any of you can see when you look at me?" I asked, wrapping my arms around my bust. "I have a mind, too, you know."

Tess dipped her head, sharing that beautiful smile of hers with the ground. I allowed myself to entertain the idea that maybe she *was* just shy, and I was overreacting.

But I *knew* I wasn't. Yet, I didn't want to know what was going on with her. I preferred the "ignorance is bliss" philosophy for once. No more chaos.

Yeah, who was I kidding? I'd be stewing on it, more than I wanted to. So much for the quiet life.

Chapter 2
Tess

Nine and ½ years ago

" . . . No time for losers / Cause we are the champions / Of the world."

We sang it loud, and we sang it proud. Several of my buddies from the football team stormed the field to celebrate my game-winning goal. Our lacrosse team just won the championship, and they hoisted me, the team captain, high on their broad shoulders. Now the world knew us not just as Mighty Lions of Santa Mesa High. We now held the label of State Champions. The skies above burned a brilliant blue. The temperature: a sweltering ninety-four degrees, just how I liked it. Hot. We paraded around the field as we belted out "We Are the Champions" at least a million times at the top of our lungs. Mud caked my red hair, along with my face and my blue and gold uniform. My voice, raw from screaming, could barely be heard, and I just didn't care. We won. The season was hard-fought, and me, a mere junior, led the team to victory. I had three full-ride scholarship offers already. And a partial scholarship offer for dance, my real love, at the small college right here in town. The world was my oyster.

"Tess! Tess!" If Mr. Vintage Southern California guy screaming out my name hadn't waved his arms frantically in front of me, I would've missed him. Not a good thing. The guy was red-hot Hollywood gorgeous, with chiseled features, tan face, blond hair—and tall. I liked tall guys. At five-ten myself, it helped.

"Tony, set me down." I tapped the head of the football player holding me several times before he glanced up.

"What, Tess?" His voice boomed above the others.

"I said put me down!" I pointed to the ground.

"We're going to make another lap," he said, as if it were obvious.

"Tony, we've circle the field three times already."

"Yeah, but if I put you down now you'll be trampled. Look at this crowd."

He had a point. My classmates now flooded the marred green field, running around, cheering, many still singing the Queen song. Some of those divots in the grass were mine and I smiled proudly. My twin sister Abby jumped up and down, waving her arms at me, screaming out my name. I couldn't hear her over the noise, but I watched as her lips formed my name. My older brother stood next to her with his arm around a pretty girl I'd never seen before. He too waved at me proudly. Remembering hot blond guy, I turned to see if he was still there but could no longer find him in the chaos. *Dang.*

Later that evening, Coach Holly and her two assistants threw a party on the beach. One of the many perks of living in the suburbs of San Diego, California: beaches. Another? Perfect weather, at least most of the time. The main reason for the party was to celebrate our victory, but it also signaled that school was about to end. I could hardly believe I'd be a senior. The past two years blitzed by.

I snagged a water bottle from the cooler and made my way to the ocean to watch the sunset. I was partied out and needed a little quiet time away from screaming girls and high-fiving guys. With graduation looming, it meant we'd lose half of our team. But I was up for it. I loved a good challenge. Getting my hands dirty and making things happen. I thrived on it. Terese Layla Selleck was not a quitter. Not ever.

Memories flooded my mind as the waves rushed the shore. I remembered my first week of ballet classes. I was six. The teacher told my mom not to waste her money when she'd asked if private lessons would help me. "This class is enough for Tess. She can get a little exercise, and have fun with the other girls, but she'll never excel in dance. She just doesn't have it."

I cried for a week. Finally, my dad sat me down and told me I had two choices. "Move on, or prove the teacher wrong." I decided on the latter. My parents checked out DVD's from the library and I spent every spare minute practicing. Three years later, an elite ballet school in the area selected me to join their troupe, and seven years later, I was the lead in Swan Lake. Nope. I didn't quit then, I didn't quit today, and I wouldn't quit next season.

Wearing only a pair of jean shorts and a green tank top, I shivered. It didn't take long for the cool ocean breeze to raise goose bumps on my body. As ribbons of red and orange painted the sky, I rubbed my hands over my arms in an effort to warm myself. I hated the cold . . . Okay, it was probably in the low seventies, but still.

"Beautiful," said a warm rich voice from behind. Startled, I spun around so fast I had to take a step to keep from tipping over. The tall blonde god from earlier, now dressed in white slacks and a white shirt, looking oh so good, stood smiling at me. The breeze pressed his shirt against him, exposing his wide shoulders and muscular chest. Impressive.

"Hi," I said, smiling stupidly. *Come on, girl, pull it together.* "And I agree, the sunset is spectacular tonight." I stiffened as he approached. I ordered myself to play it cool. The guy was obviously in college and I didn't want to look like a silly high school girl, which technically I was.

"Not the sunset, though that's beautiful also. I meant you." He smiled. His straight white teeth gleamed.

"Thank you." I adjusted my sloppy ponytail before shoving my hands into my pockets.

"My name's Garen. Garen Johnson. My cousin Jessie's on the JV team," he explained. "I stopped by to give her a ride home from the party and saw you standing out here all alone. I've wanted to meet you since the game. I hope that's alright." His eyes lit up with a smile as he added, "Great game, by the way."

"Thanks. My name's Terese Selleck, but I go by Tess." I looked into his steel gray eyes framed by dark thick lashes. Nice. The guy had a good four inches on me, too. Perfect.

"Terese is such a pretty name. I think I'll stick with that, if you don't mind." He smiled again and my heart took off. I didn't care much for my first name, which was why I went by Tess, but I wasn't about to put up a stink with hottie guy. He could call me whatever he wanted.

"So, Jessie tells me you're a junior. Is that right? I've never heard of a junior being the captain of the varsity lacrosse team before." His face held a look of disappointment if his frown were any indication. "I thought you were older."

"I'm pretty lucky, I guess. I didn't even start lacrosse until ninth grade," I explained, quickly adding, "I'll be eighteen in a few months." Okay, seven and a half.

"Nice." He added a nod.

Both of us seemed to be at a loss for words as the conversation lagged. We turned to the ocean. Garen picked up a broken seashell, turning it over a few times in his hands. He pulled his arm back, ready to toss the shell back into the ocean. I stopped him.

"Wait." I held out my hand and he slipped the shell into it, brushing his fingers against my palm. "Look. This side has waves of color, like a rainbow." I smiled into his eyes.

"If it was perfect it'd be worth saving. It's a chomped up mess." His brows pulled together in a scowl.

"I disagree. Something doesn't have to be perfect to be beautiful. May I keep it? I think it's lovely." I traced over the fragmented rainbow with my finger.

"Go ahead, but like I said, it's not worth anything." He angled back to the sunset. "So you're a lacrosse prodigy, and you like sea trash." He laughed. "Tell me more about yourself."

"I'm a dancer, ballet mostly. In fact, I hope to travel with a ballet company after college." He nodded approvingly and I continued. "I'm an ace shot with a rifle, and pretty darn good with a pistol, too."

"Guns? I'm not a fan of guns." He scowled again.

Great. I searched my brain for something to say that would impress him. "My mom hates them also. When my dad takes us kids out for target practice, she won't come along. In fact, she's never even fired a gun in her life. And if there are bullets in the gun, she refuses to pick it up."

"I do believe your mother is a very intelligent woman." If Garen was still appalled by my love of guns, he hid it behind another winning smile.

Jessie raced across the sand toward us as I babbled away about my love of surfing.

"Garen!" She jumped into his arms.

"Hey, runt. You're getting my pants dirty." He set her down and brushed off several grains of sand. It was nice to see a guy who cared about how he looked. So unlike the boys I was surrounded with at school. "Your dad asked me to pick you up. Ready to go?"

"Sure. Do you need a ride, Tess?" Jessie pressed. "Elise left with Shane about ten minutes ago. You came with her, right?"

"Ugh. Not again." Elise was my best friend, despite being uncontrollably boy crazy. It wasn't the first time we'd gone somewhere and I had to find my own way home because she'd met up with a boy.

"I'll give you a ride," Garen offered casually.

Oh yeah. Perfect. Could this day get any better?

Garen and I were inseparable all weekend. I learned he was a student at Harvard, majoring in political science. "I will be president someday," he assured me. "I have everything all scheduled out. I call it my Life Plan. I'm going to Harvard now, year round. I plan to graduate in three more years with a Masters at twenty-three. Then I plan to marry the most beautiful woman on the planet." He stroked my cheek. "Next, I'll work for a prestigious politician, and run for congress when I'm twenty-eight."

"That's an impressive plan," I said.

"Hold on, I'm not done. I'll serve two terms as a representative, then I'll become a senator. When I'm forty-one, I'll become the youngest president ever, beating Theodore Roosevelt by one year." He beamed ear-to-ear. "Oh, I almost forgot. When I turn thirty, my perfect wife and I will have a child."

I couldn't help but laugh. "You do have it all planned out."

"Sure do. And it will happen. I may have to make minor tweaks to the plan here and there, but it will happen," he said confidently. "You have to want it bad enough, and you have to be willing to do whatever it takes to achieve it. Then it will happen."

"My feelings exactly." A guy who knew what he wanted. What a nice change from the last guy I dated whose greatest ambition was to advance to the next level on some stupid video game he was obsessed with.

"Sounds as if we're soul mates." Garen nudged my shoulder with his. Instead of finding him cocky, I saw only confidence, determination. I liked it.

Late Sunday night he went back to Massachusetts. My parents were thrilled when he left. "He's in college, Tess," Dad grunted. "You should be dating boys your own age. Besides, there's something about him. I can't put my finger on it, but I don't trust him."

My father's warning fell on deaf ears. Garen mesmerized me. He was articulate, bright, ambitious. His drive to succeed, infectious. Out of respect to my parents, we only text messaged each other and talked on the phone until I graduated. Garen came down for my graduation and took my parents and I out to dinner afterward.

"Please don't rush into anything," my mother said as I got ready for bed that night. He was charming and polite all evening, but still he hadn't won my parents over.

"Mom, I'm going to Santa Mesa State University. He's in Massachusetts. I don't think you need to worry," I assured her. "Did I tell you he's not a fan of guns either?" I hoped having that in common with Garen would endear him to her.

She kissed my cheek. "Well, that's nice. Now off to bed." Not the enthusiastic response I'd hoped for, but it was a start.

Two months later, Garen flew in from Harvard on a long weekend to help me move into the dorms at SMSU. I turned down many scholarship offers in lacrosse, including one to USC, for a partial one in dance at SMSU. It was a small school and they couldn't afford full scholarships as the major universities could. But I didn't care. I dreamed of starting my own dance studio someday after touring around the world performing with a ballet company. Garen worked hard to convince me that majoring wasn't a smart move, especially since I intended to have my own studio someday. I could see his point, so I compromised with a double major. Dance and business. It wasn't what he had in mind, but he didn't press the issue . . . well, not *too* often. He also wasn't excited about me staying in San Diego for college.

"Harvard has a great business school," Garen insisted. "Don't you want to be by me?"

"I hate the cold. Correction, I despise it. And you're carrying an eighteen-hour credit load. I'd never see you anyway." None of that mattered. Unlike his, my parents weren't rich. My dad was a teacher and money was tight most times. Passing up my partial scholarship wasn't a luxury I could afford.

"That's kind of a childish reason, Terese," he complained, setting the last box in my dorm room. "What if I'm a senator in New York or Massachusetts some day? Are you telling me you won't be a part of my life because of a little snow?"

Did he just suggest marriage? Stunned, I didn't know what to say at first. Garen, not being the demonstrative type, seldom kissed me. The only reason I knew he loved me was that he sent a dozen roses for my birthday with a note stating that he did. "Of course I want to be a part of your life no matter where you end up," I said, brushing stray hairs off my face. "I'll move if your job dictates we live in a snowy climate."

"Thank you." He kissed my forehead and tugged on my ponytail. "Have you ever considered cutting your hair? Maybe a more cultivated style. You're in college now, and when I'm president, you want to look perfect, right?"

"You don't like my hair?" I tried not to sound hurt.

"I think your hair is beautiful, but you wear it like you're still a high school girl. I think you'd look stunning with it short and sophisticated." He scooped me up and swung me around, nibbling playfully on my neck. "No pressure, Terese. Just an observation."

"I'll think about it," I said as he set me down. I'd never considered cutting my hair short before. I liked it long. It only hung to my bra strap anyway. It's not like it went clear down my back.

I loved Garen. His drive, his excitement for life was infectious. Being around him, I felt as if the two of us could conquer the world. Nothing would stand in our way. But sometimes his comments hurt, bordering on insults, and made me feel as if I were fourteen and back in Ms. Liddy's dance class again. She'd insisted that her ballerinas be rail thin, and to please her I starved myself sick. I passed out at school one day and had to be rushed to the hospital where I was given an IV. My dad was livid, forbidding me to dance ever again. My mom, the reasonable one and a dancer herself, suggested I become a vegetarian instead. "She won't have to starve herself to stay slim. In fact, she'll be eating healthier than you, dear." Dad, a junk food junky, could hardly argue the fact.

After I was released, my parents sat me down at the dining room table. "Sweetie, I realize Ms. Liddy is a dictator—" Dad began before Mom nudged him. He looked at her. "Well, she is." Mom frowned. "Anyway," he growled, "your health is important to us. We understand that dancing is your life. However, as your parents, we cannot stand by and let you destroy your body by starving it. So if you're going to continue to dance, we have a couple of conditions."

"Conditions?" I rolled my eyes and crossed my arms.

"Yes. Besides dance, we'd like you to find another outlet. Your mother ran track in high school, and as you know, it didn't detract from her dance in any way, it actually helped her increase her stamina." I nodded carefully. He continued. "It doesn't have to be track. The high school has an excellent softball team." My father played ball in college. His not so subtle hint wasn't missed.

"Or lacrosse is a wonderful sport," my mother interjected.

"Yes, well, there's that." His eyebrows dipped into a vee. "Tess, you need something besides dance. You can take up sewing, for all we care. We just want you to branch out a little. Also, there'll be no more starving yourself. You can try that wacky vegan stuff if you want," my mother nudged him again, "but you will eat healthy balanced meals, young lady."

After looking over my options, I chose lacrosse. But dance was still my first love, much to Garen's dismay. He'd just have to get used to it if he wanted to be part of my life.

We continued our long distance relationship for two more years until Garen graduated and got a job working for a senator in Texas. "Marry me, Terese. I'm crazy in love with you," he begged when I flew out to see him the summer after my sophomore year. He'd just turned twenty-three. Right on target for his Life Plan.

"But I'm barely twenty. That's too young," I insisted. "What about my degree?"

"You can get your degree in Texas. Dallas has several great schools. It's not as if SMSU is some Ivy League school, anyway. What does it matter if you finish your degree in Texas?" It wasn't the first time Garen had implied that my school was second rate and that the education he'd gotten was far superior. I'd learned early on in our relationship that Garen was a school snob. I tried not to let it bother me. I reminded myself he was a driven guy, and there was no such thing as the perfect person. Everyone had faults. And being a school snob was pretty minor when it came to faults. I could live with it.

"Please move out here, Terese. Don't you love me, or have you found someone else?" His gray eyes narrowed.

"Of course I haven't found anyone else." I wrapped my hands up in his shirt and snuggled in close. "You're awfully cute when you're jealous." I smiled. "I'll think about it."

Garen pressed me at every turn for the next two weeks. He'd make a great politician someday. My parents were less than thrilled with Garen's proposal, feeling his tactics were a bit overbearing. They warned me not to take marriage lightly. "It's not to be hopped in and out of carelessly, Tess," Dad counseled. In the end, I accepted Garen's proposal. I loved him, and knew he was everything a girl could want in a husband.

My parents gave me the wedding of my dreams. How they afforded it on my dad's teaching salary was a mystery to me. I did what I could to help cut corners. I rented a dress instead of buying one, and we held the reception in my best friend Martha's backyard. Her dad was a lawyer and they had a beautiful home with a gorgeously landscaped yard. My brother Craig and his fiancée Michelle, along with my twin sister Abby, helped me decorate. We hung yards and yards of tulle and twinkling lights. My sister and her eye for decorating convinced me to accent with burlap. When she first described her ideas, I thought she was crazy. "Burlap? Are you sure? It sounds a little Beverly Hillbillies." I was wrong. It was anything but. When we finished putting everything into place, except the flowers, scheduled for delivery in the morning, I couldn't believe it. I had the fairytale wedding I'd always dreamt of. And tomorrow I'd marry my prince.

Garen was strangely quiet the entire day, as were his parents. I'd not been around them much, but I could tell they didn't care for me. During the ceremony, I worried that he'd leave me standing at the altar. We only danced three times, and he picked at his food. The photographer had to fight with him to get pictures. After the reception, he whisked me away to a beautiful resort on the beach. I was both excited and nervous. Garen wanted to wait until we were married to sleep together, and being my first time, I worried I'd disappoint him.

"Garen, this place is perfect. We have an ocean view, and a private hot tub right out the back door," I said, swallowing the lump in my throat.

"Sure beats the heck out of the country bumpkin wedding reception, doesn't it?" He carefully hung his tux jacket on a hanger and untied his bowtie.

"Country bumpkin?" I snapped as the anxiety drained from my body, replaced with annoyance. "The reception was beautiful."

"No, Terese, it wasn't." He carefully untied his shoes and placed them in the closet, lining them up perfectly with the jacket. "The flowers were pathetic and half dead. The decorations were cheap and homemade. Seriously, who uses bowls with floating candles, anyway? And burlap? It was an embarrassment. How am I supposed to use the photos when I'm campaigning in a few years? No one will take me seriously. They'll think I'm some kind of uneducated moron instead of an Ivy League graduate."

"You're being mean, Garen. Not everyone has an endless supply of money at their fingertips." I ripped the veil from my hair and tossed it on the desk in the room.

"Hang that up. Now," he demanded, pointing at my veil.

"I'll hang it up when I want." I folded my arms, fighting to rein in my anger. He was my husband, not my father, and he couldn't tell me what to do.

Garen lowered his voice. "Hang. Up. The. Veil. Now," he growled low. For a split second I thought he'd strike me.

I stepped back as he came closer, then quickly chastised myself for overreacting. "I said I'll hang it up when I'm ready." My voice quivered just a little, but I stood my ground.

I didn't see it coming, but I felt the sting against my cheek as he backhanded my face. He grabbed me by the shoulders and shoved me toward the veil, his fingers biting into my skin. I could feel the bruises forming under his grip. He shook me hard, rattling my teeth.

"I said *now*."

"Stop it, you're hurting me!" I pulled free as a tear tumbled down my cheek. He stepped closer to me and I shied back, covering my face. A small scream escaped my throat.

"Terese." Garen pulled me to his chest and stroked my hair. "Oh, Terese. I'm so sorry. Please forgive me." He pulled a handkerchief from his pocket and dabbed at my cheek. I saw a spot of blood on it as he drew back. Carefully folding the hankie, he placed it back into his pocket.

"It won't ever happen again. I swear," he promised. "It just made me crazy when you spoke to me so rudely. I have to remember we come from different backgrounds."

"Different backgrounds?" I leaned back. "If you're implying that since you come from money it is okay to hit me, you're sadly mistaken. It won't happen again. I won't put up with abuse. Understood?"

"Yes, completely," he said with contrition. He moved back and took a deep breath. "I'm sorry, Terese. It's been a long day. I took my disappointment over the simple reception out on you.

That was unfair. It won't happen again." He sat on the edge of the bed and buried his face in his hands. "I've never hit anyone before. I don't know what happened. I'm so ashamed."

He looked up at me; tears rimmed his eyes. "Garen." I sat next to him and put my arm around his shoulder as my heart softened. "It's been a long day for both of us. Let's forget this even happened." I ran my fingers through his golden blond hair.

"Thank you, Terese. I don't deserve you." He kissed my still stinging cheek ever so gently. "I promise, never again."

I nodded. "It's in the past. Now, let's get busy honeymooning." I smiled seductively, hoping I hadn't made a big mistake marrying Garen today.

Chapter 3

"Would you mind if I followed you instead?" I asked Lilah as she led us to her car. I waved to Booker—all six-foot, dimpled-grinned, deep-brown eyes of him. He freely offered back his signature part-sexy, part-playful grin. If I was going to fall for a guy ever again, it could easily be him . . . but I had no plans of going down that road. Ever.

"Tess, I noticed when you pulled in that your car doesn't sound so good. Are you sure you don't want to ride with us?" Lilah asked as Mags opened the door to the newly waxed orange bug.

"I need to go to Walgreens," I explained. "It's over by the restaurant, so if I drive I won't have to go back and forth."

"I need to get some things from Walgreens, too. We can stop on the way back," Maggie offered, adding, "Lilah's right about your car. It doesn't sound good."

"It's settled then." Lilah smiled warmly. I knew they were trying to be helpful, but I had to dye my hair again and needed to get some coloring.

"Okay," I nodded reluctantly. "Let me get my purse." I grabbed it from the trunk of my car then hurried over to Lilah's and got in.

Lilah turned a CD on low as we drove to the restaurant. I smiled to myself. Having lost her mother as a child, Lilah found comfort listening to her mother's much beloved Ricky Martin music. She sang along as Maggie laughed.

"What does Cole think about your love affair with Martin?" she teased.

"No contest: Ricky has my groove, Cole owns my heart and soul." Lilah turned the volume up and bounced to the beat as she drove.

Over the past two months, Lilah and Maggie had gone out of their way to befriend me. They invited me to do things with them at least once a week. Last week we spent a day at the mall as they shopped for a project they were working on for their new interior design company. We all got facials and manicures, too. It'd been years since I'd pampered myself like that. The last time was right before my junior prom. Another lifetime.

Since escaping from Garen four years ago, I'd cut myself off from everyone. I wanted to stay hidden—to fade into the background. Quite a metamorphosis from my high school days. Between lacrosse and my ballet performances, I'd been constantly front and center. Now I was happiest in the shadows, unnoticed. Or so I thought, until the past two months. Between these two and Booker, I realized just how lonely my life had become. Miserable, hiding and shrinking from everyone and everything. I needed my life back, to push past the apprehension that Garen might find me. The fear still haunted my days and nights.

We entered the parking lot of Veggies, a new vegetarian restaurant in town, and parked the car. "I heard this place is good," Maggie said as we walked toward the all-glass building. "It's only been open for a month but you already need a reservation for dinner."

I glanced at our reflections in the glass and couldn't help but smile. Lilah, originally from Arizona, wore a thick sweater like me, although hers was a bold burnt orange and mine more of a pale blue, to blend in. Maggie, a Port Fare native and used to the horribly cold weather, dressed only in a t-shirt and jeans. I shivered just looking at her.

"Are you cold?" Maggie asked. "I think Lilah has a sweatshirt of mine you can borrow in her trunk."

"No, I shivered because I looked at you. Aren't you freezing?" I asked as we entered the pristine building.

She laughed. "I'm used to this weather. I'm guessing you're not. Where are you from?"

"California," I said as the waitress led us to a booth by one of the outside windows. Great. Now I'd really be cold.

"You need to remember, Tess, Port Fare has two seasons: cold and colder," Lilah insisted dryly. "If you keep that in mind, you'll be fine."

"That's not true," Maggie pushed her chin up. "We have four. Summer, pre-winter, winter, and post winter. Pre-and post-winters are a hodgepodge of rain, sleet, and snow."

"And winter is just plain cold and nasty, while summer is hot and sticky," Lilah said.

"Why stay here if the weather's so bad?" I wrapped my arms around me against the cold seeping through the window.

"The people. I love the people. They're warm and friendly, even if the winters aren't. And that's a tradeoff I'll take any day," Lilah said, checking her phone.

She was right about that. I smiled, looking at my new friends as they scanned the menu. It felt good to have friends again, to be comfortable around people and not cowering all the time. I held tight to the hope of having a normal life once more. If only I could see my family, then life would be perfect. But no, not yet. *Someday*, I whispered to my aching heart. *Someday*.

A blue Ford Fusion stopped just outside the window. The driver threw the car in reverse and backed into a parking space way too quickly. Garen drove a blue Fusion. I stretched my neck to check if the license plates were from Texas, but I couldn't see them from where I sat.

I sunk down in my seat and struggled to get a better look at the driver as I tugged my purse into my lap. I carried a gun everywhere I went now. What I truly needed was a concealed weapon permit, but that meant an investigation into my life, and talking to people from both San Diego and Texas, which meant they'd have to talk to my ex. So that was out of the question.

I squinted at the car. The driver, a male, wore a cap, obscuring his face and hair. Garen never wore a hat, let alone a baseball cap. The driver kept glancing over his shoulder, as if looking for someone.

Overreacting, Tess. Calm down. I'd been doing much better at keeping my fears at bay. I was tired of living in fear. Jumping at every little noise. Cowering in corners. Like when doing yoga, I envisioned my safe place as I struggled to relax only with Maggie and Lilah sitting across from me, I couldn't very well close my eyes.

I allowed my gaze to drift back to the car. The guy took off his cap and ran his hands through his *blond* hair. I stiffened.

No. It couldn't be Garen. It'd been over four years now. Surely, he'd moved on. As I wrung my napkin into a twisted mess, I glanced again at the car in time to see it speed away, a brunette at his side. I almost sighed aloud. The knots in my stomach loosened ever so slightly.

Frustrated that I allowed myself to get worked up over nothing, I tucked the ruined napkin into my purse and picked up the menu, bracing my still shaking hands on the table. *Enough, Tess.*

"Don't they have anything with meat?" Maggie asked, flipping the menu over.

"This is a vegetarian restaurant, Mags."

"Yes, Lilah, but even the Blue Cactus over on Lightbridge Ave sells hamburgers despite the fact that it's a Mexican restaurant."

"It seems Veggies is not as considerate of carnivores as the Blue Cactus is of gringos." Lilah closed her menu.

I set mine down. "We don't have to eat here. Remember, I'm a lazy vegetarian, not a vegan, or even a regular vegetarian, for that matter." Garen hated when I called myself that. "*Get a backbone, Terese and commit.*" He'd roll his eyes. "*You're a lazy person, is more like it.*"

"No. This is good. I need to stretch out of my comfort zone. The tofu Caesar salad looks yummy." Maggie smiled up at the waitress who'd approached our table.

We all ordered a salad and flavored water, except Lilah—she ordered a Diet Pepsi.

"So, tell us, what's it like working for Booker?" Lilah asked with an impish grin.

"Great. He's a wonderful boss. Patient, kind. He has a great work ethic, and he treats his clients well. He's smart, and funny.

He makes me laugh all the time." I chuckled, remembering a comment he made about his sad little car looking like something not even the cat would drag in. Which reminded me . . . "Maggie, I've been meaning to ask you, why do you always call him by cat names?"

"Did you know Gatto means cat in Italian?" I nodded. "Well, when he was in the military and assigned to a mission, he'd have to come up with a code name. He'd choose fierce cats, like jaguar, or cougar, to pay homage to his heritage. His team would pretend to forget his code name and they'd call him things like Garfield, or Sylvester. As you can guess, he didn't think it was that funny. But I did!" She smiled devilishly. "When Seth told me about it, I felt it my duty to pick up where they'd left off. For kicks, I decided to incorporate any and all cats, whether they be from TV or literature or wherever."

"I thought of a new one," Lilah said, her eyes bright and her grin wide. "Grimalkin. He's the cat in Shakespeare."

"Good one." Maggie wrote the name down in her cell. "Which play?"

"*Macbeth*," I answered.

"You're a Shakespeare fan, too?" Lilah asked.

"No. I just remember reading it in high school," I admitted. "I don't enjoy his work. His comedies aren't bad, but his tragedies are too depressing, as are most of his love stories. Like *Romeo and Juliet*. Why in the world would you kill yourself because the one you loved died? I mean, I'd be devastated, but kill myself? Not happening."

"Booker said almost the same thing yesterday," Maggie said, her grin crooked.

"Smart and good looking," I quipped without thinking.

I glanced up at Maggie and Lilah's wide smiles.

"What?" I asked nervously.

"So, do you like Booker?" Lilah asked. "As in . . . *like* him?"

"No. I—I mean, as a friend, but not romantically. You'd have to be dead to not think he's good looking, right?"

"True," Lilah agreed. "Although he's not as good looking as Cole."

"Or Seth," Maggie interjected. Not wanting to cause a stir, I didn't point out that while their men were indeed good looking,

Booker was by far the hottest. And sexiest. And I needed to get a life.

"Book's a good person and he's fun to be around." I also liked the fact that he wore a gun. Everywhere. Added security.

The girls exchanged knowing glances. Yeah, who was I kidding? Booker had awoken feelings in me that I thought were long dead. Feelings I didn't think I'd ever have again. I was sure Garen had all but drowned them out of me, literally. A chill raced up my spine at the memory of that horrible day.

A ruddy-faced waitress with unruly brown hair brought out our meals, interrupting my private nightmare, thankfully.

"Maggie? Maggie Brown? Oh my heck! I haven't seen you since graduation," exclaimed the short waitress. "Love your hair."

"Hi, Melody. Thanks, and it's Prescott now." Maggie quickly flashed her ring at Melody. She offered the girl a smile, but it didn't reach her eyes.

"That's right. Hillary Jeffers told me you *had* to get married. You don't look very far along." She stretched her neck around to look at Maggie's stomach.

"That's because I'm not pregnant. Hillary likes to talk," Maggie said, straightening.

"So you're not pregnant?" The look of disappointment on the server when Maggie shook her head was rude, to say the least. You shouldn't judge a book by its cover, but this girl left a bad taste in my mouth. My guess was that Maggie wasn't particularly fond of her either, judging from the way she avoided eye contact with her and poked at her salad with a fork.

"Well, Hillary won't be spreading any rumors around for a while after what happened to her last week," Melody said, with a pious twist to her grin.

"What happened to Hillary?" Maggie's eyes darted up to meet Melody's.

"You don't know? Have you been living in a cave?" the waitress spurted.

"No, she's been busy finishing her degree and running an interior design business," Lilah snapped.

"Do I know you?" Melody's jaw ticked.

"This is my sister-in-law, Lilah Colter, and my friend, Tess Bennett," Maggie introduced us. "This is Melody Winkmyer. She and Hillary went to the same high school as me."

I found it impressive that Maggie said Lilah was her sister-in-law since technically Seth, Cole, and Booker were just friends. They weren't actually related in any way, although they did consider each other family.

"Hillary was a good friend of ours," Melody said to Lilah.

"A good friend of yours," Maggie corrected. "She hated me."

"True. But you did steal her boyfriend, so you can't blame her, right?" Melody tucked her hands in her apron.

"According to Seth, Hillary liked him, but the feelings were *not* mutual." Lilah took a drink of her diet soda. "Seth also said she was pretty mean to Maggie, even trying to punch her once or twice."

"She's getting her comeuppance now." Melody's eyes twinkled. "Seems she met a guy at school about six months ago and he turned out to be quite the loser. Rumor has it the guy beat her. She's sporting a cut lip and two black eyes now. I heard he broke one of her ribs, too. She had to sneak out of her dorm room in the middle of the night to get away from him. She drove all night until she got home. She's at her parents now."

It took all I had not to vomit. Every punch, every slam into a wall, every head bashing came rushing back to me. I leaned back in my chair and took deep, steady breaths to keep from fainting.

"Melody, we have to go. Get our check, please." Lilah's voice sounded a million miles away as I struggled to push memories away. Warm hands covered mine.

"Tess, are you alright?" I nodded to Lilah's question, I think. "Tess." A warm hand brushed hair behind my ear. "Tess," Lilah said again.

"What's wrong?" I turned to the new voice. Maggie had moved into the seat next to me. Only then did I realize she held my hand. I forced myself to calm down. It was only memories, horrible, vile memories. I was safe now.

"Sorry." I straightened and tucked my hands into my lap. "You know me and blood." I offered a weak smile. Neither seemed to buy the lie judging from their furrowed brows, but they didn't push it. Lilah paid the bill and we left. The cool autumn air helped clear my head, and by the time we got to the car, I felt stronger.

"Are you up for Walgreens or would you rather just head back?" Maggie asked, climbing into the backseat this time.

Not wanting to draw any more attention to myself, I said, "If you still need to go, I wouldn't mind." I unrolled the window a crack to let more cool air in as we drove.

"Feeling better?" Lilah asked.

"Yes, much. Sorry about that." I forced a small chuckle. We remained embarrassingly quiet until we reached the store. I wanted to crawl into a hole.

Lilah parked the car near the door. "Should we meet out front in, say, ten minutes?" I suggested, not eager to buy my hair coloring in front of them.

"Sure. I'm just getting a pregnancy test so I won't be long," Lilah explained. "What about—"

"Wait. You're pregnant?" asked Maggie as she pulled open the glass door.

"That's what I'm trying to find out," Lilah explained. "I'm only a couple days late, so no need to get too excited."

Maggie's face lit up. "But you are. I can see it in your eyes."

"Yes, I am." She beamed back. "But this is not the first time I've been late, and the tests have always come back negative."

"We'll think only positive thoughts then," Maggie assured her. "Alright, I'm looking for some magazines for a house we're decorating. I'll meet you guys up front in a few." Maggie turned toward the books and magazines, and I hurried over to the hair care products. I selected my usual bottle of Raven Black semi-permanent color, then searched for some shampoo, running into Lilah as I rounded the corner, pregnancy test in hand.

"Box color? Are you serious? This stuff is horrible for your hair." She planted a hand on her hips. "I can get you professional products, Tess."

"This is okay," I assured her as I mindlessly turned the box around in my hands. Maggie mentioned that Lilah had gone to hair school and was a real product snob.

She put her hand on my shoulder and said softly, "Tess, I hope you realize you can trust me. Please, tell me who you're hiding from?"

I stammered for a minute, taken aback by her bluntness. I debated whether to lie, or take a leap of faith and trust these two girls who'd tried so hard to befriend me.

But I was tired of hiding, and tired of keeping everyone at arm's length. I took the leap. "It's that obvious?" My voice was barely above a whisper. Okay, the leap was small.

"My dad was a drug smuggler. I'm sure you read about it in the papers when Booker was hospitalized after a run-in with the infamous Harry Dreser. Daddy was an expert at disguise." She frowned. "When I saw your dark hair and dark contacts, and the way you seldom made eye contact with people, I figured it out. In fact, I've known almost from the minute I met you."

"From the minute . . . D-Does Booker know?" I held my breath, afraid of her answer.

"He's never mentioned it, though I'd guess he does. He's a sharp one. It's pretty tough to fool him. Trust me, I know," she grimaced.

I took a deep breath. "The guy . . . my ex-husband, was a control freak. He controlled every part of my life. If I didn't measure up to his standard, he made sure I knew it," I said, fingering the dye. My eyes never left the box. "Like that Hillary girl, I also had to escape, and that's how I ended up here. Every time I dye my hair, I tell myself that when it fades, I'm not going to re-dye it, that I'm done hiding. But every time it fades, I re-dye it. I guess I'm still letting him control me."

"It was that bad, huh?" Lilah sighed quietly. I nodded. "The incident at the restaurant earlier triggered some bad memories, I take it."

"Nightmares. Please don't tell anyone. I don't want this to get out. I'm still afraid he'll find me. I'm not strong enough yet."

"You're a lot stronger than you give yourself credit for, Tess, but I won't say a word," Lilah promised as Maggie approached us, carrying a stack of magazines.

"Box color?" she said to me before turning to Lilah. "Breathe, Lilah. It's okay. She doesn't know any better."

"Be quiet, brat," Lilah laughed. "Come on. I want to take this." She waved the pregnancy test, crossing her fingers as she did. Looping her arm in mine, she led me to the cash register, grimacing as I paid for the hair dye.

Chapter 4

We went back to Lilah's so I could pick up my car. She had an easy recipe for stir-fry shrimp she wanted to give to me, vowing that not even I could mess it up.

"I hope you're right. I love stir-fry." I had my doubts, but figured I might as well try it. I couldn't suck at cooking forever. Someday it had to sink in.

I followed her and Maggie inside, holding tight to my purse. Booker had changed out of the dress from earlier and now wore jeans and a green Henley t-shirt with the sleeves pushed up to his elbows, looking great as always. I liked him in green. Sofia sat next to him, curled up on the brown microfiber sofa as he read *Cat in the Hat* to her, exaggerating the infuriated fish in the story.

"'No, no, he should not be here when your mother is out!'" His face twisted into a stern frown.

"Those kids are not very smart," Sofia said, scratching the tip of her nose.

"That's right. You should never let a stranger in the house, ever," Booker said.

"You shouldn't talk to them, either," Seth added as he turned to Maggie. "Correct, beautiful wife?"

"Correct." She gave a short nod.

Sofia jumped off the couch and rushed to Lilah as she closed the front door. "Mommy!" She wrapped her little arms around her mother's neck as Lilah scooped her up.

"I wonder if I'll ever get tired of being greeted like this." Lilah snuggled the little girl closer. Sofia clasped her mother's face in her hands and gave her a noisy kiss on the lips.

"Did you miss me?" Lilah rubbed her nose on her daughter's.

"Yes. Daddy made me a bologna sandwich, though."

"It's her favorite," Lilah explained to me as Cole came over to us.

"Did you miss me, too?" Lilah's eyes twinkled as she smiled at him.

"Always," he said before kissing her.

"Oh, no. Not again." Sofia wiggled out of her mom's arms and sat back next to Booker. "They do that all the time." She folded her arms in disgust. "I sit by you, Uncle Book. You never kiss girls."

"Yeah, thanks for reminding me," he grumbled. Both Cole and Seth laughed. Booker rolled his eyes. Watching the playful interaction between everyone made my heart ache even more for my own family. *How much longer do I have to stay away from them?*

My mind wandered back to the day Garen hit my mother.

Forever.

"I'd better get going." I opened the door, pushing my purse up on my shoulder. "Thanks for lunch."

"You don't need to rush off, Tess." Maggie came with me outside. "You forgot the stir-fry recipe."

"I'll get it later. I need to run a few errands." I tugged my sweater around me against the icy wind, depressed at the thought of another looming winter here. Maggie stood next to the car as I quickly slipped inside, still dumbfounded that she seemed oblivious to the cold.

"Thanks again for, well, almost having lunch." Heat flooded my guilty face as I turned the key over in the ignition. Nothing happened, just a clicking sound. "Oh, no." I tried three more times, but still nothing.

"Let me get Booker. If he can keep the POC going, I'm sure he can help fix your car." Maggie ran back inside as I tried a couple more times with no success. "Please," I muttered to the rusty Honda. "I can't afford a car right now."

Booker jogged out to me. "Pop the hood," he said. I released the hood and got out, walking over next to him. He wore the cologne I loved, and I leaned in for a whiff of leather mixed with ocean breeze as he wiggled the battery cables. He unscrewed a cap from the engine.

"I think you have a dead battery, which is an easy fix. But this, I'm afraid, could be a problem." He showed me the cap. A foamy brown liquid covered the inside. "I'm not sure, but you may have a cracked head. Didn't you say it was running a little hot on Monday?"

"Yes, but I checked the radiator like you said, and added antifreeze. It was almost empty." *Please, car, don't fail me now.*

Booker looked underneath the car and shook his head. He signaled for me to look, too. "Antifreeze." He pointed to the puddle of green liquid under my car.

"Ugh." I straightened.

"Don't panic yet. It may just be a leaky radiator. I have a friend who fixes cars. I'll have him take a look and see what he can do."

"Thank you. That'd be wonderful." I tucked my hands in the pockets of my jeans. "I can't afford a new car right now. They raised my rent again." My apartment was small, rundown, and everything was broken from the dishwasher to the A/C unit to the bathroom fan.

"When's the lease up?" Booker asked, closing the hood.

"It's up now, but I can't afford to move." I reached into the car and grabbed my purse. "Thanks for your help with the car. I appreciate it. See you on Monday." I turned for the street. Booker hooked a hand around my elbow.

"What are you doing?" His brow peaked as if bemused. "Come on. I'll take you home." He led me over to his beat-up car. The green, rusted out thing looked in worse shape than mine. The words "junk heap" came to mind as he reached for the door. "Stop scowling. She may not be much to look at, but she runs great," he assured me with a smile.

"If you say so. What does Seth call this car?" I chuckled as Booker struggled to pry the door open.

"POC Mobile. It stands for Piece of Crap, aptly name by my grandfather Samuel back in my early college days." The door finally relented and Booker stumbled back a little as it flew open.

I got in and buckled the seatbelt, double-checking to make sure it engaged. The inside of the car didn't look much better than the outside. Although clean, it had seen better days with its sun-scorched dashboard and paper-thin upholstery. I'd ridden in it several times, and each time it amazed me that it ran.

"Didn't they raise your rent not too long ago?" Booker settled in the car next to me.

"Yes. In the past eighteen months they've raised it almost two hundred fifty dollars."

"Why not move? Surely you can get a cheaper place." He turned up the heater as we approached Main Street. "I remember when Lilah lived in your complex it seemed things were always in disrepair."

"Yes, but the place is furnished and not many complexes offer furnished apartments anymore." I twisted my purse strap absentmindedly as I thought about my tight budget. "Besides, there's a little thing called first and last month's rent and a security deposit standing in the way of getting a new place. I'm afraid I'm stuck." What I hated the most was the fact that every time my rent went up, it gave me less money to put in savings. I needed a nest egg in case Garen found me and I had to run again.

"Where are we going?" I asked, as Booker turned left instead of right on Main.

"I have an idea. Maggie grew up over by Applegate Park. She and Lilah completely redid the trailer with the idea of selling it, but Mags decided to rent it out instead." Booker pulled up in front of a small green trailer. "Want to look inside?"

"It's seems nice, but again, the whole money issue, not to mention my lack of furnishings," I said, getting out.

"The place comes furnished. I can vouch for you so there's no need for a deposit or the first and last month's rent, and it's close to the office. On good days, which, believe it or not we do have once in a while, you can walk to the office if you want. It's maybe five minutes from here." He dug into the pocket of his well-worn jeans and pulled out a silver key, dangling it in the air. "I showed it for Seth yesterday to a young couple getting married so I still have the key. You want to see it?"

"Since we're here we may as well look."

"The neighborhood is pretty good since the city cleaned up Applegate Park about a year ago. It's safer than your neighborhood now." Booker opened the door and held it for me as I stepped in. He followed, shutting it behind him.

"The furnace is set on low so it'll be a bit cold, but it heats up quickly. The utilities are included, by the way." Booker stepped over to the thermostat as I glanced around. Though small, the place had a cozy charm. The colors were a bit bland, but knowing Maggie and Lilah, they were going for a neutral palate to appease a broad range of clientele.

The living room-kitchen area was not very large, which meant I'd have to move the couch and chair around to do my yoga, but everything looked clean and fresh. The place smelled of new carpet and paint. Booker showed me the small bathroom with a stacked stainless steel washer-dryer combo, a definite plus. I hated lugging my stuff to the Laundromat every week.

Another bonus? A small twelve-inch window above the shower. In the summer months I could open the window and get a nice cross breeze from the living room windows. I preferred fresh air to the A/C any day.

"Here's the first bedroom." Booker pushed the door ajar. I stepped into the tiny room. A full-size bed took up most of the space. "It's not very big, but it has under-the-bed drawers," he pointed, "and shelves in the closet so you won't need a dresser." He slid the closet doors to one side.

"The room over here," Booker led me across the short hall, "is designed for a kid. It has a loft bed with a desk underneath it. You can use it for office space or a storage room. It you want to get a roommate, I'm sure we could swap out the bed for one like in the other room."

"The place is nice and clean," I said cautiously. "How much is the rent?"

When he told me my mouth dropped open. "And you're sure the utilities are included?"

"Yes. Like I said, it's a good deal," he said with a smile.

The guy did have a great smile. Fun personality, sexy smile, and a good heart. Yup, Booker Gatto was swoon-worthy. I shook my head to break my self-imposed trance.

"You mean that?" he asked, surprised. He completely misunderstood my headshake . . . thankfully. Before I could say anything, he continued. "You're not interested in renting the place? I mean, it's a bit small, but it's a great price and close to work," he pointed out again.

"You're right. I'll take it, if you're sure about the deposit and all," I said, hoping my cheeks weren't as red as they felt.

"Great. I'll tell Maggie. You can move in whenever you want." I followed Booker out the door as he locked the trailer. "We can use my pickup. I'll help you move."

"I don't have much." We settled in his car and I continued. "Thank you, Booker. I'm grateful. I've been nervous about my bills ever since they raised the rent." I wiggled around a bit, trying to get comfortable in the threadbare seat. "Don't get me wrong. You pay me well. I'm just a bit of a savings freak, I guess." I laughed nervously. "I like to save a percentage of my salary each month, just in case. It's kind of silly to get upset about disposable income, I guess."

"That's smart. If only our government followed your example." Several minutes later he pulled up in front of my apartment. He leaned across the seat toward me as I got out. "I'll let you know tomorrow about your car. But I doubt we'll hear anything until Monday sometime. I'll pick you up for work. Sound good?"

I nodded.

I could've been wrong, but I swore Mr. Tall, Dark, and Sexy's car swaggered as he drove away.

"Too bad I've sworn off men."

Chapter 5

Booker stood at my door, his arm cocked as if he were about to knock. Startled, I flinched back out of reflex. Booker's eyes narrowed slightly. I straightened, embarrassed at my reaction.

"Morning, Tess," he said as he slowly lowered his arm.

He looked as sexy as ever in dress pants and a blue button-down shirt. That meant he wouldn't be in court today. He always wore a white shirt on those days. He hated the tie. He'd tug and loosen it constantly, mumbling that people should just conduct business in jeans and a t-shirt. As an MET agent he worked undercover most of the time, which meant no tie then either. He let me wear what I wanted, insisting pantsuits were for funerals when I asked if he preferred I wear one. I couldn't agree more.

"I was going to check my mail."

"I'm not stalking you, I promise," he chuckled, his face still tight. "Since you don't have a phone I couldn't call to see what time I should pick you up so I just guessed. You look beautiful."

"Thank you." I ran a hand over my yellow pencil skirt, smoothing it down. I'd worn the outfit many times before, but I'd take the compliment.

We walked down the pathway to the bank of mailboxes. Empty. I shouldn't bother. If anything were inside it'd be a bill. It's not as if my family could send me anything since no one knew my location. The temptation to send them a note just to let them know I was safe pulled hard on me some days. But memories of Garen's conversations with his boss, Senator Graft, about email and phone hacking reminded me of the risks. I didn't dare.

"Let me grab my purse." I ran back inside, double checking to make sure I'd locked everything before heading outside and over to Booker's car. I glanced around for anything out of the usual as he reached for the door.

"Tess, I'm okay with you not having a phone, but there are times I need to reach you." He tugged twice on the car door before it opened.

"Thanks." I settled in and buckled my seatbelt. "Are you saying I have to get a phone?" The thought made me sick. While at the women's shelter mapping out where I was going to go, one of the other ladies showed me how Garen had known where I was all the time. He'd installed a "Stalk My Buddies" app that tracked me wherever I went, and had buried the app deep within my phone so I wouldn't find it. Her boyfriend had done the same thing to her. Together, we took a hammer and obliterated our phones, a gesture that would've infuriated Garen if he knew. The memory made me smile.

Booker looked at me before starting the car. "No. I'm sure you have a good reason for not wanting a phone, but we need to come up with a way for me to contact you."

I relaxed into the seat. "I've been thinking about that, too, in fact, and have an idea that may work."

He pulled away from the curb after checking over his shoulder. "Let's hear it."

"You know how I take the laptop home to do work sometimes?" He nodded. "What if I took it home every night and left it turned on. That way if you need to talk to me you could send me an email. I'll turn up the volume so I'd hear the chime signaling me when I have mail."

"Sort of a *You've Got Mail* thingy. Brilliant idea."

"I guess I was bound to have one sooner or later," I said, chuckling.

"Tess, you have great ideas all the time." He glanced at me with an expression of genuine bewilderment.

"I do?"

"Whose idea was it to cross-file the bank reports? Who created a separate calendar of my court dates so they wouldn't get lost in our day-to-day appointments? That's saved my neck twice already. And aren't you the one—"

"Okay, okay. I'm incredibly brilliant."

"And modest," he added, a playful twinkle in his eye.

"Did you find out anything with my car?" I asked.

"Seth and I towed it last night. My buddy Dewey's going to look at it today," he explained, turning up the heat. It sputtered a little before the blower started. "Not to change the subject, but you look pretty today. Well, you always like pretty. I just like that color on you." He paused. "Did I already say that?"

I fingered the buttons on my turquoise shirt. "Yes, but it's nice to hear again. Thanks." I smiled down at the floor mats, unsure where else to look because I wasn't about to look at him.

"You're welcome." He turned right onto High Street. "I talked to Maggie yesterday. The trailer's all yours. When do you want to move in?" He parked the POC in front of a snow bank next to the office.

"That's great. I guess as soon as I get my car back." Booker opened his door and reached for mine, but I'd already bailed and made a beeline for the door. Going from a hot car to the cold outside killed me every time.

"I can help you," he offered, catching up at the menacing elevator. The building was an old structure he'd remodeled, but the elevator was still a bit sketchy. I tried to avoid it. Occasionally it'd stop between floors, and other times the doors would stick, not opening all the way. I pressed the number seven and hoped for the best. With a rattle and a groan, we ever so slowly ascended.

"I'll bring the truck to work tomorrow and we can move you after work, if that's good for you." Booker leaned against the silver handrail that circled the large elevator, looking relaxed as our tomb made its slow, rickety climb to the seventh floor.

"Booker, I don't have much. I can do it when I get my car back, but I do appreciate the offer."

The doors creaked open and we walked down the hall to the office. Lilah and Maggie had decorated the space nicely, giving the cozy room a warm, comfortable feeling, without sacrificing a professional touch.

A leather couch and matching chairs occupied the reception area, with an oversized coffee table anchoring everything together. Huge, wraparound windows filled the room with warm, natural light. A beautiful antique walnut desk stood to the right of the reception area. A brass planter with ivy tumbling over the edges sat on the top corner. My laptop was positioned in the center, along with a stack of files I needed to work on today. Both Booker's and my computer fed into a server that backed up all our information.

Booker's office was smaller than mine. It suited his personality perfectly: warm and friendly, with its antique cherry desk and leather chair. Various pictures hung on the wall and filled the top of his filing cabinet with numerous trips he and his friends made over the years. Some were of fishing trips, others were of vacations. All were of Seth, Cole, or both. To me it showed how important they were to him.

We spent the morning preparing a contract for a couple of elderly gentlemen, two old friends of Booker's grandfather, Samuel Gatto.

"Harry and John are my grandfather's oldest friends," Booker explained as we printed the document. "I've known them since I was a kid. I remember—"

A loud scuffling sound cut Booker off. I spun around to the door, my heart racing, my fingers wrapped tightly around the edge of the printer.

"It's okay, Tess." Booker placed a hand on my shoulder and squeezed gently. "It's just Harry. I saw him enter the building."

Heat flooded my face. I hurried to my desk in silence. I had to stop overreacting to unexpected sounds and people.

Booker opened the office door and a small balding man wearing plaid pants and carrying a bamboo cane shuffled into the office.

"Sammy, my boy." He embraced Booker, patting him on the head as he spoke. "Still can't believe how tall you are. Your grandfather was a little runt like me."

I chuckled to myself. I knew Samuel was Booker's given name because it was printed on the letterhead of our stationary, and he used Samuel when signing any legal documents. But Sammy was a new one.

"I ate all my vegetables like a good boy while I was growing up, Harry," Booker said as he turned to look down the hall. A few seconds later a second elderly man with white hair and almost identical plaid pants entered, gripping a walker with tennis balls anchored to the feet.

"Little Sammy Gatto, look at you," the man exclaimed, tapping Booker's cheek.

"Come on in, John. Good to see you. We have the contract ready. All you'll have to do is sign it." Booker led both men, slowly, to the couch. He laid out the contracts on the coffee table for the men to see.

"It's exactly as we talked about. Harry, you're selling John your barn and five acres for this amount of money." Booker pointed to a line in the contract.

"In my day a handshake would've been enough. Now we have to have lawyers and filing fees and whatnot. It drives the price sky high," Harry complained as he signed.

"Yes, but with you and me both having one foot in the grave, it's better for the grandkids to have a legally binding document," John said as he took his turn signing.

"And why do we care what the grandkids have to say? I say let 'em fight it out after we're dead," Harry said, red faced.

John laughed. "I like your thinkin'." He handed the pen to Booker.

"Tess, would you sign as a witness, please?" Booker passed the pen to me.

"Sure." When Booker hired me, he said I'd have to sign legal documents occasionally. I panicked at first since I used the fake name of Bennett when I was legally Selleck. I worried that it could cause legal problems if the truth were revealed. Then I realized if I wrote my name illegibly, I could use my real last name. I took the pen and signed the document, adding a curvy L for my middle initial.

"What's the L stand for?" John asked. "Lovely lady, maybe?" He added a wink with his question.

Booker chuckled while his eyes scanned the documents, making sure everything was in order.

"Layla. My dad's a huge Eric Clapton fan." I couldn't count the number of times he'd hoist me up on his shoulders or have me step on his feet, as he'd sing "Layla" while parading around the yard. Memories like that gave me the strength to keep going on during difficult days.

John's scratchy voice cut off my daydream. "Your grandfather would be proud of you, son. You've turned out well." He clasped the back of Booker's neck with his shaky hand.

"Thank you, sir. I appreciate that." Booker slipped the pen back into a brass cup on my desk as Harry gave the contract a onceover.

"Tell me, Sammy. How smart are you?" Harry asked, still looking at me.

"I graduated top of my class. Why?" Booker's tone was careful.

"I'm just wondering if you're smart enough to be dating this pretty young thing, because if you're not, I just may ask her out myself." Harry bounced his bushy gray eyebrows at me. I dipped my head and grinned.

"He's married, you old fool," John snapped the back feet of his walker on the ground and shook his head.

"I'm divorced," Booker corrected.

"Sorry to hear that, son. Too many people think marriage is disposable nowadays. " Harry shook his head. "It's a shame."

"Old man, you need to stop your yammering. His ex is in jail, remember?" John said through tight lips.

"Oh yeah. I forgot. 'Pologize," Harry said with a curt nod as John shooed him to the door. "Thank you for all your help, Sammy," he added, exiting the door behind John.

Booker tucked his hands in his pockets and smiled. "Those two are something else."

"They certainly are, Sammy." I placed the documents in a folder with the men's names on it. I gathered a small stack of files and walked over to the filing cabinet. Booker settled on the corner of my desk as I filed everything.

"You know all about my middle name now, so tell me where the name Booker comes from?" I sat in my chair after I finished and Booker turned to face me.

"Long story," he said sheepishly.

"And judging from your reluctance to share it, I'd guess it's a tad embarrassing, little Sammy?" I teased. I felt fairly confident I could tease him, but after Garen, I took nothing for granted anymore.

Booker leaned back and laughed. "I love it when you joke." He tugged playfully on a strand of my hair. "When I first joined the military, Seth's dad was my commanding officer."

"Were you a cop?" I asked.

He nodded. "Military police. And very green. I'd never made an arrest on my own. I always had a partner and they'd take the collar . . . the credit. Seniority," he explained. "When I made my first arrest on my own, a shoplifting senior citizen, I was pretty excited. I kept asking my supervisor if I could book her into custody."

"A senior citizen?" I arched my brow.

"Yes, and don't judge me." He chuckled. "At first the department was unsure about pressing charges on the elderly woman. After three hours in the interrogation room with her, and me continually asking if I could book her yet, I was finally granted permission." He rubbed a hand over his jaw. "So I booked her and placed her in the women's holding cell. I was so proud." He stood and walked to the front of my desk.

"And?" I pressed.

He buried his hands in his pockets as he chuckled low. It twisted my tummy . . . in a good way.

"Half an hour later screams bellowed from the holding tank. Several of us ran in to find my senior citizen standing in front of the toilet . . . well, peeing." He shook his head. "Turns out my perpetrator was male, not female."

"How did you miss that?"

"It was an innocent mistake. She . . . *he* had no ID on him, and his name was Kelly. I just assumed he was a girl because of his clothes, baby blue sweats and a pink baggie sweat shirt, so I checked the female box on the form without asking. Add to the fact that he was a large man with an impressive pair of man-boobs," he explained. "Anyone could've made the mistake."

Watching him as he recounted the story, his comical expressions, and the way he waved his hands dramatically in the air made me laugh. Booker pressed his lips together, fighting a grin.

"Anyway, the next day the sergeant was handing out assignments in our morning briefing. He blanked out on my name, and in frustration called me 'You, Book Her'. Well, it didn't take long for everyone in the unit to pick up on it. Within a couple hours it evolved to Booker. Like I said, Seth's dad was my commander and since I lived with them, naturally he felt it his duty to call me Booker around the house. My grandfather, Samuel, always up for a good laugh, joined in. As they say, the rest is history."

Unable to stop grinning, I dropped my head down in an effort to hide my face.

"Tess," he said, "I love your smile, don't hide it." His hand slipped under my chin and he brought my face to his. "It's infectious, sexy as h—heck," he corrected himself with a wink and a grin. He'd been working hard to curb his swearing. I couldn't remember ever hearing him cuss, but I did hear the sound of money clinking against glass coming from his office every now and then.

"I haven't sworn yet today," he said, still holding my chin. He softly caressed it with his thumb.

"It's only eleven-fifteen," I teased.

"What can I say? I'm a work in progress." He continued to stroke my jaw with his thumb as he lowered his face toward mine.

I wasn't sure what to do. Part of me, a large part, danced in anticipation. I dreamt of kissing Booker. He was the first man who'd sparked my interest since I escaped. Another part of me wanted to run and hide. I'd not allowed myself any close relationships with men, or anyone, after Garen. But I missed human contact. Coming from a boisterous, loving, Irish catholic home, we laughed, we teased, we hugged. All things Garen hated. All things I longed for again.

As Booker closed the distance between us, I held my breath..

Chapter 6

"I'm too sexy for my shirt / Too sexy for my shirt / So sexy . . ."

"Maggie," Booker half grumbled, half chuckled as he pulled back, digging his cell phone from his pocket as the magic of the moment evaporated.

"Sorry. If I leave my phone lying around at Seth's, Maggie sabotages it. Last week I had Barbie wallpaper on all my screens," he explained, as "I'm Too Sexy for my Shirt" began again. He glanced at the display. "Oh, good. It's Dewey, the guy working on your car." He pressed the phone to his ear.

I used the interruption to gather myself. Strong attraction or not, I still didn't know if I wanted to try to have a relationship again. With Booker, I felt safe, and I'd even let my guard down, opening up and letting my former self peek through. Yet fear still owned me, no matter how hard I tried to put it behind me. It didn't help that every time I took a shower, the scars across my stomach and back reminded me just how lucky I was to be alive. I ran my hand over my shirt, rubbing the healed wounds beneath—well, physically healed wounds. I doubted I'd ever heal emotionally.

"Good news and bad news. Which do you want first?" Booker asked, shoving the phone back into his pocket.

"Good?"

"Dewey replaced the battery, and he has to replace the radiator which means it's not a cracked head. The bad news is that since the car is old, he doesn't have it in stock so he'll need to order it. It'll take about three days." He shrugged. "I'll give you a ride to and from work until then, so no need to worry, and with your moving into Maggie's trailer, it'll be even more convenient for you."

"Thanks, Booker. I appreciate everything."

"I haven't done anything yet," he said. "If you need boxes, I know that Donna and Haley, the interior design duo decorating on the sixth floor, have some. You might want to run and grab them before they break them down for the recycle bin." Booker reached into his pocket. "Here." He tossed me the key. "Stick them in the car."

"Whoa," I said, catching the keys despite the poor toss.

"Sorry," he grimaced, "but nice catch."

"I was captain of the lacrosse team in high school, both my junior and senior years."

"No kidding," he said, clearly surprised. "I remembered you saying you played, I didn't know you were captain. You any good at basketball?"

"I can hold my own," I bragged a little.

"Aren't you just full of surprises today, Tess *Layla*?" he said with a nod, adding, "By the way, some of my MET gear is still in the trunk. I keep forgetting to take it in the house. Just shove it to the back."

"Okay." I reached for the door.

"I'm expecting a client so leave that ajar, will you?"

"There's no one on the calendar until two thirty." Had I messed up? My stomach tightened.

"She's not on the schedule. This is a friend of a friend," he explained. "It's not even real estate related, actually. She just needs some legal advice."

She. He'd had several female clients come in over the past two months with non-real estate questions. Since he left his office door open most of the time, I'd overheard several of the conversations. They seldom wanted legal advice. They wanted Booker. Some were more overt with their flirting, while others were more subtle, but in the end, he'd send them away. He now had me screen all his appointments so he could get his real casework done. This one must've called him on his personal phone.

I went to the sixth floor and grabbed five boxes. Haley helped me carry them to Booker's car.

"He's freaking cute, don't you think?" she asked as we approached the POC.

"Booker? Yes, I guess," I said, playing it cool.

"You guess? Either you're blind or insane," Haley said as I opened the back door. We stuffed three large boxes inside.

"Okay, he's freaking cute." We both chuckled. With the backseat full of boxes, we headed for the trunk. He'd replaced the lock recently. The shiny new lock against the banged up metal of the trunk contrasted starkly.

"Too bad he has commitment issues," Haley said as I opened the trunk. "Of course, if my ex was using me to spy on the police force so my boyfriend could steal drugs easier, I don't think I'd be too excited to get involved again either."

My mouth dropped open. "Are you serious?" I pushed the MET gear Booker told me about, a vest, empty gun belt, and a long silver case containing who knows what, to the back. I didn't buy his excuse that he forgot to take the gear in the house. I'd bet the things were a security blanket to him. He'd been a cop most of his adult life—he probably felt naked without the stuff.

Haley shut the trunk after I placed the last box inside. "How's this for sad: Booker busted his ex on their six month wedding anniversary, no less, walking in on her in bed with her boyfriend in *his* house. She ended up going to jail when everything came out. It wasn't pretty," she said as we headed back inside.

"Poor Booker. He must've been devastated." I walked to the elevators only because Haley did.

"He was pretty broken up. He divorced her in a New York minute. Her name had something to do with money, like Penny or . . . I can't remember. I can tell you, the whole thing soured him on relationships. I wouldn't get my hopes up," she warned as the elevator stopped at her floor. "I can't see Booker getting seriously involved with anyone. He's strictly a player."

She stepped out. "We just work together," I assured her.

"Right." Haley laughed as the elevator creaked shut.

Booker's office door was closed when I returned. I could hear his mumbled voice along with that of a woman's as I finished some paperwork. A couple of times the woman sniffled as if she were crying. Half an hour later his door opened and a lanky, strawberry blond woman emerged. She was angled back toward Booker and I couldn't see her face.

"Thank you, and please thank Seth for talking you into taking my case. I know you don't normally handle this type of work," she said in a sad voice.

"You're welcome, Hillary. And it was Maggie who talked me into it, not Seth," he insisted.

"Maggie? Oh, I see." She flipped her hair over her shoulder and turned, exposing the battered mess that was her face. Black and green bruises circled her eyes. I guessed them to be a few days old. Her swollen lower lip had a small cut on the left corner, and her right arm was in a sling.

I tried not to react. I tried to distance myself from my memories. I tried telling myself that Hillary had been brutalized, not me. I tried not to relive the nightmares.

I failed.

Darkness swamped the room around me. I couldn't pull my eyes away from Hillary's bruised face. Vomit raced up my throat, and I swallowed it back down. Booker continued to talk to the girl as he laid her file on my desk.

"I'll walk you to the elevator," he said, his voice a million miles away.

The office door clicked shut after them. I pulled in deep breaths, again and again. It didn't help. I stared hard at the file he'd placed there, knowing not to open it. But like a moth to a flame, I couldn't stop myself.

Pictures of Hillary lay on top, each showing angry black and purple bruises, fresh bruises. These had to have been taken right after the beating. Blood covered her mouth and shirt, and her hair was everywhere. The pictures shook violently in my hand as I relived my final beating from Garen. I struggled to breathe, as if my head were being shoved . . . I pinched my eyes shut, wincing at the pain of every kick, every blow—each feeling as real as they did four years ago.

Warm hands wrapped around my shoulders.

"Tess, you're safe now." The pictures of Hillary were pulled from my hand. I jumped as something touched my cheeks.

"It's just tissue, Tess." My eyes flew to Booker as he wiped my face. I was crying and didn't realize it. Only then did I realize my arms were wrapped tightly around me as I rocked back and forth. The photos were wrinkled in the corner from my grip.

Humiliation washed over me. I was going to lose this job, too.

"I'm so . . . sorry." The words jerked in my chest. "I . . . I . . ." I couldn't speak. I took the tissue from him and wiped the fresh tears coming down.

"Does he live around here?" Booker asked softly. He knelt at my side, concern etched on his face. I thought of lying, blaming my reaction on my struggles with blood, but I didn't.

"No," I whispered.

"I'm so sorry, Tess. If I'd known I would've arranged to meet her after hours." He took the folder and filed it in the cabinet.

"Please don't fire me," I pleaded as my strength slowly seeped back. "I . . . I need . . . this job. It won't . . . happen again."

"I'm not going to fire you, Tess. You're a fantastic secretary. Besides, it's not as if we handle cases like this all the time. I only took this as a favor for Maggie," Booker assured me. He crossed the room and poured me a cup of water from the cooler.

"Here, drink this." He handed it to me. I downed it quickly and then tossed the paper cup in the trashcan below my desk.

"Do you want to talk about it?" he asked. I shook my head and he nodded. "If you ever do, I'm here."

"Thank you," I whispered.

An hour later he left for a meeting across town, insisting he'd cancel if I needed him to. "I'm fine, I swear."

After his car pulled away, I sat in the bathroom and wept. I didn't want to be scared anymore. I wanted my life back.

Chapter 7

6 years ago

The pressure from Garen's job had him on edge more often than not. His boss, Senator Graft, had a mess on his hands after an alleged illegal deal with an upstart cell phone provider was leaked to the press. Garen ran himself ragged doing damage control. While Garen hadn't hit me again, he regularly berated me for things I'd done wrong. He loved order and demanded our townhome be immaculate at all times. The canned goods were lined up in the pantry perfectly, tallest to shortest based on label color, and the boxed foods were arranged in descending order. The towels were aligned in the linen closet with equal spacing around each stack, per Garen's orders. When I joked about his anal-retentive tendencies, he went crazy on me, pressing me up against the wall, screaming in my face.

"I'm working hard to make a life for us, Terese. Is it too much to ask that you keep a neat home?" I shrank tight against the wall as he yelled. "I'm sorry you want to live like a pig, but this is my home and you'll keep it orderly! Understood?" I nodded, afraid of saying something to upset him and he'd strike me.

"If you'd think of someone besides yourself," he said, calming himself and pulling back, "I wouldn't get so upset. I'm beginning to believe you enjoy provoking me." He tugged a strand of my hair. I assumed he meant it as a playful gesture, but my head jerked sharply to the side, nevertheless.

His obsessiveness carried over to the dirty laundry, of all things. The soiled clothes were to be folded in neat stacks in the hamper until they were washed. His dress shirts were to be dried for exactly forty-two minutes, then immediately pressed.

"Why don't we just send them out to be dry-cleaned?" I asked a few weeks after my anal retentive comment. I'd lost track of time while studying for a math exam and let a shirt sit too long in the dryer. He wasn't happy.

"Why? I think you know full well why, Terese. All our extra money goes to pay for your silly bachelor's degree, in *dance*," he snapped. "Oh, and in business. Like everybody and their dog doesn't have a degree in business. Great choice." His snarky tone infuriated me.

"Silly? My degree is not silly." I took the shirt I'd been ironing and tossed it at him. I wheeled around to leave the room when his hand slammed down on my shoulder and he twisted me back to him. He planted his hands above the collarbone on either side of my neck, and with his forefinger and thumb squeezed my shoulders. The stabbing pain drove me to my knees.

"I will not be spoken to in that manner, is that understood?" he said through clenched teeth.

"Stop it, you're hurting me," I pleaded. His jaw ticked twice before he let go.

I stood, rubbing my tender neck and shoulders. This had to end. I'd tried to make our relationship work, but his temper made our chance at a happy marriage impossible. I decided to broach the subject of counseling. He was more receptive and usually more reasonable after one of his outbursts.

"Garen, I've been thinking." I chewed on my bottom lip. "Maybe you should talk to someone about . . . about your anger management issues." He said nothing as I unplugged the iron and neatly wrapped the cord up. I took a slow breath in then blew it out and continued. "Your temper seems to be getting worse lately. I'm questioning whether you and I will survive as a couple, you know? I mean, if you're going to continue to hurt me—"

"You're giving up on us?" He stepped toward me. I planted my feet shoulder width apart, standing my ground, even if my hands trembled. "A few mistakes and you're calling it quits? Terese, you're a fighter, you never give up. It's one of the reasons I married you. Even though your parents forced you to pick up lacrosse, you worked night and day to become the team captain." He wrung his hands as he paced in front of me. His face was tight, and he looked worried. Knowing he wanted to make our marriage work took me by surprise since all he'd done was point out my shortcomings. I didn't realize I had so many before marrying him.

He continued. "Didn't you tell me that you used to get only three or four hours of sleep, weeks on end, so you could keep your grades up because you wouldn't give up dance? You maintained a four-point-oh through it all." He stopped and turned to me. "I need a wife who's going to stand by me. I mean, I know I struggle with my anger sometimes, but I can't believe you want to call it quits already. I love you."

I felt terrible. And ashamed that I'd even considered divorce. He was right. I didn't quit, ever. "I'm sorry. It's just that I don't want to live in fear, either," I said softly.

He pulled me into his arms. "I'm sorry, too. I shouldn't take my bad days out on you. We have to stick together, Terese. A divorce is definitely not part of my Life Plan." He kissed my forehead. "I can't think of anyone who'd make a better first lady than you." He apologized once more, insisting it wouldn't happen again. "It wouldn't bode well for my political future if it got out I had to get therapy for anger management. I'll do better. I mean, it's not like I'm one of those crazy actors who beat up paparazzi." He chuckled. Relieved at his renewed commitment, I let the issue drop.

~*~

"Perfect." I set a bouquet of white roses in the center of the table. Being our six-month anniversary, I wanted everything to be special. I'd hurried home after taking my last final of the semester and prepared all of Garen's favorite foods. The eggplant Parmesan recipe was tricky, at least for me. I couldn't cook to save my life, but I hoped that this time it'd work. I followed the recipe exactly and even watched a YouTube video of a French chef preparing the exact dish.

I removed a pair of silver candlesticks, a wedding gift, from a long slender box. I set them on either side of the flowers and lit them as his car pulled into the driveway of our small two-story townhouse. I did a quick check of the living-dining room combination to make sure everything was in its place. The gray linen couch and chair sat exactly at a ninety-degree angle. I'd dusted the torch lamp, made sure the flat-screen TV hung perfectly straight on the wall, and dusted the photos from our wedding, spacing them equally on the side table. Nothing was out of place, which meant Garen should be pleased. A perfect evening.

The door flew open and Garen stormed in, his overcoat tucked neatly under his arm alongside his briefcase. Nervously, I smoothed down my apron, wishing I'd thought to remove it. I wore my white button down shirt and plaid blue and green skirt Garen liked.

"I hope dinner's ready. I'm starved." His eyes narrowed on me before he guided his briefcase into its spot next to the living room chair along the wall, and hung his coat in the closet.

"How was your day?" I untied the apron and placed it neatly in a kitchen drawer.

He angled his head and said, "How do you think it was, Terese? Do I look like I'm in a good mood?" He spun away and went into the living room to watch the news. Like he always did. He hadn't noticed the beautiful table I'd set, or commented on how delicious the eggplant Parmesan smelled as it baked in the oven.

I stepped next to him as he sat on the couch, being careful not to block the TV. He hated when I interrupted the news. I waited patiently until the commercial.

"Happy anniversary, Garen." I smiled, settling in next to him and placing my hand on his knee.

His eyes stayed on the TV. "It's not our anniversary." He dropped his head back against the couch and rubbed his temples with his middle fingers. When I tried to do it for him, he slapped my hands away. I rubbed at the sting.

"It's our six-month anniversary. I made eggplant Parmesan and apricot turnovers." I smiled as his eyes met mine in a sneer.

"You actually cooked?" he snapped. "So I guess that means we'll be getting our stomachs pumped for dessert?" He pushed to his feet and strolled into the kitchen. I followed, letting his snide comment roll off my back. I wanted tonight to be perfect. I fought hard for us the past six months. Tonight I wanted to remember why I fell in love with him.

"Maybe you'll be surprised. I've really tried to make it a special night." I smiled proudly as he picked up one of the turnovers and examined it. A moment later he tossed it callously onto the plate.

"I'll wash up. If this crap totally sucks, there's leftover Chinese in the fridge we can eat." Without so much as a glance my way, he headed straight for the bathroom, taking my dreams of a romantic evening with him.

I increased the temperature to 450° on the eggplant to brown the top, setting the timer for five minutes. I slumped against the counter, my arms folded, and wondered what it'd take to please him. What was wrong with me? It felt like I was back in ninth grade taking dance from Ms. Liddy again. Trying and trying, yet never quite meeting her expectations.

"Terese, come here, please." Garen's voice echoed low and threatening through the small townhome. I swallowed hard and ran to him. This couldn't be good. I entered the small bathroom to find him standing in front of the linen closet, his arm pinned to the doorframe, his face, blood red, his breath, heavy.

"What's wrong?" I stayed out of reach. I knew what was coming.

"How many times do I have to explain how the closet is to be organized?" His eyes met mine. Fire burned within them. He answered before I could. "This closet is twenty-six inches. If the towels are folded properly into thirds, each measuring eight inches across, then we can have three stacks of towels, with an inch between each stack." He drew in a deep breath. "Having space around the towels allows for airflow, thus keeping the towels from smelling stale and musty."

"I did measure them. They're eight inches." I made sure. I always made sure.

He stepped back and jabbed his hand at the towels. The center stack had tipped over to the right, knocking all the towels out of alignment. "But . . . I . . . ." I shook my head, then remembered. I'd placed the center stack on the shelf as the timer on the dryer went off. I hurried to remove his shirts before they wrinkled. I meant to come back and align the towels, but got busy with dinner and completely forgot. I didn't dare explain it to Garen. He hated excuses. He considered them weakness.

"I'm sorry." I dropped my head and stepped to the closet to fix the towels.

"You did this on purpose, didn't you?" He stood so close to my side his breath beat on my cheek in short puffs.

"No, I swear. It was an accident." Garen's hands fisted into balls. I swallowed hard. "I'm sorry. It won't happen again." I straightened the towels using the ruler Garen had tacked to the inside of the door.

He turned to the sink and washed his hands as I measured and refolded. He shaved his face again, not an uncommon thing for him. He often shaved twice a day. Only today the hum of the electric razor drowned out the beeping of the timer in the kitchen. Garen smelled it first. The unmistakable odor of burnt food filled the air. He darted out of the bathroom and turned for the kitchen. I stood frozen. I knew what had happened. The eggplant was burnt.

The sound of the pan crashing into the sink jolted me. I busied myself with the towels again, hating that my hands shook as I did. Garen's thundering footsteps did little to quell the fear rising inside me.

"Ruined. Burnt to a crisp. What possessed you to turn the oven up so high, you moron?" He shoved his face into mine as he railed. "Eggplant is expensive this time of year. At least ten dollars now gone," he snapped his fingers in my face, "just like that."

"I—I was going to be right there. I set the timer, but didn't hear it over your razor." I replaced the ruler on the nail inside the door and bravely turned to face him, even though I felt anything but.

"So this is my fault?" Spittle flew from his mouth and I flinched back. "I suppose the skewed towels are my fault, too?" I shook my head. He shoved his hand toward me and I flinched, only he didn't hit me. Instead, he grabbed a handful of towels from the pantry behind me and tossed them across the room. He repeated the action until all the towels lay scattered across the room. "I will not be blamed for your shortcomings, do you understand?"

"But—"

"Also, I thought we had a deal," he interrupted. "You're to clean the bathroom on Monday, Wednesday, and Friday in the morning so I won't have to smell that horrible cleaner you insist on using. What day is it, Terese?"

"Friday. And I did clean it," I lied. So busy preparing for our anniversary, it slipped my mind.

"Oh? Where's the dirty rag then?" He pointed to the empty rack he'd installed on the inside of the bathroom cabinet door for drying soiled rags so they wouldn't mildew.

Before I could answer, he grabbed a handful of my hair and dragged me to the toilet. He lifted the seat and shoved my head into the bowl, stopping an inch short of the water. "Does that smell clean to you, Terese?" I didn't dare move, afraid my face would touch the water. "I guess this won't bother you either since it's clean." He shoved my head down into the bowl, submerging it. I grabbed the rim of the toilet and pushed upward, desperate for air, but he held me firmly.

"I. Will. Not. Be. Lied. To." His words were muffled by the water that filled my ears, but I still heard each and every syllable. My head hit the bottom of the bowl with each anger-filled word. Finally, he jerked me back and shoved me to the floor. "Clean up this mess. And don't ever lie to me again."

I lay on the floor, gasping for breath as he stomped from the room. My silent tears mixed with toilet water as I cleaned up the mess. How could I go on living like this? How?

After rechecking three times to make sure I put everything in its proper place, I stripped off my wet clothes, hanging them on the hook on the back of the bathroom door to dry, and slipped into the shower.

Hopelessness enveloped me as the water ran over my trembling body. He was never going to get his temper in control. I cried into my hands, feeling like a complete failure. *I can't do this anymore. I just can't.*

After exhausting my tears, I dressed in pajamas before quietly slipping onto my bed and staring mindlessly at the ceiling of the dark bedroom. Only a few minutes passed before a soft knock at the door jolted me back from my stupor.

"May I come in?" Garen asked softly. He had a tray of Chinese food in his hands along with the roses from the table. "I thought you might be hungry."

I carefully sat up quickly as he set the tray on the nightstand. "I cleaned up the mess and refolded the towels, Garen. I triple checked everything. And my wet clothes are hung on the hook to dry so they won't mold in the hamper." My heart beat like a caged bird.

"Yes, I saw that. It looks very nice." He sat next to me and took my hand in his. "Terese, I'm so sorry for losing my temper." Tears tumbled down his cheeks as he brought my hands to his lips and gently kissed them. "Work's been a beast lately. Then coming home to all of this just set me off." The tears flowed hard now, followed with breathy sobs. "I'm begging you to forgive me. I don't know why I went crazy. It's not like me. I promise it'll never happen again."

"You've said that before, Garen." My tears began. "You scared me. I thought . . ."

"Shhh." He pressed his fingers to my mouth. "It'll never happen again. I'll get counseling if you'll just say you've forgiven me. We can get through this, Terese. Just give me another shot, please. I'm begging you. It'll get better from here on out. I promise."

I stared into the sad gray eyes I'd fallen in love with back in high school. The eyes I still loved, despite his temper. I didn't want to let him go. I didn't want to fail. I hoped to make our marriage work. I knew I wasn't the first person to be in this situation. Certainly there had to be a way to make it work.

I wiped the moisture from his face. "If you promise to get counseling, I'll stay. I can't live like this, Garen. I just can't."

"I will, Terese, I promise." He smiled. "Things will be better around here from now on."

Chapter 8

Present day

"Four boxes?" Booker asked, placing the boxes in the back of his pickup. I came home after work yesterday and packed my apartment. It felt good to be moving. I'd lived here since escaping Garen and wanted to move on, let the nightmares go. Having a new place with my new job would be a fresh start. This apartment was my escape from Garen. The new place would be my new beginning.

"Yes." I laughed at his frown. "Remember, it's a furnished apartment. All I need are my personal belongings and linens. Even the kitchen came furnished."

"Oh yeah. Didn't think about that." Booker set the last box in the truck and the top popped open. "Sorry." He started to intertwine the flaps on the box and then stopped. "Is this entire box full of shoes?" He pulled the flap back as I reached inside and grabbed my favorite pair of flip-flops.

"I sort of have a thing for shoes." I waved the bright pink and blue sandals at him.

"You haven't even worn some of these." He held up a black spiked pump. The tag flapped in the breeze.

"I have no place to wear them." I took the shoe from him and placed it back in the box alongside the flip-flops.

"Now those you could wear." He pointed to the knee-high black boots. They too had tags.

"Those are a little ostentatious. I shouldn't have bought them." I quickly twisted the flaps shut.

"Ostentatious?" His mouth ticked up in the corner. "I like 'em."

Embarrassed and not knowing what to say, I pushed the box up next to the others as he closed the tailgate. He opened the passenger door and held my hand as I climbed into the black F-350. What a contrast to the POC.

"I don't think Maggie's place has pots and pans." Booker turned the key in the ignition and the truck roared to life. "I have some extras. Do you mind stopping by my place to pick them up?"

"If you're sure," I said hesitantly, buckling my seatbelt.

"Positive. I believe I have some dishes you can have also." He turned the radio on low and slipped in a Tim McGraw CD. "Do you like country music?" he asked as we rounded the corner near the center of town several minutes later.

Hated it. I smiled and lied. "Sure."

He chuckled. Okay, so I didn't lie very well. "How about Lifehouse?" He inserted another CD.

"You can listen to country. I don't mind."

"No big deal. I'm a song person more than a genre. If I like the song, I listen," he insisted. "Do you have a favorite?"

"Neoclassical," I admitted. Garen hated neoclassical and I seldom listened to it. He insisted on straight classical. After moving to Port Fare, I purchased a few CD's for the car. My new favorite was Jennifer Thomas. I loved to put on her CD and blast the music. I'd choreographed several dance routines in my head that I was dying to try out in the gym at the local recreation center. My tiny apartment made yoga impossible, let alone dancing. I missed dancing.

"Neo what?" Booker asked.

"Neoclassical. It's classical crossover," I said. "Oh, yeah! And I just discovered Lindsey Stirling. She's a dubstep violinist. She's incredibly talented." Never in my wildest dreams would I've imagined mixing classical violin music with dubstep to be a good thing. But it was. "I love her music. It has incredible energy," I gushed.

He cringed. "Dub . . . Well, I don't have either of those."

"Don't judge without hearing them, little Sammy," I teased.

"If you promise not to call me that in front of Magpie, I promise to give them a try," he said.

"Deal."

The leaves on the trees had turned from green to golden yellows, bold reds, and burnt oranges. They tumbled to the ground with the slightest breeze. It seemed to rain leaves as we drove down the road. He pulled into the driveway of a beautiful red brick two-story home with white colonial pillars. Gold and burgundy mums framed the front yard, and a huge oak tree that still held its leaves despite the cool autumn air. "This is the abode. Come on."

The inside was lovely. Clearly, Booker loved wood. The dining room had a stunning dark wood table. I'd never seen anything quite like it, sporting detailed carvings on the legs. A matching China hutch stood against the wall. He led me to the kitchen. Breathtaking, dark gray cabinets showcased the room, and white marble countertops with veined gray streaks topped them off. A row of windows above the sink made the room feel part of the backyard.

"This is beautiful." I caressed one of the cabinet doors.

"Thanks. When I'm uptight or bored, I build," he said with a shrug.

"That's right. I forgot you worked with wood. Lilah showed me the cabinets you built for Cole." I nodded to the handcrafted kitchen island. "Incredible. You could make a fortune doing custom cabinetry."

"No. I'm too slow."

I laughed. "I find that hard to believe. You set your office up in two days. You drive . . ." I trailed off, not wanting to offend him.

"I drive like a madman?" He chuckled as my face flooded with color. "When I'm doing something I enjoy, I never rush. Some things shouldn't be rushed, not if you want it done right."

I couldn't help but stare at his mouth, with his full bottom lip and his sexy dimples as he spoke, and wondered if that included kissing. I imagined it did. *I need to stop imagining that.*

"I'm game if you are," he said.

"Game?" I swallowed hard, jerking my eyes from his mouth.

"I said we'll need to dig through some of the boxes in the basement to find a set of dishes for the trailer, but I'm game if you are." He pointed to the basement door.

Oh yeah, completely embarrassing. "That'd be great, if you're sure it's not a bother."

"Not at all." He opened the door.

"Would it be alright if I used the powder room first?"

"Nope, sorry." He went down two steps and angled back, a grin filling his mischievous face. "Second door on the right down that hall." He pointed to a hallway off the family room.

"Get your hormones under control," I lectured my reflection in the bathroom mirror as I washed my hands in the marble sink. A pink liquid soap bottle with a picture of Hello Kitty sat on the counter. Maggie, no doubt.

I made my way back down the hallway, noting the collection of pictures on the wall. He had some from both Maggie and Seth's wedding, and Cole and Lilah's. A picture of Booker with an older gentleman caught my eye, too. They stood in front of a car that all through high school my brother insisted was the best car ever: an Aston Martin. The older man had a grin from ear to ear.

Another photo, slightly yellowed with age, one I assumed was his family, hung next to it. Booker and the man in the photo looked almost identical, from their dark wavy brown hair to their soulful brown eyes. It had to be Booker's dad. The woman was pretty, and tall, almost as tall as her husband. What I assumed was a young Booker and a girl, probably his sister, stood in front of the parents. Booker couldn't have been more than eight. His teeth were too big for his face, having not grown into them yet, but you could tell he'd be a looker even then. His sister had dark hair and eyes, but she was quite a bit smaller. I guessed her to be about six.

"That's my family," Booker said, startling me. I stepped back. He held out a glass of lemonade.

"Thanks." I took the glass. "You look like your dad," I said, sipping the delicious drink.

"Everyone tells me that. He smiled. "He died when I was ten. Cancer." He let out a hard breath. "And my mom and sister were killed by a couple of thugs who broke into our home looking for drug money. I was sixteen."

"Booker, I'm so sorry." I placed my hand on his arm as pain twisted his face.

"My sister and I were twins," he said.

"I'm a twin, too. A sister. And I have an older brother." We softly bumped fists. We were both twins. What were the odds? I missed my family something awful. I ached to hear their voices, to hug and hold them again. Afraid of tearing up, I pointed to the picture of Booker's sister. "I wouldn't have guessed you were twins. Your sister's tiny."

"Sara had asthma. The doctors struggled to control it. It stunted her physical growth. If that wasn't enough, when she turned twelve she developed juvenile diabetes. The poor thing just couldn't catch a break." The sadness in his eyes broke my heart. I couldn't imagine his loss; at least I had hope of seeing my family again, someday. Hopefully.

Time to change the subject.

"So, I take it those are the dishes." I pointed to the box sitting on the counter.

"Yup. They were in the first box I checked. Guess it's meant to be that you have them." I followed him into the kitchen and he opened the box, pulling out a white plate with a thin silver line around the rim, and blue flowers in the center.

"Forget-me-nots." I traced the pretty blue flowers with my finger.

Booker's eyes widened in surprise. "Correct. Most people mistakenly call these violets. My grandfather gave the plates to my grandmother for their thirtieth wedding anniversary. They were her favorite flower."

"My dad's an avid gardener. He has the most beautiful flowerbeds I've ever seen. He also grows vegetables. You should taste his tomatoes." I closed my eyes, remembering the taste. "I used to help him plant the garden when I lived at home."

"The trailer only has a small yard, but there's enough room to grow a few things if you'd like." He wrapped the newspaper around the dish and set it carefully into the box.

"Maybe I will, although the growing season is quite short here. Did you know this area gets on average ninety-two inches of snow a year? Yuck!" And the exact reason why I chose the Rochester, New York, area to escape to. Garen knew how much I hated the cold. He'd never think to come looking for me here . . . at least that was my hope.

"Ninety-two inches? I didn't know that. Sounds like you're not a fan of the snow. Why stay?" Booker pressed.

I stammered for a minute, not knowing what to say. "It grows on you, and it's beautiful. Green and lush."

"When it's not snowing," he pointed out, closing the box. "Look, I know these plates have seen better days, so if you'd rather buy new, it won't bother me in the least."

"I feel bad, taking them. I'm sure they have sentimental value to you."

He pointed to the stove. One of the plates had been mounted on the wall above it. "Mags did that for me. She says my place is too masculine."

"Or she's a sweetheart and knows how much these mean to you."

"Knowing Magpie, I'd say you were right. But seriously, I need to de-junk around here. If you don't take the plates I'm donating them to the local thrift store along with seven other boxes in the basement."

"Are you sure? It'd be nice not to have to dip into my savings."

"Positive." He set the box on the floor next to the counter. "Okay, tell me what you like to cook and I'll see what kind of pans I have for you."

"Booker, I don't want to take—" He threw open a large pantry filled to the brim with pans. My mouth dropped open.

"Don't judge me." He chuckled. "Seth's worse, just for the record."

"Judge you? Remember my box of unworn shoes?"

"Good point. Alright, what do you like to cook?"

"I hate to cook. I'm terrible at it." I shrugged, feeling guilty looking at all his pans and knowing he clearly enjoyed it.

"You hate . . ." He dramatically stretched his arms across the pantry doorway. "She didn't mean it," he said to the pans, while glancing playfully at me over his shoulder. "Okay. Even haters have to cook a little." He pulled out a couple of small pans, saucepans he called them, and a frying pan, and set them on the counter. When he reached back in the pantry for more, I stopped him.

"Booker, this is plenty."

He faced me. "Wow, you don't like to cook." He closed the doors. "I guess that's it then. I'll take—"

A large black dog came bounding around the corner, barking. I all but jumped into Booker's arms, staring at the huge dog with huge teeth. "She won't bite. She may lick you to death, but she won't hurt you. You're safe." We stood there, arm in arm, staring into each other's eyes before the dog broke the trance. She jumped up, placing her large paws onto Booker's back. He stumbled forward, pulling me into his arms even more to keep us both from falling over.

"Sorry," he mumbled, backing away. "Rude, Daisy May." He chastised the dog with a playful rub of her ears. I could've sworn she sighed with joy. "Come on." He walked her to the patio door and let her outside.

"Let's get this stuff loaded." He picked up the box and I grabbed the pots.

"She's a pretty dog."

"Daisy is actually Maggie's dog."

"Why is she here? Are you dog-sitting her?"

"Long story," he said way too casually as I followed him to the garage. "I got Daisy for her a few years ago from an unscrupulous breeder. He was going to put her down because she wasn't perfect. She has some brindling on her legs and chest."

"Brindling?" I had no clue what that meant.

Booker set an empty box in the back for the pans and shut the tailgate when I finished folding the flaps over. "If you look at her legs you can see yellow streaks running through her otherwise black fur. That's called brindling. Her father is a black lab, and her mother's a yellow lab."

"That's horrible," I said.

"I told him I'd take her and he sold her to me, full price, mind you. Some people have no scruples," he grumbled. "I have to let Daisy in, then we can head over to your new place."

I watched him through the door as he tossed a ball to the dog before bringing her in and giving her a bone to chew on while he was gone.

I had to stop crushing on that man.

Chapter 9

Despite its small size, the trailer turned out to be a godsend. It was clean, and everything functioned properly, especially the heater. An added bonus? A small nightstand next to the bed with a hidden drawer. It made for the perfect location to keep my gun at night.

For the next few days, Booker gave me a ride to work until Dewey completed the repairs on my car. "It's on my way," he said, brushing off my concerns about burdening him. Since we had our first snowfall already, most days he drove the truck. Worked for me. I loved his truck. But by the end of the week the snow melted and we were back to the POC.

Since the move was a new beginning for me, I decided it was the perfect time to work harder at pushing past my fears. I forced myself not to constantly look around whenever I went out. I allowed a quick check of the area when I arrived, then that was it. At the office I refused to overreact to awkward noises and random strangers. It'd be a lie to say I had no reaction, but they were more like tiny . . . alright, medium-sized twists in my gut and not all-out meltdowns. I still cringed just thinking about the persistent salesman who had me near tears until Booker showed up and kicked him out.

The best part about the trailer was its proximity to the recreation center. I could walk there, which saved me gas money. This past summer I'd volunteered to teach yoga to the senior citizens in the area two days a week. Not the most strenuous of workouts, but usually the manager allowed me to stay after if the room wasn't booked and run through a more vigorous routine. Some days I played around with choreography to my new CDs.

Today was one of those lucky days. Tired of the internal turmoil over my growing feelings for Booker, I hoped an hour of strenuous yoga would burn off the angst. We'd spent the day putting together documents for an important deal he'd been working on. Side-by-side we verified signatures, copying and printing reports, and arranging the documents. We'd crossed hands, pressed by each other in the cramped working space, and bumped noses as we tried to go opposite ways. More than once I turned to find him looking at me before he averted his eyes. I had a strong suspicion that he too struggled with his attraction to me as much as I struggled with mine to him.

Instead of concentrating on a calm peaceful place in my yoga routine, all my thoughts were of Booker, and they were anything but calming. I felt like a silly, lovesick schoolgirl by the time I finished my workout.

Joyfully exhausted, I showered, taking the time to blow-dry my hair since it was already freezing cold outside, and left for home. I cut across the parking lot, cinching my backpack up on my shoulder, and remembering a joke Booker told me earlier as I made my way to the sidewalk. Distracted, I tripped over a lip in the concrete and landed in someone's arms. A muscular, well corded set of arms. Arms I'd seen once too often in my dreams, holding me, wrapped around me—

"Falling for me, are you?" I looked up into the eyes of my obsession as I righted myself. What were the odds?

"Sorry, Booker." I pushed my backpack back up onto my shoulder. Booker kept his arms around my waist. My inner voice told me to back away and put some space between us. Thankfully, I didn't listen. I did, however, get lost as I noticed flecks of dark honey in his otherwise deep brown eyes. His damp hair held the scent of shampoo, as if he'd just showered. "Do you work out here?" I asked.

"Yup. I keep meaning to put a gym in my house so I don't have to pay the outrageous fees they charge here, but obviously I've not done it yet." He smiled tightly. I swallowed hard. I'd seen that tight smile before. Many times today, in fact.

"Obviously you work out here also." His eyes searched my face, stopping at my mouth. Yeah, he felt what I felt.

"I teach yoga to seniors. Teaching a class gives me a place to work out without having to get rid of my couch," I chuckled. His eyes didn't stray from my mouth. "C—come January I'm done, though. No one signed up for the winter class. I may have to move the desks around at work and use the office after hours." I again chuckled nervously. Only then did I realize I was staring at his mouth. *Stop staring!* My self-chastisement was about as effective as it was during my yoga workout earlier. I found myself moving closer to him, instead of away.

"Sounds like a great—" Booker didn't finish his sentence because he was too busy kissing me. I bit back a groan as his lips brushed over mine in a slow, unrushed kiss, as if he were memorizing each curve, each dip, each corner of my mouth. His unhurried manner sent my pulse racing at hyper-speed. With Garen, it was always fast and rushed, as if to finish was the goal. Not Booker. He seemed content enjoying the journey. A very delightful journey.

I thought he was done until he buried one hand in my hair, and tightened the other around my waist as he angled his head just enough to deepen the kiss. Why I did not spontaneously combust mystified me.

Oh. My. Gosh.

When he finally released me, I stuffed my hands into my pockets to keep from grabbing him and pulling him back to me. How could this be? I hated kissing.

"Sorry. Got a little out of hand there." He dipped his head. "Can I give you a ride home or do you have your car here?"

Unable to speak, I only nodded.

"So which is it?"

"Sorry." I pulled my eyes away. "I walked. A ride would be great."

We drove in silence. Now, with time to think, my inner demons set me in full panic mode. Did I want to take a chance getting involved with Booker knowing that at any minute Garen could show up and I'd have to run? And leaving Booker behind would be hard, that much I knew.

And what of his demons? Didn't the designer from his office tell me he too struggled after the fiasco with his ex-wife?

I drew a weary breath. I'd better nip this in the bud now, before either of us fell too hard. But . . . how could I tell him that? He'd probably think me some sort of nut after kissing him back like I had not more than three minutes ago.

"Do you have the Broadbent file?" he asked, breaking the deafening silence.

"Yes. You asked me to prepare the documents for court on Thursday, remember?" He pulled up to the trailer and turned off the truck.

"Oh, that's right. No wonder I couldn't find it. Would you mind if I grabbed it from you? I have a few things I need to work on," he said, already getting out of the truck. "I'll bring it back Monday."

I nodded, working my way up the small pathway to the door. He followed me in as I set my backpack on the couch. "I believe it's right here." I stepped over to the kitchen counter, pulling it out of the small stack I'd brought home, and handed it to him.

"Thanks. You're as bad as me about taking work home at night, I see." He pointed to the pile. "I guess we both need to get a life." He chuckled nervously. Neither of us seemed to know how to handle what happened in the parking lot. Maybe he too regretted it. The thought made me a little sad, which was ridiculous since I'd just decided to tell him that I didn't want to get involved. *You're psycho, Tess.*

"I like what you've done with the place." He glanced around the room.

I hadn't done anything. It looked the same as when I'd moved in.

"Thanks." I folded my arms. "I'm thinking about moving the couch over to this wall. The glare from the window makes it impossible to see the TV. Not that I watch much TV," I admitted.

"I'll move it for you, if you'd like." Before I could say yes, he set the file down and moved the couch to the other wall with ease. I enjoyed watching his biceps bulge more than I should. "Better?"

I stepped to the side. "No. It looks crowded. Unbalanced."

"I'll put it back," he chuckled.

"Sorry," I said sheepishly.

"How about we put the TV on this wall?" he suggested. We tried several different combinations before returning everything to where it started.

"Are you trying to wear me down so you can ask for a raise?" he said, wiping perspiration from his forehead.

"Oh, you've figured out my evil plot." I poured him a glass of ice water.

"Thanks." He took the glass and downed it in three swallows. "Well, hate to move furniture and run, but I have a date tonight so I'd better get going."

His comment hit me like a fist to the gut. A date? How dare he kiss me like there was no tomorrow, then tell me he had a date?

But then again, it was just a kiss. *Calm down, Tess.*

"It's with Sofia, Lilah's daughter, remember?" Booker chuckled, stroking my cheek. Judging by his soft tone, and the fact that he'd closed the distance between us, he sensed my indignation. I wanted to crawl into a hole and die. "Cole and Lilah are going out and Sofia begged me to babysit."

"That's right. I forgot you mentioned that yesterday." Warmth flooded my cheeks.

"I'm not a scoundrel, Tess," he said gently. "I very much want to kiss you again." And he did. This time he kicked the heat up a notch, if that was possible. He cradled my head in his hands and pressed his mouth onto mine, his lips still cold from the iced water. My eyelids fluttered closed, and this time I failed to stifle my sigh. He pulled me closer. I was lost. Any thoughts of telling him I didn't want a relationship were shoved to the furthest corner of my mind. He pulled back, his breath haggard.

"I should go," he said, resting his forehead on mine. "How about you come over to my place and I'll make us some lunch tomorrow. I'll pick you up around one?"

"I'd like that."

Then he was gone. I paced to the kitchen then back to the living room, anxiety surging through me now that he wasn't around clouding my brain. "You've been dying to kiss him. Why are you freaking out?" I snapped to myself.

My fears hit me like a sledgehammer. It wasn't just the fear of Garen finding me that had me in knots. The fear of getting into something I couldn't get out of tore me up inside. The fear of being trapped again. The fear of opening myself up to another person on such an intimate level again. Garen's abuse involved more than his fists. He'd taken away my freedom. Destroyed my feelings of self-worth.

If I even looked at another man, no matter how innocently, he overreacted, insisting I was a whore. I had to give Garen a detailed agenda of everywhere I went. Often he'd show up just to make sure I was where I said I'd be. And there was the tracking app he secretly placed on my phone. I never wanted to feel that way again. Never. I'd lost myself with Garen. I was still somewhat lost no matter how hard I'd tried to move past everything.

"I can't do this again. I'm not ready." I sank to the floor. "Why did I think I could do this?" I wrapped my arms around me as deep sobs wracked my body.

Chapter 10
BOOKER

"Crap." I smacked the steering wheel. "Forgot the folder and I have to have it." I looked at my watch, frowning. I was going to be late. I made a U-turn and headed back to Tess' place.

A wide grin filled my face. Tess' kiss could drive a man to his knees. Not what I expected from someone so timid. Part of me worried she'd slap my face. Luckily, she didn't, though if she did, it would've been worth it. "Wow, what a great couple of kisses."

I debated for days whether to do it or not. My train wreck of a past with women kept me from putting myself out there again. But Seth reminded me I didn't have to fall in love. "Just have fun. Share some laughs."

"Yeah, might've gone a little past that." I blew out a breath as my nerves gnawed at my gut, hoping I wouldn't regret my choice.

I pulled up in front of Maggie's old trailer. How different it looked from the first time I'd seen it almost four years ago. The MET suspected Maggie and her mom of being part of a heroin ring. Thankfully, we were wrong. I'll never forget the first time I met her on that cold January day. Skinny, pale. The walking dead had more color. Now she was married to my best friend, and the haunting look that held her eyes that day, gone.

I set the emergency break and stepped out. As I approached the trailer, sobs, Tess' sobs, could be heard through the closed door. Instinct kicked in. I crouched and grabbed the Glock strapped to my calf under the leg of my jeans and crept up to the trailer. Adrenalin, my drug of choice, surged through my veins. I hadn't realized just how much I'd missed the rush of police work until right this second. Too bad the stress about killed me.

I stood slowly and looked through the living room window from the porch. Tess was crouched on the floor, crying into her hands. She appeared to be alone.

I pounded on the door and watched her reaction. She only looked at the door, which meant if there was someone else in the trailer, they were by the door, or she really was alone, and I'm an overreacting idiot. Probably the latter. So why was she crying? Since she didn't have a phone she couldn't have gotten bad news, and she said her mail wouldn't be forwarded to her new address until Monday.

She jumped up, wiping her face. I stepped back to the door and said, "Tess, are you okay?" No answer. I could hear her muffled cries still. I pulled the gun tight to my chest. "Tess, are you okay? I can hear you crying."

"Yes," she finally answered. "But I'm not dressed, I was in the shower. I'll talk to you Monday." She added, "Sorry."

Monday? We talked about her coming over for lunch tomorrow. Something wasn't right. Was she trying to send me a message? "Tess, I'm coming in. Either you unlock the door or I'll shoot it open."

The door immediately flew opened. "Don't shoot. I'm fine." She dried more tears with the back of her hand and signaled for me to come in. I stepped in the doorway and scanned the room. "I said I'm fine. You can put your Glock away."

"You don't look fine." I slipped the gun back into the holster, tugging my pant leg back over it. I glanced into her pink face as I straightened. Her wobbling lower lip betrayed her gallant effort to stop crying. "What's wrong?" I asked carefully.

"I can't do this," she whispered. "I thought I could, but I'm not ready." Tears again tumbled down her cheeks.

I stepped to her and wrapped my arms around her shoulders. She fell onto my chest and the waterworks began once more. Only then did I notice her trembling. I held her tighter. "Please tell me what's wrong, Tess."

"I thought I was ready. I thought I could move on," she said against my chest. "Over the past few months, I've tried to let the past go, and I honestly thought I was ready." She pulled back and looked into my eyes. "I'm not. I'm so, so sorry."

"Does this have anything to do with your disguise and the person you're hiding from?" I asked, handing her a tissue from the box on the counter next to me.

"Does everyone know I'm in disguise?" She pulled away, tossing her arms up and sinking onto the couch, burying her face in her hands again.

"Everyone who's a highly trained detective for the past twelve years, yes."

"And Lilah," she said, exasperated.

"Yes, well, Lilah has her own reasons." I sat next to her. "Do you want to explain what's going on?"

Why did I know I didn't want to hear this? Oh yeah, because I'm the guy with the Midas touch . . . except with women. With the fairer sex I was the black plague. Case in point: Tess. We hadn't even started a relationship yet and she was about to dump me. I just couldn't seem to get it right when it came to women. If I had half a brain, I'd plug my ears and start humming right now. Or better yet, I'd leave and let her work this out herself. She's probably PMS'ing anyway. Crying was the best thing for her at her moment.

And that thought alone was exactly why I sucked when it came to women. *You have the sensitivity of a mountain goat, Gatto.*

I inhaled slowly and waited for her to blow her nose.

"I was in . . . an abusive relationship." She pinched her eyes shut. "He was a monster," she whispered. "I'm trying to move past the nightmare, but in my gut, I'm petrified he's going to show up again."

"By abusive, you mean physically?" My stomach knotted. I knew the answer, deep inside suspected it from the beginning, I only hoped I was wrong.

"Very much so. I barely escaped with my life. Not only was he abusive, he was a control freak. I had no freedom. He controlled and monitored my every move. If I went shopping, he'd check the receipt to see what time I left the store." Tess straightened and took a deep breath, forcing the tears back. "He'd installed a Stalk my Buddies app on my phone without my knowledge to track me." She dropped her head back on the couch and let out a heavy breath. "In the end, I was literally a prisoner in our home."

"I'm so sorry, Tess." I wrapped my hands around hers. "I'm guessing that's why you don't want a cell phone?"

She nodded. "Booker, I'm not ready to get involved with anyone yet. I've made some great strides in my life lately, but I'm not there yet." She wiped the tears from her eyes before continuing. "I . . . um . . . think it'd be best for me to find a new job. I'll stay until you find someone else, but I can't stay."

"You're quitting? Why? Tess, you don't think I'd ever hurt you, do you?" The thought of not having her in my life was too bitter a pill to swallow. We could be friends. Just friends worked for me. Anything was better than not having her around at all. I couldn't let that happen . . . nor could I force her.

"No. I can't imagine you ever hurting me. But I'm not ready for a relationship either."

"We'll keep it platonic," I bargained.

"Unless I've misunderstood your body language over the past couple months, you're as drawn to me as I am to you. Booker, the attraction between us is too strong."

I stood and paced to the window, pushing the curtain aside to see out. I saw nothing. My brain focused only on the thought of losing Tess. There had to be a way around this. She came next to me.

"Maybe when I'm stronger we can try this again, a relationship, I mean," she said gently. "If you're not involved with someone else by then, of course."

Yeah, like that would happen. It'd been five years since I found a woman I wanted to have any kind of relationship with. I turned to look into her eyes. They carried so much pain. "Tess, please don't quit on me. Business is starting to pick up. I need you. You're the best secretary I've ever had."

"I'm the only secretary you've had," she correctly pointed out.

"Technically. But I've worked with many secretaries at police headquarters. Trust me. You're remarkable. In fact, you deserve a raise." I wasn't proud at my attempt to bribe her, but I couldn't let her slip through my hands either.

"Booker, this won't work. We're too drawn to each other." She sat back down on the couch, crossing her arms over her middle.

I paced the floor. There had to be a way to make it work. *Come on, I'm a lawyer. Loopholes are my specialty. Think.*

"Why did you come back anyway?" Tess asked.

"I forgot that file. I need to do some work tonight on the con . . . tract." I spun to face her. "That's it. We'll make a contract. No, better yet, I'll make a promise. And you know I'm good at keeping my promises. Remember that day at Lilah's? How many men would go so far as to wear chaffin to fulfill a promise?"

"Chiffon," she corrected, with a slight twinkle in her pained eyes. "But I don't see how that is going to help."

"Simple. I promise not to kiss you again. We'll keep our relationship platonic. I promise." Then I coyly added, "As long as you work for me. If you quit, the deal's off. In fact, if you quit I'll send love notes and roses to your new job, every day. I'll drive your new boss nuts, and you'll be fired. Then what will you do?"

"You will not." She rolled her eyes.

"Yeah, okay. You're right." I dropped my shoulders. "But we can make this work."

"Booker, this is crazy. Why torture yourself? Isn't it better if I'm not around every day, reminding you that we can't have a relationship?"

Think, Gatto. I smiled. "So you're telling me that you're afraid you can't handle yourself around me. That all this," I waved a hand over my length, "is just too tempting for you to control yourself."

Finally a laugh. She buried it behind her hands, but at least it was a laugh. "It's not going to work," she said, serious again.

I pulled her up off the couch, taking her hands in mine. "Tess, I'm begging you not to toss us aside without giving it some time. You're right. I'm attracted to you. Very attracted. But I'm willing to wait." She opened her mouth to protest and I added, "Even if it takes a hundred years. Just don't say no."

"But what if I'm never ready?" Her eyes dampened again.

"I'll risk it." I cupped her face in my hands, realizing I was putting a lot of pressure on her. I had to give her an out. Otherwise she'd stay for all the wrong reasons. "Tess, I'm not going to force this on you. This is your decision. I'll respect whatever you have to say. I mean, I know I'm begging," I teased, kinda, sort of, "but in all honesty, you have to do what is best for you. I'll understand."

Her eyes searched my face. "My decision. My ex-husband, Garen, seldom let me decide anything. I appreciate you saying that."

"You were married to the . . .?" I bit down to keep from swearing.

"For eighteen months. It seemed a lot longer." She curled her slender fingers around my wrists. "I think you're insane for wanting to torture yourself like this, but I'll give it a try."

My heart flipped in my chest. "Thank you." I reached in to kiss her forehead, then stopped and stepped back. "See?" I said proudly. "I'd better get going. I'm late." I turned and picked up the file I'd left behind and turned for the door.

"I'll see you on Monday, then." She held the door open for me.

I wanted to remind her we'd set a date for tomorrow, but decided not to press my luck. "Yes. Monday. And would you mind wearing that pink shirt with the blue flowers? You look pretty in it," I said. Her hands snapped to her hips and her eyes narrowed. "Just kidding." I smiled. "I'm here if you need a friend to talk to, Tess."

"Thank you," she said quietly, closing and locking the door behind me as I left.

~*~

"Well, I made it a month," I snarled, slamming the filing cabinet in my office shut and folding my arms on top of the cold metal. A whole month with no flirting, no ogling, no touching . . . okay, maybe not the touching part. I did put my hand on her shoulder when I looked at the computer screen whenever we worked on a document together. And, of course, when we left the building together I'd touch the small of her back as I guided her out. It was the gentlemanly thing to do. So, yeah, I touched her. And I'd better cross off the no ogling thing too, because I *most certainly did* ogle her whenever she came into my office. Or walked past my door. Or when I peeked out of my office to . . . ogle her. At least I kept my longing stares private . . . and stalker-like.

I dropped my head down onto my arms. The only thing I succeeded at for the past thirty days was not kissing her. Rocking my head back and forth I grumbled, "I suck."

"Hello, I'm here to see my husband."

No! I cringed at the voice coming from the outer office. It couldn't possibly be . . . I jerked my head up and in two strides all but ripped the door off the hinges as I jerked it all the way open. There stood my own personal nightmare, all five-foot-three inches of her, dressed in a short pink skirt and white shirt. Vintage Nikkolynn outfit: too tight and too provocative. Still too sexy for her own good. The only difference was that her long blond hair had been cut short. And she'd aged. Prison life's not for wimps.

"Ex-husband, Nikkolynn. What the he . . . eck are you doing here?" Okay, I deserved to take a quarter out of the curse jar for not cussing at my lying, two-timing, manipulative ex-wife.

"Bookie!" She smiled her sassy little grin. There was a time I'd have melted on the spot when she did. Not anymore.

"Prison life been good to you?" I snipped back. "How did you get out already? Who'd you use this time, Nikkolynn?"

"Bookie, I haven't seen you in five years and that's all you can do, insult me?" She pouted and strutted my way. Tess sat frozen, her eyes wide. Her mouth twitched. Not sure if she fought a laugh or tears. I stepped aside and signaled for Nikkolynn to come in. She sashayed past me, shaking her moneymaker. Didn't even faze me.

"If anyone calls, if anyone comes in needing to see me, if Mormon missionaries come knocking with promises of eternal life, please interrupt us." I winked at Tess as she pressed her lips together, fighting a smile for sure this time.

Girding up my loins, I turned to my bombshell of an ex and snapped the door shut. "Why are you here, Nikkolynn?" I asked, no hint of caring in my voice.

She sashayed up to me. "Call me Nickel like you used to, baby," she said in her infamous dumb blond voice as she walked her fingers up my chest.

I rolled my eyes and plucked her hand off me, dropping it in the air. "I repeat, why are you here, Nikkolynn?" I folded my arms over my chest.

"Still working out, I see." She smiled and bounced her eyebrows. I paced to my desk and sat down, picking up a magazine with Justin Beaver, or whatever the heck his name was, on the cover that I'd been meaning to look over. Yeah, right.

"Okay. No need to be rude." She plopped onto the corner of my desk and crossed her legs. Her skirt rode up, barely covering her—

"Bookie, I came to apologize for what happened with, well, you know who." She shifted uncomfortably on the desk and her skirt rode up even higher. I reached over to the corner chair and grabbed the jacket I'd tossed there earlier and laid it across her legs.

"I still get to you, don't I?" she said smugly.

"No, Nik. Not even a little bit. You're embarrassing yourself, is all." I turned my attention back to the magazine. Why do people read this drivel?

"Come on, Bookie. It was you I loved, not Josh," she insisted.

"If that were true, and it's not, you had a funny way of showing it," I snorted, slapping the magazine closed and tossing it in the garbage where it belonged as I stood. "You married me hoping to get confidential information about cases I worked on to help Josh, drug dealing Josh," I reminded her. "You set me up. I could have lost my job if I hadn't found out in time." I pushed a hand through my hair. I needed a haircut. It was past my ears. I'd gotten lazy about it since quitting the MET.

"I admit I used you at first. But by the time we got married, it was you I loved, not Josh." She tossed in a pout with her lie.

"And yet you still slept with him, in our bed, I might add, and you still tried weaseling information out of me to help him avoid being caught." I didn't mean to raise my voice, but the bitter taste of betrayal fueled me.

"I know, Bookie. You're right. I should've come clean when we got married. It was a lapse of judgment on my part."

"You think?"

"I've paid my dues. I'm here to ask, no, beg you for another chance." She sauntered in my direction, looking up at me through her thick fringe of lashes.

"Good bye, Nikkolynn," I said stoically.

"But . . . but I love you," she said. She actually had the nerve to force a few tears down her cheeks.

I softened my tone somewhat. "But I don't love you. Not anymore."

Nikkolynn dried her face, stomped past me, and bee-lined straight to the exit. "I'm not giving up on us, Bookie." Dramatically, as per her usual style, she flung the door open, and with a turned up nose, left.

I turned to Tess. "Suppose you heard all of that?" I said, knowing how thin the old building's walls were.

"I tried not to listen," she said with a guilty edge to her voice.

I exhaled loudly. "You and me, we know how to pick 'em, it seems."

She chuckled. "I do believe you're right. She doesn't seem your type. What drew you to her, if you don't mind me asking?"

I chuckled. "I'm embarrassed to admit it but three things: short skirts, smoldering eyes, and great kissing."

"That'll do it every time," she said with a wide grin.

I set my hands on her desk and, being the sadomasochist that I was, leaned in, hoping to catch the scent of her hair. "I'm starving. Do you want to go get some lunch?"

"So that's it, huh? You got a thing going with your secretary." Nikkolynn's shrill tone reverberated in my ears.

"We're just friends, not that it's any of your business." I straightened.

"Right," she said, her arms stiff at her side.

"Why are you back?" I demanded.

"I forgot my coat." She snatched up a white furry-looking coat from the chair in the reception area, glaring at Tess as she left.

"Sorry about that. She's harmless." Tess nodded stiffly. I wanted to tell her that not everyone dealt with their issues using violence, but I'd had enough of Nikkolynn for one day. I'd had enough for a lifetime.

"Grab your coat. I'm treating you to steak," I teased. Sort of. She could eat her veggies. I had every intention of having a thick juicy steak.

Chapter 11
Tess

Five years ago Garen insisted I go to counseling with him, pointing out that I too had faults that needed to be addressed if we hoped to have a healthy marriage. He asked me not to mention the physical abuse to the counselor, fearing that somehow it'd be leaked to the press. Reluctantly, I agreed, although I told him that it'd be hard to get the proper help if we weren't honest with the therapist.

After four sessions Garen stopped going, and demanded I quit, claiming the therapist blamed everything on him and not the underlying reason for our troubles: my inability to measure up. His agitation with my imperfections grew daily. He criticized everything from the way I cleaned the house to what I wore. It didn't take long to lose myself under his visceral criticisms.

Gone was the girl who, in high school, had the world by the tail. In her place an uncertain screw up remained. I struggled to understand why Garen didn't love me enough. Was I that bad of a wife? Had I disappointed him to the point that he no longer loved me? I truly believed that if I just loved him enough, everything would be better. Clearly, I failed. That guilt hung around my neck like an albatross.

One day, in the midst of one of his rages, he tossed all my clothes away. If it were possible, I'd have sworn the guy had

PMS. He purchased boring pantsuits for me as a replacement. They weren't exactly my style, and when I tried to gently mention that he said, "If it's good enough for Jackie Kennedy, it's certainly good enough for you. My wife will not dress like a slob." It was a slap in the face. I liked the way I dressed. But then again, he did have a point. The conservative pantsuits did look more professional and I'd be looking for a job soon. I guessed it was time I stopped dressing like a teenager. I swallowed my pride and wore them . . . as if I had a choice.

If anything was out of order at home, he still lost it, but never like the day on our half-year anniversary seven months ago. He'd just shove me against the wall and yell in my face, or push me down onto the couch in fits of anger. By far better than being hit.

When I received a B- in a math class, he went on a tirade yet again. "I won't have a stupid wife embarrassing me," he said, jabbing my breastbone with his index finger. I was bruised for a week. My already fragile self-esteem slipped even lower. My drive to succeed, to never give up, had lost steam.

To make matters worse, my father was diagnosed with prostate cancer. I didn't dare burden my parents with my troubles and we seldom talked anymore, fearing they'd catch on. They had enough to deal with. They didn't need my failures to weigh them down, too.

It didn't matter anyway. We were on a strict budget and therefore had the cheapest cell phone plan available. Garen would only allow me limited minutes on the phone each week because he needed the lion's share for work. I did write them regularly, and Garen mailed the letters from work since he didn't want to squeak out the money for stamps. "I pay taxes. These can be mailed on Senator Graft's dime."

"Graft's coming to dinner tomorrow. I want you to prepare a spectacular meal. He's considering making me head of his reelection campaign. Oh, and he's a strict vegan. No dairy, or meat, not even fish. Got that?" Garen laid out his demands before he even put his briefcase down. "None of your lazy vegetarian crap either. Unlike you, Graft has self-control."

Studying for a final at the table, I angled my chair to him. "Maybe we should go out for dinner. As you well know, I'm a disaster in the kitchen."

"That's not the only room you're a disaster in, mannequin." I bit my tongue at his reference to the bedroom. Apparently, I was a disappointment there also.

He took off his tie and unbuttoned the top button of his shirt. "Maybe it's about time you learned to cook, Terese. Between spending all of our disposable income on your ridiculous degree," he pointed to my books, "to teaching you how to set up a proper household, I've been the only one giving in this marriage for the past thirteen months. I give and you take."

"That's not true, Garen."

"Oh? Tell me then, what do you give in this relationship?" He sank his hands in the pockets of his pants as his foot tapped impatiently.

I didn't know what to say. Not wanting to bring up the physical abuse, fearing it'd give him ideas, I sat there, forcing myself not to run out of the townhome and catch the next plane home to my parents. The counsel my father shared with me as we walked down the aisle together rang in my head. *Tess, the first few years of marriage are tough as you merge two people from different upbringings into one family. More than once I wondered what I had gotten myself into after I married your mother, and she felt the same way about me at times. But with patience and love, things got better,"* he assured me. *"We Selleck's are not quitters, remember that."*

"I'm waiting for an answer, Terese."

"I'll try harder," I assured him quietly. After dinner, I drove to the library and checked out a couple of vegan cookbooks. I found a recipe for summer squash soup that looked fairly easy, and a recipe for an avocado salad that require no cooking, of course.

I stopped at the market to pick up the ingredients on my way home. Garen wanted to know why I'd taken so long, demanding to see the grocery receipt. More and more he'd check the time stamp at the bottom to see if I'd gone anywhere else than the store. I found it insulting, but didn't dare say anything about it. It was easier to just let it go.

I made the soup twice the next day, and both times it turned out terrible. I tossed the disasters into the garbage disposal, not wanting Garen to know. I went to the one and only neighbor I knew, Juli Coldwell. I didn't dare talk to the other neighbors. Garen had a fit if I even looked at anyone of the opposite sex, but Juli, a single mother of three girls, was safe. In lieu of cash, I bargained several hours of English tutoring for her fifteen-year-old daughter in exchange for four meals along with desserts from Greens, a high-end vegan restaurant in Dallas she worked at. I placed everything in our crystal serving bowls as if I'd made the meal, and ran the containers out to the dumpster so Garen wouldn't know.

"This is fantastic, Terese. It tastes just like the squash soup from Greens." Senator Graft smiled broadly as he served himself up another bowl. My nerves were on end and I couldn't eat much, leaving extra soup for him. "I'll need to get the recipe for my wife, although I don't know why. She can't cook to save her life," he added with a chuckle. "You're a lucky man, Garen."

Garen offered a terse grin, but said nothing. He knew. Somehow, he always knew. After dinner, I set out raspberry tarts, also courtesy of Greens. The men migrated to the living room as I excused myself to clean up dinner.

While loading the dishwasher, I could hear them talking about Graft's reelection plans. The man was a dishonest slimeball. In other words, a typical politician. Graft spoke of illegal voter registration, paying off counting judges, even hacking into people's emails and cell phones. When he left an hour later, I stormed in the living room as Garen typed away on his laptop.

"The man is a scum," I pointed out needlessly.

"Politics is brutal," he said with a shrug.

"You're seriously going to work with him after everything he said?"

He shrugged again as his fingers flew across the keyboard.

"Garen, he plans on spreading lies about this opponent at the last minute so she won't have time to defend herself. How can you support that?"

"Terese, Graft has ideas that can help this country, only most people are too stupid to realize that yet. He knows what's best for America, and I, for one, am going to help him." Garen closed his laptop and set it on the coffee table as he stood. "Graft's going places and I'm going with him."

"He's dishonest!" My bravery surprised me. I seldom confronted him anymore, fearing his wrath.

"*He's* dishonest? What about dinner tonight, Terese? Do you expect me to believe you made that squash soup?" He came next to me. Instinctively I tensed.

"I didn't want to disappoint you," I swallowed hard.

"Yeah, well, seems that's all you do anymore. I'm used to it. I married beneath myself, that's for sure." He folded his arms over his chest.

Before I could stop myself, I said, "You know, you can be a real jerk sometimes."

Garen's fist plunged into my stomach. I doubled over as the oxygen purged from my lungs. He wasn't done. He grabbed a fistful of my hair and jerked my head up, shoving his face in mine. "You'd better watch the way you talk to me, do you understand?" he growled, low and threatening. Still gasping for air, I couldn't answer. "I said do you understand?" He backhanded me across the face. I fell to the floor, tasting blood as I landed in a heap.

He slapped my head and back repeatedly as he crouched over me. I begged and pleaded, promising I'd be a better wife. After several minutes he stopped, as breathless as I was. He straightened and tugged his dress shirt back into place and smoothed his hair.

"I deserve someone better than you, you stupid whore." He kicked my backside and grabbed his keys. Scooping up my cell phone from the counter, he hurled it against the wall. Bits of plastic and circuits rained down onto the floor as he stormed out.

I lay on the floor, unwilling to move for a long time. Finally, I forced myself up, each move met with pain. A little dizzy, I walked slowly to Juli's townhome at the end of the hall. I'd had enough. Time to bring the police in and get some help. Only Juli wasn't home, and I didn't know any of my other neighbors, certainly not well enough to appear on their doorstep bruised and bleeding. I worked my way back to my townhome and dropped onto the couch as my body and mind gave out.

~*~

"Terese, wake up, sweetie." The voice pulled me from a dark, disturbing sleep. One filled with nightmares and pain. I stirred, my stiff body protesting, as if I'd run a marathon. Or been slapped around. The dull throb in my head nauseated me. I opened my eyes, cringing as they met Garen's. I slowly sat upright, and pulled into the corner of the couch, wondering what he'd do this time. He grimaced as if he felt badly before sitting next to me. I knew what was coming. Pleas. His, this time, as he begged for forgiveness. I'd heard it all before.

"Terese, please forgive me. I'm so sorry." He took my hand gently in his and pressed it to his lips. "I've been under a lot of pressure at work with Graft's reelection in jeopardy and everything. If I can help him win, he's promised me a spot on his cabinet. It's a step closer to the White House, Terese, and our dreams. Our Life Plan is alive and well if Graft wins." He had tears in his eyes now. Tears I'd seen one too many times before. "I can't believe I hurt you like this. If you'll forgive me, I promise, it'll never happen again."

"You've said this before, you've even promised to go to counseling, but you quit. I just don't see an end to all of this." Only because of his penitent state of mind did I have the courage to stand up to him. I shifted on the couch. "Maybe we were a mistake, Garen. I disappoint you in every way. Maybe we should just get a divorce now and call it good." I wanted out. It was too much for me.

"No, sweetie, please." He dropped to one knee in a panic. "I'll do whatever it takes. I'll go to counseling again if you want, and I won't quit this time, I swear. I love you. Please don't tell me we're through." He dropped his head in my lap and sobbed like a little child, pleading and begging more. Making promises that I knew deep down inside he'd never keep.

Pulling himself together, he straightened. "I got you a gift. A token of my love." He nodded to the kitchen table before taking a hanky from his pocket and drying his face. In a lovely crystal vase sat a dozen white Calla lilies, *his* favorite flower. He'd never gotten me flowers before. Although I preferred poppies, the gesture touched me. A little.

"And I thought we could take a trip into town and you can get your nails done, maybe even get your hair cut." He kissed my temple. "And I got you this, too." He reached into the pocket of his pants and pulled out a cell phone. "It's the latest and greatest model."

We stood as he tucked my hair behind my ears. I knew I must look horrible, but for once he didn't complain. Guilt's not always a bad thing.

"I planned on getting you a new phone for graduation, but, well, after my disgusting temper tantrum it's the least I can do," he said in a soft voice. He placed the phone in my hands. "Please tell me it's not too late. Please tell me you forgive me."

"I don't know, Garen. I'm afraid the next time you get angry, you'll just hurt me again, or worse." I twisted the phone nervously in circles.

"Sweetie, please, don't act like this. My job is stressful right now." He wrapped his arm around my shoulder. "When you don't support me, it makes things difficult. Don't you see, I was worried that Graft would find out you didn't make that dinner. And then when you went off about his political tactics, well, the pressure was too much and I freaked out. But it won't happen again. If you put undue pressure on me, I'll find a healthy outlet from now on. I'm a changed man. You'll see." Garen's favorite thing to do after he went psycho on me was to blame it on everyone and anyone but himself. *I* caused the beating.

"I have some exciting news, Terese. I know how much you've wanted to move so I talked to Graft about it this morning. He has a small home in west Texas that he owns. It's about thirty minutes from his office. He's offered it to me, rent free if we'll fix it up for him." He pressed his lips to my forehead. "Do you realize how much pressure that will take off me not having to come up with rent every month?"

Our own place. Well, not our own, but anything had to be better than our tiny townhouse. Garen did stress about money constantly. Maybe this would help. "Rent free? That will loosen up the budget quite a bit. How bad of shape is it in?"

"It needs little things like paint and the yard weeded. It's a tax write-off for him. Win-win for both of us. He uses it as a write-off so we'll get it rent-free. It's some sort of incentive to help the less fortunate. We'll need to use your social security number for the application since I have a job. I guess it's a good thing you don't work, after all. Now we can get this place and save some money. There is even room for a garden, just like you've always wanted."

I wanted to point out the dishonesty of it, but I held my tongue. Maybe with freeing up our income a bit, he'd not be so stressed. It was only for a little while anyway. When I graduated in three months, I'd get a job of my own. And with that money, I planned on leaving Garen. If I didn't leave him . . . he'd kill me. I felt the truth of that in the marrow of my bones.

Chapter 12

Present day

"Thanks for lunch." I shoved Book's passenger car door closed, frowning at the thing that should've been put down years ago.

"Yes, you're right. I need to replace my car," Booker said, as if reading my mind. He stepped around and pushed on the door to make sure it was secure.

"Did I scowl?" I asked, embarrassed.

"Maybe a little." He chuckled. "I love this car. It's only been in the shop once since I bought it ten years ago." He lovingly patted the hood. "Sorry, sweetheart. It looks like it's time to put you out to pasture. But never forget, I'll always love you."

"I'm sure she feels much better knowing that," I said as we headed inside. He sighed dramatically and turned for the stairs instead of the elevator. "Good idea. We'd better take the stairs. You need to work off the half cow you had for lunch."

"Don't be knocking my carnivoreistic ways," he teased. "Personally, I don't know how you can survive on a salad with 'the dressing on the side.'" He made finger quote marks in the air.

"You know I'm teasing about your eating meat, right?" I said, unsure if I'd crossed any lines. "Just because I choose to be a vegetarian, albeit a lazy one, I certainly don't think everyone has to be."

Booker waved a hand. "I know you were. In fact, I've noticed you joking around a lot more lately. Good job." He playfully tapped my shoulder with his.

"I'm trying to loosen up and relax, not be so jittery. Believe it or not, I knew how to shine at one time." I dropped my head, disappointed in the woman I'd allowed myself to become. "I was a prima ballerina in high school. Now look at me."

"I see a beautiful woman who's recovering from a tragic situation." He squeezed my hand. I chastised my heart for hammering in my chest. The past month had been hard. I tried not thinking about him in any way other than as a boss and a friend, but I often found myself staring at his mouth when he spoke, or felt stirrings in my belly when he laughed. Booker was doing much better than me at keeping our relationship platonic. Some days I wondered if he'd completely moved on, figuring I just wasn't worth the effort.

Instead of heading upstairs after entering the building, he led me down toward the basement. "I'd like to show you something." At the bottom of the stairs was a new door with a glass window on the top half. Booker pushed on the door, and motioned for me to step inside.

The space, maybe thirty by thirty feet, was pretty much empty except for a wall of mirrors with a ballet barre running the length of it. "This was a ballet studio back in the eighties," Booker said, stepping over to the mirrors. "The basement had an inch of water when I bought it. I had the warped wood floors ripped out, so it's just cement now." He ran his hand over the splintered barre. "And this railing is shot."

"Barre," I corrected, running my hand gingerly over the wood. "I studied ballet most of my life and dreamt of teaching ballet after I finished touring." Memories washed over me like an old friend. Dancing in recitals and pretty costumes covered in sparkles. Blistered toes and endless hours of rehearsals, the smell of new leotards and pointe shoes; sweet, beautiful memories.

"You should see your face," he said, watching me intently. "I don't think I've ever seen you look so blissful. What made you change your mind about dance?"

"Garen, my ex." I wrapped my hand carefully around the weathered barre again. "I regret giving it up. I wanted to have my own studio."

"So don't give up on the idea," Booker said.

"Maybe someday."

"Why someday? Why not now?"

"Money, for one," I said. "It'd probably take a good ten, maybe fifteen grand to get started." I shrugged. "Like I said, maybe someday. Right now I'm happy having the rec center to teach and work out at."

I met his eyes and could almost see his mind working. "What's going on in that . . ." *sexy, gorgeous,* I settled for " . . . head of yours, Gatto?"

"I've been thinking a lot about the day in the park." He cleared his throat and tugged on his blue tie. "You said then that your yoga class was ending soon, so I thought: why not create a space to workout in here? I've wanted to install a gym in my home, but with all this space going to waste, it'd be perfect here." He pointed to one end of the basement. "I could put gym equipment and free weights there, and a place for yoga, or ballet for that matter, here, by this mirror."

"Are you serious?" I snapped my mouth shut.

"Yes. I've already talked to Magpie and Lilah about it and they both said they'd help design the space, but they'll need help with the specifics." He folded his arms and leaned against the mirrors. "I can do the gym part, but would you mind helping with the yoga-dance area?"

"Yoga . . . Dance . . . Are you serious?" I repeated. I'd have a place to work out. No more trying to find a free room at the rec center. Feelings of excitement and hope rushed through me.

"Yes. In fact, I've been thinking about opening it up to the entire building. A gym may draw in new tenants. Seth and I have talked about teaching self-defense classes for women, too."

"Self-defense classes?"

"Both of us miss our work with the MET. Magpie thinks we have a savior complex going on." He rolled his eyes. "She takes one psychology course at the college and suddenly she's an expert at diagnosing people."

I didn't want to rain on his parade, but from the little I knew about the two guys, Maggie hit the nail on the head. I smiled and nodded, as if I agreed with him.

"Anyway, Mags suggested we teach women self-defense classes as a way to feed our complex. Whatever. Personally, I think it's a great way to empower women," he said it as if he were trying to convince himself that was the real reason. I suspected it was a little of both.

"I'd love to help." Without thinking, I flew at Booker, hugging him. He wrapped his arms around me, holding me close to him much longer than a friendly hug, before finally letting me go. Maybe he struggled more than I thought with our platonic arrangement.

"We'd better get back to the office," he said, walking to the door. I followed silently, embarrassed at my over exuberance.

The next evening Lilah invited me over to her place. She and Maggie wanted to get going on the design for the gym. Booker gave them a list of the equipment he wanted. Maggie had pictures of each piece on the table in front of a layout Lilah drew of the space on a board.

Lilah wore thigh-high boots and black tights with a short skirt. Maggie, her opposite—and part snowman, I decided—had on a simple t-shirt and a pair of capris. I wore jeans and a button down shirt, along with a turtleneck underneath, and a bulky sweater to top it all off . . . and I was still cold.

"Book said he wants to open the space up to the entire building so I think we should have at least three treadmills and three ellipticals," Maggie explained as she added pictures of each machine to the board.

"What about a couple of bikes?" Lilah suggested.

"Great idea. We certainly have the budget for it." Maggie wrote bike twice on the layout.

"Hello, sleepy." Lilah smiled as her daughter came over to the kitchen table we were gathered around and climbed onto her mother's lap. Sofia stuck her thumb in her mouth and laid her head on Lilah's shoulder as Lilah stroked her hair.

"Any luck in the baby-making department?" Maggie asked Lilah, waving at the droopy-eyed little girl.

"Not yet, but it's only been three months." Lilah's attempt to sound casual failed. I rubbed the ache in my stomach, knowing I'd never carry a child.

"I'm still adjusting to Sofia, so it's okay. Sometimes, at night, Cole and I sneak into her room and watch her sleep." Lilah laid her cheek on the now sleeping child's head. "Okay, back to work."

"How is Innovative Interiors coming along?" I asked Maggie.

"Slow. But we've decided not to push it too much until I graduate in April." She grinned widely at Lilah and added, "In five more months. No more tests, no more papers. And most importantly, no more math. I'm done."

"Then watch out, Port Fare," Lilah beamed, as she should. The two of them recently decorated Cole's house and it was beautiful with its warm greens and browns. They'd accented with a few pops of orange that to my surprise looked terrific.

Maggie nodded and drew our attention to the drawing. "Tess, we thought this area would be good for yoga and the self-defense classes the guys plan on teaching. What kind of flooring do you think—?"

Cole, Booker, and Seth burst into the room. I had no idea that Booker would be there and the surprise put a smile on my face.

"Not happening, Cole," Seth said with a loud laugh. Sofia's head popped up and Lilah shushed them. She pointed at her daughter as the child settled back to sleep. "Sorry," Seth said, pressing a finger to his lips.

"Did you tell them our exciting news, Maggie?" Seth whispered, kissing her cheek.

"Not yet," she said softly. "I planned to after we finished laying out the gym."

"Tell us what?" Lilah straightened in her chair. "And hello, Booker. I didn't expect to see you tonight."

"Cole invited me over." Booker nudged Cole in the shoulder with his fist.

"Seth has an announcement and he asked me to invite Booker over so he can tell everyone at once," Cole explained. "Go ahead." He signaled Seth.

"I'm opening a restaurant," Seth grinned ear-to-ear.

"He and Maggie are heading out to New York next week to a restaurateur's conference to figure out what they need to get up and running," Cole added.

"Next week?" Maggie turned to Seth. "But that's the week of Thanksgiving."

"It is. I figured we'll get a turkey dinner at one of the local restaurants," Seth explained. Oddly, instead of their conversation sounding spontaneous, both Seth and Maggie's words were stiff, rehearsed.

"And what about Booker?" Maggie stood, facing him. Her eyes darted to me then back to Seth.

"Lilah and Cole will be here. Not to mention Sofia."

"No, we won't. We're flying to Louisiana for a family reunion," Lilah explained, in the same rehearsed tone. They were up to something. Lilah continued, "We can't cancel. It's the first time Sofia and I will meet his brothers and their families. Yeah, I'm petrified," she added.

"They'll love you," Cole reassured his wife. "We're also having a ring ceremony for everyone while we're there since they missed the wedding. Remember I told you about that last week, Seth?"

"That's right. I completely forgot." Seth smacked his forehead with his palm. "Wait, Tess, do you have plans for Thanksgiving? Maybe you and Booker can get together for dinner."

So that's what they were up to.

"And the Academy Award for truly the worst acting job on the planet ends in a four-way tie." Booker folded his arms and frowned.

"What are you talking about, Booker?' Maggie stood and walked over to Seth, wrapping her arms around his waist as he wrapped his around her shoulders.

"Well, Magpie, that'd be your first mistake," Booker said. "If this were a genuine spontaneous conversation, you'd have called me Garfield or . . ."

"CC." Pretty much everyone greeted Cole's reply with blank stares. "CC, stands for Copy Cat or Carbon Cat depending on who you ask. It was the first cloned cat."

"You're making that up," Booker insisted.

"No. I read an article about it in the New England Journal of Medicine just last week," Cole said, taking the sleeping Sofia from his wife. She smiled up at him.

"Who knew smart could be so sexy?" Lilah stretched up and kissed his cheek.

"Thank you, beautiful wife." Cole bounced his brows at Lilah.

Booker tossed his head back and grumbled something under his breath. "Tess, so we can put an end to our misery and stop all this PDA'ing—"

"PBA'ing?" Cole interrupted.

"PDA, sweetie. Public Display of Affection," Lilah informed him.

Cole smiled. "Yes, of course. PDA, something I am rather fond of."

"Please say you'll spend Thanksgiving with me so I can get out of here before I have to throw up?" Booker asked me. "I'll even make you a tofu turkey."

Not so sure Thanksgiving alone with Booker was a good thing. Being in an intimate setting, like his home, with just the two of us, may prove dangerous.

On the other hand, I'd spent the last four Thanksgivings . . . and every other holiday for that matter, alone. It'd be nice to have someone to share the day with.

Booker wrapped a hand around mine. "Tess," he said quietly, "no pressure. If you have other plans, that's fine."

"No. I'd like to spend Thanksgiving together, but only if you promise no tofu turkey."

"Lazy vegetarians eat turkey, I take it."

"Since I made up the term I guess I can set the rules down. Seriously, Thanksgiving just wouldn't be that same without a turkey."

"Then turkey it is." We glanced at his friends as we fist-bumped. Each had an ear-to-ear grin. Booker turned back to me. "Just ignore them. I do."

Chapter 13

Thanksgiving morning I ran to the store and bought a readymade pumpkin pie and veggie tray before driving to Booker's. The weather, its typical freezing cold, had me wrapped up in two sweaters and a thick coat before leaving the house. The nasty wind laughed at my vain attempt to block its harsh lashes as it easily cut through my clothing and stung my skin. Despite cranking the car heater up all the way, I still shivered. I pulled into Booker's driveway as the snow started. I thumped my head against the headrest with a groan. "I hate snow."

Grabbing the food, I scurried up the steps of the red brick home and pressed the doorbell, dancing around to help keep warm. Booker answered wearing jeans and a burgundy Henley shirt with a blue one layered underneath. A black apron with the words "Real Men Cook" hung from his neck.

"Come on in." He held the door open, taking the pie and veggie tray so I could remove my coat.

"Store bought pie on Thanksgiving, Tess?" He scowled. "You do know this is a criminal offense. In fact, the last person who tried it is still in jail." I followed him into the kitchen. "This isn't part of your lazy vegetarian criteria, is it?

"No. I told you before, I can't cook. I'm absolutely hopeless in the kitchen."

Booker set the pie on the counter with a look of disdain. "I don't believe it. I bet I can teach you to cook."

"I bet you can't," I grumbled. He took an apron from a hook inside the pantry and handed it to me. It was covered in pictures of kittens, cute fluffy kittens, playing and tumbling. I slipped it over my head and tied it at the waist. "From Maggie?"

"How'd you guess?" He chuckled. "Now, what do you say to baking the most delicious pumpkin pie you've ever eaten?"

"Alright, but I'm warning you, this is not going to turn out well." I took the red bowl he held out to me.

"Bet you're wrong. In fact, loser does dishes, deal?" he suggested. "And before you agree, you should know that I've never lost a bet. Not ever."

"Never?" I asked, debating. I planned to do the dishes anyway since he'd done all the cooking so I had nothing to lose. But I also knew how hopeless I was in the kitchen. Betting him would be unfair.

"How about we make this a promise instead of a bet: you promise to do the dishes if I fail to make an edible pie. If I succeed, I promise to do the dishes. Okay?"

"Don't you think that's picking at straws, calling it a promise instead of a bet?"

"I'm just trying to protect your winning streak," I said in my best martyr tone. I even added a dramatic sigh.

He laughed. "Deal—ah, promise," he amended quickly. "I wanted to watch the football game after dinner and you just made that possible," he added, rubbing his hands together.

"Pretty confident, aren't you, Gatto?" I set my hands on my hips.

"Yup. Here's the recipe." He handed me a battered cookbook, opened to Grandma's Pumpkin Pie recipe. "Add the first five ingredients to the bowl. Most everything you'll need is in the pantry." He pointed to a walk-in pantry next to the refrigerator. "Go ahead and start. I need to baste the tofu turkey," he teased. At least, I hoped he teased. I hated tofu. He glanced back before opening the oven door. "You do know how to use measuring cups, right?"

"I'm ignoring your comment," *you extremely sexy, even in an apron, man.*

I stepped into the pantry, worried I'd get lost. The room, truthfully the best word to describe the space, was bigger than my bathroom. Cans and boxes of all sizes and colors aligned perfectly on the many shelves. Each label faced forward and like-things stood next to each other. Nothing was out of place. My thoughts went immediately to Garen and his obsession with order. Nausea wrapped around my stomach. I closed my eyes to block out the memories.

"I forgot to tell you, the pastry flour is in the red cans . . ." I jumped at the sound of Booker's voice. "Tess, are you okay? You're pale." He slipped an arm around my waist.

"I'm fine," I lied.

"Tess," Booker pressed, his brows forming a vee.

"I . . . um . . . My ex . . . He had a thing for neat, orderly cabinets . . . He's sort of a neat-freak." I glanced around the tidy space again.

Booker immediately began pushing cans over and shoving boxes onto their side.

"What are you doing?" I asked, my eyes wide with confusion.

"I stayed up late last night organizing the pantry so you wouldn't think I was a slob." He scattered a few more cans.

I grabbed his hands. "It's okay. Don't mess everything up on my account." I smiled. "But thank you."

He nodded soberly and grabbed the red canister before heading back to the kitchen. I quickly straightened the cans, touched by the simple act of compassion he'd offered. *If you're not careful, Tess . . .*

"Okay, you've added everything just like it said?" he asked as I mixed in the salt several minutes later.

"Exactly, but I'm telling you, it's not going to work," I warned for the fourth or fifth time.

"Can't wait for the kick-off," he all but cooed.

"It says I need two cups of pumpkin, but I couldn't find the can in the pantry."

"Canned pumpkin? Disgusting." He opened the stainless steel fridge and removed a second red bowl. "Fresh pumpkin. Seth brought this by before he left. He didn't want it to go bad. I cooked it up this morning. You'll need to add the chunks to the blender to puree it before scooping it into the mix." He set a blender on the counter and I added the orange chunks to it while he gathered the pie tins.

"How long should I blend them for?" I asked.

"Thirty, maybe forty seconds."

I pressed the lid in place and pushed the puree button. The blender roared to life. Booker looked through the glass when it stopped before removing the blender from the base, lifting the lid. He inspected the pulverized pumpkin.

"Better give it another twenty seconds." He handed me the blender, brushing his hand along mine. Goose bumps raced up my neck. While setting the blender back on the base, I knocked the recipe to the floor with my elbow. He pressed the puree button and it roared to life once again as I bent to pick up the recipe.

That's when something went horribly wrong. The lid flew off the blender and smashed into the refrigerator, sending pumpkin everywhere, including clear up to the ten-foot ceiling. Booker slammed his hand down on the base, turning the blender off. He was covered in the orange goop. It landed in his hair, on his neck, all over his shirt and apron, even a little on his jeans.

I stood in horror, my body shaking. I stepped out of his reach. "I . . . I . . . I'm so sorry." The words about choked me. I began speaking quickly. "I'll clean it up, all of it, I promise. You won't even know anything happened." My breath came in short gasps.

Booker just stood there, his mouth twisted tight, his eyes radiating a murderous glare. He stepped forward. I cringed, waiting for the blow, the slap, the punch. My hands shot up in front of my face. Pure instinct took over as I cowered.

I never thought Booker would've hit me, yet there he stood, teeming with anger. Maybe I was the problem after all, just like Garen always claimed. Somehow I brought out the worst in people.

But instead of a punch, Booker pulled me into his arms. "Tell me his name," he demanded, holding me tight against his chest. "No, don't, because if you do, I'll kill him."

Only then did I realize I was crying. I felt foolish and forced myself to get control. "I'm getting mascara on your shirt." I pulled my head back and dried my face as the panic leeched from my body. Booker laughed softly as I dabbed at the spot. "What?" I asked.

"You're seriously worried about a little mascara." He pointed to the pumpkin blob on his shoulder and apron. My apron now, too, had pumpkin from his hug.

I wrinkled my nose. "Point taken." I took a deep calming breath as Booker lifted my chin to his face.

"I wish I could take the memories away, Tess. If I live to be five hundred I'll never understand how a man could hit a woman." He pinched his eyes shut and shook his head slightly, before opening them again. "I'm—" a chunk of pumpkin dropped from his hair onto my nose. I pinched my lips together. "I guess we should get this mess cleaned up, after which I'll excuse myself and take a shower."

"I'll clean up, you go shower. This is not your fault. I forgot to tighten the lid," I said hesitantly.

"Tess, it's my fault. I know better than to turn on a blender without putting my hand on the lid. The sheer force of the food being tossed around—" Another chunk of pumpkin fell from his hair. I grabbed a paper towel and removed the pieces still in his hair, well, the big pieces anyway. The small stringy ones would have to be showered out.

"Thank you." He stroked my cheek. Fire burned inside me at his touch. "You had some on your face."

We cleaned up the stringy puree. Booker blended a fresh batch and I poured everything into two piecrusts and set them in the oven while he showered.

I sank onto the couch and cried, completely humiliated. Humiliated over the mess I made with the pumpkin and humiliated at my reaction. I wondered if I'd ever truly put Garen and all he did behind me and move on. I dried my face and resolved to let the pumpkin incident go. I didn't want Booker to know I'd been crying.

"Garen's out of your life. Let him go," I muttered to myself, applying a fresh coat of mascara.

Book came back fifteen minutes later, looking sexier than ever in dark blue pants and a white t-shirt. Daisy trotted along at his side.

"You're taking a chance wearing a white shirt. I may decide to explode cranberries next," I warned, proud of my joke, despite the guilt still churning in my belly.

"I'm willing to risk it. Besides, both me and my clothes are washable," he assured. I couldn't help but compare how Garen would've reacted to the exploding blender. I shoved the thought out of my head, vowing not to give that creep one more second of my thoughts today. We gathered the food and set it on the table, along with red and green Christmas plates.

Daisy came and sat quietly near the head of the table, waiting. "She's a quiet dog." I rubbed the Lab's head. Her mouth dropped open and her tongue flopped out, clearly pleased at being petted.

"Daisy is a wonderful dog, but she prefers to spend most of her day sleeping, unless there's food around," he explained as he carved the turkey—a *real* turkey. He tossed the dog some skin, which she immediately inhaled. "Happy Thanksgiving, Daisy May."

I swiped a piece of the turkey Booker cut up also, moaning as I chewed.

"So lazy vegetarians eat turkey." He chuckled as I stuffed another much too big piece of the bird in my mouth.

"That's the beauty of being lazy. You get to pick and choose which rules you follow," I said after swallowing.

"But no beef or pork?"

I scrunched my nose as I shook my head. "Not for me."

As we sat, Booker poured us each grape juice. "Sorry," he said. "I don't drink. I should've asked you if you wanted something. I could've picked it up for you."

"Juice is fine. I rarely drink either," I said. "I'm afraid I can't handle my liquor. I usually end up sick so I seldom drink." He passed the potatoes to me. "Are you a lightweight when it comes to alcohol, too?"

"No. I'm afraid my reasons are a little more complicated," he said, solemnly. "I told you my mom and sister were killed during a home invasion robbery, right?" I nodded. "Afterward, I went off the deep end for a while." He set the juice down and picked up the gravy bowl. "I didn't handle their deaths well and started drinking, heavily. It was pretty bad. Seth's family took me in after they died and I gave them a rough time of it. My grades slipped. I seldom went to classes, barely graduating."

I didn't know why he poured gravy on the moist turkey, and then I tasted the gravy. Incredible. I added it to my turkey, eating everything way too quickly. The guy could cook.

"So what happened after graduation?" I asked.

"A couple of my buddies talked about wanting to join the military. I spoke to Seth's dad, Eric, and he encouraged me to join. No doubt he thought the military would force me into straightening up my act."

"Did it?" I asked, slipping Daisy a piece of turkey.

"Spoiled." He waved a finger at the dog. Her tail beat rhythmically against the wood floor. "Unfortunately for me, you can legally drink on base at the age of eighteen in the military. Though I never drank on the job, nor did I ever go to work under the influence, all my free time was spent in the on-base bars.

"Eric pulled a few strings and got me stationed under him, but I lived in the barracks so he seldom saw me outside of work. One day I got completely wasted and somehow ended up at their home. To this day I don't know why I went there. Out of habit, maybe." He put his fork down. "Eric found me early the next morning, passed out in his driveway in a puddle of my own vomit. He helped me inside, and into the bathroom where I took a shower and cleaned up. I went into my old room and crawled into bed. Before I fell asleep again, Eric came to me and said, 'Sam, those men robbed you of your mother and sister. Don't allow them to take any more from you.' I'll never forget that."

Booker's words hit me like a freight train. Garen robbed me of years of my life, and I'd allowed him to take even more by hiding, by not living how I wanted to live. "I'm guessing that's when you stopped drinking?" I asked.

"Nope," he said softly. "Though his words were in my head almost every waking moment, I didn't get sober until Eric and his wife died. Seth was only sixteen at the time and needed me. I was no longer active duty. I bought a house with money I'd saved and Seth moved in, along with my grandfather. I never drank again and I let the anger go."

"And things are good now?" I asked.

"Yes," he nodded. "Sometimes I still struggle with the memories. That's the main reason I left the MET. Nightmares I hadn't had for years were back with a vengeance. When I started the law practice, they stopped again. I'm in a much better place now."

"I'm glad," I said as the buzzer went off in the kitchen, breaking the tense mood.

"The pies." Booker jumped up and removed them from the oven. They smelled tempting. We cleared off the table as they cooled.

"Looks like you'll be doing dishes," he prodded. "The pie is going to be incredible."

"We'll see. You haven't tasted it yet," I warned.

"No, but I did wear it for a bit—part of it, anyway," he said grinning. "I think orange just may be my color."

Booker sliced us each a piece. "On three," he said. He took a large forkful, as I scooped up a small bite on mine. "One, two, three." We both bit into the pie. It was disgusting. I spit mine into my napkin. Booker forced his bite down his throat. "It has an interesting texture," he said, laying his fork on the plate. "And the spices enhance—"

I stood with a shake of my head. "Forget it, Gatto. It sucks. I win. I'm going to watch the game. Hurry and load the dishwasher and maybe you can catch the second half." I waved and walked into the family room with Daisy at my side.

My stomach fluttered at Booker's warm chuckle.

Chapter 14
BOOKER

I shoveled the driveway so Tess could leave. Too bad only a few inches of snow fell, otherwise I'd have a strong case to insist she stay the night. My eyes raked over the empty prison most people lovingly call home. Prison might be too strong an analogy, but at times it felt like solitary confinement. I loved my home. I just hated the overbearing emptiness that threatened to crush me when guests left. I already felt the emptiness creeping in and Tess wasn't even out the door yet.

"All ready," I said, dipping my head back inside. Tess slipped on her thick parka, looking as if she were preparing for the Iditarod instead of driving across town. With a steel grip on her purse, she made her way to the car, flinching at a brutal gust of cold air.

"Oh! I hate the cold," she grumbled to herself more than me. I held her car door open and she tucked inside, shutting it and opening the window a tiny crack. "Thanks for warming up my car while you shoveled."

"Thanks for helping with the dishes after I lost the 'promise.'" I made quote marks in the air. I stooped, eye to eye with her fake brown eyes, and couldn't help but wonder what they looked like without the dark contacts.

"It was a sucker promise, anyway. I knew from the get-go I'd win. I've a long, painful relationship with cooking," she admitted. "I'm hopeless in the kitchen."

"I hate to think anyone is hopeless," I pressed.

"Great. I'll bring dinner over tomorrow. Would you like charred scrambled eggs or soupy hamburgers?"

"Soupy ham . . . ah, maybe you just need some lessons," I assured her. She laughed and rolled up her window after thanking me again for Thanksgiving dinner.

I went inside, wrapped up the last of the turkey, and put it in the fridge after making a turkey sandwich. "Soupy hamburger," I chuckled to myself. Scooping up the remote, I plopped down on the couch to watch the football game I'd recorded earlier, but couldn't concentrate. My thoughts centered on Tess. Her warm smile as we set the table, her look of joy when she tasted my stuffing. Seth's recipe, actually. I also remembered the look of sheer terror in her wide eyes when the blender exploded. Her entire body trembled. It made me sick to think what caused such a vehement reaction. Good thing I didn't know who her ex was. I'd pummel him for every blow he'd given her. The look on her face reminded me of my mom and sister's faces that horrible day. I could still hear their screams.

Now sickened, I tossed my sandwich on the plate and set it on the ground for Daisy, who promptly inhaled it, tail a-wagging. "You're one lucky pooch." I rubbed her ears as the doorbell rang.

Hoping it was Tess, I raced to the door. "Did you forget . . . What are you doing here again, Nikkolynn?" I braced my arm on the top of the doorframe, hoping it sent the message that she wasn't welcome.

Her white fur coat draped her shoulders, and despite the row of black buttons, her hand pinched it shut. Something red poked out just above the collar. "I know it's a little early, but . . ." She let go of the coat, and it dropped to her feet as she tossed her hands in the air. "Merry Christmas, Bookie." She'd wrapped herself up like a present. Red paper covered in little Santa Clauses twisted around her body, and a red bow sat under her chin. "Aren't you going to open your gift?"

There was a time she wouldn't have had to ask. Nikkolynn was built for speed that started at the top, with her full mouth begging to be kissed, and ran clear down to her red painted toenails. She had a knockout body, probably from teaching some exercise class she used to talk about ad nauseam. What did she used to call it? Zimble, or Zumba maybe? Whatever the reason, she was too smokin' hot for her own good.

Now what I felt inside at seeing her standing there in nothing but some paper and ribbon couldn't light a candle. I felt nothing. Not a flicker of desire, not a whispering of love. Not a spark of fire. Not even hate or anger over what she'd done to me.

"Well, don't just stand there, I'm freezing. Invite me in," she demanded in her vintage princess tone. A tone I used to find cute. What was I thinking?

I stooped and picked up her coat, handing it to her. "Go home, Nik. Like I told you that first day in my office when you showed up, and each and every time you've dropped by my house since then, I'm not interested." I started to shut the door, when her arm shot out, blocking it.

"If you don't let me in, I'm going to sit here naked on your porch and freeze to death. And it'll be all your fault." She stomped her foot, as if that would intimidate me. I shook my head. I could be just a stubborn as her.

"It's a holiday, Bookie. I don't want to be alone." Her sexy little body may not do a thing for me, but that pout did. And that fact that I *knew* she'd sit on my porch all night, naked.

Resigned, and clearly a sucker, I said, "You can come in, but not dressed like that."

"I brought some clothes for in the morning, you know, in case I got lucky." She wagged her eyebrows.

"You're not spending the night. I'm watching the football game. You can join me if you want and have some pie, then you're leaving. Understood?" I said firmly. She nodded and hurried to her car for a grocery bag.

"My clothes," she explained, waving it. I nodded and led her inside.

"You remember where the bathroom is, I assume," I said, debating whether to give her some of the store bought pie Tess left. My conscience got the better of me and I pulled a banana crème pie from the fridge.

"I'll change here." She dropped her coat to the floor and set her grocery bag of clothes on the counter next to the pie.

"You're not changing in my kitchen, Nik."

"Fine." She took four steps back, now barely inside the family room, and peeled off the Christmas wrapping. I busied myself with the pie. The girl had moxie. I gave her several minutes to dress before looking up.

Nik sauntered to the counter in a barely-there lacy nightie, not much better than naked really. Still, I felt nothing. Maybe I'd been celibate for so long, I'd killed my drive. Or maybe the memories of finding her in bed with another man killed it.

"There was a time you couldn't have looked away," she purred.

"That was before I caught you in my bed with what's-his-name," I said dryly. "I lost interest after that."

"Bookie, you don't understand, I had to—"

"You're right, Nikkolynn, because when I said I loved you, and subsequently married you, I thought you knew that meant we were exclusive. And I don't want to talk about this again."

She pouted and dropped onto a barstool, glancing over at me, no doubt hoping the pout would work as it had so many times before. It didn't. I ignored her and ate my delicious pie. Nik's head tipped back and I looked up to see what had caught her short attention span.

"Is that pumpkin on your ceiling?" She squinted at the orange blob.

I laughed, remembering the explosion again. "Tess and I were pureeing pumpkin and the lid blew off the blender. What a mess."

"Tess was here for Thanksgiving? Who else? Seth, I assume." She sneered Seth's name. They never got along. He saw through her long before I had.

"Seth and his wife are in New York City. It was just Tess and me." I had no idea why I shared that information with her.

"I thought you weren't dating her." She gave me the death glare, another one of the tools she used to get her way.

"Tess and I are friends. She has no family around here, and all mine were out of town, so we shared the day," I said in my best 'drop the subject' tone. "I'm going to watch the game. You can stay or leave. Honestly, I don't care which." I paced to the couch, snatched up the remote, and settled onto the couch. The front door slammed as I hit play. "Thank you," I muttered to the ceiling.

~*~

"Hey, Book, that thing you wanted has been installed," Maggie said, yawning. "Want to come see?" She yawned again.

"Can you stay awake long enough to show me?" I teased.

"You want to invite Tess down, too, since technically this is for her?" Magpie asked before opening the office door.

"Great idea," I said a little too eagerly. Maggie glanced over her shoulder at me, flashing a twisted grin.

Tess sat at her desk typing up a report, her fingers flying across the keys as she worked. She wore a white turtleneck underneath a red sweater. I glanced down at her feet hoping she'd worn the boots from the box I'd seen the day she moved. Nope. Brown flats.

"Tess, give your poor fingers a break and follow us," Magpie said.

"I have to get this done. Booker needs it for a meeting this afternoon." Her fingers continued to type as she spoke, her eyes glued to the computer screen.

"It'll only take a minute, I promise," I said.

She nodded and stood. "If it's not ready in time . . ." she warned.

It'd be ready. In the three-and-a-half months since I opened my practice, she'd never been late with anything. In fact, quite the opposite. The girl had perfectionism down to a science, finishing every project way ahead of schedule. I made a mental note to tell her mistakes weren't punishable by death.

We took the elevators to the basement. Tess fidgeted with her sweater the entire time. "Tess, relax."

"Sorry." She tucked her head. "I have another two pages to type up. I just don't want to disappoint you, that's all."

"You haven't yet," I assured her. "Well, maybe once." Her eyes popped open wide. "Your pumpkin pie needed a little help."

I rubbed my stomach and leaned against the elevator railing as if weak.

"A little?" She laughed and nudged my arm. "I warned you."

Magpie stood watching us from the corner of the elevator, smiling ear to ear. The doors opened when we reached the basement. I took Tess's arm. "Okay, close your eyes."

"Booker, I've been helping Maggie and Lilah down here every night after work. I've already seen the space."

"Not everything. Now close your eyes." Reluctantly, she submitted to my request.

I slipped my arm around her waist . . . Okay, I could've held her arm, but my masochistic ways wouldn't allow me to miss an opportune moment to be a little closer to her. I guided her through the door of the workout room and led her to the mirrors. Lilah came over from the other side of the room where she'd been wiping down one of the new treadmills.

"Open your eyes," I said in Tess' ear, stealing a whiff of her hair.

"Oh." She stepped back. "I didn't realize we were so close to the mirror." She glanced around. "What am I looking for?"

Magpie turned her back around to the mirror, while Lilah chuckled. Tess studied the mirror, then her eyes landed on the barre. Her mouth dropped open. "You replaced the barre, Maggie?" She caressed the shiny wood with her hand.

"Booker's orders," Magpie said.

Tess turned to me, a look of confusion knitting her brow. "I thought you might want to get back into ballet since playing lacrosse in winter around here's pretty tough." She flew into my arms as I explained.

"Thank you!" She squeezed me tight. I hugged her back, glad to have my arms around her again even if it was for only a few moments. It felt as if everything in the world had righted itself. She pulled her head back and wrapped her hands around my jaws. "That is the sweetest—"

"Just friends, huh?" Nikkolynn's shrill tone killed the mood. Tess moved away as Nik stomped toward us. I wheeled around, sick and tired of dealing with her.

"Hate to leave, but I'm exhausted. I'm going home to take a nap." Maggie raced out the door. She had the misfortune of meeting my ex the other day. Nik was hired by a local restaurant supply house to demonstrate a new juicer they were featuring. Mags ran into her while Seth and I were picking out appliances for his restaurant. Since getting out of jail, Nikkolynn had only been able to find a few temporary jobs. A felony conviction will do that for you.

"Maggie's trying to do too much," Lilah said, undaunted by my ex's presence. I chuckled to myself at her moxy. "She's helping Seth set up the restaurant, doing the design business with me, and this week and next she has finals."

"You're right. That's too much," I complained.

"Tell me about it." Lilah pointed to the treadmills. "Yesterday we had an early appointment to pick up those. She looked like death warmed over when she got in my car. Halfway through the appointment she excused herself and ran outside. When I came out a few minutes later, she was white as a sheet. I took her straight home and told her to go back to bed."

"That's not good." Tess stepped closer to me.

"Don't worry," Lilah insisted. "I've stopped taking any more jobs until after Christmas. If she's still overwhelmed with school and the restaurant, we'll wait until she graduates in April."

"Excuse me!" Nik's voice grounded our conversation to a halt. "I do believe I was speaking to Booker first."

"Nik, why are you still here? In fact, why are you here at all?" *And why did I ever get involved with you?* I wondered for the millionth time. A lapse in judgment I'd be paying for for a long time.

"I'm here to ask you for a letter of reference." She sneered at Tess while holding out a slip of paper to me.

"You're joking, right?" I scowled at her incredulously. "A letter of reference, as in, 'Nikkolynn is my ex-wife. I caught her in bed with another man, and she tried to use me for insider information to help said man in his drug dealing business.'" Tess coughed to hide her laugh. Good ol' Lilah laughed right out loud. I couldn't help but grin myself.

"Always the comedian," Nik grumbled. She pressed against me, and ran her hand up my arm, aiming for my hair, only I pulled back before she reached it. "I've never seen your hair this long. I like it." She wagged her brows at me and bit her bottom lip playfully.

"I'm getting it cut tonight, right, Lilah?" I stepped out of her reach. "Now, seriously, why are you here?"

"I told you, I need a letter of reference." She stomped her foot. "And stop rolling your eyes and hear me out." I signaled for her to continue. Why not? I enjoyed watching a train wreck as much as the next guy.

"You know how great I am with fashion, like, ya know, with clothes, purses, shoes, right?"

I nodded. "Yes, my bank account and I remember your obsession with spending my money."

"Bookie, please," she complained, her teeth clenched. I waved her on. "There's a prestigious fashion house in New York City accepting four apprentices, and I need you to write and tell them I'm a good risk. With my criminal record and all it's been difficult. Like you said, the crimes were against you so I'm hoping if they see you've forgiven me, maybe it will help persuade them." She dropped her gaze to the floor. "You've forgiven me, right?"

Now I felt like a jerk. No, I hadn't forgiven her. She used me. She never loved me, ever, yet I did love her, very much. "Let me have the paper."

"Thank you, Bookie. I knew I could count on you." She attempted to hug me. I angled coyly to the side and stepped closer to Tess. "I see your email address is on the form. When I'm done, I'll have Tess shoot you an email and let you know when you can pick it up."

"You can drop it off at my mom's. I'm staying there temporarily," she said, walking out the door.

"I'll have Tess email you," I reiterated. Nik was horrible, but her mother . . . I shivered. I wrapped my hand around Tess' elbow. "We should be getting back to work. It's looking wonderful in here, Lilah."

"Thanks, Bookie. See you at dinner tonight." Lilah's chuckle could be heard all the way to the elevator.

"That was nice of you," Tess said as the elevator doors creaked closed.

"Don't put me on a pedestal, Tess. If Nik's in New York City that means she won't be hanging around here bothering me." Tess hid her grin behind her hand as I pressed the seven. I hated when she hid her smile.

Chapter 15
Tess

Nearly five years ago

Our new home, courtesy of reelected Senator Graft, stood in the middle of nowhere. It took an hour and a half each way to get to and from school using public transportation. I'd always used the bus system before because we could only afford one car, but being so far from school meant more than double the commuting time. Thankfully, I'd graduate soon.

Despite Graft's win, Garen didn't get the cabinet seat as promised. He was livid. Up until then he'd controlled his temper fairly well even though he'd only completed three sessions with an anger management counselor before quitting. He quietly redid the household chores that hadn't measured up to his standards, with only a twitch of his jaw. Once I heard him muttering about what a disappointment I turned out to be, and he should've married up the social ladder and not scraped the bottom. It hurt to hear, despite the fact that I'd be leaving him soon.

After the election his temper escalated daily, and he began shoving me around, even slapping me once. He stayed out later and later, not coming home some days until the early morning hours. We hadn't slept together in weeks. Thursday while doing the laundry, my suspicions were confirmed. I found a hotel receipt in his pocket from the Hansford Inn, in town. He'd told me he had a weekend conference in Houston. I sank to the floor, stunned and raw. I told myself it didn't matter, I was leaving him, but the betrayal stung nevertheless.

Later that evening, I made the mistake of confronting him. "You're asking me if I'm having an affair? Tell me, Terese, where do you go every other afternoon from five to six thirty? Don't you impose your guilt onto me when you're the one who's been unfaithful."

"I'm taking a yoga class in town. Remember, you said my butt was getting saggy," I explained, exasperated that he'd turned this back on me. "How did you know, anyway?"

"I have my ways. I knew you couldn't possibly be taking care of this place. I've had to redo the towels daily. And we won't discuss the mess you call a pantry." He jabbed a finger at me. "If I stay away it's your fault for making this place a nightmare to come home to." He pushed past, shoving me roughly aside. I stumbled to the floor, smacking my elbow.

He made love to me that night, if that's what you want to call it. It was cold, sterile, and harsh. After he finished, he crawled off and headed for the shower to "wash your stink off of me," he muttered. He seldom touched me after that, and for that I was grateful. Our "bedroom time," as Garen called it, had never been stellar.

A couple months later, I finally graduated. Instead of taking some time to celebrate, Garen had me running errands for him in Dallas. Having not eaten all morning, I felt queasy, and decided to splurge and stopped at Greens for a quick lunch, braving Garen's wrath. I'd call it a graduation gift to myself if he complained. While waiting to be seated, I discovered Garen sitting in the back of the restaurant, kissing a thin blonde girl. Unlike the time I discovered the hotel receipt, this time I felt nothing. I just didn't care anymore. I took my salad to go and ate it on the bus ride home. With any luck, they'd check into the Hansford Inn, and I've the house to myself for the night.

The new phone Garen bought me was a joke. It seldom worked and had to be constantly repaired. That meant I hardly ever got to speak to my family. Whenever I did, Garen was right there listening. I felt cut off, isolated. With my father in chemotherapy, my parents couldn't make it to my graduation. I was heartbroken. I really needed to see them.

To my surprise, for my graduation gift Garen said I could fly home next Christmas. That helped take the sting out of not having them there for the ceremony, even if Christmas was still months away. Part of me wondered if the only reason Garen offered was so that he and his mistress didn't have to hide, but again, I just didn't care.

My plan now was to work until then, saving all my money, and then once I got to California, I'd file for divorce. I'd have enough money to stand on my own and not burden my parents. My sister shared with me during one of our brief conversations that my dad had to take out a second mortgage on their home to pay for his cancer treatments.

It sickened me to know I'd failed at my marriage, having rarely failed at anything, but I didn't know what else to do. My self-worth lay at my feet in a crumbled mess. I second-guessed everything I did to the point that I'd gotten my one and only "C" the last semester in my dance theory class. I knew the material inside and out, yet still choked on the test, doubting even the simplest of questions. For the first time in my life I felt myself falling into a depression. I wanted to sleep all the time, nausea and fear were my constant companions, so much so I was an emotional basket case, crying over every little thing. But never in front of Garen. I desperately needed to find a job and break free.

I didn't mention any of the job interviews I went on to him. I didn't want to endure his ridicule if I wasn't hired. But somehow, he always seemed to know as if he were having me followed.

Today I'd spent the day filling out applications at several of the local dance studios downtown. A last ditch effort before trying the dreaded fast food chains. Whatever it took to escape Garen.

The local dance school advertised for a new instructor and I jumped at the chance. I dreamt of teaching dance to children, and hoped someday to own my own studio. In all, twenty-three people vied for one position. The school's owner arranged for auditions at the Marriot hotel in downtown Dallas since their studio had classes all day. When we arrived, they taught us all a dance routine. We then had to dance it back for them. The interview process was brutal. I felt both exhilarated and nauseous, but I pushed my way through it, pleased with how well I'd done.

Afterwards, a few of us stopped at Mike's Pub and got sodas to celebrate—diet, of course. Not one of us dared gain an ounce, a big no-no in dance. I went home and waited for the call offering me the position, but it never came. Heartbroken, I dreaded the thought of Garen coming home more than usual. The last thing I wanted was to walk on eggshells because he'd had yet another bad day. Rumors of illegal use of campaign funds trickled into the news of late, threatening Senator Graft's seat. He took out his frustration on Garen, who, of course, took his frustration out on me.

He arrived home an hour early in a full rage. He shoved his briefcase in his usual spot, went to the bathroom and washed his hands. I heard the pantry door open and knew he was checking the towels to make sure. He stormed out of the bathroom, still not having said a word to me.

"How was work today?" I went to the fridge and removed the salad I'd made earlier and added some fresh tomatoes, Garen's favorite.

"Graft got caught dipping into campaign funds, and he made me the scapegoat." He sank into a kitchen chair.

"Scapegoat?" My body tensed. This was not going to be a good night.

"He claimed I mishandled the funds and suspended me for a month, without pay." He scrubbed his jaw and shoved his hand through his hair. "He can't fire me outright because I've information that could be damaging to him if anyone found out. The suspension is his way of giving the press a bone, but in truth, it's a warning to *me* not to mess with him." Garen slammed his fist onto the table. "I won't be treated like this, Terese. He's going to be sorry he did this to me."

"I'm sorry, Garen. You've worked hard for him. You deserve to be treated better." I did my best to soothe him, strictly out of fear, not compassion.

"That's exactly right!" He slammed his fist even harder on the table, rattling his much beloved salt and pepper shakers. He had a fetish with salt and pepper shakers, spending months trying to find the perfect set. They either poured too quickly or not quickly enough. When he'd found those, he was like a kid in a candy store.

"Graft has messed up my Life Plan. I'll have to lay low until the press moves on to another scandal. Do you know how hard it's going to be to get a job in DC now?" He stood and shoved his chair under the table. "I was supposed to be working for a federal senator by next summer. No more messing around with some rinky dink state senators. I was moving on to the big boys, where the real power is." His eyes met mine, his nostrils flaring as he grounded his teeth. "You're as much to blame as Graft for messing up my Life Plan. You and your selfish refusal to move to a place with snow. 'I hate the cold, Garen. I refuse to live anywhere that has snow'," he mocked me. The conversation didn't go down like that in the least. I bit my tongue as my anger surged.

"I'm so—"

"What's his name?" Garen planted his knuckles on the table as he leaned across toward me.

"Whose name?" I asked cautiously, spinning the bowl of salad in my hands.

"Don't play games with me, Terese. You've been all over town today. The Marriot downtown, Mike's Pub."

How did he know where I'd been? His eyes scrutinized me as he waited for my answer. "You're following me. How dare you, when you're the one having an affair. I saw you at Greens the other day kissing a blond." Outraged, I slammed the bowl down on the table, knocking his precious saltshaker onto the floor, shattering the glass. My stomach sank.

His eyes burned with anger as he paced slowly toward me. His glare going back and forth between the broken shaker and me. I backed away. My first instinct was to run, only we had no neighbors. I wondered if that was why Garen insisted that we move here; no one would hear my cries for help.

My body trembled, and I sent up a silent prayer begging for protection from what I knew in my heart was going to be bad.

He flew into a rage, slamming me into the wall. I slid to the floor as lights flashed behind my eyes and my head pulsated. Dampness ran down my hair. Blood. He'd split my head open.

He grabbed my shirt and dragged me to the ruined shaker, rubbing my nose into the scattered grains of salt and glass on the floor.

"Garen, please stop! I remember where we got those. I'll get you another set tomorrow." Blood droplets splattered onto the floor. My head now bled heavily.

"I'm on suspension, Terese, without pay. Where do you think the money's going to come from to cover your clumsiness?" he shouted in my ear.

"I had a job interview today with one of the dance studios. I'll buy a new shaker with my first paycheck." I tried pulling away, but Garen held my face to the floor.

"A job interview for a dance studio in a hotel? I don't think so. I know you're meeting your lover, Terese. I'm not a fool. Tell me, do you lay there like a mannequin for him, too?" He grabbed my arm and dragged me in the living room, ripping my t-shirt off me and pushing me down.

"Garen, stop. I'm not having an affair. I swear!" I wrapped my arms instinctively around me as I scooted backward on the hardwood floor.

"What about the other place, Terese? Mike's Pub? Tell me, why were you there?" He grabbed my pants around the ankles and with a couple hard shakes, jerked them off me.

"Garen, you know I can't drink alcohol. It makes me sick. Please, stop and think." I scooted to the couch, having nowhere else to go. Shaking so badly now, I had to wedge my tongue between my teeth to keep them from chattering. "I swear I'm not having an affair. Garen, get control of yourself!"

His eyes flashed red. "If I'm out of control, it's your fault, you whore." He pulled his shirt off and his trousers, tossing them onto the floor, a first for him. His actions reminded me of a wild man, someone completely out of control. "Well, now you're going to get what you deserve."

The rape was quick. He was rough, insulting me, slapping me, clawing at my skin the entire time. When he was done, he spit in my face and immediately went to shower. I lay on the floor, shocked and humiliated.

After he finished, he dragged me into the shower, demanding I wash off the other man's filth. When I stepped out of the shower ten minutes later, he grabbed my wet hair, his fingers thumping against the cut on the back of my head from earlier. I flinched.

He tossed me on the bed, and pressed his face to mine as I lay shivering on top of the blankets. "You're mine, do you understand me? No man can ever touch you but me, do I make myself clear?"

"I swear I wasn't—"

This time, instead of a backhand across my face, came an all-out punch to the head, not once but three times. Thankfully, I passed out.

When I woke, I was cuffed to the bed and Garen was raping me again. He continued all night. Punching, violating, insulting me. "You worthless piece of trash." "Selfish, evil woman." "Vile sick whore." Over and over. I stopped defending myself, crying silent tears as he violated me in ways I didn't know were possible. I felt filthy, nauseous, empty.

The next morning, after he showered, he dragged me into the bathroom. "Clean yourself up."

Sitting on the shower floor, cold water pelting my skin, I cried, my knees to my chest and arms around them, rocking back and forth, unaware of how much time passed. I didn't budge until the shower curtain flew open and he dragged me back to the bed, naked and wet. This time he only cuffed one hand to the bed. He shoved a tray of food at me, leftover salad from the dinner we never ate last night, and a cup of peppermint tea. The smell of food made me sick and I turned my head.

"Eat." Garen thrust my face into the food. I fought back the bile in my throat and forced down half of the salad, and all of the bitter tea. He removed the tray and I lay back on the bed, sick and dizzy.

He came back, this time cuffing both my hands to the bed. I thought he was going to rape me. Instead, he put on his suit. "Have some things I have to do. I'll be back before dinner."

"You're going to leave me cuffed to the bed until dinner?"

"Don't want you calling your boyfriend over, Terese." He readjusted his tie, as if he hadn't a care in the world.

"What if the house catches on fire? I won't be able to get out." As soon as the words left my mouth, I swallowed hard, hoping I hadn't planted an idea in his wicked mind.

He shrugged. "Guess you'd better hope it doesn't." He turned to me, laughing as a yawn escaped my lips. "Besides, with as much Ambien as I put in your tea, you'll sleep through a fire."

"You drugged me?"

"Sure did. How else am I supposed to keep track of my tramp of a wife?" He turned and strolled out of the bedroom, leaving me naked and cold on the bed without a blanket.

I lay shivering, my mind floating in and out of reality before the pills took completely over.

I don't know how long I lay there, but it was dark when he came home. The assault started once more, violating me over and over. I didn't fight him to avoid being punched. Sometime during the ordeal, he shoved me into the shower, and when I came out forced me to eat and drink more drug-laden food. Then it began all over again. Thankfully, I passed out.

Days turned into nights, and into days again. A thick fog held my mind because of all the drugs. I remember being uncuffed at one point and forced to walk, or at least try to walk, around the house while Garen followed me, acting as if he were worried about my state of mind. "Terese, are you alright? What's wrong?" I brushed it off as delusions from the drugs, but to be honest, I just didn't care anymore. I wanted him to kill me, to be done with it all.

I woke up to sunlight slipping through the slats of the blinds in our bedroom. I was alone, but could tell from the sound of the birds chirping it was morning. Of what day, I had no idea. Though still drowsy, my mind had cleared significantly. I twisted around to the alarm clock on the nightstand. It read seven-oh-three. I lay listening to the birds, wondering how long I'd be left in peace before my sick pervert of a husband came in, starting the nightmare all over. Tears slipped down my face, running through my matted hair, soaking my pillow. How much more would I have to take before I died? I drifted off to sleep, waking to a loud slam of the bedroom door sometime later.

"Good afternoon, whore." Garen strolled causally across the room, tossing his coat into the chair along the wall. In the eighteen months we'd been married, never had I seen him toss his coat in a chair, or anywhere for that matter. He always hung it up. Always.

"I had an early afternoon meeting with Graft today." He dropped into the chair where he'd tossed his coat. "I've decided to take charge of my life and my goals. I'm not about to let that scumbag destroy my dreams." Though he acted calm and confident, eeriness sharpened his eyes, as if he'd lost his mind. Fear ratcheted up inside me, to the point of utter hysteria. I scooted further back on the bed, as if somehow I could get away from him. He continued laying out his plan to me, oblivious to my actions.

"I convinced Graft that keeping me suspended wasn't a good idea." He smiled the sadistic smile I'd seen so many times over the past however many days I'd been cuffed to the bed. He pulled out his cell phone. "You see, I went above and beyond what was expected to help him get elected. And being the scumbag that he is, I knew he'd turn on me someday, so I made sure to tape several of our conversations." He chuckled. "He wasn't too happy, but he saw the light and reinstated me."

He stood and came over to the bed. "Which means you and I are back to playing a loving couple."

Okay, he had completely lost his mind. If I got out of here alive, I was gone. No way would I stand by him now. No way. I'd walk back to California if I had to.

"I know what you're thinking, Terese. You think I'm crazy and that as soon as I uncuff you, you plan on . . . what? Leaving me? Calling the police, maybe?" He pushed a few buttons on his phone then turned it to me and pressed play. It was a video of me, wandering through the house naked, stumbling and falling, and blabbering incoherently. But Garen's voice was loud and clear.

"Terese, you got more drugs from your brother, didn't you? Angel, you have to stop this. It's destroying your life." Garen's voice sounded tender, compassionate, as his hand reached out to me when I fell, my head shaking vehemently. *"Angel, look at yourself. You're a mess. I know this is hard, but there are wonderful rehab programs we can get you into. If you agree to enter a program, I promise to not tell anyone your brother's been mailing you the pills. We can get through this, but all family ties must be severed. It's the only way."*

"Why you doin' t'is?" the me in the video slurred out while inching away from Garen and the camera.

"I warned you if I found you like this one more time, I was going to tape it so you could see how genuinely sick you are. Angel, come on, let me help you into bed."

The me in the video began screaming and kicking as he reached for me, then the video ended.

I remembered none of it. Horror overwhelmed me. My disheveled hair, my stumbling naked body, clearly under the influence of something. And Garen, the twisted maniac, kept the lights down low enough you couldn't see the numerous bruises on my face and body. I just looked like a poor, homeless drug addict.

Tears streamed down my face. This would never end. If I went to the police, my brother would be brought into it. His medical practice would suffer. He could even lose his license.

"I always get what I want, Terese." He tucked his phone into the pocket of his pants and uncuffed me from the bed. He grabbed my arm and led me to the bathroom. "Time for a shower. I hope the last five days have taught you a lesson."

Five days? I've been held like a slave for five days?

It was another cold shower. I washed myself quickly and stepped out. Garen stood there, arms over his chest, glaring. He lowered his face to mine. "I own you, whore. And if I ever find out you've been sleeping with someone else, I'll kill you next time." He shoved me and I fell backwards into the cabinet, my flailing arms grabbing onto the counters for balance. Two rolls of toilet paper and a box of tampons spilled out of the cabinet and onto the floor.

"I'm sorry." I hurried and scooped up the toilet paper and set the rolls inside. As I reached for the tampons, Garen's hand clamped down over my wrist.

"This box is unopened," he growled in my ear. I nodded, having no idea why that was a problem. "I bought them two months ago."

Two . . . "No. It can't be." I thought back over the last couple months. Oh no. Please, no! Depression hadn't caused my nausea, my lack of energy. I was pregnant.

Garen dragged me up to my feet and backed me into the wall. "Who's the father?" He shook me hard, slamming my head against the wall. "Who's the father?" he screamed in my face, spraying me with spit.

"You, I swear," I whimpered. This couldn't be happening. How much more could I take? I'd never escape him now.

"You're a liar!" He grabbed my uncombed hair and whipped my head back and forth before shoving me onto the floor. He crouched over me as I curled into a ball. "This is not my child. We used protection, whore. You got careless with your lover."

He kicked and punched me repeatedly in the back and legs. I wrapped my arms around my head as he worked his way up my body. He grabbed a handful of my hair again and shoved my head into the toilet, smacking my forehead against the bottom of the bowl. Water filled my ears as he continued his profane-laced diatribe. Garen never swore, ever. He considered it beneath him, lower class.

I grasped desperately at the rim of the toilet in an effort to fight my way free. I needed air. I kicked at him, hoping to knock him off his feet. It just made him angrier. He jerked me back and pushed me to the floor as he kicked at my stomach repeatedly. Becoming winded, he stopped kicking and again shoved my face into the toilet. I fought frantically until my breath, my life, slipped away.

No more pain. No more Garen.

Chapter 16

"Thanks." Nikkolynn snapped the letter out of my hand. It'd been two days and four emails since she'd asked Booker for a recommendation. All the emails coming into the office go through me first, a little fact that drove Nik crazy. She took the opportunity to include a few love notes, as I called them, directly to me whenever she emailed back. "He's mine, remember that", and "hands off him, dumb snit". I wasn't sure if the last one was a typo and I didn't ask. But my favorite note from Nik had to be, "he'll realize it was a mistake to let me go, oh dyed haired one". That inspired me to stop dying my hair. Clearly, everyone saw through my lousy dye job. I also thought it was rich for her to accuse me of dying my hair when hers was heavily highlighted. No one is that blond without a little help from peroxide.

"So where is he?" she asked, tucking the letter in her purse.

"I told you, he had a meeting." Okay, he didn't. Booker saw her coming and slipped out the back door.

She leaned closer, her boobs, like biscuit dough ready to bust from its container, practically popped from her low scooped-neck shirt. "I plan on winning him back, so you know," she sneered.

"We're just friends," I said quietly, in case he was nearby.

"So you say." She straightened. "Just remember, I'm not giving up." She turned and stomped out the door in her barely there skirt. It was only twenty-four degrees outside. She was going to freeze.

Ten minutes later, Booker strolled back into the office. "Darn, I missed her."

"Poor baby." I smiled and handed him the file I'd been trying to finish for his meeting in an hour. "Just in time, right?"

"Um . . . Mr. Hart canceled until next week," he said, adding, "Sorry. But how would you like to go to Rome with me instead?"

"Rome? I don't have a passport." I looked at him, confused. We didn't handle real estate outside the United States. Not to mention with my fake ID I didn't dare apply for one.

"Pass—no," he laughed. "Rome, New York. It's about two hours east of here. A friend of mine built a resort hotel there and invited me to the ribbon cutting ceremony. Originally I couldn't go because of the meeting, but now that it's been postponed, I'd like to go."

"I had no idea there was a Rome, New York," I said, closing my laptop.

"There's also an Egypt, Liverpool, and Greece, New York, to name a few." He sat in the chair in front of my desk as I neatly stacked the papers I'd been working on. "So what do you think? Can you handle four hours in a car with me?"

"I think I can manage." Oh, shoot me please. Four hours of trying not to gawk, touch, or drool over Booker, in the confines of a small car, no less. It'd be a long day. And the twisted soul that I was when it came to Booker Gatto and torturing myself, I could hardly wait to get going.

~*~

"Wow. This is a big deal." I stood next to the POC and stared at the crowd. There had to be six hundred people, along with a news van.

"Yup, real big deal. They're hoping to revitalize the area. It was hit hard when the economy tanked." He pointed to the beautiful new hotel. It had the look and feel of days gone by. The whitewashed wood building reminded me of an old southern mansion with its stately pillars and black shutters. "It has an indoor spa, tennis courts, and a pool. Each hotel room has a different theme."

"Theme?"

"Yes. One room—"

"Booker, my friend. Thanks for coming. If it weren't for you, I never would've done this." A tall Hulk-like man with flaming red hair and a freckle peppered face smiled broadly. He embraced Book in a powerful bear hug, if the bulging eyes on Booker's face were an indicator.

"I made a suggestion. You took the ball and ran with it." Booker twisted his shoulder around as if he were putting it back into joint. He winked at me as I laughed silently.

"You're still driving that POC thingy?" He pointed to Booker's car with his mammoth hands.

"It's a good car," Book defended.

He frowned. "Bro, that car doesn't instill confidence in your clients." Red then turned his attention to me. He took my hand and buried it between his. "Who's this lovely creature?"

"Wayne, this is Tess, my secretary." Booker spoke directly to my hand still cradled between Wayne's.

"Secretary. Good. Then I can ask her out and you won't mind." He turned to a photographer standing nearby. "Hey, Jimmy, snap my picture with Gatto here. This was all his idea in the first place." Within minutes, Booker and Wayne were smothered with cameras and newspaper reporters.

The ceremony was short. After a few hundred more pictures, Wayne made his way back over to us. "How about a private tour of the place," he offered.

Booker took my arm before Wayne could. "Love to," he smiled.

We walked through a large brick archway that spanned the road. Hanging from the center was a wood sign encased in an ornate metal frame that read The Fantasy Inn in large curvy lettering. Underneath in small caps it said, TURNING YOUR FANTASIES INTO REALITIES, ONE ROOM AT A TIME.

As Booker and Wayne talked business, I lost myself in the setting. Beautiful maple trees lined the banks of the lake that ran along the hotel. Despite that fall was coming to a close, the remaining leaves on the trees still burned rich with reds and golds. This area of the country held nothing for me when compared to Southern California, except for the falls. In autumn, New York shined. A light breeze sent leaves fluttering to the ground, and filled the air with their sweet maple scent. I inhaled deeply. Too bad it couldn't be autumn all year round.

We walked up the porch, and Wayne pushed open the tall white double doors. We stepped into the lobby, and back in time.

Rich burgundy and gold arabesque style wallpaper lined the walls. A grand staircase of wood and ornate iron made the perfect centerpiece for the entryway. A bellhop dressed in a red jacket with shiny brass buttons stood like a royal palace guard at the bottom. A long wooden reception desk was off to the right, with several different size brass bells the desk clerk used to summon a bellhop for the guests.

"I'll show you some of my favorite rooms." Wayne guided me up the stairs by my elbow. Booker stayed glued to my other side. Wayne stopped in front of a solid wood door and fished out an oversized gold key from his pocket.

"Keys instead of cards to unlock the doors? Nice touch." Booker nodded his approval.

Wayne unlocked the door and pressed it open, signaling us in with a wave of his hand. "Welcome to Swan Lake."

Breathtaking would be the best word to describe the room. An oversized white poster bed stood in the center of the room. White wisteria and tulle tumbled down and around the metal frame. A silky deep blue comforter with oversized white pillows completed the perfect picture. A full wall mural of the lake similar to the one next to the hotel covered the inside wall. Two swans, one black, one white, sat in the middle of the lake with their necks intertwined, curved into a heart shape.

"This is beautiful." I nodded to the wall.

"It cost me a pretty penny." Wayne beamed at the hand painted mural.

"But well worth it," Booker said, admiring the painted maple trees up close.

"You think this is beautiful, wait until you see the bathroom." We followed him to the next room. Huge skylights flooded the room with natural lighting. The mural extended to these walls also, but that was not the focal point. The large sunken tub that resembled a pond was.

The attention to detail in the room astounded me. Soap and shampoo dispensers fashioned after swans sat in a wicker basket next to the tub. On a large flat rock the swans from the mural in the other room had been replicated with towels.

"Towel origami," Booker chuckled. "This is impressive, Wayne. Makes me want to dive in." He nodded to the tub. Diving into water was the last thing I wanted to do. One too many times of having my head forced down the toilet and not being able to breathe left me with that phobia. I much preferred a shower.

"Come on. I'll show you some of the other rooms." Wayne went to place his hand on the small of my back to lead us out of the door, but Booker beat him to it.

"We already have plans to expand this place if it takes off," Wayne explained as we followed him. "We're going to add a wedding chapel and a reception center. We'll offer wedding and vow renewal packages that will include the wedding, reception, and a room of their choice."

"This place is a goldmine," Booker said as we stopped at another door. "Wonder if we could find a place near Port Fare to build one," he said, half to himself.

"This room is my favorite," Wayne opened the door and stepped back as Booker took my hand. We went inside via a gangplank. "We call this Shipwrecked."

At the end of the short gangplank, we stepped through what looked like a giant hole torn into the side of a ship. The walls were planks, much like the inside of a small boat and the windows were portholes. Artificial palm trees lined one side of the room, but you'd never guess they weren't real. The headboard of the king-size bed was an aquarium, teeming with colorful tropical fish. It ran from the floor and arched over the head of the bed to the floor on the other side.

Wayne put his hand on my shoulder. "What do you think?"

"Unbelievable. It feels like you're on an island in the middle of nowhere." I could hardly take in all the details there were so many. Coconuts in the palm trees. Starfish and coral light fixtures. Even the carpet looked like rippled sand.

Wayne took my arm and guided us to the bathroom. Booker wedged his way in between us as we stepped into the lagoon with lush greenery and a rock wall. Wayne pressed on a coconut mounted to the wall and water poured over several large rocks near the ceiling.

"A waterfall shower," I said with a grin. "I love it."

Next Wayne showed us a room fashioned after a disco. The bed was up on a platform and had chaser lights around the frame. A disco ball hung from the ceiling. "I had to double the insulation in this room. The sound system is so good the floor actually vibrates."

We also toured a jungle room with vines hanging from the ceiling, and a bed up in a tree house.

Wayne flirted his way through the tour, touching my arm, winking, hinting that we go out sometime. Booker all but broke his teeth from grinding them.

While checking out the motorcycle themed room, which had a genuine Harley Davidson as the headboard, Wayne's assistant rushed into the room.

"The governor wants to take some pictures with you," said the overly excited girl.

"Tell him I'll be there in a while, I'm giving a tour right now." He looked at Booker. "I didn't even vote for the guy. Starting a business in New York with all of its ridiculous regulations and laws was cumbersome, to say the least. This state literally chases businesses away."

"He's leaving. His helicopter just arrived. He said you'll need to hurry." She opened the door further, waving him on.

"I'd better go or he'll raise my taxes even more," Wayne grumbled. "Thanks for coming, Booker." The two men shook hands. "You're welcome to stay here anytime. In fact, pick a week and you can try out a different room every night."

"Will do," Booker said, slipping an arm around my shoulder as Wayne took my hand in his.

"I'll call you," he promised me before leaving.

"This is a beautiful place," I said as we made our way outside and over to the reception area.

"The guy's going to make a killing."

I went straight to the car as Booker said goodbye to a few people he knew. I turned on the car and cranked up the heat.

"Here. I got you some contraband." He handed me an egg salad sandwich as he got in. "These are pure heaven. I talked the girl into giving me the recipe for Seth's restaurant."

"I'll bet you did." No doubt the poor girl was putty in his gorgeous hands. I took a bite and groaned. "Pure heaven is right. And thank you," I said around the ecstasy in my mouth.

He dropped half a sandwich in his mouth. "I have more." He pulled a small bag from his jacket and waved it at me.

"I'm good, thanks."

"Would you mind driving then so I can finish these?"

"I can't drive stick," I admitted, scrunching my nose.

"You can't drive . . . Well, no time like the present to learn." He placed the sandwiches in the backseat and got out of the car.

"No, I tried. It was a disaster," and it cost me an elbow in the stomach and a shove to the ground by Garen.

"That's because I didn't teach you." He took my hand and guided me out of the car. "I promise to be kind and patient. And do I not keep my promises?"

I nodded, swallowing the lump in my throat. "Okay." I started for the driver's side when he took hold of my arm.

"No pressure, Tess. You can say no."

"I know. And thanks for saying that." I wanted to throw my arms around him and thank him for all the kindness he'd shown me, and for the restraint he used in not pressuring me into going out with him. Instead, I nodded and got into the rusty green car and double-checked my seatbelt. I was taking no chances.

"I'm assuming you know a little about how to use the clutch and gas pedal?"

"Yes, but I can't seem to get the timing," I explained. "Either I let the clutch out too fast and jerk all over the place or I kill the engine."

He explained about listening to the engine and getting a feel for it, all the things that Garen had explained, except Booker's voice held no condescension. I turned the engine on after engaging the clutch.

"Slowly let off the clutch and press on the gas pedal at the same time." I did exactly what he said and the car bucked forward and died.

Booker chuckled. Not what I expected. I'd take laughing over punching any day. "You'll get it. Try a little more gas and a little less clutch."

Twenty minutes later we'd made it to the mouth of the parking lot. "I'm hopeless." Exasperated, I turned the car off.

"No. You're frustrated. We've made it clear across the parking lot," he pointed out as if that were some grand feat.

"Seriously? I've gone fifty feet in twenty minutes. At this rate it will be nine-thirty on Monday before we get back to Port Fare."

"You know, Tess, if you want to grow old with me, pretending you can't drive a stick is going about it the hard way." He looked at me sternly, as if he meant every word. I dropped my head back against the headrest and laughed. "I do enjoy that laugh," he said, brushing a strand of my hair over my shoulder.

I turned my head, facing him. He twisted sideways, an arm wrapped around the headrest. Our eyes locked, then his gaze fell to my lips. I could feel my breath catch. He reached over and tugged a strand of my hair. "I'm trying real hard not to break my promise here. Maybe we should get going."

"Good idea." I took a cleansing breath. "Okay. First gear is here?" He nodded. "Let off the clutch slowly and give it some gas," I said to myself for the hundredth time. The car jerked forward, but it was the smoothest of my attempts so far. I drove to the throughway and kept going. By the end of our two-hour drive, I'd gotten the whole shifting thing down pretty good. Granted, we were on the freeway so I seldom had to shift, but I felt proud. I'd conquered a stick shift. I pulled up in front of my trailer and maneuvered the car between a snow bank and a tree.

"Great job." Booker smiled.

"Thanks," I said proudly, forgetting to leave my foot on the clutch. We jetted forward into the snow bank.

Booker chuckled. "Guess you get to try reverse," he said, looking over his shoulder. "The tree is about ten feet behind us so it shouldn't be a problem."

"'Shouldn't' being the optimal word," I grumbled, restarting the car. It took me three attempts to get it into reverse.

"Ease up carefully," Booker instructed.

I jerked us back a few inches and killed the engine again. "Tess, more gas pedal. We're on ice so it may take a little more but don't gun it."

I nodded as we continued jerking back ever so slowly. "More gas pedal," he said again.

So I did. And we hit the tree. My heart jumped up my throat. I hurried out of the car and ran to survey the damage. His trunk and fender had a six-inch crease, there was no way he could open his trunk, and the muffler had fallen completely off.

Booker came around. "Are you hurt? You're whiter than the snow."

I looked at him, my eyes wide, my mouth hanging open, waiting for the explosion when he saw the damage. He wouldn't hit me, but he would be furious. I could feel the tremors taking over. I wedged my tongue between my teeth to keep them from chattering. I stepped back as he glanced at the damage.

"I'll pay for it I've money in savings I've enough to cover the damage in fact, I can replace it and you can have my car until yours is fixed I'm so sorry." My words were one long run-on sentence through chattering teeth. Booker looked at me, his brow tight. He took one long stride toward me.

"What did that scumbag do to you?" Anger rolled off him as he cupped my face in his hands. "Tess, I'm not going to hurt you. Please tell me you know that." I nodded as he wiped the tears rolling down my cheeks and pulled me to him. "It's a piece of metal. Not even metal, more like fiberglass. And rust anymore. I'm not worried about the car. I'm worried about you. You're trembling. And I don't believe it is because you're cold."

I shook my head, ashamed of my reaction. "You must think I'm an idiot. I'm trying to forget him. I'm doing better. When I'm in public, I force myself not to search for him. But a part of me still lives in fear. Every raised voice still draws my attention. You have no idea how hard I've been trying to put it all behind me."

"I just might understand, Tess, at least on some level." Pain filled his tight eyes. I remembered him telling me his mother and sister were killed right in front of him. Maybe he did understand.

"Is it alright if we go inside so I can call a tow truck?" I nodded, and then he added, "I've something I want to share with you. Maybe we can help each other move on."

Chapter 17
BOOKER

I settled on the couch as Tess handed me a mug of hot chocolate. She'd used little envelopes of store-bought cocoa mix. I forced myself not to cringe. "I love hot chocolate." A pained smile tightened her pale face. Crashing my car did a number on her.

I took a sip, shoving a groan back down my throat at the watery drink. *Yuck.* "I make a killer homemade hot cocoa that will ruin you for other cocoas," I promised, forcing down more of the vile liquid. "I can make us up some if you'd like." Keeping my voice from sounding desperate wasn't easy.

"Remember, non-cook here. I don't even have cocoa." She pointed to herself as she sat down on the opposite end of the couch. "I'm sorry about your car. Like I said, I've enough money to pay for a new one."

"I've been thinking about getting a new car, actually. Seth's been after me, insisting clients won't have any confidence in my skills if they see me driving the POC." I shrugged. "He's got a point. I'd pretty much decided to go and look next week, though now you may have to drive me around to the car lots," I teased.

Tears fell down her cheeks again as her lower lip wobbled. I slid over next to her, putting my arm around her shoulder. "Hey, I was teasing." I kissed her temple. "Now look what you made me do. I just broke my promise not to kiss you. I never break a promise."

She laughed through her tears. "You honestly expect me to believe that you've never broken a promise, ever?"

"I'm far from perfect, but in all honesty, I do my best to keep my promises. You can blame my dad." I pulled my arm back and set it on my lap. The less touching I did, the better. "He was a stickler for honesty and integrity. He ground the values into me from an early age. After he died, my mother picked up where he left off."

"How old where you when she died? I know you told me, but I can't remember." Tess took a swallow of her watery cocoa and smiled, as if the stuff actually tasted good.

"Sixteen," I said soberly. "Tess, I'd like to share something with you I've never told anyone. Not even Seth knows all the details. But I'm hoping my ordeal will help you deal with your past."

"Okay. And I promise to not repeat it," she vowed.

"Thank you." I took a deep breath, not wanting to relive the nightmare, but hoping it was for the good in the long run. "When I was sixteen, me and my buddies, the Im brothers—"

"Im brothers?" Tess brow wrinkled in confusion.

"Their real names were Jim and Tim, but I call them the Im brothers as in *Jim* and T*im*." I chuckled as she playfully rolled her eyes. "Come on, Tess, I was sixteen after all. Besides, the Ims deserved it. They called me Sam I Am after the Dr. Seuss book." She mumbled something that sounded like boys, and waved her hand, signaling for me to continue. "The brothers and I were fishing up on Lake Ontario. It was a hot and sticky July afternoon."

"Sticky, I believe, but hot?" she questioned.

"Ha-ha. As I was saying, a couple of rough looking guys, in their mid-twenties, I'd guess, came over wanting to sell us some weed. None of us did drugs, but the older guys were intimidating, not to mention persistent. I wanted to leave, get away from them as quickly as possible. Tim, always quick on his feet, made up a story about growing his own weed, hoping they'd think we were not in the market and leave." I shook my head. Who knew what a big mistake that would be? "I joined in, elaborating on the plants and lights I had hidden in the closet in my room. We laid it on pretty thick. It worked. They hung around for only a few more minutes, then left. We went back to fishing, not giving the guys another thought.

"Two weeks later, I paid dearly for my lie." I rubbed my chest as the vivid nightmare flooded my brain. Every gruesome detail, front and center, as if it were happening all over again.

"Samuel, stop teasing your sister and set the table. Dinner will be ready in ten minutes." Mom led Sara to the bedroom for a breathing treatment. Her asthma had been acting up all day. I began setting the orange plates out when someone knocked at the door.

"Sam, get that, please," Mom yelled from the bedroom.

"Yup." I crossed the dining room and jogged down the hallway, flipping on the lights. My gut sank when I opened the door. The marijuana guys from Lake Ontario stood on my doorstep dressed in baseball caps and oversized jeans. They rushed forward, each carrying a bat, and shoved me back up the hall.

"Dude, it's one of the pukes from the lake," the tall blond one said, grinning ear to ear.

"Where do you keep your stuff, twit?" asked the shorter one with brown hair. He slapped the bat in his palm, leaving little doubt what would happen if I didn't cooperate.

Why had I lied? They were going to kill me. My heart beat so hard it bordered on painful. "Um . . . I don't have any drugs. I was lying at the lake."

The blond pitched the bat into my gut and I doubled over with an oomph, stumbling back against the wall.

"Glen, don't hurt him just yet. Let's check out his room, maybe he's lying." The shorter one grabbed my elbow. "Where's your room?"

"I . . . I swear, I was lying," I said, struggling to breathe still.

"Where is it?" Glen screamed, punching my chest. My shoulder collided with the wall, and I slid to the floor.

"None of us do drugs. We were afraid of you, so we lied to get you to leave." I staggered to my feet.

"Kevin, have him show you his room. I'll look around in here and see what I can find." Glen jogged toward the family room.

"My mom's here, and my sister. If you come back tomorrow they'll be gone and you can search the entire house," I bargained.

Kevin turned to me and slapped the bat on his palm. "You ever heard of a home invasion robbery, liar?" I nodded slowly. "Well, this is your home, and we're invading it." He raised the bat and I turned, covering my head as it came down across my back, knocking me to the floor. He laughed and left me lying there.

"Sam, who was at the . . . I don't believe we've met." My mom shoved Sara behind her. She spotted me as I struggled to stand. "Sam!"

Kevin swung his fist into my mom's face and she stumbled back onto the floor, taking Sara with her. I weaved toward my family and took a swing at Kevin, missing. The force threw me off balance and I fell to the floor.

Glen came back into the room, carrying my mom's jewelry box under his arm. "No one's growing drugs in the closet. He did lie to us." Glen kicked me as I crawled to my sister. I ignored the pain and covered her with my body to protect her. Kevin grabbed me by my hair and pulled me back.

"Please, don't hurt my children!" My mother sat up and wiped blood from her lip with her fingers. "I have money. It's in a shoebox in my closet. It's all we have. Take it and leave."

Kevin signaled with a nod to Glen who dropped the jewelry box onto the recliner and jogged back down the hall. "Stay put," Kevin demanded as he crossed to the kitchen, pounding his bat on the counter. "You move again, lady, you all die." I turned to see my mom sit back down.

Kevin pulled drawer after drawer in the kitchen out and dumped the contents onto the floor. He jerked open the drawer where we kept the tape, and smiled. He grabbed a roll of duct tape as Glen came back carrying a brown and red shoebox.

"Jackpot, dude. There's at least five hundred dollars here." Glen opened the box and grabbed a fistful of money, waving it at Kevin.

"Good." Kevin held up the duct tape. *"We need to take care of these guys."* Glen stuffed the money back in the box and set it next to the jewelry.

"Please, just take the money and leave. We won't even call the police," my mom promised as Glen shoved her to the floor. They laughed.

Kevin jerked me to my feet. In my desperation to protect my family, I threw several punches at him, despite the fact that I knew it was a foolish act. One of my wild punches landed on his jaw. He shoved me to the floor before pulling a gun from his pocket.

"We can do this the hard way or the easy way, punk," he said, rubbing his chin. *"Now, get up."* I stumbled to my feet and Kevin forced me onto a bar stool, his gun held firmly in his free hand. He wound layer after layer of the duct tape around my legs, binding me to the stool.

"Why are you doing that?" Glen asked, as he knelt next to my mother. *"I thought we agreed to robbery only. I don't want to spend the rest of my life in jail for murder if we get caught."* He rubbed his face, obviously frustrated. *"I knew I shouldn't have let you talk me into bring guns."*

"Dude, we're not going to kill them, but that liar over there needs to be taught a lesson," he explained, walking back over to Glen. *"Besides, look how pretty this girl is."*

"I like the way you think." Kevin grinned malevolently before turning to me. *"We're going to take care of her first. I want the pleasure of seeing you watch. Then I'm going to beat you senseless."*

"I'll never forget those words." I pinched my eyes shut. "They violated my mom and sister like only foul, disgusting perverts would. My sister's asthma kicked in, and she didn't survive the brutal attack. A blessing, really. That freaked them out, especially Glen. That was when they decided they'd have to kill all of us to keep from being caught. Kevin tried to make me watch, part of my punishment, he said, but my mother pleaded with me not to. I shut my eyes, but could still hear it all. Each hit, each tearful plea." I dropped my head back against the couch, exhausted. Tess wrapped her hands around mine. "They came at me next. I have no idea why they didn't use their guns nor do I remember much about what they did to me except that they beat me good. I woke up in the hospital a week later, with Seth's parents at my side." I released a heavy breath. "I carried the guilt of their deaths for a long time." *Still carry it some days.*

I looked at Tess' tear-bathed face for the first time since I began. I saw pain in her eyes . . . and recognition. She knew, from bitter experience, exactly how I felt. It made me sick. She brushed the tears away and pressed her cheek to mine.

"I'm so sorry," she whispered softly in my ear. I put my arms around her and held her next to me as I pushed the memories away. I'd learned years ago that reliving the nightmare only damaged me. I seldom thought about it anymore, but when I did, the hurt was just as raw, just as crippling as it was all those years ago.

"Did they ever find the guys who did it?" she asked against my cheek.

"Nope. I like to imagine they doubled-crossed their drug supplier and were murdered, violently and slowly." I shrugged. "But that's only my hope."

Tess pulled back and looked into my eyes. I could see the dark rim of her contacts. She gently touched my cheek with the back of her hand, her eyes wide with compassion. A few tears tumbled down her cheeks again.

"Tess, I didn't tell you my story to make you sad. I just wanted you to understand that I know somewhat of where you're coming from, and that you have a friend in me. Someone you can trust. Someone who can relate to your pain."

She nodded. "Thank you. It does help." She smiled tenderly. "We're a pretty damaged pair, you and me."

"I like to think of us as survivors." I tucked a strand of hair behind her ear.

"Yes. Definitely survivors. And I need to try harder to do more surviving and less cowering."

Chapter 18
Tess

4 ½ years ago

The throbbing in my head paled against the sharp stabbing pain in my lower abdomen. I groaned and tried twisting onto my side.

"Hold still, Terese. I'm here now. Everything will be fine." Garen's false reassurance chased an icy chill up my spine as I tried to figure out what was going on through the haze in my mind.

Why am I in pain? Where am I? I forced my eyes open, only to shut them against the bright light.

"What's . . . Where am I?" I sputtered out weakly. Someone tugged on my feet, separating them, and setting each onto something hard and cold.

"You were attacked, Mrs. Johnson. Do you remember anything that happened?" a woman's voice asked.

"Attacked?" I opened my eyes, guarding them from the light this time with my shaky hand.

I glanced around as things slowly came into focus. The room was stark white, and a small steel cabinet sat in the corner. Gauze packets and several bottles lined the top. A hospital. The emergency room? A nasal cannula, strapped to my face, fed me oxygen. Another tube, an IV, was taped to my right arm. I looked down between my legs and saw a woman dressed in a blue paper gown, sitting there with her head down. Another woman, another doctor or maybe a nurse, stood next to her. I tried to remember what happened, but my thoughts were patchy at best.

Garen's face appeared between the doctors and me as he leaned over my chest. "Don't you remember, Terese? I came home from my business trip and found you on the bathroom floor in a pool of blood. You said a man broke in, demanding money and drugs before he attacked you." Garen's earnest face seemed so real, as if what he said was the God's honest truth. Only I knew better. I didn't remember everything that happened, but the memory of being cuffed to the bed and icy cold showers were vivid.

"I don't remember," I lied, though I had no idea why. Now would be the perfect time to expose Garen. I was in a hospital, for crying out loud. There'd never be a safer place. But I couldn't. My fear of him choked back the words. I'd have to wait until he wasn't around. Then I'd expose him for the monster he was.

"It'll be okay, Terese. Don't you worry. We'll catch the man who did this, I promise." He planted a dry kiss on my forehead. Both fear and anger tightened my stomach. I nodded dutifully. *Just you wait, you foul pig. Just you wait.*

"I'm sorry, Mrs. Johnson." The doctor between my legs stood. "I can't get the bleeding to stop. We're going to have to do surgery. Immediately. You're in serious danger of bleeding out." She tugged the blood covered paper gown off and tossed it into the garbage while giving orders to the other doctor and a nurse who'd entered the room. As she added something to my IV my brain started to go hazy again.

"Is the baby . . ." Garen asked. He had the tenacity to sound upset.

"I'm sorry. It's too late." Next I heard the doctor say something about a possible hysterectomy, but before I could scream out in protest, Garen shot to his feet and grabbed my hand.

"My wife and I desperately want children. Please do whatever it takes to keep from having to doing a hysterectomy, I beg you." Even as my vision blurred I could see tears on Garen's ugly face. Why did I ever think he was good looking? "Please, only do the hysterectomy if you have to, to save her life. She means more to me than anything."

I couldn't take his false pleas any longer. I tugged my hand free as I too protested. "Please, not a hysterectomy, doctor. I want to have children." The drugs slurred my speech.

My frantic protests and Garen's demands were the last things I heard before surrendering to the abyss.

When I woke again, my nightmare had gotten worse: I'd never have a child. They'd done the hysterectomy. The reality threw me into a tailspin of sorrow and anger. All because of Garen. I couldn't eat, and I couldn't stop crying. Every time Garen put his arm around me to comfort me, I wanted to throw up. To scream. To punch and kick him. I settled for medication, getting the pain meds as often as I could. They helped me not to feel.

Over the next two days, the memories of what happened slowly returned. Every ugly word, every painful blow. I remembered the despicable things he did to me. I remembered having my head shoved into the toilet, over and over, as I fought for my life.

"You didn't eat much of your dinner." Garen removed the tray from the bedside table and handed it to a nurse outside my door. "You had major surgery two days ago, Terese. You need to rebuild your strength."

I wanted to say, 'For what? So I can be healthy enough to endure another one of your vicious attacks?' I settled for, "Not a big Jell-O and watery soup fan, I guess."

"Compared to your cooking, this is a virtual feast." He chuckled and rubbed my head playfully, as if he were joking. Right.

"So, how are the memories coming? What do you remember so far?" He sat in the chair next to my bed, doing his best to look relaxed, with his hands tucked behind his head, and his feet stretched out in front of him, crossed at the ankles. His ticking jaw and tight eyes betrayed him.

"Still nothing," I lied, as if I had any intention of telling him. "Like I told you when you asked me after the surgery, the last thing I recall was you removing the handcuffs for me to shower. That was Thursday, right?" Thursday was the first day of my imprisonment. I pretended to have no memory of anything after that.

"Yes, Thursday. That's it, then." He leaned forward, setting his elbows on his knees. "You have no memories of how we talked about taking a cruise this summer, and inviting your parents to come along?"

I bit my tongue to keep from screaming out at his lie. "I'm sorry. I guess cooking isn't the only thing I'm terrible at."

"Don't stress about it, Terese." He reached over and squeezed my knee through the blanket. "The doctor said it's common to lose memories after a head injury. He also said you may never get them back."

Two could play his little game. "I guess that's a good thing considering how brutal my injuries were. It takes a sick, twisted mind to hurt another human being like that, don't you think?"

"Or maybe someone highly stressed." He stood and paced to the window. "It's over now, and you're safe. Let's just move on from here and not dwell on it." He turned back to me. "Don't wear yourself out trying to remember, Terese."

I pressed my call button and asked for some pain meds. I needed to escape the monster, if only for a couple hours.

The police showed up later that evening, but I'd just been medicated again and could hardly keep my eyes open. They handed Garen a business card with instructions to call after I was released from the hospital to file a report to try to find who attacked me. In my drug induced haze, I pointed at Garen. He scooped up my hand and kissed it.

"I love you, Angel." He didn't let go until the police left.

Garen played the dutiful husband well. Flowers adorned much of the free space in my private hospital room. He insisted I have my own room "for solitude as she grieves over the loss of our baby."

Only I knew the real reason. He was scared spitless that I'd remember and tell the police. He should be, because the second he left me alone that was exactly what I intended to do.

Done. Finished. The girl who never gave up, who never quit, was defeated. My marriage, if you could call it that, had come to a tragic end. I refused to live the nightmare any longer.

Garen stayed by my side, night and day, for four days. The man who insisted on showering daily, sometimes twice, hadn't showered since I got here. He also hadn't shaved. I laughed to myself every time he scrubbed at the paltry growth on his jaw, knowing it drove him crazy.

The hoodwinked hospital staff, which now believed he could walk on water, took pity on him and brought him fresh scrubs to wear each morning, along with a disposable hygiene kit, which consisted of a small can of deodorant, a toothbrush, and a mini tube of toothpaste. It also included a razor, but Garen, used to an electric razor, didn't dare try it, afraid of cutting up his pretty face.

Every day I had to listen to the staff gushing about Garen. Today a perky student nurse with deep brown eyes offered her opinion about my better half. "You're so lucky to have a wonderful husband like him, Mrs. Johnson." She slipped Garen a flirty grin. "I don't suppose you have a brother?"

Playing his part masterfully, Garen all but ignored her and stroked my hair. "I'm the lucky one. No man could ask for a more forgiving and loving wife."

I twisted gingerly onto my side. "I need some pain medication, please."

As the nurse left, Garen moved in closer. "I meant every word, Terese. You're the most important thing in the world to me. I'll do whatever it takes to win your trust back for handcuffing you that day." He kissed my cheek. I clenched my hands to keep from scratching his eyes out. He still had no clue I remembered everything.

"I've decided that as soon as you're on your feet again, Terese, I'm going to see an anger management specialist. Not some random counselor, but a specialist."

Yada yada yada. Heard that a million times over before.

"I need to learn how to deal with the things you do that anger me. It'll never happen again. I promise." He gave my lips a quick peck as the nurse came back in with my pain medicine. Prefect timing, no doubt planned.

"Oh, how sweet. Like I said, you're so lucky," the nurse prattled again as she injected the meds into my IV. I instantly faded away. Medication. My only escape from my "wonderful" husband.

"Good morning, Mrs. Johnson, I'm covering for Dr. Miron today. My name is Dr. Moore." Dr. Moore, a tall, lanky middle-aged man extended his hand with a broad smile. Garen jumped to his feet and shook the doctor's hand before I could. Always schmoozing. I swear Garen was born to be a politician.

"Your lab work from this morning came back. Everything looks good. I'd like to check the incision. If it looks as good as I hope, we can send you home tomorrow." He grabbed a pair of latex gloves from the box on a shelf near the door.

I went into panic mode as he busied himself removing the dressing. Tomorrow? No! I couldn't leave with Garen. He'd kill me next time I did something wrong . . . like breathe.

"This is healing nicely." Dr. Moore smiled reassuringly. "Looks like we'll be setting you free."

"I'm not—I'm not ready." I forced my voice to stay calm as fear clawed inside me like a rabid dog. "I'm still in a lot of pain. Could something else be wrong?"

The doctor pressed carefully on my stomach. I winced dramatically a few times to make it look good even though the pain was minimal. "If you're in that much discomfort, maybe we'd better keep you for another day or two, just to make sure you're not getting an infection. I'll order a few tests, also." I sighed heavily as he wrote something in my chart. Two more days. I'd have to find a way to get help.

"Mrs. Johnson, I know this is a delicate matter, but I wanted to go over the attack with you."

That perked Garen's ears up. "My wife can't remember anything. We've already told the police this." His knuckles blanched as he wrapped his hands around the bedrail.

"I understand, but this is not about the attack, per se. Mrs. Johnson, my daughter was raped while she was away at college, by her boyfriend, no less. I don't know if you're aware, but most victims of sexual assault know the perpetrator. Anyway, like you, she showered and washed away all the evidence. Because it was a 'he said, she said' situation, the boy walked free. He had a solid alibi. His mother, of all people." He paused as his lower lip wobbled for just a second. "If anything like this ever happens again, heaven forbid, it is best not to shower." He squeezed my hand.

Garen's agitation grew with each word coming out of Dr. Moore's mouth. I enjoyed watching the creep squirm as the doctor continued. "Please don't misunderstand me, you did nothing wrong. I completely understand why you'd want to shower. But with DNA, we can nail scum like the man who hurt you. Personally, I'd like to see men like him fry in the electric chair."

"Dr. Moore," a nursed rush into the room. "They need you in the ER, stat."

He nodded. "I'll be back this afternoon and we'll talk more," he promised, dashing out the door.

"Well, he was a little over the top. I'll see about getting you a new doctor right away."

"No, Garen!" His eyes widened at my reaction. *Calm down, Tess, or you'll raise his suspicion.* "It's embarrassing enough having someone poking around at my half naked body. I don't want to have another doctor looking at me. Besides, it's only for a couple more days, so what does it matter?" I forced myself to squeeze his hand.

"I'll think about it." Garen sat quietly for a moment. "This could've been avoided if you'd not had a hissy fit about going home tomorrow. Graft asked me to do some things and I need a secure Internet server, not this lousy public server the hospital provides." Garen sank into the chair.

"Graft gave you your job back?" I asked, playing dumb. I remembered all too well him telling me about getting his job back the day he tried to drown me.

"Oh, yeah. I forgot to tell you. He rehired me a few days ago." His body seemed to relax. His shoulders drooped a little and he had a content grin on his face, as if he'd just gotten away with something.

"You can leave if you have work, Garen. I understand. Besides, that stubble on your face is driving you crazy." I touched his arm. "But don't be long. It's been nice having you so close." I about choked on my lie.

"It'd be nice to have this gone." He scratched his jaw again. "No. I'm not leaving you, Terese. Graft will have to wait." Garen patted my hand.

I slumped down into the bed. At this rate, I'd never be free from the monster. I needed to stop waiting for the opportune moment, and just make it happen. Maybe I could tell one of the nurses. I had to. No way could I leave with him in two days. As my fears escalated, tears fell down my cheeks. I batted them away quickly, but not before Garen saw them.

"Terese, what's wrong? Are you in pain?" He grabbed my hand as a nurse walked in.

"Hello, Mrs. Johnson. My name is Lian Liew, and I'll be taking care of you today." The petite nurse dressed in blue scrubs marched over and set a package of gauze and some tape down on the bedside table before grabbing gloves from the same box the doctor had earlier. "Dr. Moore asked me to redress your incision."

"Thank you." I frowned. The five-foot nothing of a nurse wouldn't be my ticket out of here and away from my husband. I needed the big brute nurse from yesterday who took care of me. "Is Bo here today?"

"Who's Bo?" Garen pressed, his eyes narrowed slightly. "Wait, he's the nurse who took care of my wife yesterday, correct?"

"Yes," Lian said as she applied the gauze. "He's off until next week. He and his wife are on a cruise. Lucky them."

No! I crossed my ankles to keep from jumping up and running out of the hospital.

"Are you okay?" Lian asked as she added a strip of tape to the dressing.

"She's having some pain," Garen said. "Can you get her something, please?" Garen brushed my cheek.

"I'll check her chart when I'm finished here." She applied another strip of tape as Garen's cell phone rang.

"It's Senator Graft, Terese. I need to take this, but don't worry. I'll be right by the door." Garen's tone held more of a warning than anything else. He walked to the door, but stayed in the room, keeping me in full sight.

"I'm supposed to remove the IV, but I can give you something for pain first if you'd like. Otherwise I'll have to give you a shot." As she leaned closer to add another strip of tape to the dressing, her head blocked my view of Garen.

"Help me," I whispered. Her eyes shot to mine. Thankfully she didn't move. "Please, help me. My husband's the one who did this to me, not a stranger like he keeps telling everyone. I'm afraid he's going to kill me." Her soft brown eyes hardened.

"He's the one who attacked you, who beat you up?" Her voice was as low as mine. I nodded ever so slightly.

"Is everything okay?" Garen edged his way between the bed and the nurse.

"No, actually. Everything is not okay." Lian turned to face Garen. My hands fisted the sheets. Did she honestly think she was a match for Garen? "Your wife's in a lot of pain. When I asked her to rate it on a scale of one to ten, she said twelve." Lian stuffed her hands in the pockets of her scrub top.

"I guess you'd better get her something for the pain then," Garen snapped, scooping my hand in his. His palms were damp. She nodded curtly and left.

"What where you talking about?" he asked as the door closed.

"Um, like she said. My pain level." I shifted in the bed.

"So why was she leaning so close? I couldn't even hear you talking." He let go of my hand and folded his arms, stretching to his full height. Not good.

Think, Tess.

"She lowered her voice because you were speaking to Graft and she didn't want to disturb you. She's a big supporter of his. Voted for him twice." I chuckled, hoping it didn't sound forced.

"She's a bit star struck. I thought she was going to ask me to get her an autograph."

He nodded, a wistful look in his eyes. "Someday I hope to evoke that kind of awe in people."

A light tap and the door opened. Lian entered carrying a syringe. "My wife tells me you're a fan of Senator Graft."

My stomach tightened needlessly. Without missing a beat Lian said, "You told him." She flashed Garen an embarrassed grin.

"Don't worry," Garen insisted. "It happens all the time. I'm used to it."

"Still, not very professional of me." Lian removed the cap from the syringe. "Dr. Moore ordered a second pain medication for what is known as break through pain." She injected the medicine into the IV tubing. "With your wife being in so much pain this will be best. No sense in letting her suffer. She's been through enough." She patted my hand. I looked at her bewildered. How did doping me up help me escape from Garen?

However, unlike the other times I received pain meds, this time my mind stayed clear. She'd lied to Garen. The thought gave me hope.

"I should warn you," she faced Garen, "she'll be out cold for a good three or four hours. I mean completely out of it. A nuclear bomb won't wake her. Altamelidene is our strongest narcotic."

"I've never heard of it." Garen scratched his jaw again.

"Just approved by the FDA." As she continued, I pretended to battle my eyelids as if they weighed fifty pounds each. I even yawned. "See what I mean? Some of my colleagues jokingly call it the horse tranquilizer. While I don't feel that's professional, it's accurate."

"So she'll be completely out of it?" Garen asked, as I fluttered my eyes shut.

"Yes. It's twice as strong as her regular pain med, and you know how drowsy that makes her," Lian said. "She won't even know you're here."

She must be trying to get him to leave. Now if Garen would take the bait. I had my doubts.

"She'll be that out of it, for sure?" He sounded intrigued. "So I could go shower and she'd never know I was gone? I mean, after what happened to her, I haven't dared to leave her alone. You know, I don't want her to be scared."

"The staff is right, you're a wonderful husband," Lian cooed. "And yes, you can go home and shower, even take a nap if you'd like. She's not going to wake up. And judging by the way you are scratching that stubble, I'll bet you'd enjoy a good shave right about now."

The next thing I knew, Garen grabbed my hand and lifted up, then let go. I let it fall lifelessly to the mattress.

"She's out cold," Garen said. "Maybe I'll go shower." I heard his shoes tapping on the linoleum floor as he walked away from me, then the sound stopped. "I don't know." He sounded hesitant. "I'd hate for her to wake up and find herself alone."

"Mr. Johnson, I've been a nurse for over ten years. I guarantee she'll not wake up. You deserve some down time. You're wearing yourself ragged. Now go," Lian insisted, reiterating, "She's lucky to have such a devoted man in her life."

It was silent for a moment. "One hour. That's all I need." He opened the door and left. I struggled to sit up, my incision pulling.

"Don't move." Lian put her hand on my shoulder and gently pressed me back to the bed. "Close your eyes. Let's make sure he leaves." I heard her feet pad to the window. "There he is. He's running toward a blue car, a Fusion." A few moments later she added, "and his Fusion has left the parking lot."

I slowly sat up again. "Thank you," I said, feeling as if the world had been lifted from my shoulders. I could almost dance. Tears welled in my eyes. "I don't even feel drowsy. What did you give me?"

"Saline." She shrugged. "Please tell me I understood you right. He did this to you?"

"Yes. He tried to kill me." As I blurted out what had happened, Lian removed my IV after calling security, who called the police. Two officers showed up, as did the doctor from earlier.

"Mrs. Johnson, I wish I'd known," Dr. Moore said soberly after I answered Officer Clark and Thomas's questions, recounting what had happened. "I'm so sorry. He was so attentive." He handed me a fresh tissue. "He's a good actor, I'll give him that."

"I'd like to call my family." I blew my nose for the hundredth time as Lian handed me her cell phone.

"Thank you." With shaky hands, I took it and punched in the number to my dad's phone.

Garen burst into the room before my dad answered. I snapped the phone shut and scooted carefully off the bed, ducking behind Officer Clark. Officer Thomas, a large brute of a man, stepped up to Garen.

"I demand to know what's going on." Garen had the audacity to look confused. "Did she steal drugs from one of the nurses? She has a huge drug problem."

"That's a lie," I said, still safely hidden behind Officer Clark.

"A lie?" He laughed a short hard laugh. "I have it on tape. She's an addict and her brother's her supplier."

"No, that's not true." I shook my head.

"Turn around, Mr. Johnson, and put your hands against the wall," demanded Officer Thomas.

"For what? Loving my wife? For staying by her side through her addiction?"

"You're being charged with several things, one being attempted murder." Thomas spun Garen to the wall and cuffed him after frisking him.

"You'll be sorry," Garen screamed as they hauled him out.

Chills racked my battered body. The relief I felt just moments ago evaporated.

Chapter 19

Present Day

Seth stopped by the office after lunch and persuaded Booker to go with him to a restaurant supply store. My afternoon dragged on without Booker around. Since sharing the story of his tragic loss of his mom and sister with me, we'd grown close. We had an unspoken bond. A deep trust. I found myself even more drawn to him, and it grew difficult to not take our relationship to the next level.

I locked the office door and headed to my car. Booker's poor car sat next to mine, with its now duct taped bumper. The trunk was permanently stuck shut. The shiny new muffler looked out of place on the pathetic thing. I couldn't help but smile at the POC as I scraped the snow off my windshield.

Nikkolynn pulled in next to Booker's car. I groaned silently. She'd been a thorn in my side these past couple months. She learned my first name was Terese from my email signature and now insisted on calling me that, when she wasn't using more cheerful names for me, like home-wrecker. She reminded me of Garen with her mind games, only she was nowhere as good as him. I'd decided not to show the emails to Booker, hoping to avoid any more trouble with the girl. If she got the internship in New York she'd be leaving soon and would be out of our hair. Booker laid it on pretty thick in his recommendation letter.

"You do realize with a letter this nice, she'd be accepted into a convent," I commented after proofreading it for him.

"Exactly." He smiled broadly. Loved that smile.

Unfortunately, this afternoon Booker saw the latest smack down letter she sent me before I could delete it. He asked how long she'd been doing it. His cheeks flushed with anger when I told him.

"I'll talk to her tomorrow. This won't happen again," he vowed on his way out with Seth.

"Good. You're leaving, Terese. Booker and I can be alone." Nikkolynn strutted passed me. I didn't acknowledge her. The snow crunched under her feet as she made her way toward the building.

"Booker's gone for the day," I said quietly, *after* she went inside.

I jumped in my car, cranked up the heat, and left before Nik came back out, driving straight to Maggie's. Lilah eagerly agreed to meet me there to help me in my quest to reclaim at least part of my life.

I sat in the driveway debating for a solid two minutes before Maggie stepped out on the porch and waved me in.

"Are you excited?" She took my coat and hung it on a hook by the door.

"Sure." I chewed at my lower lip. She laughed and led me to the kitchen. I couldn't help but admire the beautiful cherry cabinetry.

"Booker built those." Maggie pointed to the cabinets. "Talented, don't you think?"

"Very." And sexy and funny and . . . *Yeah, I need a life.*

"Lilah's upstairs getting everything ready." As we climbed the grand staircase, which, she pointed out, Booker also built, I noticed how her shirt practically hung on her. She'd grown so thin over the past few weeks, and I wondered if she'd been sick again. Not wanting to sound rude, as in, "Hey, Mags, you look like crap. Are you sick?" I kept my opinion to myself.

Before we entered the room she turned to me. "Lilah's a little down. They thought she was pregnant this month, but she's not. She's trying to act as if it's no big deal, but . . ."

I nodded as she opened the door. We went into the master bathroom, my eyes landing on the grand tub in the center of the room.

"Wow," I said.

"I know, right?" Lilah said with a smile that didn't touch her eyes.

"Hi, Tess." Sofia stood next to her mom, applying a wide ring of lipstick to her lips.

"Don't you look lovely?" I sat in the stool in front of an oak vanity, almost eye to eye with the child now. I could see that she had at least three other colors of lipstick on already.

"Do you want some?" Sofia held the tube up to me. Maggie and Lilah smiled.

"Maybe later," I said as Lilah picked up a red brush and began pulling it through my hair.

"Are you sure about this?" she asked my reflection in the mirror.

I nodded weakly. "No . . . but yes."

"That's what I like. A woman who knows her own mind," Lilah said with a smile.

"I'm ready. But let's hurry before I change my mind."

Maggie snorted a laugh. "It'll be okay. Lilah's great with hair. You should've seen how pathetic mine was before she rescued it from certain death." Maggie fingered her pretty brown hair. I had a hard time imagining it looking anything but great.

"Let's get started." Lilah took a cup and a long paintbrush-looking tool and started painting whatever was in the cup onto my hair. "Oh, yeah. I forgot to warn you. This stuff stinks," she said as Maggie gagged and opened a window.

Lilah worked quickly, covering my hair with the stinky solution. Maggie stayed rooted at the windowsill, frequently sticking her head out for fresh air. The smell was ten times worse than the bottled hair color I normally used. Halfway through, Mags excused herself, claiming she needed to check on dinner. Lucky girl.

Sofia set the makeup down and followed Maggie. "You stink," she said to me, plugging her nose.

"Sorry. I need to strip out all this nasty box color," Lilah said as she dabbed on more solution.

After letting the stuff sit on my hair for thirty minutes, I knelt over the tub so she could rinse it out. It took all I had not to freak out as Lilah held my head under the water spout to rinse it. I concentrated on the trail of dark water running from my hair, down the drain, and out of my life. Goodbye bad memories.

"Okay," Lilah said when the water ran clear. She wrapped a towel around my hair and led me back to the vanity. "If the stinky stuff did its job you should be back to your true color. If not, we may have to dye it your natural color for a bit." She combed through my hair, added some kind of yellow creamy stuff "for volume," she said, before blowing it dry.

Maggie and Sofia came back as Lilah finished. Mags propped the door open and stood there to avoid the fumes still hanging in the air.

"What do you think?" Lilah held her hands out as if presenting me. Maggie smiled broadly. Sofia stomped her foot and fisted her hands at her side.

"What's wrong? Don't you like it?" I asked her.

"Now Booker will love you and not me," she declared, a pout on her cherub face.

"Sofia, please be nice," her mother said firmly, to which Sofia folded her arms and knit her brow in silent protest.

"Ready to see it?" Lilah asked. I nodded as she turned my stool around to face the mirror.

I gazed into mirror, taken back at seeing my natural red hair color again. I ran my fingers through a few strands, twisting my head from side to side. "Something seems off." I didn't quite look like the old me. I leaned in closer before realizing what it was. The contacts. They were dark brown, and my eyes were a blue-green.

I removed them, placing them in a small paper cup Lilah handed to me. "Perfect." Now I looked like me. I smiled at my reflection, before turning to Lilah. "Thank you. This looks better than I'd hoped."

She stared back at me, her mouth hanging open. "What?" I turned back to the mirror.

"Booker's a dead man," she said, looking at Maggie.

"Lilah, give Booker some credit. He doesn't just like a woman because she's pretty," Maggie defended, pinching her nose against the smell.

"I know. But I think we can all agree that he is already attracted to her," she said. "All he ever talks about is Tess this and Tess that. I'm just saying."

With her nose still plugged, Maggie came next to me. Both her hand and her mouth dropped. "Booker's a dead man."

"See!" Lilah grinned triumphantly.

I looked back in the mirror. I knew I was pretty. I'd heard it most of my life, but I had no idea my disguise hid that much. "Maybe this isn't such a good idea." My heart raced in my chest. Garen would spot me for sure now. I grabbed the cup with my contacts.

"Tess," Lilah placed both hands on my shoulders. "Why don't you give it a couple days? If you still feel this way, I'll recolor it for you." I looked at her reflection in the mirror. "It's a big change. It probably feels overwhelming right now."

I nodded. Of course she was right. Besides, what were the chances of Garen showing up in Port Fare, New York? He worked for a Texas state senator. He'd have no reason to come here.

"Seth's made eggplant parmesan for dinner. It's a new recipe he wants to try out for the restaurant. Please stay and have some," Maggie insisted.

"Thank you." I loved eggplant Parmesan, despite Garen. I steadied my nerves and pushed away the fearful thoughts.

"Goodie. I can't wait to see Booker's face when he sees you." Maggie all but skipped out of the bathroom.

"Booker's coming?" I stood and slid the stool under the vanity.

"Yup. And I'm with Maggie. I can't wait until he sees you." Lilah hurried out the door.

"But . . ." I said to no one. Even Sofia had stomped away. "Positive thoughts, Tess. Only positive thoughts."

Chapter 20

As I finished setting the table, the guys showed up. I stepped off to the side hoping to avoid being the center of attention. Maggie came up behind and nudged me out front. "Nice try," she giggled.

"I just don't want everyone to make a big deal is all," I explained.

"I understand." She patted my shoulder. "In the family room there's a cabinet along the far wall. We keep our nice glasses in there. Do you want to get them? It will buy you a couple minutes."

"Thanks."

I hurried out of the room as Seth and Booker's voices filled the kitchen.

"I think you're going to want the bigger fridge," Booker said.

"Yeah, you're right," Seth answered. "Mags, how's the eggplant coming along?" Soon everyone chattered way. The sounds of laughter and lighthearted teasing filled the air. They sounded like a family.

I gathered seven glasses and carried them quietly into the kitchen, setting one at each place setting. The voices quieted as I set the last glass down.

A whistle cut the silence and I looked up at Seth. He whistled again. "Like the red hair." He nudged Booker.

"Hello, Tess." Booker's smile was one of pride. Not at all what I expected. He gave me a hug, saying softly in my ear,

"Congratulations on taking the first step to reclaiming your life." Of course he'd know how hard this would be for me and do what he could to minimize my fears.

"Not a very big step," I whispered.

"It's a step forward, Tess." I nodded. "Now, you do realize we're going to be under the spotlight for the next hour or so? These clowns are going to scrutinize every little thing we do and say."

"You should see them gawking at us now," I said, frowning.

"I should just kiss you and really give them a show," he said with a wink. He turned to everyone. "Okay, show's over. Let's eat." And the awkwardness ended that quickly.

"You outdid yourself, my friend," Cole said to Seth after he served up a flaming dessert that was out of this world. Sofia, who was planted on his lap, yawned. "And I believe it's someone's bedtime." Sofia gave her mother a drowsy kiss, and Cole placed her on his shoulder. "Spare room okay, Mags?"

"Yes." She raced up the stairs after him, opening the bedroom door.

"I can't wait for Christmas." Lilah cleared the plates as I cleared the glasses. "It'll be our first one together. She's going to be one spoiled little girl."

"Wait 'til you see what I got her," Booker said, a gleam in his eye.

"It had better not be a gun, Crookshanks," Maggie said as she came down the steps.

"What about water pistols?" he asked, straight-faced.

"You're impossible." Maggie slumped into a chair.

"What? You can never have too many guns." He shrugged a shoulder. "In fact, I just bought myself a new one for Christmas."

"Did you get the Glock with the laser we were looking at last week?" Seth straightened, all but drooling now.

"Maybe. You'll have to wait and see what Santa brings next week," Book teased.

"You two are obsessed with guns." Maggie wiped the table as Seth finished wrapping up the leftovers. "Have you seen all the guns he has?" she asked me.

"No. Just the Glock he keeps in the calf holster." I pointed to his right leg.

"The Glock." Lilah's eyes fixed on me. "You know what a Glock looks like?"

"My dad used to take me and my brother and sister shooting all the time. I'm a good shot. I can outshoot my brother, but not my dad. He's the best." I bragged a little. "In fact, I've been eyeing a new gun myself. The Gen four. Small, but powerful." And easier to hide in my purse than the one I now carried.

"Are you talking about the Glock Nineteen Generation Four?" Booker asked, his face lighting up.

"You're an expert with a gun." Maggie's comment sounded more like a statement than a question. "Booker, did you hear that?"

"Yes, Magpie. I'm right here."

Maggie began rattling off a list. "Red hair. Tall. Can shoot."

"Anyone care for some strawberry-limeade?" Booker asked, pouring himself a glass and taking a sip. "It's very good."

"What's your blood type, Tess?" Lilah asked.

"My . . . um, AB negative. Why?"

Booker choked on his drink, Maggie and Lilah both laughed.

"Did I miss something?" Cole said, stumbling down a couple steps.

"Careful," Lilah said. "We just learned that Tess has AB negative blood."

"Hmm. Booker does, too." Cole pounded on Booker's back. "In fact, only one percent of the population has AB negative blood. Small world, right, Book?"

"Yup, and getting smaller every day."

I had a strange feeling I was missing out on an inside joke. Booker handed a plate of cookies to both Maggie and Lilah.

"Here. Eat," he said firmly, clearly trying to stop them from talking.

"No thanks," Maggie said through a yawn. "I'm stuffed."

"You okay, Magpie? You looked exhausted." Booker's eyes scanned her face.

"We've been working like crazy getting everything ready to open the restaurant," she said.

"I've begged her to take it easy, but you know how she is," Seth complained. "And with Christmas coming she's running around like a chicken without a head."

"Speaking of Christmas, Tess, would you like to come over for dinner on Christmas? Seth has some vegan recipes he wants to try out for the restaurant," Maggie asked.

"See?" Seth pointed to his wife. She waved him off.

"You're doing vegan on Christmas?" Both Cole and Booker whined.

"Just a couple side dishes," Seth assured them.

"I have to tell you, I've enjoyed being your guinea pig over the past several weeks." I stood. "I can't remember having eaten so well."

"You're the only vegetarian we know, and Seth is a stickler for details." Maggie yawned again.

"I certainly can't ask these two carnivores if a vegan dish tastes good," Seth nodded to Cole and Booker. "You gotta go to the source."

"True," I said. "I also need to get going. My boss is a real slave driver and I have some work I need to finish. Thank you, Seth, for the wonderful dinner. And, Lilah, thanks for the makeover."

"Anytime," Lilah said with a short wave.

I turned to thank Maggie, but she'd fallen asleep in the chair. Booker helped me get my coat on and walked me out to my car. I groaned when I saw an inch of snow on the ground.

"Get in and start the car. I'll scrape your windows," he said as I fished the keys out of my pocket.

"You always scrape my car." I handed him the scraper.

"I like the snow. You don't."

"Thank you."

When he finished, he opened the door and handed me the scraper back. "Tess, you do look beautiful. Is this color real, or another disguise?" He tugged playfully on a strand.

"Real."

"I like it, a lot. And your eyes, too. They remind me of the Caribbean Sea." He sighed dramatically. "I have a hard enough time concentrating on work with you in the next room. Now it's going to be near impossible."

I dipped my head. "Thank you," I said, embarrassed.

"Don't worry, Tess. I'm not going to break my promise."

"I know you won't." I looked at him and smiled. *But I wish you would.*

"But I may drool a little," he warned, adding his Cheshire Cat grin. "I never promised not to drool."

~*~

The next day Maggie stopped by to show us how to work the new sound system in the workout room. We made our way to the elevator as Booker argued with Nikkolynn over the phone. He demanded that her nasty emails to me end or he'd withdraw his recommendation letter. They were still arguing when we left. Maggie chuckled as the sound of clinking coins hit the bottom of the curse jar.

She looked even worse today. Her cheekbones were sunken in and her hair was pulled up in a ponytail.

"How are you feeling?" I asked.

She pressed the B button and the elevator rattled to life as we slowly descended to the basement. "I'm fine, don't worry. After Christmas, I'm going to sleep for two we . . . eks," she said through a yawn. "The restaurant opens in February, and Lilah said we're holding off on any more design jobs until I graduate, so all is good."

The elevator rumbled to a stop and the doors groaned open. "That doesn't sound good." She shook her head and led me to a box in the room next to the mirrors. "We can't open the gym up to the rest of the building for a few more weeks. To get anything done in New York requires a mountain of paperwork and a mile-long list of fees and permits."

The room looked incredible. Shiny new stationary bikes and ellipticals lined one wall. A metal stand off to the left held rows and rows of dumbbells. Four treadmills faced two flat screen TVs on the right, and juice and water stocked a refrigerator with a glass door. A metal rack lined with white towels and a large hamper sat next to it for soiled towels.

"This is perfect." I admired the foam floor and ballet barre yet again.

Booker came rushing in. "Am I too late?"

"Nope. I was just about to show Tess how to use the sound system."

"Good. I haven't heard it yet." He folded his arms. "You still look like he . . . heck, by the way. I thought you were going to sleep in today."

"Thank you, Mr. Bigglesworth," she growled.

"Okay, you made that name up," Booker insisted.

"Google it," Maggie snapped.

"No need to get snippy." Booker's eyes narrowed as they went from playful to concerned. "We can do this tomorrow, Magpie, if you'd rather."

"I said I'm fine." She turned back to the box and pulled on a knob. "You open this door and there's a—"

A putrid smell oozing from the box forced us back. Maggie and I slapped our hands over our mouth and nose while Booker reached inside and removed a green moldy ham sandwich. I cringed. Maggie ran to the bathroom in the back corner of the gym and threw up. I followed her, rubbing her back.

"Probably one of the workers left it by accident. I'll take this out to the dumpster," Booker said, hurrying out with the moldy sandwich.

I watched as Maggie slid down the wall and sat on the floor, knees bent, arms draped over them. She dropped her head onto her arms.

"How far along are you?" I asked. I handed her a cool damp towel to wipe her face.

"How did you know?" She pressed the towel to her neck.

"You're tired all the time, you've lost weight, you've been a little . . . uptight lately—"

"You mean grumpy," she admitted, dropping her head back down. "Please don't say anything to Booker yet."

"I won't."

"I don't know how to tell Lilah. She and Cole have been trying for four months now. We haven't been trying and, bam, I'm pregnant. This is going to devastate her." Tears welled in her sad blue eyes.

"She'll be happy for you," I assured her, wrapping my arms around her and patting her back again as she stood. "She may be a little sad that she's not pregnant, but she'll still be happy for you." Maggie nodded. "I'm happy for you."

"Thanks. We wanted to wait until I was done with school, but . . ." She rubbed her tummy, a tender smile on her face. The outer door opened and Mags placed a finger to her lips, reminding me not to say anything.

"That was disgusting." Booker washed his hands in the sink. "The entire room smells like rotten meat now. I'll get an air freshener and you can show us the sound system tomorrow." He studied Maggie's face as we got back on the elevator.

"I'll come by before lunch tomorrow," she said, getting off on the main floor.

"Go home and go to bed," Booker said as the door shut. He narrowed his eyes, clearly worried about Maggie.

Chapter 21
BOOKER

"Thanks, Book." Seth slapped an arm around my shoulder and gave me a side hug.

"Thanks for what?" I asked. "I just told you your wife looks like crap."

"And that you are concerned for her." He opened his refrigerator door and grabbed two cans of Diet Pepsi, tossing me one.

"Thanks, and if this explodes you're cleaning up the mess." I sat the can on the counter.

"Sometimes adding someone to the complex dynamics of a family can mess everything up. I'm grateful that you've accepted Maggie into the family." He opened his soda and took a swig, and then looked at the can and shook his head. "I'm a chef about to open my own restaurant and I drink this stuff. Do you have any idea what all these chemicals can do to you?"

"Are you trying to avoid talking about Magpie? Is there something wrong with her?" I pressed.

"Nope. In fact, she went to the doctor yesterday morning for a checkup. They gave her some vitamins, and told her to rest. She's enjoying a lazy Saturday afternoon nap as we speak."

I sank onto a barstool and risked opening my soda. A small squirt shot out of the can and landed on my new, blue t-shirt. Seth chuckled and handed me a damp sponge. "Good news about your wife. After Cole's cancer scare this summer, I've been worried."

"Yeah. Cole's illness had us all on edge. He had a follow up scan last week." Seth took another drink. "Lilah's been pretty stressed out waiting for the results. He thinks that's why she's not pregnant yet."

"Could be. Stress can kill ya." Of that I knew personally. As much as I missed police work—and man, did I miss it—I was enjoying my peace of mind so much more.

"What's going on with you and Tess?" Seth asked. He tucked his hands into his jean pockets and perched himself against the counter, a stupid grin on his face.

"Not much. She doesn't want a relationship right now, so I've been kicked to the curb." I still thought about her night and day. At the office I found myself looking for excuses to talk to her. *Idiot.* I laced my fingers behind my head and leaned back, doing my best to look as if I hadn't a care in the world.

"Nice try," Seth laughed. "I've seen the way you look at her. You got it bad."

I shifted forward, planting my hands on my knees. "Seth, I haven't felt this way about someone in a long time," I finally admitted aloud. "I think Tess feels the same, but she had a pretty abusive relationship before and she's scared." I took a swallow of the soda and set the can down with a clank.

"As in physical abuse?" Seth asked, his jaw tight. We'd both witnessed domestic abuse while we worked for the MET. It turned Seth's stomach as much as it did mine.

"Yes. And from what I've gathered, it was bad," I said, frowning. "So I wait, for who knows how long. I'm pathetic. Why do I always pick the wrong girl? What's my problem?"

"Sorry," Seth said. "I can fix you up with this new waitress I hired. She seems nice." He grinned hopefully.

"No thanks." Tired of my little self-inflicted pity party, I said, "Of course, if you told me the secret ingredient in your Beef Burgundy, it just may cheer me up." I'd been trying for years to get him to reveal it, but he wouldn't. I added a long face to my plea in hopes of invoking sympathy.

He snorted. "Not even, bro." He tossed a dishtowel at me. "So where's Tess now?"

"Probably doing her dancing in the new gym. Or maybe yoga. She's been down there every evening after work since it's been finished doing one or the other." I looked at my watch. She planned on stopping by there today around three. That was ten minutes ago. I stood and slid the chair under the table.

"Thanks for the soda." I tossed the empty can into the recycle bin. "I'll see you around five for our annual Christmas Eve dinner." I started for the door.

"Where are you going?" Seth asked, following me to the truck. The roads were pretty slick with a fresh coat of snow. The tires were much better on the truck then the POC. Frankly, everything was better on the truck. I needed a new car.

"I'm going to the gym to get a workout in before inhaling all the fattening food we'll be eating tonight." I zipped up my coat and pulled on my gloves as Seth laughed behind me.

"Good luck, Romeo."

"I hate that play. They were cowards who gave up," I said, jogging down the porch.

"I know. You tell me that all the time. I wouldn't let Cole and Lilah hear you, though. They'll get you coal for Christmas."

"True that." I waved. "See you later."

I drove home and changed into sweats and a gray sleeveless t-shirt. I brushed my teeth and put on some fresh deodorant. *Yup, I'm a glutton for punishment.* I planted my shameless butt in my truck and hurried as fast as I dared drive on the snow packed roads to the office.

I parked near the front of the building and, tucking my sneakers under my arm, jogged slowly across the parking lot. I took the stairs to the basement, stopping at the door to look inside. Tess stood stretching in the center mat wearing her "yoga pants"—as she informed me they were called on Friday before changing into them. Not going to lie, I did like her yoga pants. I could hear classical music playing over the sound system. It was the Jennifer Thomas music she loved listening to. Whenever we worked after hours, she'd turn the CD on low.

I sat on the steps and changed my sneakers, not wanting to get the floor all wet with my snow-covered boots. I set the wet boots aside and reached for the door, stopping when I looked through the window at Tess again.

She now danced around the mat, a graceful angel. The way she waved her arms and moved her body, I stood mesmerized at the elegance. Her body moved as if she were using it to tell a story. The look on her face—pure joy. I couldn't ever remember seeing her like that. No fear, no worries. Just sheer pleasure. Tess was born to dance.

Feeling like a stalker, I reluctantly pressed the door open. The look of peace evaporated from her face. She stepped over and turned off the music.

"Hello, Booker. I didn't expect to see you here today." She removed a white towel from the barre and looped it around her neck.

"Seth's making some amazingly fattening, a.k.a. delicious, food for our annual Christmas Eve dinner. I wanted to work out a little so my clothes would still fit on Monday." I looked around for the thermostat. The room was an oven. "I think the heater's malfunctioned."

"I did that, sorry." She jogged across the room and turned down the heat. "I wanted to do some Bikram yoga. It has to be hot, like a hundred-five. I was stretching a little while I waited for the room to heat up."

"Berkram Yoga?"

"Bikram," she corrected. "It's a pretty intense workout. You should try it."

"Yoga is good for girls; men need weights to challenge them." Yup, I actually said that aloud. *You're going to be alone forever, Gatto.*

"For girls?" she said, with an edge. An edge that I found quite sexy, to be honest. Wanting to see how far I could push her, I continued in my un-PCness. "Yes. You can't get muscle like this from touching your toes and breathing deep." I flexed my biceps.

She tugged the sleeve of her shirt up and flexed an impressive bicep of her own.

"From yoga?" I asked, impressed.

"Yup." She tugged the sleeve back down and grabbed the ends of the towel around her neck. "I'll bet I can outlast you in Bikram yoga poses by . . . let's make this challenging. Let's say four poses."

"A real live bet this time, not a promise?" She nodded firmly to my question. "And all I have to do is hold four poses longer than you. Seriously?" I snorted, and then added, "Deal." It took all I had not to kiss her and her cocky attitude. I'd never seen her like this before. Clearly this hot yoga thingy was her element, her domain. Well, that and dance. Watching her strut around the padded floor, I could see that this girly yoga gave her a sense of pride. It made me smile to know that her jerky ex hadn't stripped everything from her.

Tess turned on some yoga-y chanting music and faced me. "To show you my heart's in the right place, we'll do some easy moves first, to warm you up. Then I'll crush you."

I held my hand out to the mat. "Crush away." *Oh yeah, very sexy!*

"This first move is called the Utkatasana." She set her feet about six inches apart, then squatted somewhat. "It's similar to sitting in a chair," she pointed out.

"Easy." I followed her example.

"Your butt's sticking out," she said. "Straighten your back." She ran her hand up my spine. I about fell over as a chill followed her fingers. I straightened, and noted the pose wasn't as easy then. "Now lift your arms. Keep them straight and next to your ears."

That was a little more difficult, nevertheless, still easier than working out with weights. She stood across from me and copied the pose.

After several deep breaths she said, "Good. I'll turn the heat back up so we can get the full benefit of the yoga. We'll try another simple pose before moving on to the challenging ones."

She turned the heat up and tossed me a clean towel from the rack. "You're going to need it," she insisted.

Next she showed me the Pasa-Ha . . . something or other. It was a straightforward pose. Bend over, press your head to your knees . . . more or less.

"Easy stuff's over. Ready, Gatto?" Her eyes twinkled.

"If I fall asleep, don't be offended." I said it with a straight face, which earned me an eye roll from her beautiful Caribbean blue eyes.

"This is called the Danday—"

"Do any of these have English names?" I interrupted.

She laughed. "In English, this is called the Standing Separate Leg Stretching Pose."

Like a graceful butterfly, she set her feet at a wide stance, wrapped her hands around the outside of her feet, and put the top of her head on the mat. Knowing I wouldn't look half as graceful, I swallowed my pride, widened my stance and copied her pose, or tried to, anyway. My legs were nowhere near as stretched out as hers and I could only grab my ankles. I toppled to the side, unable to hold the pose.

"Strike one, Gatto." She straightened and bowed, a hint of a gloat firmly planted on her pretty face.

I tried one last time and fell on my butt. She slapped her hand over her mouth to keep from laughing.

She held out her hand and helped me up. Still a little dizzy from having my head down, I stumbled. She grabbed me around the waist.

"Are you okay?" Tess asked.

"I am now," I said with a grin.

She pushed me away playfully. "One down, two to go. This is called the Tad . . . ah, Tree Pose."

We went through several poses, and I did pretty well. A couple times I messed up on purpose so she'd have to correct me. A hand on my back, a gentle twist of my head. I loved every correction. I loved the closeness of her, the touch of her breath on my cheek.

As she stood behind me and shifted my arms to the correct position in the Half-Moon Pose, I knew I was a fool for accepting her challenge. Having her so close and not being able to kiss her, to wrap her up in my arms, messed with my head. I stumbled, and again she wrapped her arms around my waist.

"Maybe we should go over by the mirror so I can use the barre for balance." I didn't wait for an answer. I needed space between me and the intoxicating Tess. I marched over to the corner next to the mirror and the wall. That way if I fell, I'd have both the mirror and the wall to catch me.

"Ready to ratchet it up a little?" she said with a devilish smile that looked oh so good on her.

That wasn't ratcheted? *I'm a dead man.* Putting on my game face, I shot her my mischievous grin and said, "I wondered when this was going to get difficult." My comment would've been ten times more effective if a bead of sweat hadn't rolled down my forehead and nose at that exact moment. She pinched her lips together.

"That's from the heat." I chuckled, wiping my face dry with the towel around my neck.

"Of course it is." She shrugged casually, her face still perfectly dry. "This pose is pretty tough. Are you ready?"

"Bring it on."

"Bringing it." She squatted low, brought her left leg up on top of her right knee, and then lifted up onto her tiptoes. "It's called the Toe Stand Pose."

I started sweating before I began. I squatted, but for the life of me could not bring my foot up onto my knee. After four attempts I tumbled over onto my side. "My body is not meant to bend like that."

"Strike two." She laughed, extending me her hand. How was she not sweating? Ridiculous.

Exhausted now from not only the extreme heat, but also from the ludicrous poses, I staggered to my feet. I stepped too far forward and bumped into Tess as I stood. I grabbed her shoulders to keep her from falling. Her hands wrapped into my t-shirt for balance also.

We stood there, nose to nose, neither of us moving for several seconds.

"You are so beautiful," I said, breaking the silence.

Her head dipped, then she looked up at me through those incredible long thick lashes of hers and smiled. "Thank you," she said softly.

Kiss her! Now! I took a deep breath . . . and stepped back.

"What's next on your list of torture?" I asked, my voice shaky.

"You're not admitting defeat?" She playfully cocked her head sideways.

"I'm admitting this is a pretty tough workout, and I was wrong. But I'm not admitting defeat, so bring it on."

And she did. Two more poses, both tough, but doable. She then stepped back, stretched up tall, and proceeded to twist her body into the most convoluted position I'd ever seen.

"Now you're just making poses up." I folded my arms defiantly over my chest. She still hadn't broken a sweat.

"It's the Eagle Pose." She took a deep breath and settled into her stance. Her left leg draped over the right one, and wrapped around it at her calf. Her arms were completely wrapped around themselves, and her palms, twisted as they were, pressed together.

I slumped my shoulders. "How many more are there?" I asked, sure I didn't want to know. There was no way my body would twist like that.

Tess untangled herself. "There are twenty-six total, and we've done ten. Come on, you have to try."

Resigned, I began twisting my body in ways that had to be illegal. All the while, Tess circled around me, giving me pointers. "Hands need to be higher." I moved them up. "This leg needs to cross over higher on that thigh." I adjusted my leg.

But when she placed her hand on the small of my back and ran it up to my shoulders with the instruction to straighten my spine a little more, I lost my balance. I toppled over, taking Tess with me. We collided with a thump against the wall, Tess with her back to it. I tumbled into her, straight-arming the wall in time to keep from crushing her.

"Are you okay?" I asked.

"Yes," she chuckled. "And you?" I was about to pull back and give her some room when her hands slipped around my waist. My heart all but stopped.

"I'm good." I lowered my elbows to the wall, leaning closer to her. She pulled the towel from around my neck and wiped my face and neck dry.

"Thank you." I said, taking the towel from her hand and tossing it to the ground.

I brushed several small strands of hair from her face, allowing my hands to caress her cheek as I did.

"Tess, do you ever feel like we're trying to swim up a waterfall in our effort to keep from getting romantically involved?" I asked, wondering if she was as weak as I was at this moment.

"Yes," she whispered, her eyes on my mouth, which didn't help my resolve, at all. "Angel Falls."

"What?"

"Angel Falls, in Venezuela. It's the world's tallest waterfall," she explained, licking her bottom lip. *Just shoot me now.* "It's something like 3200 feet." She laughed softly. "I had to do a report on waterfalls back in college."

"Definitely Angel Falls then. All 3200 feet of it. And then some," I said, stroking her hair again. "I love the smell of your hair." I leaned in and inhaled her scent.

"Summer Rain." She dropped her head back against the wall, looking as angst ridden as I felt, with her eyes now shut tight as she breathed short breaths.

"Summer Rain?"

"Lilah bought me some shampoo. The scent is called Summer Rain." Her Caribbean eyes popped open, searching my face again.

"Yes. Summer rain is exactly what it is." I inhaled her yet again. I needed to leave. Never in my life could I remember wanting to kiss someone this desperately.

"Book, just how important is it that you keep your promise?" she asked, before inserting a knife in my gut with the words, "because I wouldn't mind if you broke it."

"You're not afraid anymore?"

"A little, but not enough to keep me from taking the risk."

Hope and fear twisted inside me as I buried my hands in her hair. I lowered my head—just as someone pounded on the door. Both Tess and I jumped.

I dragged myself back as Cole, with Sofia on his hip, came in.

"Hi," he said. He set Sofia down and she raced to the mirrors, making goofy faces at her reflection. "We just finished up some Christmas shopping and were on our way home when Sofia saw your truck. Lilah's been talking up a storm about the new gym so I thought we'd stop and check it out."

"Come on in and look around." I stepped back as he crossed over to the treadmills.

"Why is it so hot in here?" Cole asked, slipping off his coat.

"Tess does Bikham yoga," I explained, turning down the thermostat.

"Bikram yoga," she corrected.

"Is it called hot yoga, also?" he asked her. She nodded. "Lilah's been thinking about getting into that. I'll tell her to talk to you." He slapped a hand on my sweaty back. "Sick." He grimaced while drying his hand on his jeans. "Alright, Book, I only have a few minutes. You'll have to give me the five cent tour."

As I showed him the gym equipment, I watched Tess teach Sofia some simple dance steps.

"It looks great. The girls did an awesome job," Cole said as we walked over to Sofia and Tess a few minutes later.

"Watch, Daddy," Sofia said, jumping up and down. "I'm a ballerina. Tess showed me how." Sofia put her hands on her head and spun in a tight circle on her toes.

"Perfect." He clapped and gave her a hug. "You'll have to show mommy when we get home." He took her hand. "You're still coming to dinner, right? It's in forty-five minutes."

"Is it that late? Yes." I grabbed another towel and wiped down my face again. "I have to shower. I'd better get going, too."

"See you there." Cole started for the door and stopped. "Tess, you're welcome to come."

"I can't make it, but thank you for the offer." Tess slipped on her winter boots and coat next to the door. "I need to get going also." Cole held the door open for her. My heart tightened as she headed out.

"Thanks for the yoga lesson," I joked.

She smiled at Cole's wide-eyed expression and left. I followed Cole out after locking the building. Tess was long gone by the time we got outside.

~*~

"Delicious dinner," Cole said. "And I'm sure no one's surprised." Everyone nodded lazily as they stood and migrated to the family room. I couldn't say if the food was good or bad. I couldn't even remember what we ate. Tess owned all my thoughts as I replayed the afternoon.

Cole took his wife's hand and stood in front of the fireplace. "Lilah and I wanted everyone to know the brain scan showed no abnormalities, so I'm still cancer free. I won't need another scan for a year." Cole's announcement brought claps from Sofia, who probably had no clue as to what it all meant, and hugs, along with a few tears, from the girls. Seth and I offered high-fives.

"Since we're making announcements," Seth said next. Maggie came up to him and he slipped his arm around her shoulders. "As you have all noted, Maggie's not been feeling well lately. When she went to see Dr. Robertson a few days ago, she confirmed what we pretty much already knew. We're having a baby!"

Lilah flew at Maggie, hugging her tight. "How exciting! I wondered if you were when you kept getting sick," Lilah said, all smiles.

"I didn't know how to tell you," Maggie answered, blinking back tears. "I know you guys have been trying. Seth and I haven't, and then surprise, I'm pregnant. I'm sorry."

"Mags, I'm happy for you. It will happen for us. And even if it doesn't, I certainly don't expect you not to have children." Lilah pulled Maggie into her arms and they both cried.

Females. They confused me on every level.

I stepped over and hugged Seth. "Congrats, bro. You're going to name it after me if it's a boy, correct?"

Maggie pulled away from Lilah. "I am not naming my son Boo Boo Kitty."

I gave her a hug. "I'll chalk that rude comment off to your raging hormones, Magpie."

"Can I see your baby?" Sofia asked, tugging on Maggie's green and red shirt.

"Next summer you can. It's still inside me." Maggie rubbed her stomach.

"You ate your baby?" Poor little Sofia, her eyes wide in horror, stepped away.

"No!" Maggie laughed. "It's growing inside me. When it gets bigger, it will come out."

"How did it get in there?" Sofia's eyes narrowed on Maggie's stomach.

"Umm," stammered Lilah and Cole simultaneously.

"Sofia, I thought you were going to show me your new room after dinner." I held my hand out to her and wiggled my fingers. Her face lit up with a grin and she grabbed my hand, dragging me to the stairs.

"You owe me," I mouthed to her parents.

"This is my new veil," Sofia said, after we entered her room. She pointed to some mosquito netting stuff wrapped around a hoop over her bed. Flowers had been weaved into the netting, making it look all girly.

She pointed to an even girlier dresser. "And me and Mommy painted my dresser pink and put princess stickers on it."

"Awesome," I said. "You and your mom did a great job in here."

"Sit in my new chair." She pushed me to the corner of the room into an overstuffed pink chair. I sat; my manhood took a hit.

Sofia pulled out a book from a basket next to the chair and crawled up onto my lap. "Will you read this to me?" She handed me her favorite book, a tattered copy of *Rapunzel*.

"Don't you know this story by heart already?" I asked. She nodded her head against my shoulder and slipped her thumb in her mouth.

I chuckled, opened the book, and began. "Once upon a time . . ." She was asleep before they lived happily ever after. I laid her in her pink bed, covering her with a pink quilt, making a note to get her something *not* pink for her birthday. The place looked like a pink Smurf had exploded.

As I crept quietly to the door, a sleepy voice called out, "I love you, Uncle Book."

"I love you too, sweetheart." I smiled at her and her droopy eyes as they closed.

Cole was one lucky man. And now Seth was going to be a dad. I thought I'd be married with kids long before now. My love life was nothing more than a series of unfortunate events— unfortunate, lousy, pathetic events. Was I that much of a loser?

I closed the door behind me and headed down the stairs, my Scrooge attitude firmly in place. Cole and Lilah were all curled around each other on the couch, Lilah giggling as Cole whispered in her ear. I turned for the kitchen. It was worse. Seth had Maggie up against the fridge kissing her with his hand on her pregnant belly.

I walked out the back door and went straight to my truck, tired of being the fifth wheel all the time. Tired of having no one. Tired of eating dinner alone. Tired of watching TV alone. Tired of sleeping alone.

And most of all, I was tired of my stupid promise to Tess.

I shoved my truck into second gear and peeled out of the driveway, drowning in self-pity.

Chapter 22
Tess

I grabbed a sweatshirt and turned up the heat. It was freezing and the little trailer didn't stand a chance against the winter storm beating against it. I sank into the recliner. "Another Christmas eve alone." I shook my head. I should have gone with Booker, but I was already going over to Seth's tomorrow and didn't want to wear out my welcome.

I dropped my head back and laughed. "Who are you kidding, girl? You're afraid of being around Booker because you're crazy about him." If Cole hadn't shown up . . .

I was tired of being alone, and of my empty life with no one to love. And I was sick and tired of feeling sorry for myself. I chose to live the life of a nun. No one forced me.

"Hot chocolate." I jumped out of the chair and went straight to the kitchen to fill my teapot. I held my hands an inch from the pot and let the warmth radiate around them.

"Okay, Terese Layla Selleck. For Christmas you are giving yourself a backbone. You're going to tell Booker how you feel and that the promise is done . . . finished . . . kaput." I smiled to myself before adding, "Merry Christmas."

I so wanted him to kiss me at the gym today. My lips tingled as I remembered his kisses in the rec center parking lot and my apartment. That seemed like a million years ago. I took a deep breath and exhaled loudly. I felt like a fifteen-year-old schoolgirl with her first crush.

Only this wasn't a crush. I had strong feelings for Booker. Strong enough it both scared and thrilled me at the same time.

"I should have kissed him. I should have grabbed him by the sexy tee he had on and kissed him." I smacked my fist on the counter. "Urgh!"

A gentle knock at the door sent a chill down my spine. Who would be stopping by at ten-thirty at night? Carefully, I pulled back the edge of the curtain and saw Booker's truck parked out front. My heart leapt in my throat. It seemed Santa was delivering my backbone early.

"Okay." I exhaled slowly. "Do it. Just grab him and kiss him. Right on that sexy mouth."

"Tess, it's me, Booker," he said through the door. "I know it's late, but I need to talk to you. May I come in?"

I rubbed my hands together, every nerve ending in my body tingled as my heart beat against the wall of my chest. I opened the door. His hands rested on either side of the doorframe as if he needed support. He looked as frazzled as I felt. We stared at each other, neither one of us speaking. Heated glances bounced back and forth. I noticed he was breathing in short rapid breaths at the exact same time I noticed I was, too. Time to make my move. I straightened and said, "I quit," as he said, "You're fired."

We collided in the doorway and he captured my mouth in an intense, demanding kiss. My hands tangled in the front of his jacket and I pulled him closer. With a throaty sigh, Booker plunged his hands in my hair, cradling my face to his. He steered me inside and kicked the door closed, his mouth never leaving mine. The urgency of his kiss shook me to my core. Never, ever, had Garen kissed me with this much passion. They were short, dull, and unimaginative.

Not Booker's. The blood coursed rapidly though my body as if I'd run a marathon. I was no longer cold either. My toes curled in my slippers as he continued his masterful kiss, turning his head to deepen it. Just when I was sure my bones were going to melt, he groaned and dragged himself away from my mouth, resting his forehead on mine.

"That certainly was worth the wait," he said, his voice a little shaky.

"Yes," I whispered. "But let's not wait that long again."

"Agreed." And he kissed me again, my poor mind reeling by the time he stopped. His hands were now around my neck as his thumbs caressed my jaw.

"I'm afraid I'm falling for you, Tess." His brown eyes met mine. "You're probably not ready to hear—"

"I feel the same, actually." What would be the point in denying it? "But," I hastened to add, "I'm still scared. Not because I worry that you'll hit me, but with Garen my life was like a prison. I don't ever want to feel that way again. I don't see myself ever marrying again." He needed to know. I'd seen the way he admired his friend's relationships. That wouldn't be in my future.

"Would you be okay with me trying to change your mind?" He held a finger to my lips, stopping my answer. "Not by force, Tess. I promise."

I took a deep breath and said the words I'd never said aloud before. "I can't have children. Garen . . . he . . . I—I can no long have children." I didn't want the memory of that night to spoil the moment. "I don't want to talk about that right now."

He touched my cheek tenderly. "Agreed. Tonight it's just you and me." He kissed me once, twice, three times before pulling back, shoving his hands through his hair. "I think I'd better go."

I nodded and opened the door. "By the way, am I still your secretary?" I asked with a sheepish grin.

"No, Tess. I made a promise. And I always keep my promises." A Cheshire Cat grin cut across his face. "However, I could use a new office manager."

"What's the difference?"

"With my small practice, nothing. But as office manager you are entitled to a nice raise," he said, fishing the keys out of his jacket pocket.

"I don't want a raise. You already pay me well."

"Tess, rule number one in business: Never turn down a no-strings-attached raise." He stepped closer and kissed me again.

"Merry Christmas, by the way. I'll pick you up for Seth's around noon?"

"Merry Christmas," I said with a nod.

~*~

For the first time in a long time it didn't feel as if the weight of the world was on my shoulders when I woke the next morning, despite the fact that it took me forever to fall asleep. I showered and dressed in my green shirt with the pearl buttons. Booker'd made a comment more than once that he liked the shirt. I added a denim skirt and my mid-calf Fuggs, as Lilah called them. As I waited for Booker, I went through the stack of mail on my counter. Another note from Nikkolynn. She'd been mailing them to me at home since Booker had gotten after her about her noxious emails. They were always addressed to me using my full name and never a return address. The first one was just plain juvenile.

He's still mine. Don't forget that, slut. I will win him back.

Short, and to the point. She even signed it "Nikkolynn Gatto". She'd make a lousy serial killer.

The next one was more imaginative. She'd glued letters from magazines together inside a Christmas card:

Merry Christmas, whore.

That one irritated me, reminding me way too much of Garen. In my anger, I called her and told her if she sent another note like that, I'd show it to Booker. She denied knowing anything about the notes. When I reminded her that she'd signed some of them, she hung up, but that was okay. I felt proud that I'd taken that step.

I shoved the Christmas card aside, refusing to let it bother me. I debated showing it to Booker, then decided when he brought me home I would. Enough was enough, and he was the only one Nikkolynn would listen to.

I set the letters in a stack, tossed the junk mail, and went to brush my teeth. Booker came as I added a Christmas bell pin to my shirt.

"Hello," he said before taking me in his arms and kissing me. Oh, man, could this guy kiss. "Merry Christmas, again." He wore a brown sweater and jeans, and he looked so delicious.

"And to you." I pointed to the counter. "Will you grab my gift for Sofia, please?"

I gathered my coat from the small closet in the bedroom. When I came back out, Booker had the envelope from Nikkolynn in his hand. He held it out to me and I took it. "I knocked this on the floor by accident. No return address," he noted, averting my eyes.

I wrapped my arms around him and pulled him close. I knew by his tight jaw that the pain of what Nikkolynn had done to him was still fresh. Even though he'd moved on from her, the sense of betrayal he felt over her affair was very much a part of him still. I kissed him soundly. "Never in a million years will I cheat on you." I ran my hand through his dark brown hair.

"Am I that obvious?" he asked softly.

"My ex wasn't faithful either. It's not hard to guess what you're thinking. The letter's from Nikkolynn. She's been sending them here since you told her not to email me anymore." Anger light up his eyes. "Book, let's enjoy the day. I've been alone for four Christmas' now. I don't want this to spoil it."

"Alright. But I'm going to talk to her later."

I handed him the letter back. "For evidence. She denied sending them when I called her, even though she'd signed some, though not all. I tossed all but these ones."

His jaw ticked, but he said nothing more. He shoved it in his pocket, and helped me with my coat. Holding my hand, he led me outside, stopping for me to lock the door. "I can install a full blown, no holds barred security system in here if you'd like."

"Thanks. I'd like that." I climbed in the truck and Booker cranked up the heat, knowing without having to ask that I was already freezing.

As we walked up to the door at Seth's, he chuckled. "Let's not let on that we're a couple just yet. Maggie and Lilah have been going crazy trying to get us together."

"Playing a little cat and mouse game, are we?"

He smiled ear to ear. My joke was not lost on him. The door opened and Lilah greeted us with a couple glasses of eggnog.

"Mischievous, thy name is Booker," I whispered as Booker took the glass and we stepped inside.

"Please don't go quoting Shakespeare, too. I get enough of that from those two." He pointed to Lilah and Cole.

"You like Shakespeare, too?" Cole said, giving me a hug before taking my coat.

"No. I mean, Romeo and Juliet are horrible examples if you think about it. Killing yourself because you can't have the one you love." I scrunched my face at the stupidity of it.

"Booker feels the same way, don't you?" Maggie greeted us both with a hug and led us into the kitchen.

Booker walked behind her, patting her on the head. "Now, now, Prego."

And the games began. Lighthearted teasing, and several not so subtle hints that Booker and I should hook up.

"Where's Sofia?" Booker asked, deflecting yet another veiled suggestion that we go out on a date.

"Napping in my room," Cole said automatically. "Well, I guess it's not my room anymore." He bent down and kissed his wife's neck.

"Enough of that," Booker said. "There are young impressionables in the room." He pointed to Maggie.

"This young impressionable is two months pregnant. I think it's okay," Maggie said, still looking a little under the weather with her drawn cheeks and eyes.

"Cole used to live here?" I asked.

"Yes, just for a little while," Cole said, taking a piece of ribbon candy from a bowl on the counter.

"Seth and I wanted to wait until we were married," Maggie explained. She glanced quickly at Booker then back to me. "We had Cole come and stay with us until we got married, sort of like insurance."

"That's nice," I said. "I admire you. I'm sure it wasn't easy."

"Nope," Seth laughed. "But we survived."

"Cole and I waited," Lilah piped in.

"Pshhh. Two and a half months," Booker scoffed. "Who couldn't wait two and a half months?"

"He has a point," Cole said.

"Yeah, on his head," Lilah replied. "I'll bet you can't wait. I'll bet when the right girl comes along, you won't make it two days."

"I didn't sleep with Nikkolynn before I married her," Booker said defensively.

"Bro, you met and married her in just over two weeks." Seth shook his head. "I'm with Lilah on this, except I have more confidence in you than Lilah. I know you can handle two days. But I'll bet you can't wait until you're married."

"I'm in, too. How much are we betting?" Cole asked.

"We'll need to make it a large amount or Booker won't do it." Cole grabbed a paper and pen from the desk in the kitchen.

Booker stood there shaking his head. "Now wait just a minute—"

"I'll bet fifteen hundred dollars," Cole said.

"I'll match it," Lilah piped in.

"That sounds good to me." Seth wrote down their names and the amounts, all while Booker stood to the side, chuckling to himself. "Mags and I will bet five thousand."

"Speak for yourself," Maggie said.

"You want to bet higher?" Seth asked.

"No. I'm taking Booker's side. I think he can do it." She smiled at Booker and he grinned proudly.

"Thank you, Magpie. I'm glad someone has a little faith in me." The smile then fell from his face. "Yours is a pity bet, isn't it?"

Maggie shrugged. "Maybe." Guilt hung in her eyes.

"May I join in?" I asked. I'd been on the receiving end of Booker's kisses. There was no way he would win this bet, and I could use the money. "I can only afford two hundred fifty."

"Okay, stop." Booker stepped over next to Seth and looked down at the list. "I never agreed to this. I never even hinted that I'd agree to this."

"Chicken?" Lilah asked.

"No!"

"Oh, then you're saying you don't have enough self-control?" Lilah took the sheet of paper and wadded it up. "That's what I thought."

"Hold on. I am not lacking in self-control. In fact, that's one of my best qualities," Book insisted.

Lilah straightened out the paper. "So the bet's on, then?"

"I'm being railroaded," Booker said.

"Yes or no," Seth said. "Are you man enough?" Booker rolled his eyes.

"It's okay, Book," Maggie said. "We understand if you don't feel up to the challenge. Your little brother can kick your butt when it comes to self-control. We get it. Not everyone can have his incredible stamina." Seth beamed proudly at his wife's words. She kissed his cheek and said, "Come on, everyone, it's Christmas. Let's open some gifts." We all turned for the family room and the large Christmas tree in the corner as Booker grumbled under his breath, his lips curled.

"Ugh! Fine. Deal," Booker growled. Everyone, myself included, turned to Booker, our eyes wide. "I'm more than capable of controlling myself, thank you." He folded his arms triumphantly over his chest.

"Book, you're letting your pride get in the way again," Seth counseled. "You need to stop and think this through. You know how you get. You're like a dog with a bone when it comes to making bets. You hate losing. In fact, you've never lost."

"Yeah, I was mostly teasing anyway, Book," Lilah said, patting his arm.

"The deal is on," Booker said firmly. "Unless you're all afraid of losing your money, then by all means, chicken out. I'll give you all one last chance to not be part of the deal."

You could have heard crickets chirp. No one changed their mind. Lilah broke the silence first. "I'm not interested in backing out, but can I up my bet?" That earned a few smirks, myself included.

Booker ignored us. "To prove to you all," he said glaring directly at me, "I'll double the bet."

"So if we win, we now get double that?" Lilah pressed.

"Exactly," Booker affirmed.

Maybe I should bet more.

"This is all premature," Seth said. "Booker hasn't dated anyone seriously since Nikkolynn. At the rate he's going, we'll all be dead before he gets even gets a girlfriend, let alone marries her."

"Dang, I hadn't thought about that," Cole said, frowning. "Too bad, I wanted to upgrade my motorcycle."

I chuckled to myself. Cole and Harley's were two things I'd never put together, and yet he owned one and rode daily until the weather got bad.

Seth tucked the paper in the drawer. "You got my hopes up, bro." Seth's mouth turned down, clearly disappointed.

Booker rolled his eyes. "You all are pathetic actors. Each and every one of you. Oh, and p.s., Tess and I are dating. Game on." He looked at me and shrugged.

Lilah and Maggie grinned from ear to ear. "I knew it. I could tell when you walked in," Maggie swore.

"You could not." As he and Mags debated whether or not she could tell, I helped Seth set the table for dinner.

"He's a great guy, Tess," Seth said. "We tease a lot, but I don't know a better person. Mags told me you had a rough marriage and I want you to know, Booker would never hurt you like that."

"I know. I trust him." And I did.

~*~

Seth's restaurant was going to be a hit if Christmas dinner was any indication. The tofu salad was out of this world, and I hated tofu usually. Sofia was the big winner of the day, scoring so many gifts she was a grumpy mess by the time evening came due to overstimulation.

"Merry Christmas," Cole yelled above Sofia's screams as they left.

Seth turned, leaning against the closed door and said, "Just think, Mags. That could be us next Christmas."

"I can hardly wait," she smiled.

"We'd better get going, too." Booker helped me with my coat. "We have work tomorrow and this one's boss," he squeezed my shoulders, "is a Scrooge if we're late. . ." His eyes widened in mock fear.

We said our goodbyes and exchanged Merry Christmas' again and left. "I thought the office was closed tomorrow," I said as we drove away.

"It is. I'm hoping you want to spend some alone time with me." He took my hand. "I have something for you at my house. Do you mind if we swing by?"

"Sure. With the bet in place, I have no need to worry about any ulterior motives."

"Don't remind me." He muttered something under his breath again, but the music on the radio drowned him out as we drove to his house.

"Here." Booker handed me a small gift wrapped in red and gold paper after letting Daisy May outside.

"Thank you, but you already gave me a bonus." I took the gift and tugged on the gold ribbon, looking at him as I did.

"That was from your boss," he explained as I peeled the paper back. "This is from the devilishly handsome guy in your life."

"You forgot modest." I chuckled.

"And humble."

I open the box. Inside was a picture of a gun. I looked at him, confused.

"It's the Glock nineteen you said you wanted," he explained.

"The Gen four?" I smiled wide.

"I love it when you talk guns," he growled into my neck before running a trail of kisses across to my lips. "Monday we'll go pick out the exact one you want and fill out the mountain of paperwork now required to get a gun, and start the process going. If you want, you can get a concealed weapons permit."

"Thank you," I said, hugging him, and wondering how I was going to fill out the paperwork with my fake ID. I'd have to tell him the truth.

"I hope you'll feel a little safer with one of these in your purse," he said, pointing to the picture. "When the weather warms we'll go do some target practice. Heaven knows we won't have anything else to do."

~*~

"We can head over to the gun shop tomorrow. Sound good?" Booker kissed me before I could answer. "You're intoxicating," he said heavily, opening the door to the trailer and stepping onto the front steps. "I'll see you tomorrow."

We came back to my place after I opened my gift and spent the night talking. It was now two-thirty in the morning. I enjoyed every minute of it. I turned and went inside, watching him drive away before shutting the door completely. I missed him already.

Before going to bed, I decided to send Booker a quick email.

"Thanks for making my Christmas wonderful. I miss you."

I hit send, but didn't close the laptop, in case he answered. I brushed my teeth and washed my face, then checked my email. No messages. He probably hadn't checked his email.

"Unlike you, Tess, he's gone to bed." Exhausted, I turned my Lindsey Stirling CD on and fell asleep quickly to the vibrant melodies of the violin, happier than I'd been in a very long time.

I awoke to hands wrapped tightly around my neck.

Chapter 23

Four years ago

"Mom." I threw my arms around her neck and held her tight while my sister grabbed my one and only suitcase from her car. Tears streamed down my mom's face as we stood outside the red brick rambler I grew up in.

It hadn't changed. Even the Hawthorne tree looked frozen in time with its bright pink flowers and rough bark. I tipped my head back and let the sun bathe my face as I wiped my tears away.

My mom cupped my still bruised face in her hands. "Sweetie, I'm so sorry. I wish you would've told us."

I looped my arms in hers and my sister's as I nudged them toward the house. "I should have. I know that now. I just didn't want to admit I'd failed. Plus, with Daddy being sick and all . . ."

"Failed? I hardly call this failing, Tess." The look of indignation on my mother's face gave me comfort. Dark circles hung beneath her eyes, and her hair had grayed significantly since I'd last seen her, probably because of my father's cancer.

I opened the screen door and stepped into the living room. It hadn't changed either. Same green couch. I ran my hands over a misshapen cushion and smiled. Same huge TV sitting on a rickety stand. We kids tried relentlessly to convince Dad he needed to upgrade to a modern, sleek flat screen right after I got married. Dad, ever the saver, simply refused. "Not until this one stops working," he'd say, patting the monster TV proudly.

A shadow caught my eye and I spun around quickly, fearing Garen had followed me. The sudden action pulled at my still tender incision and I winced. I smiled when I realized it was my dad.

"Sugar Cube." He ambled toward me. It'd been a lifetime since I'd heard him call me Sugar Cube. He pulled me into a hug. He looked good, better than I'd imagined. Thinner and with less hair, but his skin had a healthy glow. "I wish you'd shared with us what was going on. You deserve so much better." He pressed a kiss to my temple.

"I should've listened to you, Dad. You were right about Garen." I pulled back and dried my face with my hands again.

"None of us knew he was a monster, Tess." As he carefully turned my face side to side, his bright blue eyes darkened. "I know the good book says we are supposed to forgive, but I'm struggling with that right now."

"Me, too. The past eighteen months have been a nightmare." I sank back into his arms. "I'm so happy to see everyone. I don't want to talk about him right now."

"Go ahead and put your suitcase in your old room." Mom kissed my cheek again. "Freshen up. I'm making grilled salmon for lunch."

Abby grabbed my hand and dragged me down the hall to the old bedroom we'd shared. Unlike the rest of the house, this room looked completely different. A queen bed and a faded, floral print quilt replaced our twin beds and silky pink bedspreads. The room no longer screamed a couple of teenage girls live here, that's for sure.

Abby laughed and plopped down onto the bed, crumpling the bedspread. "Grandma's old quilt, remember?" I smiled at the faded old thing as she picked up a corner and showed me where my grandmother had hand stitched her name and the date.

"When did all this happen?" I gestured to the room as I sat next to her.

"After I got married." I missed her wedding. Garen insisted we couldn't afford to go. She leaned over the side, grabbing something from under the bed. "But I saved these."

She handed me a CD and my old ballet shoes from when I danced in the Nutcracker as a child. "My Taylor Swift CD." I remembered Abby had given it to me for Christmas right after I got married, but Garen didn't care for country music. Being newly married, I didn't want to rock the boat so I asked Abby to keep it for me until I could soften Garen up a little. That worked out well.

I flipped the CD over and smiled. Taylor stood there, her curly blonde hair flying everywhere. The word "Fearless" was printed across the bottom. It was exactly how I felt at the time.

How things had changed.

Abby went over to the white dresser and took a pushpin from a small glass bowl and pressed it into the wall. She tied the ribbon from my ballet slippers together and hung them over the pin.

"Thanks, Abby," I said, setting the CD on the dresser. We lay back on the bed and stared up at the ceiling, neither of us speaking for a bit.

"Life sure didn't turn out how I'd imagined it." I twisted carefully onto my side. "Are you and Calvin happy?"

"Yes," she said softly. "He's a wonderful guy, Tess. He treats me like a queen. He . . . ah . . . he has a brother that's single. After your divorce is final we thought it would be fun to fix you two up."

"No. I'm done. I'll never marry again. I doubt I'll date again either." I cringed at the thought. "Lesson learned."

She sat up and crossed her legs. "You can't judge all men by Garen. Calvin's never hit me. He's never even come close. He wouldn't."

"I know they're not all evil like Garen, but I'm not so lucky when it comes to men. Remember Tim Soren in tenth grade? He was a loser, too." Tim never hit me, but he did struggle with telling the truth and stealing. "Last I heard he was serving time for car theft."

"Tess, you dated the guy for two months," she pointed out.

I shrugged. "No more men."

"After the divorce is final, and you've had some time to heal, you'll feel differently," she said with confidence. Not wanting to burst her bubble, I let the subject drop.

"Dad talked to Martha's dad, Mr. Velazquez. He's agreed to help with the divorce. From what Mom was saying, he's pretty sharp."

The Velazquez family had hosted my wedding in their backyard. We'd come full circle now. They were there to help me celebrate my wedding, and they'd be there to help me end the nightmare.

"Garen's going to cause problems. It's going to get ugly, and expensive. He considers me his property. No way is he going to let go easily . . . if ever."

"Dad said Michael Velazquez would work his fee into the settlement. It won't cost you a thing, considering the circumstances," she added softly.

"Good luck with that. Garen's pretty tight with his money. We always seemed to have money when he needed something, but never when *I* did."

"Tess, how did it happen? You used to be confident and sure of yourself. Why didn't you leave when he started hitting you?" Abby asked softly.

"I don't know," I admitted. "At first it seemed insignificant. A slap here, a shove there. I brushed it off, thinking it wasn't a big deal." She started to say something and I stopped her. "I know. Major mistake. Hitting and shoving are never okay." She settled back down.

"He picked away at my self worth, little by little, every day. I doubted myself and my abilities. I kept trying to please him, to make him happy. I thought if I could get him to see I wasn't a total mess up, or a waste like he told me I was too many times to count, he'd love me as much as I loved him." Rubbing my temples to relieve the pounding in my head did little to subdue the pain I now felt from rehashing my failure. "I lost myself." I tucked my hair behind my ears. "Finally, I realized I had to get out or he'd eventually kill me. I was trying to get a job so I could save enough money to come home when . . ."

"Don't worry. The worst is over." She wrapped my arm in hers and squeezed.

I lay back down on the bed as my stomach knotted. My family had no idea what we were up against.

As I predicted, the divorce proceedings were ugly. I tried shielding my parents from Garen's lies, worried about my dad's health, but they overheard enough to figure it out. Garen not only gave his lawyer a copy of the video he'd made of me drugged up, but he had pictures of me that fed his paranoia. The situations were innocent enough, helping a random stranger pick up some spilled groceries, or a lunch with friends. But somehow everything looked salacious simply by the angles of the shot or they'd been cropped to create an intimacy that just wasn't there. The photo of me having a soda after the dance tryouts was the worst. Whomever Garen hired to follow me positioned the shot so it looked as if I were whispering into one of the male dancer's ears, which was not the case at all.

"You have no case, Velazquez. This is one of many men she was having an affair with," he bellowed during a meeting with my lawyer. He slapped the picture down on Michael's large oak desk, and I jerked back. Garen demanded the meeting to try and work out our problems without lawyers. He claimed that he wanted to reconcile. I refused to meet without Michael present, which angered him, but he agreed anyway.

I picked up the photo and pointed out that I was talking to someone next to the dancer, and that the dancer he said I was having an affair with was, in fact, gay. Garen produced several more pictures, most were clearly manipulated, but a couple were damning.

When Michael stepped out into the hall to take a phone call, leaving the double doors wide open, Garen came next to me. I stood my ground, fighting with all I had not to flinch. "You're my wife, whore. I'll destroy you before I let you go. Capiche?"

"Move away from my client now or I will have you arrested." Michael had placed a restraining order against Garen, angering my soon to be ex to no end.

Garen spun around, shooting daggers at Michael with his eyes. "I will destroy you and your client. You've been warned." Garen scurried out of the room like the rat he was, slamming the door behind him.

I dropped my face into my hands, flooded with feelings of hopelessness. "This is never going to end."

"Tess," Michael said, passing me a tissue, "it will, we just need to get something on him. He has a lot of damaging photos and videos—"

"All false." I shot to my feet and crossed the room, staring out the window at the ocean.

"Be that as it may, they do make you look bad." He picked up a yellow notepad and sat in his leather chair. "We need something on him. Something big."

"How about the fact that he tried to kill me?" I spit out.

"Unfortunately, that's your word against his. He's still claiming your house was broken into." He rubbed his forehead in frustration.

Garen went all out to make it look like we had a break-in. The front door to our little house had been kicked open, shattering the doorframe. Our living room furniture was in complete disarray, with the couch flipped onto its back and the chair onto its side. He'd emptied the contents of the dresser drawers onto the floor, and pushed the mattress off the box springs. Garen even went so far as to file a police report.

"Okay, he works for Senator Graft, who has a pretty shoddy reputation himself. Did Garen ever talk about questionable tactics he participated in? Maybe election fraud or illegal use of power?"

I spun to face Michael. "Several times. One evening after dinner, they talked about illegal voter registration, and about hacking into emails. Oh, and they said they were going to pay off some judge."

A smile grew on Michael's face. "This could work. I know a top-notch private detective that specializes in political investigations. Let me give him a call and see what we can come up with."

It didn't take long. Two days later Michael came by the house with not only photos of Garen and Senator Graft with a notorious crime boss, but phone records as well.

"These records are not admissible in court," he waved the paper at me, "but now that we know what Garen's been up to, we can request a search warrant and obtain them legally," he chuckled. "My guess is that Graft will cover his sorry butt and put pressure on Garen into signing the divorce papers, mostly to cover his own skin. Graft's not going to want this to get out, not with his dream of becoming Governor."

That was all we needed. Garen crumbled, just as Michael predicted, though he didn't go quietly. He called me the night before I signed the papers and laid into me, swearing he'd get even for my threat to expose him and his criminal acts. My dad grabbed the phone, reminding Garen we had a restraining order against him and he'd better not call me again.

"Here and here, also." Michael pointed to the last two places I needed to sign the divorce document.

"I don't trust Garen. He's going to come after me. He hates losing. He's a major control freak, if you haven't already guessed." I set the pen down and slid the documents across the desk to Michael.

"I thought the exact same thing, so I hedged our position. I contacted Senator Graft directly and told him if Garen comes within five miles of you or your family, or if any of the photos or the video mysteriously gets out, my information would be turned over to the attorney general's office in Texas, ASAP." Michael beamed proudly.

I sat back in my chair, relaxing a little for the first time since leaving the hospital. "So this is it. My maiden name's been restored, and no more Garen Johnson to worry about?" Michael nodded. I wanted to dance around, shout for joy, but part of me still didn't believe it was over. I knew Garen too well. He didn't lose, ever.

It'd been seven weeks since the divorce became final. Six months since I left the hospital broken and crestfallen. Garen was back in Texas working for Graft again, who'd announced his bid for the office of governor. I never heard from Garen. Not a text, not a phone call. Nothing. Life was slowly getting better. My sister was pregnant, and my dad's cancer treatments had finished. My mother celebrated his success, while dad celebrated that his hair no longer fell out.

I applied for and got a job teaching ballet to five year olds at a local dance studio, and loved every second of it.

"Mom, I'm going to get started on the garden," I called out, grabbing some work gloves and a floppy straw hat.

"Okay. I have to pay some bills, but I'll be out soon," she said from the office.

The sun shone bright. I turned my face upward and soaked in the warmth. Exhilarating. I worked the soil along the edge of the garden spot. Dad loved to garden. I decided to plant one for him this year since he didn't quite have the energy to do it himself. I loved watching his face as the vegetables began sprouting. He got such a kick out of it.

I turned over the soil and smoothed out the clumps. After an hour, my stiff back and tight shoulders demanded a break. I speared the shovel into the soil and twisted at the waist to loosen my back.

"Hello, whore."

My knees gave out at the sound of Garen's voice. My heart beat so hard it reverberated in my ears. His shoes crunched on some loose gravel scattered across the driveway. I turned to face him.

"Stop," I croaked while trying to regain my composure. Garen chuckled the sick depraved laugh I'd grown to hate. "The restraining order is still in effect."

He shrugged. "Not a problem. I have women who will vow I was with them when you died. In fact, Senator Graft will vouch for me."

He lifted his hands up. Only then did I notice the rope wrapped around them. I couldn't scream. I couldn't run. I stood frozen, staring at his hands twisting the rope. "Guess you should have brought your gun out here with you, whore. Then you just may have surv—"

"Get off my property before I call the police." My mother stood firm behind Garen, her feet planted shoulder width apart, and dad's favorite Glock in her hand. Only it was no good. Garen knew my mom hated guns and had never shot one. I doubted the gun was loaded.

Garen turned to her and grinned warmly, as if greeting an old friend. "Hello, Jenny."

"It's Mrs. Selleck to you. Now leave before I make a mess of your freshly pressed shirt."

"Tsk, tsk." He stepped closer to her. She lifted the gun higher, pointing it at his chest.

Garen raised his hands, letting the rope dangle from one. "Mrs. Selleck, I thought you and I were on the same side of gun control."

"I'm on the side of protecting my family from scum like you. Now leave." My mom's voice oozed anger. Garen had a good six inches on her, and yet she didn't flinch.

"Sorry. I have something to take care of first." He pointed to me. "She's mine. She left me, *and* threatened me. She needs to be taught a lesson."

Garen looked back at me; my mom never saw him coming. Like the wind, he twisted around and ripped the gun away from her, punching her in the face, and knocking her into the side of the house. She slid to the ground. He raised his fist to hit her again, only I was faster.

I grabbed the shovel from the garden and ran at him, bringing it down onto his head with all I had. He fell to the ground, hitting the concrete with a thud. Blood poured from the back of his head. He didn't move. I ran to my mom and helped her up.

"Are you okay?" I looked at her jaw with its angry red streak, courtesy of my crazy ex-husband.

"I'm fine. Grab the gun." She pointed to the gun that was now just out of Garen's reach. I scooped it up, surprised to find it loaded.

The back door opened and my father came out holding his favorite rifle. "I thought I heard that scumbag's voice. Is he dead?"

My body shook violently as the adrenalin wore off. "Dead?" I turned to Garen's body. A small puddle of blood now lay next to him. "There's so much blood." I'd never been bothered by blood before, but that . . . that was so much, too much blood. I fell to my knees and vomited on the driveway.

My dad went over to Garen's body and felt for a pulse. "He's alive." Disappointment hung in his voice. He pulled out his cell phone. As he spoke to someone on the other end, my mom wrapped her arms around my shoulders.

"Come inside, Tess." She stroked my hair.

"This is never going to end. He's not going to stop until I'm dead." My brother's car came tearing into the driveway a few minutes later.

"Why is Craig here?" I asked. My brother jumped out of his car and ran over to Garen and felt for a pulse.

"Tess, your father and I worried that Garen would come back so we created an emergency plan in case he did," Mom explained. "We need to hide you, or you're right, he'll kill you." She swatted away a tear.

"Is the bag in the house?" Craig asked Dad.

"Yes, under our bed," Dad answered.

"What is going on?" I asked, still sick to my stomach.

"Craig's going to take you to the women's shelter in town. There's ten thousand dollars in the suitcase, along with some clothes. There's also a number you can call . . ." Tears rolled down Dad's cheeks. "This guy, he can get you some . . . new ID. A driver's license, a Social Security card." He broke down in my arms. "Be safe, Sugar Cube."

No. I didn't want to go. I was back with my family. I looked at my mother's jaw. The red streak had started to turn black.

I had to leave.

"I love you, Daddy," I said as our tears mixed. He led me to the car as my mother threw her arms around me one more time.

"I love you." Her words were muffled against my neck. I tightened my arms around her.

"The shelter will help you to relocate, Tess." Dad opened the car door. "Pick somewhere Garen will never guess. And whatever you do, do not tell us or anyone where you are going."

All this was so unfair, yet I had no choice. Garen would never stop, not until I was dead. Never. Knowing that didn't make it easier. Both my parents drew me into another embrace.

"Please be careful," Mom said, letting go. "Please."

"I love you, Mom." I hugged them both, squeezing with all I had.

I glared back at the motionless Garen on the driveway as Craig put my suitcase in the backseat and got in the car. "Wait. What about him?"

"I got it all covered." Dad patted my shoulder. "Garen attacked your mother when he came here looking for you. I grabbed the first thing I could find to protect her, the shovel, and hit him over the head with it." My father seemed proud of his story. He wiped the shovel clean of my fingerprints with his shirttails as he spoke. The man who prided himself on honesty was about to perjure himself.

"What if he dies? That's murder," I said. No way would I allow my sick father to go to jail for me.

"He's not going to die," my brother said, grabbing my hand and pulling me into the car. "We have to go. The ambulance is on its way." A siren cut through the air as he spoke.

"Daddy, I can't—"

"Tess." He took my hand through the window. "I'm not going to force this on you. Maybe I'm wrong." He looked at the unconscious Garen, then back at me. Doubt weighed heavy in his eyes. "You know Garen better than all of us. Do you believe he's going to stop coming after you?"

Tears tumbled down my cheeks. "No. You're right. I have to leave." Mostly because I feared what Garen would do to my family in an effort to hurt me. I couldn't let that happen. I had to protect them. I had to hide.

He kissed my hand. "If that pig kills you, it will destroy me." I saw something in my father's eyes I'd never seen before. *Hate.*

"I love you." I squeezed Dad's hand and let go. "And you too, Mom." As my brother backed down the driveway, my mom cried in my dad's arms. My own tears clouded my vision as we drove away.

Chapter 24

Present day

The hands tightened around my throat. "Hello, Terese." My stomached lurched at the sound of Garen's voice. I gasped for air, scratching at his hands as my feet kicked frantically. He pulled one hand off my neck and backhanded me across the cheek. My vision flashed white as he dragged me from the bed and shoved me to the floor. I scurried backward to the wall, having nowhere else to go. A single beam of light shone from the living room through the bedroom door and fell on the face of the man I feared most.

Instead of his pristine shirts and sharply creased pants, Garen wore dirty sweatpants and a ripped t-shirt. His hair stuck up everywhere, as if he'd run his hands through it several times. His appalling body odor reminded me of a sweaty gym shoe.

He came at me again. I jetted my legs out and kicked at him, catching him behind the knee. His leg buckled and he dropped down. He roared out in pain, twisting around to face me. My stomach dropped when I saw the rage that held his eyes to mine.

He forced me flat to the ground as I fought him, and straddled my hips. He delivered several well-placed punches to my ribs, forcing the air from my lungs. I struggled to draw breath as he punched my head repeatedly. I stopped fighting. Why did I think I stood a chance against him? He outweighed me by close to eighty pounds. *How stupid.*

He climbed off as sweat striped down his face. "You should know better, whore." His spit splattered my face as I lay back, defeated. He stalked over toward the bed and grabbed a butcher knife from the top of the nightstand he must have placed there, and stabbed viciously at the mattress and sheets. I huddled tightly against the wall, in pain and speechless as wave after wave of nausea crashed over me. I couldn't scream, I couldn't move. *This can't be real. It has to be a dream. Please be a dream.*

As he continued viciously hacking my bed, a deep gut-wrenching chill wrapped around me. Horrifying images of Garen doing the same thing to me filled my head. I cringed each time the knife plunged into the mattress.

My heart broke as I thought about Booker and all he'd been through, all he'd lost. Now he'd have to bury me, too, because no way would Garen allow me to leave alive. I only prayed Booker wasn't the one to find me. I didn't want to add my butchered body to his bitter memories.

Garen turned and hurled the knife at me. It embedded into the wall mere inches from my head, and wobbled back and forth. I wished it had pieced my heart and hastened my inevitable doom. What a fool I'd been. Why did I ever believe I could escape him? What a stupid, stupid fool! I'd never be free of the monster. Ever. I sank lower as all hope seeped from my heart.

"Where's your gun? And don't lie, I know you have one," Garen demanded, wiping sweat from his forehead onto the shoulder of his t-shirt.

I said nothing, I couldn't. The knife, so close, beckoned to me, and yet it might as well have been miles away. Terror kept my arms useless. Instead, I pinched my eyes shut and prayed I'd wake from the nightmare.

"Tell! Me!" he screamed. I cringed, hearing him stomp my way and waited for the punch. I received a kick to my thigh instead. One turned into four, and still I couldn't speak. I just shook my head, repeating *wake up, Tess, wake up, Tess,* over and over again. Garen kicked me one more time before storming back across the small space. He flipped over the mattress, and then the entire bed in his frenzied searched for the gun. Next he kicked over the nightstand. The knob-less drawer slid open and the gun tumbled out. He snatched it, and in his rage, kicked viciously at one of the stand's legs, snapping it off. He spun around, his eyes wild, wielding the gun at me. I flinched, still too terrified to scream.

"Next time I ask you a question, you'd better answer me, whore." His voice was low and threatening as he tucked the gun into the waistband of his pants.

He jerked the knife from the wall. "Gonna need this." He smiled gleefully before gripping my upper arm and dragging my trembling body into the living room. He shoved me next to the front door where he'd wedged a kitchen chair under the doorknob. "That chair isn't going anywhere so don't even think about running." He kicked it to prove his point. The thing didn't move.

Garen took the knife and proceeded to slice away at the couch like he had the bed. With each plunge of the knife he cursed me for ruining his life.

"I lost everything because of you," he said, slashing along the back of the couch. Stuffing tumbled out onto the floor. He bellowed random words. "Selfish. Tramp. Disappointment. Ignorant." His volatile anger continued to fuel him on as he attacked the chair next.

I pushed tighter against the wall, wishing I could bury myself inside it. Wishing I could disappear. *This nightmare's never going to end. I'll never escape the madman.* I pulled deeper into myself. It felt like I was watching a movie. A horrible, sick movie, and I desperately wanted it to end. But it'd only just begun.

Garen straightened, panting as he glanced around the small trailer. When his eyes landed on the kitchen, they lit up like a child's on Christmas morn. "I'll bet it's a disaster in there," he said under his breath, as if the thought excited him.

He all-but ran into the kitchen. I cringed as he tossed the gun on the stove before opening the cabinets. He threw his head back, laughing in delight. "Just as I expected. Still a disappointment in here, too."

He busied himself arranging the cans and boxes, shortest to tallest, by color, perfectly, laughing with glee as he worked. He'd lost his mind. He'd completely lost his mind.

I curled into a ball, my knees pressed to my chest, my hands clamped tight over my ears as feelings of deep despair paralyzed me. I rocked back and forth, praying silently he'd kill me quickly when the time came.

When he finished, he dragged me to the kitchen and shoved me into the corner next to the stove. "This is how you properly arrange a cabinet." The amusement in his voice was now replaced with hatred. He reached into the cabinet, and with one swipe, emptied the shelves. Cans and boxes flew everywhere, some landing on me. I hardly felt them.

Next, he tore the dish cabinet open and seized a stack of plates, dropping them onto the counter. I heard several crack. Garen emptied the cabinet of all the dishes, meticulously lining them up on the counter, despite the fact that several were now broken. He turned and jerked me up by my hair. "Unsophisticated mess," he complained about my hair before hurling me across the room. I stumbled backward, falling onto the destroyed couch. Springs jabbed me in the thigh and back. I sat still.

"Don't move," he chuckled, grabbing a cast iron skillet from the sink and smashing the dishes on the counter. Pieces of glass flew through the air like razor sharp snowflakes, some hitting his face. Like a madman on a mission, Garen didn't flinch once. Within seconds the dishes once belonging to Booker's grandfather lay in hundreds of shards. Next, he turned to the glass table and, with a fierce swing of the skillet, shattered it also.

In his fury, he snatched the gun from the stove and placed it atop the broken glass pieces on the counter. With a sledgehammer he must have brought with him, he repeatedly hammered away at the gun. Breathless, he stopped and picked it up with his finger and thumb, the once round barrel now smashed almost flat. "I guess you won't be using this piece of evil again." He tossed it recklessly on the floor. The absurdity of Garen's comment was lost on him.

I curled my legs under me as I continued to shake violently. I pinched my eyes shut as he ran toward me and pulled me to my feet by the shoulders of my pajamas. Heat radiated off his body in waves.

"Please don't do this," I whispered, my voice wobbling.

"Don't do what, Terese?" His arm snaked around my waist and he jerked me into him. "Don't ruin your life like you've ruined mine?" Garen ran his hand over my hair, fisting it, and jerking my head back. His vile breath beat against my face. "I've lost everything. Graft fired me, said I was too volatile, mentally unbalanced. He thought my obsession over finding you put him at risk." Garen's jaw ticked. "Should have known. After everything I've done for him, the little leech. You can never trust a politician."

"Please," I begged as he crushed me tighter.

"You destroyed my Life Plan, you and that sleazy lawyer of yours." Garen laughed. "I've already dealt with Velazquez. He got what he deserved."

"What do you mean?" With every fiber of my being I didn't want to know the answer.

"Seems someone broke into his office and torched the place. Sadly, Velazquez didn't make it. He may or may not have been tied to his desk." Garen shrugged. "They'll never know because everything was burnt beyond recognition. The authorities had to use dental records to ID him."

"You killed him." The very thought sickened me. Michael Velazquez was my friend's father. He helped me not only to divorce Garen, but he did his best to assist me as I got back on my feet.

"The two of you destroyed my life, Terese. He had to be taught a lesson. Now it's your turn."

I was staring into the face of an insane man. "Please don't do this. What about your dream to be president?" Not that he could possibly achieve that now, but I was desperate.

"Gone, Terese. All my dreams, all my plans, destroyed." He shoved me backward and my head hit the wall with a thud. "It seems Graft spread his lies about me to his contacts. No politician will hire me now. All my dreams, gone up in smoke. All." He jabbed his finger into my breastbone. "Because." *Jab.* "Of you." *Jab.*

"I'm sorry," I said, struggling to normalize my trembling voice. "H—how did you find me?"

"Pure dumb luck. I was sitting in the dentist's office waiting to have my teeth cleaned when I picked up a copy of *USA Today*. There was an interesting article about revitalizing depressed areas, and low and behold, I saw a picture of my wife, in Rome, New York, of all places, at the opening of some swanky hotel."

He wrapped his hand in my hair again and twisted, jerking my head back. "I wasn't sure it was you at first. The dark hair threw me a bit. And the fact that you came so far north. Never in a million years did I think you'd go somewhere cold, knowing how much you hate it. Good one." He jerked on my hair once more, forcing my head sideways. "Your hair looked better black."

"Garen, can we put the past behind us—"

He cut me off and continued as if I'd not said anything. "The article featured the developer, Wayne Bushman, who gushed on and on about some attorney named Gatto and how he helped him get the project started." He pushed me tighter against the wall, wedging his forearm on my throat. "At first I thought, no, that can't be Terese. Then he mentioned that Gatto and his secretary *Tess* Bennett had come from Port Fare, New York, to help him celebrate the grand opening. That's when I knew. Tell me, did you legally change your last name or did you marry some other poor sap?"

"Changed my name." I didn't even think about the pictures making the national news. One little mistake was going to cost me everything. "Garen, can't we part as friends? A good looking and successful guy like you can have any woman he wants. You certainly don't need to settle for a loser like me."

He pressed his arm tighter against my neck. "I see you've moved on. I watched you making out on the porch with the scumbag lawyer." Growing lightheaded from the lack of oxygen, I began sliding down the wall. Garen let go and I dropped to my knees, coughing.

He laughed. "Did you like my Christmas card?"

"Christmas card?" I sputtered between coughs.

"It was pretty clever, if I say so myself. I cut out letters from magazines and pieced them together into words before gluing them all into a lovely Christmas card. Kind of serial killer-like, don't you think?" He sat on the arm of the dilapidated couch.

"That was from you?" I asked. A proud grin split his face. "You're going to kill me, aren't you?"

"Not right away. I have some plans for us first." He stood and went into the kitchen. He returned with the sledgehammer in his hand. I screamed and scurried tight against the wall.

"Don't worry." He chuckled. "This isn't for you." He held the hammer like a baseball bat and swung it into the wall. After two swings, he'd made a decent size hole.

"There it is," he said, nodding to the two-by-four stud behind the wallboard. He reached in the hole and grabbed the wallboard, jerking it back. A large section tore away from the studs, exposing the framing in the wall. "That's for later, after I teach you a lesson or two."

Pulling me to my feet, he dragged me across the broken glass to the kitchen again where shards cut into my feet. He picked up a sharp knife he'd thrown on the floor earlier and clutched a handful of my hair and hacked away at it. The tugging of the knife hurt my head as he chopped at my hair, but I didn't give him the satisfaction of knowing. I kept my face stoic as large sections of my hair fell to the floor.

"Tsk, tsk. What have I always said about long hair?" He patted my head, as if I were a dog.

I didn't answer.

When he finished butchering my hair, he took the knife and slipped it under the edge of my pajama top. Closing my eyes, I waited for him to plunge it into me. He didn't. Instead, he cut off my pajamas.

"Before I kill you, I'm going to mark my territory, if you will." He chuckled at his vulgar analogy. "I want my face to be the last thing you see as you die." He shoved me to the floor in the living room, next to the hole he'd made earlier. "But first, your punishment." He tugged off his belt. It rippled through the loops with a swooshing sound I doubted I'd ever forget. I closed my eyes and curled into ball on the floor, waiting for the beating to begin.

"Relax. This part won't be as bad as you deserve. I want you fully cognizant for the grand finale."

Despite his words, the beating was intense and littered with crude profanity, though nowhere near as savage as the beatings had been in the past. Nevertheless, all hope of ever being free, of ever being happy seeped from me as I curled into a ball, not caring anymore how much it hurt. I just wanted to die so I could finally escape him.

After the beating, he savaged my body, my heart . . . my soul. When he finally crawled off, he shoved my face into the carpet before reaching into his discarded jeans and removing a pair of handcuffs. He hooked my arm and I braced for another beating. Instead, he shoved me against the wall, and cuffed my right wrist. He looped the cuffs around the bared wall stud then cuffed my other wrist.

As I lay naked, tethered to the stud, he gathered his clothes and headed for the bathroom, calling over his shoulder, "Don't go anywhere while I wash your stink off me."

I began shaking, unsure if it was from the cold or fear. I noted the sun had risen. I'd lived through the night, something I hadn't expected. Exhausted, I closed my eyes as tears tumbled down my face to the floor.

I must have fallen asleep, or passed out, because the next thing I knew Garen, fully dressed, stood by the door twisting sheets and towels into rope-like strands.

"Good morning. Did you sleep well?" He chuckled to himself as he placed the sheets around the front edge of the living room. "What am I doing, you ask?" He spoke the question I was indeed thinking. "I'll tell you, Terese. Have you ever talked to someone who's been badly burned?"

I tried to sit up, forgetting I was cuffed to the stud. I didn't like where this conversation was going.

"I have. He told me it was excruciating. Well, at first. Once the burn goes deep enough, the nerves are dead so the pain ends." He squatted down next to my battered body. "I'm going to watch you burn until it gets to that point."

"You're insane," I spit out. "Absolutely insane."

"That comes from having your dreams destroyed." He smacked my forehead. "Now, if you'll excuse me, I need to board up a few windows." He went outside and returned with a small toolbox, from which he removed a hammer, a screwdriver, and a box of nails. He removed two doors from the kitchen cabinets and walked into the bedroom. I heard him pounding on the wood. He came back out and removed two more, taking them into the other bedroom.

"There. The windows are covered so you can't get out of the trailer, just in case you somehow break free." He pointed to the sheets and towels. "As you can see, the front of the trailer will have a wall of flames keeping you in, so we're good. I'll light the towels in front of the door on my way out so I have an escape route." He smiled proudly, as if he'd done a good thing. He took a long blue lighter like the kind I'd seen my dad use to light the barbecue from the toolbox. "I was going to use gasoline, but I worried about the fire moving too fast. Fast is not my objective here. Slow and painful is."

I struggled fruitlessly against the cuffs. Thankfully the sheets wouldn't catch. "Maybe a *little* accelerant won't hurt." He jogged to the bathroom and returned with a bottle of clear nail polish and some polish remover. He sprinkled the sheet furthest from me with the remover. It sparked to life. "Whoa, too much." He chuckled and stomped out the flames. Garen took the hammer and smashed the polish, smearing it along one of the towels before carefully sprinkling remover over the sheets.

"See this window?" He jerked one of the curtains down. "When it gets too dangerous for me in here, I'll watch from outside."

"Garen, please don't do this," I begged. "I have money in the bank, I'll give it all to you, and I can send you more every month until you're back on your feet again."

He flew to my side, dropping down eyelevel with me. "You don't understand. This is about payback. You destroyed my life, my dreams. I'll not be satisfied until you're six feet in the ground. Get it?" His lips pulled tight over his teeth. "If by some miracle you live through this, I'll keep coming after you until I succeed. I won't stop until you're dead." He stood and kicked me in the stomach as my computer chimed, signaling that I had a message.

"Seems you got mail." Garen casually picked up the laptop he'd long ago shoved to the floor. I couldn't believe it still worked.

"Well, well. It's from your lover. I'll read it to you." He stepped over near me.

"Hey, sleepyhead. I hope you're up." I could almost hear Booker's voice saying the words. *"I'm on my way over, and I'm bringing breakfast: a veggie croissant and some of my special hot chocolate. I'll be there in a few so you'd better get dressed."*

Garen raised the laptop over his head with a scream and tossed it against the wall shattering it. "I can't catch a break with you." He kicked my thigh before punching the wall. "Now I'm going to have to rush this." Garen spewed obscenities as he doused everything with the rest of the remover and a bottle of hand sanitizer he found under the kitchen sink. He lit the sheet and the fire roared to life. He turned and repeatedly kicked the chair he'd wedged under the doorknob until it shot out. He opened the door and stepped outside, starting the towels there on fire. I glanced at him through the flames. "Just remember, whore," he said. "If you survive this, I will hunt you down. You're going to pay." He locked the door and slammed it shut.

I twisted on my side as the smoke thickened, choking me. The remaining curtain was now fully engulfed. The flames spread quickly along the entire front of the trailer, including the kitchen.

As the flames shot higher, I closed my eyes. Garen had won, just like I knew he would in the end.

Chapter 25
BOOKER

I made a right onto Tess's street as a crazy driver in a blue Fusion raced past me, practically forcing me into a snow bank.

"Idiot." The road still had a thick layer of slick snow from the storm earlier this morning. I hoped she hadn't looked outside yet. I held tight to the wheel as I made my way to the trailer.

Fresh tire tracks led away from her place, along with a set of footprints from her trailer to the road as if someone had just left. "That's weird." Her car parked out front was covered in a good six inches of snow so they couldn't be her footprints and besides, they were too big.

I swallowed hard at the memory of coming home early and finding Nikkolynn in bed with her boyfriend not so long ago. While staring at the footprints, the snow reflected flickering Christmas lights shining from inside the trailer.

"Breathe, Gatto. Tess barely speaks to anyone. She's not cheating on you." Shaking off the sickening feeling, I headed up the short pathway to her door. Only then did I realize the twinkling wasn't Christmas lights, but flames. The trailer was on fire.

I jerked frantically at the locked door. A sense of dread gripped my insides. I leaned back and kicked twice before the door gave way. Flames shot out and I stumbled back into the snow. I pulled out my cell phone, dialed nine-one-one, and requested police and fire as I slipped my coat off.

"Tess!" I yelled again, shoving the phone in my pocket. She didn't answer. For a split second I debated about going inside. Maybe the footprints were hers. I looked at them again. No, *not hers*. Nausea welled up when I realized she might be inside.

I searched through the flames. My heart stopped when I saw a body lying on the floor next to the wall. Tess. Thankfully the flames looked to be concentrated around the door and hadn't reached her yet. Covering my head with my coat, I jumped through the fire, praying I hadn't made a deadly mistake. Smoke stung my eyes and scorched my throat. I dropped to my knees. Squinting, I crawled to where Tess lay naked on the floor.

Long red marks streaked her face, and her left eye was swollen. Her beautiful red hair had been chopped off, helter-skelter.

No, not again. Please don't take another person from me.

I jerked the cuffs. They refused to give. Pulling the coat up to cover her face, I took my Glock from my calf holster and fired three times, severing the stud. I pulled the handcuffs free and grabbed Tess to my chest. Fire completely engulfed the front of the trailer and the kitchen. I buried my nose and mouth in my shoulder and raced to the bedroom. We'd have to go out the window.

But no. Someone had nailed cabinet doors to both bedroom windows. *What's going on?* I had no other options. I ran into the bathroom. I set Tess inside the shower and turned the water on warm. I pulled out my cell phone and called nine-one-one again as I jerked down the shower curtain and pressed it between the floor and the door to help keep out the smoke. "This is Captain Gatto of the MET," I stated out of pure habit. I ordered additional fire, police, and an ambulance. "We're stuck in the bathroom on the backside of the trailer. I'll hang a yellow shirt from the window. They're going to have to use the Jaws of Life to cut us out," I instructed the operator as I ripped off my shirt and wedged it out the window's twelve-inch opening.

Smoke seeped through the side and top of the door. I picked Tess up and stepped inside the shower, aiming the stream of water out into the small room. I pulled her closer. "Tess, please.

Fight. Hold on." She moaned in my arms. "Who did this to you? Was it someone you know, or a stranger?"

"Garen," she whispered.

My eyes flew open wide. "He found you? How?"

"Please, Booker, please just let me die. I can't do this anymore . . . I can't . . ." Her eyes rolled back in her head as she passed out.

"No! We fight," I demanded as the sirens grew louder. "We're in this together now, Tess. I'll be by your side. You're not alone anymore."

Chapter 26

I sat next to Tess, forcing back a panic attack. I had to remain in control. Her injuries, though brutal, were not as bad as I first thought. An oxygen cannula was strapped to her nose and an IV ran into her arm. "She's going to be okay," Cole said after settling her in the room.

"Physically, yes. Emotionally, not so much." I took her hand in mine. "She asked me to let her die."

"She's been through a lot in the past several hours, Booker. I'm sure once she's had time to recuperate, she'll be fine." He squeezed my shoulder as he left.

She groaned a few times, and tugged at the oxygen. She hadn't opened her eyes since we brought her in. I spent the next three hours pacing her room, waiting for her to wake.

I leaned over and pressed my lips to her forehead. "I love you, Tess. I hung my head, not stirring again until I felt Tess's touch as she lightly stroked my hair.

I straightened. "How are you feeling?" I took her hand in mine.

She tried to speak, but coughed instead. I got up and took the small pink water pitcher with a straw in it from her bedside table and held it to her mouth. She greedily drank from the straw. "Thank you," she said, her voice raspy. Her hand went to her throat as she tried to clear it.

"You inhaled a lot of smoke. You'll sound that way for a bit," I explained.

"Are you okay? You didn't get burned, did you?" Her eyes scanned me as her voice whispered painfully.

"No. My coat was singed, but I'm fine." Tears welled in her eyes. "You're safe now, Tess." I carefully wiped her bruised cheek dry. The red welts had faded, exchanged for bruises.

"No. I'll never be safe, ever. Garen vowed that if I survived he'd hunt me down and finish the job." Her face scrunched in agony and she coughed again. "Why didn't you let me die? I can't live like this anymore. I'm tired, Booker. I'm tired of hiding, of worrying. I'm tired of being alone. I quit."

"But you're not alone anymore. I love you, and I'll be by your side," I vowed.

She shook her head. "Garen wants to control, dominate me. He wants me a cowardly mess, groveling at his feet. Well, he's won."

"Tess, please don't give up." I pressed her hand to my lips, holding back my own fears. "We can get through this together."

She cupped my cheek. "I do so love you," she whispered. "But I can't."

"Ple—"A tapping on the door interrupted me as Cole entered.

"Hello," he said, setting a tablet on the foot of the bed. "How are you feeling, Tess?"

"Okay," she said soberly.

"I'd like to check your lungs and make sure they're clearing." She nodded. Cole pressed the stethoscope to her back and listened to her breathing. When he finished, he checked her eyes. "You sound better. I think we can remove the oxygen. We'll check your O_2 levels first, to be safe." Tess looked away with a shrug, ignoring him.

"Do you want more water?" I asked. She shook her head.

"I need to review her medical history for our records, Book. As you know, due to privacy laws you'll need to lea—" Cole began.

"Booker can stay," Tess interrupted.

"We'll be discussing some very personal things, Tess," Cole said, picking up the tablet.

"He can stay," she reiterated.

"As you wish." He removed a stylus from his breast pocket and tapped on the tablet a few times. He briefly recounted her current injuries, reassuring her that she'd make a full recovery. "Mostly bruises and a few lacerations. Surprisingly, the injuries are fairly minor, considering his intentions."

"Doesn't surprise me. Garen wanted me fully aware so that when he set fire to my place I'd feel the fire as it burned me alive," she said flatly.

Cole's face went as rigid as mine. He looked at me, then back at her. "He said that?" She nodded. Cole swore softly under his breath, something I'd never heard him do before in all the years I'd known him. I turned and paced to the window, desperate to get my hands on Garen.

"We were able to collect some DNA from the sexual assault. That should help." Cole tapped several times on the tablet before speaking again. "I need a little medical history, if I may. The x-rays show numerous breaks, all old injuries. Let me see. There was a break to your left collarbone. Numerous skull fractures, along with several broken ribs. Your spleen's been removed." He paused, looking up from the tablet. "I'm hoping you're going to tell me you were involved in a very serious car accident at some point."

"No. Those are all from Garen, including a lacerated liver, and a few other various injuries," she said.

"Garen did all that?" I barely controlled my anger.

"Yes."

"Why's he not in jail?"

"Are you serious?" She looked at me and for the first time I heard something flicker to life in her voice. "Oh, I had a restraining order against him, but those things are a joke. Do you have any idea what little the courts do to protect victims of domestic violence? Criminals have more rights than victims do."

She dropped her head down and pulled mindlessly on some loose threads from her blanket as she told us about the abuse that finally led to her escaping Garen. She didn't go into details, stating everything matter-of-factly, and in generalized terms. *He kicked* or *he punched*, but it was enough to make my blood boil.

"They arrested him for putting you in the hospital, I hope." Cole looked at her in disbelief. Me, I wanted to leave and go find the soon-to-be dead man.

"Sort of. He told everyone that someone broken into our home and that the intruder attacked me. I couldn't remember what had happened at first, but I knew he was lying." She laughed a short, hard laugh before coughing again. Cole handed her the water pitcher. She took a couple more sips and set it on the table.

"In the hospital, Garen stayed by my side, night and day, looking ever the devoted husband as he set up his alibi.

"When he got a phone call the day before I was supposed to leave, I took a chance and mouthed to the nurse that Garen was the reason I was in the hospital, not a random stranger. Thankfully, she believed me and pretended to give me some powerful meds. She then told Garen I'd be out cold until morning. As soon as she was sure he'd left, the nurse called the police."

Cole stood. "Tess, do you feel up to talking to the police about what happened at the trailer? I'd like to increase the odds of catching this guy, the sooner the better. No pressure. If you're not ready . . ."

She shrugged. "Go ahead and call them. It really doesn't matter."

Cole glanced my way before walking out of the room. Anger still burned in his eyes.

I wrapped my hands around hers. "How long was he in jail?"

"Less than twelve hours," she said. "The senator covered for him, claiming he and Garen were in meetings all day. Graft stated that I was unbalanced and had caused problems more than once for Garen. He even backed up Garen's claim that I was having an affair."

I ground my teeth to keep from yelling. "Why would a senator do that?"

"Garen held something over him." She shrugged again. "The only reason Garen finally agreed to the divorce was because of my amazing attorney Michael. He hired a PI and learned that they were both involved with some pretty low-life characters. Michael worked a deal that he'd keep quiet about what the PI had found out if Garen agreed to an amicable divorce."

"I'll bet the weasel took that deal," I snapped.

"But it cost my attorney his life." Tears rose in her eyes, but she blinked them back. "Garen told me he set fire to Michael's office, and burned him alive. *Punishment*, he claimed."

With considerable self-control, I held my temper in check. She needed someone to talk to, not a raving lunatic. I pressed her hand to my lips. She didn't react. She wouldn't look at me, but she didn't pull her hand away. She remained flat, expressionless. "I assume you went into hiding after the divorce, fearing he'd come after you."

"Actually, I didn't see or hear from Garen for six months. I thought the nightmare was over. Then one sunny afternoon I was working my dad's garden so he could start planting some vegetables." She straightened. "Garen showed up, a rope in his hand, vowing revenge. My mom heard him and came out with a loaded gun, demanding he get off our property. My mom hates guns, but there she stood, pointing it straight at him." She closed her eyes for a moment. "He hit my mom, catching her by surprise, and she fell against the house. I freaked. I picked up the shovel and hit him over the head with it. There was blood everywhere. I thought I'd killed him. My father came running, took one look at Garen, and called my brother, who whisked me off to a women's shelter." She pulled her blanket tighter around her, as if it offered some sort of protection.

I shoved my hands through my hair again as I paced to the window and then back to the bed, grinding my teeth. *I'll find this pig and tear him apart, slowly and painfully.* I scrubbed my face with my hand.

"That was the last time I saw my family. I didn't dare contact any of them, fearing Garen would somehow find out." A tear rolled down her cheek, finally. "I mapped out a place to relocate while at the shelter. I decided to go somewhere cold. Garen knows how much I hate the cold, so I hoped it'd be the last place he'd think to look. New York holds six spots on the Top Ten Snowiest Places list. I picked Port Fare because it was not so big that people wouldn't notice if I didn't show up at work, yet not so small that my presence stuck out."

"Wait, what about your last name? And your social security number?" I asked. "Why didn't he track you through that?"

"I bought new ID, and a gun."

"So your real name isn't Terese Layla Bennett?"

"I only changed my last name. Garen took so much from me, I kept my first and middle name so I'd have some connection to my past." She looked up at me. "My last name is Selleck. And so you know, whenever you had me sign my name to any legal documents, I did sign Selleck. I scribbled it so you couldn't tell."

"Tess," I said, giving her a gentle hug. "That is the last thing I'm worried about right now."

Cole came back as Tess lowered the head of the bed while rubbing her eyes, clearly exhausted.

"The police are on their way. I'm afraid you won't be able to sleep just yet." Cole came over to her bedside. "We need to catch this guy."

"You won't catch him." She shut her eyes.

Her calmness only ratcheted my fury. "What's his last name?" I asked.

She snapped upright. "No! You're not going after him. He'll kill you."

"You underestimate me. If anyone is going to be killing someone, it'll be me," I vowed.

"Booker—" Cole began.

"Great. So then you'll be in prison. Wonderful alternative to being in a grave." She rubbed her head and dropped back to the mattress with a groan.

"Are you alright?" I stooped over her, stroking the choppy strands of hair from her face.

"Please promise me you will not go after him," she begged, her fists wrapped tight in the front of my shirt.

"Tess," I shook my head. "I—"

"Promise me," she demanded.

For the first time since my family's brutal murders—I lied. "I promise." She sighed softly and released my shirt.

Cole's eyes narrowed. He knew. No doubt I'd be getting a lecture when we were out of earshot of Tess. He nodded to the door. I ignored him.

The cops came in, two women I'd worked with over the years, saving me from Cole's stare down.

Tess reiterated what had happened in the trailer yesterday. After I promised her yet again I'd stay away from her ex, she gave the officers his last name.

You're about to meet your maker, Garen Johnson.

Chapter 27

I met up with Seth and Maggie at the trailer later. My nose wrinkled at the wet smoky stench that clung to the wreckage. It was a complete loss; only the metal frame where the north-facing wall once stood remained upright.

Maggie's gloved hand flew to her mouth with a gasp as she stepped out of the car. "I'm sorry, Magpie." I gave her a quick hug.

She shook her head. "Don't be. The place was jinxed. Nothing good's ever happened in that nightmare of a trailer. I should have torn it down instead of remodeling it."

Seth wrapped his arm around her. "We'll have it hauled away and sell the pad space if you're ready to part with it," he said.

"Yes. Good riddance," she said bitterly. "How's Tess?"

"Not good," I said solemnly. "She's given up. She told me I should have let her die."

"Not good is right," Seth said. "Maggie and I have been talking. We'd like to invite her to stay with us until she's back on her feet."

"That'd be great. I'll talk to her and see how she feels about it. Your security system should give her some comfort, too." I'd have her stay with me, but I didn't plan on being around much since I'd be hunting down the scumbag ex. Tess would feel safer with people she knew. Besides, I didn't want her to know what I was doing.

We moved around the rubble. Nothing survived. I rummaged through the charred ruins and found what was left of her wallet—the zipper and a melted plastic credit card. The barrel of her gun had been beaten flat.

"Garen's handiwork would be my guess," Seth said. I cocked back my arm and threw it into the back of my truck. "How are you doing?" His eyes scanned my face.

"I'm going after him. I'm going to . . ." I glanced at Maggie and drew in a deep breath. "I'm going to find him, then I'm going to kill him."

"And then you're going to jail," Maggie said, her hand cocked on her hip. "Then Tess is going to fall in love with someone else and spend the rest of her days with him instead of you. And her nights," she added pointedly.

"Let the cops do their job, Book." Seth kicked a piece of burnt rubbish. "We've worked with these people. They're good at what they do."

We'll see.

~*~

The hunt for Garen Johnson was nothing but dead-end after frustrating dead-end. The police learned that his latest ex-girlfriend was also in hiding, fearing for her life. Her mother told the police of the bruises and welts she'd seen on her daughter, all courtesy of Garen Johnson. She refused to give the police her daughter's location out of her own fear for the girl's life.

Tess made steady progress, physically. Emotionally, she was still withdrawn and fearful. "Good morning," I said, entering her room. Finally, after five long days, Cole gave the okay to release her. He'd kept her there a little longer than needed because he too worried about her flat emotional state and ordered a psych consult to be safe. When I told her about Seth's offer to let her stay there for a while, she accepted with a blank nod and a thank you.

"Are you ready to go?" Her lips turned up ever so slightly and she nodded. I handed her a large bag from some girly shop in the mall. "Lilah got you some things. I make no promises.

Knowing her they'll be cutting edge and bright." At last a real smile crossed her lips. The tightness that gripped my chest since the fire eased up minutely.

Tess took the clothes and went into the bathroom, coming back out a few minutes later in a simple pair of jeans and a green sweater. She then pulled out a hat with bold splotches of greens and blues. A large pink flower of some kind sat on the brim. She gave me a crooked grin and plopped it on her head. Had to give Lilah credit—Tess looked amazing in the silly thing. I guided her arms into a blue coat, also picked out by Lilah, and we left.

"Any news on him?" Tess no longer referred to Garen by his name.

"No, but we'll find him."

"We'll?"

"I meant the police," I assured her. "Lilah and Cole are at Seth's. We thought a quiet New Year's Eve dinner might be nice." She said nothing.

Okay, Plan B. Instead of turning for Seth's, I drove to *The Dragon Noodle*, one of my favorite Chinese takeout joints. "Are we picking up food for the party?" she asked as we got out of the truck.

"Yes." I didn't mention it was now a private party of two. I ordered the shrimp chow mien she loved and the beef chop suey for me. I paid for the food as she studied a map on the wall by the door. I wondered if she trying to conceal her bruised face from the workers, or if she was making plans to run away and hide again. Neither thought thrilled me.

"That's all we're getting? I don't think that will feed everyone." She climbed back in the truck and set the food on the seat between us.

"I made an executive decision." I said, leaving the parking lot. "We're going back to my place for a quiet dinner for two. Does that sound alright to you, or would you rather go to Seth's?"

"Your place sounds perfect." She squeezed my hand. The forced smile on her lips didn't touch her eyes.

We ate dinner in virtual silence. Even the dog seemed to sense something was wrong. She stayed on her pillow next to the couch and slept, never once begging for food. I put the leftovers in the fridge as Tess used the bathroom. When I came into the family room, she was petting the docile Daisy.

"Want to watch a movie? We have a good three hours before the ball drops." I picked up my guitar off the couch that I'd left there earlier.

"I didn't know you played." She ran her hand over the instrument's curve.

I slipped the strap over my head. I just may have found a way to put a smile on her face. "The past couple nights," *while I've been missing you like crazy*, "I've taught myself how to play *Layla*."

"The Eric Clapton song?" She smiled. "My dad used to sing that to me when I was young."

"I only know the unplugged version." I plucked out a few of the song's cords.

"That's my favorite. Let's hear it." Mild excitement tainted her voice. I'd take it. Anything sounded better than complacency, no matter how small.

"Impressive," she said after I strummed the intro. "Do you know the words?"

"I do, but I'm not a very good singer," I warned.

"Somehow I doubt that." She sat on the arm of the couch and waited.

'*What will you do when you get lonely*
When nobody's waitin' by your side?
You've been running and hiding much too long.

I didn't realize just how close to home the words hit, but she didn't seem to notice. Hopefully she'd escaped into in a happy childhood memory. She sat quietly, her arms braced on either side of her, as I continued singing.

"*Layla, you got me on my knees.*
Layla, I'm begging darling please.
Layla, Darling, won't you ease my worried mind?"

She clapped as I removed the guitar strap from around my shoulders and bowed. "Most excellent, Booker." She kissed my cheek. "What about the rest of the song?"

"You really want me to?" She nodded.

I picked up the guitar and played a few cords as I thought about some of the lyrics and decided to reword a few spots. The next couple lines reminded me of Garen, a place I didn't want to go tonight.

"You shook my world up with your smile;
Your gentle caring ways abound.
Like a fool, I fell in love with you;
You turned my whole world upside down.
Layla, you got me on my knees.
Layla, I'm begging darling please."

She said nothing about the changed lyrics as I set the guitar down and took her by the hands, pulling her into my arms. I hummed the tune softly in her ears as we swayed to the music.

"You can dance, too?" she asked.

"Yes. Don't you remember Seth's wedding? We danced together," I reminded her.

"That's right. Can't believe I forgot that." She moved in closer and rested her head on my shoulder, her cold nose pressing against my neck.

"Layla, Darling, won't you ease my worried mind?
Let's make the best of the situation,
Before I finally go insane.
Please don't say we'll never find a way
And tell me all my love's in vain."

"I do love you, Booker Gatto," she said softly. We stopped dancing as her tears began, and the dam broke.

She purged her soul of the atrocities Garen had inflicted on her for over a year-and-a-half, details she'd not shared with Cole and me in the hospital. I never wanted to let her go. My chest hurt as the vulgarities spilled out of her mouth. My gut knotted in anger, and I forced my hands to keep from fisting. Memories of my mom and sister's last moments tried to break in, but I shut them out. Tess needed my undivided attention. She shook so badly I guided her to the couch. After crying herself out, she fell asleep in my arms.

I didn't sleep. My mind replayed her words over and over again. They ate at me, festered. Garen would pay for the putrid things he'd done to Tess if it were the last thing I did

Chapter 28
Tess

I woke the next morning, still nestled in Booker's arms, as we lay stretched across his recliner sofa. His chest rose and fell with the rhythm of sleep. Sometime during the night he'd covered us with a blanket. Not wanting to wake him, I lay quietly.

Daisy didn't share my thought. She paced back and forth in front of the patio door, clearly needing to be let out. As carefully as I could, I moved Booker's arm, or I tried to, only he held on. I tickled his nose with my fingertips, hoping he'd swipe at it with his hand. He did, only with the *other* hand. Hadn't thought of that.

When poor Daisy whimpered, I had no choice but to wake him. "Booker, the dog needs to go out." I nudged him with my hands. "Booker."

He sat up straight, eyes wide, fists clenched, ready for a fight. "Is everything alright?"

"Yes." I hurried as fast as my bruise body allowed to the back door. "Your dog is about to have an accident."

"Hold on." He darted to the keypad, punching in the code. The bell rang twice, signaling the all clear, and I opened the door. The dog raced outside, but didn't clear the deck before relieving herself.

"And that's why you should never eat yellow snow," Booker said, coming over next to me. We watched as the dog bounded across they yard, diving into piles of snow. Daisy seemed oblivious to the icy cold. Better her than me. I rubbed my arms at the thought of the white powder on my skin.

"How are you doing this morning?" He rubbed my arms also.

"Better. Sorry about unloading like that," I said, embarrassed at my mini breakdown.

"No need to apologize," he said, brushing off my outburst. "I'm just sorry you had to suffer because of your ex."

"We missed the dropping of the ball." I slipped my arms around his waist and rested my cheek on his shoulder.

"I guess we'll have to welcome the New Year in with a good morning kiss," he said.

"You'll want me to brush my teeth first." I looked into his brown eyes.

"I'll risk it." He kissed me softly. "Not too bad. I've smelled worse."

I smacked his chest and he laughed. "Come on. I think I have a spare brush you can use." He took my hand and led me down the hall. I stopped dead when we entered the bedroom.

The gargantuan bed took my breath away. The headboard had to be six feet tall, and constructed of wood, which didn't surprise me knowing how much he enjoyed woodworking. What did surprise me was the wrought iron insert.

"I just finished this last month," he said. "I have this weird fascination with iron, and when I saw this piece I knew I had to have it."

I stepped over to the headboard. "It's beautiful." I stroked the curved lines of the iron. "I love this stuff, too. My brother used to tease me because no matter where we were, vacations, school clothes shopping, whatever, I'd hunt out the wrought iron stores." I laughed.

"Me, too." Booker tugged at the crooked bedspread, embarrassed. So unlike him. "When I first built it, the iron blended in and you couldn't see it very well. Lilah suggested I mount a mirror behind it." He pointed out a mirror I'd not noticed. "She and Maggie keep trying to get me to girly the place up." He went to the closet and came back with three very girly pillows, complete with white ruffles and roses. "Look what they want me to put on the bed." He all-but shoved them at me, as if holding them burned his hands.

I set them on the deep green comforter. "I have to admit, they do look really good on the bed," I said. Booker rolled his eyes and went into the bathroom, signaling me with his hand to follow.

A large, brown travertine tile shower dominated the space with its glass doors and four showerheads. "It has a steamer, too." He smiled proudly as my mouth dropped in awe.

"Did you install this?"

"Not the plumbing, but Seth and I did the tile work. Took forever, but it turned out great." He handed me a new toothbrush. "It cost me a pretty penny."

I squeezed a bead of toothpaste on the brush as he folded his arms and leaned against the sink.

"I have a proposition for you."

"Caving on your bet already, Gatto?" I teased, nodding to the bed.

He looked at it and frowned. "Yeah, don't remind me. Don't know what I was thinking." I chuckled at his long face. "It's good to see you laugh again, Tess."

It felt good to laugh again. For the past week I'd felt like an emotionless zombie. I'd hardly allowed myself to feel anything until I cried on Booker's shoulder last night. "Thanks again for letting me get that all out."

"Anytime." He kissed my temple. "I'm glad you trust me enough to unload like that. I've been pretty worried about you." He brushed his teeth as I did mine. It felt natural to be next to him, sharing the bathroom, like we'd been together forever.

"I feel better, and strangely enough, stronger." I dried my mouth and set the brush on the counter. "I don't want to go back to how I was before, cowering at every sound. I don't want to allow him to take my peace of mind again. I'm going to be stronger, braver."

"Good for you . . . which brings me back to my proposition." He put his brush in a silver holder and hung up the towel. "Since Garen knows where you are, there's really no sense in hiding from your family anymore. I thought maybe we could fly out to California and you could see them, if you're comfortable with that."

My heart leaped for joy as I jumped into his arms while holding back tears. I'd cried enough. "I'm taking that as a yes." I nodded against his chest, unable to speak. "Good. We can look over flights while we have breakfast."

"Thank you, Book." I kissed him, catching my reflection in the mirror as I did. "Oh, wait. I can't go home looking like this. My parents will freak." I fingered the rough locks of hair sticking out everywhere. "They've been through so much. If they see me like this it will devastate them, especially my mother."

"Maybe Lilah can help."

"I don't think anything but time can fix this. And the same goes for my bruises." I gingerly touched around the still tender yellowing bruise.

"Let's see what she can do, then you can decide. Honestly, Tess, I think your parents will be happy to see you no matter what your hair looks like." Booker took my hand and led me to the kitchen.

"Happy? Undoubtedly. I'm more concerned about upsetting them. They haven't seen me in four years and I walk in looking like this?" I sat on the barstool as he gathered some eggs, bread, and milk.

"It's your call, but like I said, I think they'll be overjoyed to have you back and simply won't care."

"Let me see what Lilah can do before I make any commitment."

~*~

"Hi, guys. Missed ya yesterday." Lilah greeted us at the door.

"Sorry. I wasn't up for company," Booker said, bee-lining it into the family room and plopping down on the couch next to Seth.

While the guys watched football, Lilah and Maggie sat at the kitchen table going through magazines, looking at decorating ideas for a baby nursery.

"Who's playing?" I asked, tugging nervously at my hair.

"Who cares," said Lilah, waving her hand in the air.

Maggie laughed. "What she said. Judging from your intense stare at the TV, I'm guessing you like football?"

"It's alright. I enjoy lacrosse much more. And basketball. I love basketball." I grinned at Lilah's scrunched face. "I played lacrosse in high school. I guess that's where I get my love of sports from."

"You were captain two years in a row," Maggie added. "Book's been bragging about you."

"Come on, dream girl. Let's do your hair so you can watch the game." Maggie took my arm and we followed Lilah up to the bathroom.

"Maggie, I want to apologize again—"

"Tess, you apologized at the hospital, and I'll repeat what I said there. It wasn't your fault. Stop torturing yourself about it," she said softly. "Besides, I think the trailer was possessed anyway." She gave me a hug.

"Thank you." I sat in the chair in front of the vanity.

"Mags, you're going to have to put a salon chair in here as often as we do hair up here," Lilah joked.

"Seriously," she nodded.

Lilah laid out a set of black scissors, a cape, and a small plastic box of makeup. She worked on covering the bruise on my cheek first. "Not bad." She held up a small mirror for me.

"You can hardly tell." I grinned, twisting my head toward the light for a better view.

"This stuff is a miracle worker." She handed me a small black tube of liquid foundation. "Don't leave home without it. Now for your hair. When we stripped the black dye out I remember you mentioning that you preferred your hair long, correct?" she asked, fingering the butchered mess. I nodded. "I won't cut much off then. I'll blend in some of the shorter pieces. What do you think?"

"I'm thinking I have no choice," I said grimly.

"But you will soon. In a month, maybe six weeks, depending on how fast your hair grows, we can add extensions. You'll never know," she vowed. "And I can dye them to match your hair."

It didn't take her long to finish, not that she had much to work with. Ten minutes later, she stepped back. "What do you think, Mags?"

Maggie painted a phony smile on. "Not bad at all."

She and Lilah's eyes met soberly. Lilah turned back to me and ran her fingers through my hair again. "Do you have any clips?" she asked Maggie.

"I do." She opened the drawer of the vanity and fished out a couple of rhinestone clips. Lilah put them in my hair, on either side of my part.

"That's cute," Maggie said with a genuine smile this time.

Lilah turned me to the mirror. "What do you think?"

I turned my head from side to side. "Pretty good for someone who's had all her hair hacked off by a butcher knife." I smiled at my weak joke.

Lilah pressed her cheek to mine. "I'm so sorry, Tess. Please know we're here for you." I nodded as she hugged me.

"Thank you. You did a great job for what you had to work with." I tugged on a strand of my hair.

"I think it looks cute with the clips. Maybe after dinner we'll run and get you some more since all I have are those two." Maggie led us down stairs.

"Sounds great." And a complete waste of money since I'd be dead soon. Booker told me on the drive over that they had no leads on Garen.

"I'm excited you've agreed to move in with us. Seth's come up with even more vegetarian recipes he wants your opinion on for the restaurant." She chuckled. "Horrible thought, right?"

"My thoughts exactly." We bumped knuckles. Seth could *punish* me any day with his recipes. "How are you feeling, by the way? You look better."

"I feel better. I'm a little sick in the mornings still, but not bad," Maggie said.

We were greeted with a cheer as we entered the family room. "Touchdown!" Cole and Booker shouted. Seth tossed a potato chip at the TV.

"They're playing like a bunch of girls," he sneered.

"Excuse me?" Maggie crossed her arms in front of her.

"Sorry, my beautiful, pregnant wife." Seth scooped her up and peppered her face and neck with kisses. "Will you forgive a mere man for making such a narrow-minded remark?"

"Yes, if you'll give me an extra serving of pie after dinner," she said, her fingers twisting in his hair.

"I'll give you the whole pie," he promised.

"Hold on. I want some." Booker came up to me as he groveled for pie.

"Sorry, bro." Seth went to the kitchen, Maggie followed.

"Your hair looks really nice." Booker squeezed my hand. "And I can't see the bruise at all."

"Lilah did an amazing job." I tugged self-consciously at my hair.

"Good enough you'll go visit your family?"

"If you'll come with me," I said. Since we had no idea where Garen was, I didn't dare go without Booker. Besides, a part of me wanted to show him off to my family. I wanted them to meet the man who restored my faith in men. Well, most men.

"I'd be honored."

Chapter 29

"You okay?" Booker asked as we disembarked in San Diego.

"I'm fine," I tugged nervously on my hair for the millionth time.

He was able to get us direct flights the next day. We'd flown all night, and I hadn't slept, but I was home. We decided it best that we stay for only one night in hopes that Garen wouldn't find out. I worried he'd seek revenge on my family. Booker agreed completely.

When I called my mother she cried so hard I could hardly understand her. I decided not to tell her about Garen's latest attack, instead focusing on seeing everyone again. Booker suggested we keep it low key, telling only my family and not any of my friends I was coming. He promised we'd come back and visit whomever I wanted once Garen was arrested. We got into a cab and the driver took us directly to my parent's.

"You're right," Booker said, as the taxi turned down my street. "The weather here's a bazillion times nicer than Port Fare."

"Don't remind me." So frantic to see my family, I'd hardly noticed the clear sunny skies and warm weather. I turned my face to the sun shining through the open window and drew in a deep breath, filling my lungs with the salty smell of the ocean, only a block away. I smiled at the palm trees that lined our street, trees I'd taken for granted growing up here.

The front door of my parent's house opened and my mother flew out, wearing khaki shorts and a blue button down shirt. I ran, collapsing into her arms. I don't know who cried harder as we clung desperately to each other in the front yard. Booker guided us inside as he constantly surveyed the area for any sign of Garen. Since he couldn't bring his gun on the plane, I knew he felt naked. I promised to lend him one of my dads' to carry while we were in San Diego.

"Oh, Mom, it's so good to see you." I stroked her tear-streaked face. "It feels like a lifetime since I left."

"It has been," she assured me. Deep creases lined her pretty face now. Her hair was heavily peppered with gray and white strands also. "He hurt you again, didn't he?" She touched my cheek by the bruise. I hadn't thought about my tears washing the makeup away.

"Yes."

"And he did this to your hair, too?" I nodded to her insightful question. Should have known she'd figure it out. She turned to Booker. "Just because Garen did this, don't be getting any ideas." She shook her hand at him, her face fierce, like a lioness protecting her young. Booker's face tightened, no doubt sickened at being compared to Garen.

"He's nothing like Garen, Mom. Nothing at all," I assured her. I stepped over next to him and looped my arm around his. "This is Booker Gatto. He's my boss in Port Fare."

"Your boss?" Mom eyed our intertwined arms.

"Hello, Mrs. Selleck." Booker took a step forward and stretched out his hand to Mom. He added his Cheshire Cat grin. They shook hands under Mom's narrowed eyes.

Seeming self-conscious under her glare, he stepped back next to me. "Your daughter's an amazing office manager," he said, tugging nervously on the collar of his shirt.

"Not surprised. She's excellent at everything she does." Mom grinned proudly. "She was captain of the lacrosse team her junior and senior year. That's never happened at her school, before or since. She was also vice president of her senior class. She did all that and still participated in dance competitions cross the state."

"Okay, Mom," I said, embarrassed.

"Okay nothing," she said firmly. "Tess never quit at anything she did. She worked hard at everything, including fighting to make her marriage work to that foul barbarian of a man." Tears welled in her eyes.

I rushed to her side and wrapped my arms around her. "It's okay, Mom. I'm here now."

"For how long? I miss you, Tessy." Her breath caught in her throat. "Every day I've wondered where you were and if you were safe. Every night I've begged God to protect you and keep you hidden from that monster."

"Mom, I only have two days here. Let's not spend it talking about him." I rubbed her back as I spoke.

"Is that really you?" I turned to see my twin, Abby, racing out the front door to my side. We embraced, each of us crying. I hugged her husband Calvin next. "And these are my children. Jaxton, he's three and a half, Gabe, eighteen months, and Ciel, our little surprise baby," she said, pointing to the bundle in Calvin's arms. More hugs and kisses before my brother Craig and his family showed up. We went inside as Craig introduced his two boys to me. I'd missed so much in four years.

"Where's Dad?" I asked.

"Sugar Cube." I turned to the door as my father came in carrying a couple bags of groceries. He dropped them on the table and rushed me. "Oh my, Sugar Cube, how I've missed you." He scooped me up and spun me around. His hands went right to my hair after he set me down. "I like the new hairdo," he said with a weak grin.

"He did it to her," my mother snapped, grabbing the groceries and taking them into the kitchen.

"Well, it'll grow back. I kind of like it, actually." He tapped a clip. "Those look real nice." He kissed my forehead.

"Dad, this is Booker Gatto." I tugged Book next to me.

"Yes. I've wanted to meet you." He shook Booker's hand, grabbing his arm with his other hand. "I can't thank you enough for saving my little girl." Tears welled in my father's eyes again. "When she called yesterday and told us what had happened . . ." He batted at a tear that escaped.

Booker, for the first time since I'd known him, was speechless. No jokes, no teasing, no confident grin. Just a sweet humble nod to my dad. I fell in love with him even more.

Dad gave Booker a small caliber pistol to carry. It fit perfectly in his calf holster. I could almost see Booker sighing in relief. Mom prepared a full-on turkey dinner. We sat around the table talking about old times and laughing at the childhood mayhems we encountered, or more often than not, created. The broken arm my brother received after jumping off the roof of the garage wearing his Halloween costume—a superman cape; the stitches to Abby's knee when she crashed her bike trying to jump over me, daredevil style, as I lay on the sidewalk; the bloody nose that would not stop after a giant wave face-planted me into the sand when we were body surfing. No one wanted the day to end. Abby and her baby stayed the night with me. Booker, being the good sport, graciously accepted the couch for a bed since my brother's room had been converted into a study.

"Is Ciel a good sleeper?" I asked after she finished nursing the baby.

"Thankfully, yes." She went to lay her down in a port-a-crib my mom had set up when I reached for her.

"May I hold her again?" I asked.

"Of course you can." She set the two-month-old infant into my arms. I stared down at her, enjoying the little miracle.

"How were your pregnancies? Did you have morning sickness?" I cuddled the baby close. She smelled of lavender from the lotion Abby had rubbed on her chubby arms and legs.

"My pregnancies are a breeze." She grinned from ear to ear. "In fact, I love being pregnant. I have tons of energy, and I feel so alive. Calvin says I was made to have babies, although Ciel was a surprise. We wanted to wait another year."

"I can't believe I'll never have children." I kissed Ciel's jet-black hair, compliments of her father who was of Chinese descent.

"I know, Tess. I'm so sorry." She squeezed my forearm. I got up and lay the sleepy baby in the crib, covering her with a pink blanket.

"Okay, tell me all about the sexy Booker Gatto." She sat cross-legged on the bed, patting the mattress, signaling me to sit next to her.

"I know, right? He's gorgeous," I agreed, lying beside her and propping myself up on my elbow. "And he's the nicest guy, too. He's the complete package. You-know-who's opposite."

"And?" she pressed.

"And yes, I love him," I admitted. "Very much. I never thought I'd find love again, but he's been my rock these past few days after . . . everything."

Pushing away negative thoughts, we lay back and I drew the blanket from the foot of the bed over us, just like we used to do as kids. We talked and giggled quietly until we couldn't keep our eyes open. Neither of us stirred until the scent of French toast drifted into the room. I dressed while Abby fed the baby.

"You realize how lucky you are she sleeps though the night, right?" I said as she fed her.

"Shh. She'll hear you. I don't want her getting any ideas." Abby playfully covered her baby's ears.

"I do believe Booker's cooking. I can't make any promises, but I'll try and save you some," I teased, making my way out the door. A burp cloth flew my way, but I shut the door before it landed.

As predicted, Booker was in the kitchen making breakfast. My mom, who'd eyeballed him suspiciously all night, was warm butter in his hands this morning. She laughed freely at his jokes, and was taken in by his charm.

"You've beguiled my mother," I said when she left to set the table.

"Haven't met a woman yet who doesn't succumb to the Gatto charm." He smiled broadly. "And she likes meat." He pointed to the bacon sizzling away on the stove.

"You won her over with breakfast meat," I teased. "You're lucky she enjoys dead animal carcasses."

"I prefer to think my smile won her over." He flashed a grin. I tucked myself under his arm as he finished frying the pig flesh.

Soon the house filled with family again, laughing, eating, enjoying. No one spoke of the elephant in the room. All too soon it was time for us to leave. Booker offered to move the tickets back to tomorrow, but I didn't want to risk putting my family in any more danger than I already had. Through tears and unrelenting hugs, we said our goodbyes and made our way to the cab after Booker gave Dad back his gun.

I fought back more tears as we got in the taxi and headed down my street, wondering when, if ever, I'd see everyone again. The taste of my salty tears reminded me. "I wanted to see the ocean." I dried my face. "Maybe next time." I struggled to sound optimistic, as if there'd be a next time.

Booker leaned forward. "We need to make a stop at the beach," he instructed the driver who then made a U-turn.

"Will we have time?" I looked down at my watch. We'd already left later than we were supposed to.

"We can probably squeak out ten minutes." He sounded confident, but his tight brow said otherwise.

We slipped off our shoes in the cab and rolled up our pants legs to save time. The driver dropped us as close as he could to the ocean side and we hurried to the water. I ran to the edge as a small wave rolled in, splashing up over my ankles. My phobia of water screamed at me and I backed up.

"Afraid?" Booker asked softly.

"Yes. I've let him take so much from me," I said soberly.

"If you're ready to reclaim this," he pointed to the ocean, "I'll help you however I can."

I looked at him, then back at the waves. Memories of the hours I'd spent in the ocean growing up washed over me. I took a deep breath. "I'm reclaiming this." I said it proudly, despite the nausea eating at me.

"It's colder than I remember," I said, stepping a few inches deeper into the water.

Booker laughed. "California or not, it is still January."

As I waded in deeper, I felt free. I lifted my arms in the air next to me and threw my head back, letting the salty wind rush over me.

"You're not going to yell 'I'm king of the world', are you?" he asked, undoubtedly referring to the *Titanic* movie I loathed.

I turned, laying my head on his chest. His arms came around me. "Thank you for the past two days. You've given me the strength I need to keep moving forward." I looked up into his chestnut brown eyes and kissed him. He gently kissed me back.

"I'm glad to see your smile again. I've been worried about you." He ran his hand over my ugly hair.

"Is that why you've not kissed me since all this happened?"

"I've kissed you," he scoffed.

"Innocent brotherly kisses, but never with passion," I insisted as we backed out of the water. "Is it because of what Garen did to me? Does it disgust you? You can be honest, Book. I won't be upset, nor would I—"

"Is that what you think?" he interrupted. "No, Tess. That's not it at all. I don't want to bring back bad memories. Besides, I can only imagine what is going on inside your head after that pig . . ." he shook his head. "My only thought is to let you heal."

"Promise?"

"Promise."

"Then kiss me, I mean really kiss me. Push every nightmare out and fill it with thoughts of only you."

So he did. He wrapped his arms around me and covered my mouth with his, but he held back still. I pushed him. I fisted my hands in his hair and held his face tight to mine, crushing my mouth hard to his. His hands cradled my head as he groaned my name. I hadn't realized my toes curled until my foot cramped. I pulled back first, and he didn't fight me. He rested his forehead on mine as his breath slowed.

The cabbie honked twice. "We'd better get going," he said, taking my hand.

I looked over my shoulder for one last look at the beautiful blue water. My heart was full from not only spending time with my family, but also knowing we were still in a good place despite my scummy ex. I turned my gaze to Booker. "I love you."

Chapter 30
BOOKER

"Welcome back, Book." Seth tossed a shovelful of snow at me as I walked up to his house. I scooped up a handful and chucked it at him, which he deflected with his shovel.

"I'm going back to San Diego," I complained, brushing the snow off my coat.

Seth pushed the cap he wore up his forehead and laughed. His cheeks and nose burned red from the cold. "Tess said the exact same thing this morning when she looked outside."

"I'll bet she did." She pretended all was good when I drove her to Seth's last night from the airport, but I knew she struggled with being back. Between the snow and her fear of Garen finding her, I don't think she felt the town had much to offer her. I only hoped I'd be enough to keep her here.

"She looks better than she did when she left. The trip was a good idea. She actually smiled at breakfast." Seth planted the shovel in a snow bank and removed his wool gloves, shoving them in the pockets of his coat. I followed him up the steps onto the porch where he brushed away icy crystals from his jeans. He straightened and rubbed his hands together. "Should have waited to take my gloves off."

I stood on the mat next to the door once we went inside, not wanting to track snow into the kitchen. Seth sat on a bench and removed his boots. "I'll get Tess," he said, rubbing his hands together again while walking into the kitchen. Maggie made her way down the stairs, meeting Seth halfway.

"Book's here," he said, slipping his arms around her waist.

"Tess is on her way," Maggie said, leaning in to kiss him, only he had other plans. He slipped his freezing cold hands up the back of her shirt. She squealed, pushed him back, and ran down the stairs to the sink. "You do that again and I'll use the squirter thingy on you." She pulled the side spray out and aimed it at him. "Fine, but hot water, please," Seth insisted. "I'm freezing."

Tess came down the stairs, interrupting the show. "Sorry, Booker. I'm still on California time, I'm afraid." She hurried over to the fridge and removed a paper sack, her lunch I assumed, and rushed toward me.

"Garfield, I didn't see you." Maggie waved at me from the sink, the side spray still in her hand.

"Mornin', Prego. How you feeling?" I helped Tess on with her coat as Seth quietly crept toward Magpie.

"Great. No more nausea. And the exhaustion's pass—"

"Maggie, over your right shoulder," Tess warned Mags of her encroaching hubby. Maggie, with notoriously poor aim, sprayed toward Seth, missing him completely.

"Hurry. Let's get out of here before we get wet." I grabbed Tess's hand and we darted out the door. Once inside the truck, I cranked up the heater.

"Those two are cute together. They're so happy," Tess said wistfully.

"They're perfect for each other. As are Lilah and Cole."

"I love Lilah." Tess laughed softly, no doubt at some crazy memory involving Lilah. It warmed my heart to see her happy.

"I thought the truck was for when we had deep snow. There's only six inches on the ground. Spent too much time in sunny Cali, Gatto. You're getting soft," she teased. I loved it when she called me by my last name.

"The heater's going out in my car."

"We can drive mine." She pointed to the rusty Honda covered in snow as we drove away.

"No thanks. I want to make sure we get to the office in one piece."

"Rude." Tess playfully pushed my arm.

"Honestly, I've had two people over the past week comment that I must not be a very good lawyer if I have to drive the POC. Enough procrastinating. I'm going to have to get a new car." I shook my head dramatically adding, "I'm going to miss the old POC mobile."

"Just breathe. It will be okay," she assured me. After a few silent moments she asked quietly, "So, any news on . . ."

"No. Not yet." I took her cold hand in mine. "We'll get him," I assured her. She said nothing else about him.

She jogged from the truck into the office building, and we took the elevator to our floor. "It's freezing in the office, too," she groaned, making a swooshing sound as she rubbed her hands over her down coat.

I tapped on the thermostat. Fifty-two degrees. I twisted the dial but the furnace didn't turn on.

"Maybe you should call the owner," she grumbled. "Tell the cheapskate to fix the elevator, too."

"Hey," I said, crossing over to her. I wrapped her up in my arms. "I resemble that remark." I kissed the tip of her frozen nose. "And what's wrong with the elevator?" I seldom used it. Like she said, too creaky and slow.

"Are you kidding me? My grandma can walk up the stairs faster than that thing moves, and she's been dead for ten years." She snuggled in closer. "It also has more creaks and groans than my grandmother did. It doesn't sound very safe."

"It's not that bad."

"Not that bad? Did you not pay attention while we were riding up it just now?"

"Nope. I was lost in those beautiful blue eyes of yours."

"You are a charmer, Booker Gatto." She gave me a quick peck on the cheek.

"I'll call a repairman." I started for the phone only she wouldn't release me.

"Warm me up first," she said, wagging her eyebrows.

"Whatever it takes to keep my renters happy." I dropped my mouth to hers.

An annoying shoe tapping and a female clearing her throat trashed a perfectly good fantasy. I pulled back and turned to the tapping. Nikkolynn.

"Yes?" I said as Tess went to her desk and turned on her computer, zipping her coat higher.

"I need to talk to you, away from Terese's ears." Nik pointed to my office and strutted past me.

"Why does she call you by your full name?" I asked Tess.

"Probably hoping to intimidate me. Don't worry about it." She waved her hand in the air.

I scrubbed my jaw and followed the two-timing liar into my office. She started to close the door, but I stopped her. No way was I allowing Tess out of my sight, not until Garen was found.

"This is personal," Nik pressed.

"Sorry. You'll have to talk quietly, then." I folded my arms and sat on the corner of my desk with Tess firmly in view and signaled for Nik to continue.

"Bookie," she said stepping directly in front of me and walking her hand up my arm. "I know I've done some pretty lousy things to you—"

"Ya' think?"

She continued, undaunted by my sour expression. "I *am* really sorry. I'm here to beg for your forgiveness and to ask that you please give me another chance. We were good together, Bookie. You know that. Besides, I'll bet I'm more exciting than her." With a jerk of her chin, she pointed at Tess, who busily typed away.

"Nikkolynn, Tess is not the reason I won't take you back." I stood and paced across the room. "I can't trust you. It's that simple. And whether I'm dating her, or anyone else for that matter, has nothing to do with it. If Tess were to dump me tomorrow," *heaven forbid*, "I wouldn't take you back. If a relationship doesn't have trust, it has nothing."

"But—"

"But nothing, Nikkolynn. I will not take you back. I forgive you for cheating on me and for using me, but I'm sorry, we're through."

She stood there, tears wetting her makeup covered cheeks. I stepped next to her and wrapped my arm around her shoulder, brotherly like. "Nik, I thought you were going to that fashion school in New York." I patted her back.

"It doesn't start until spring. But it doesn't matter. I can't afford the tuition since no one will hire me thanks to my record." She pulled away and reached for a tissue on my desk, which she used to dry her cheeks and blow her nose.

I went to my desk and pulled out my checkbook. "How much is the tuition?" I asked.

"$22,000," she said with a sniffle. I wrote her a check and handed it to her. She looked at it then at me. "This is for a lot more than tuition."

"I added money for room and board." She tried hugging me, but I stepped back. "Start your life over, Nik. Do well at school and put your past behind you."

"I will, promise. Thank you." She headed out the door, then stopped and angled back to me. "I'll always love you." She said it loud enough that Tess glanced up from her computer.

"Good luck, Nikkolynn," I said. Her lower lip trembled as she left.

"Tess, will you bring me the building file?" I wheeled around toward my desk. "I need to call the furnace guy before we freeze to death." I was tackled from behind before I reached my desk.

"You are a real sweetheart, you know that, right?" Tess's arms were around my shoulders, squeezing me tight, her cheek resting on my shoulder.

"Once again, you're putting me on a pedestal when I don't deserve it." I twisted around in her arms. "I gave her the money so she'd leave town."

"Whatever," she said, kissing my neck with her icy cold lips, chasing a shiver up my spine. "I'd like to think that was because of my sensual kisses, but it's probably from my cold lips."

"Maybe both," I said diplomatically.

"I'll get the file." She pulled away. I missed her already, cold lips and all.

I called the manager at Port Fare Heating and they sent a repairman out immediately. He went to the furnace room on the main floor and returned to my office ten minutes later.

"Hello," I glanced at the name tag sewn on his shirt, "Hank, what did you find?"

"Do you want the good news or the bad," he asked, glancing at Tess and winking.

"Just tell me what's wrong," I said, *and keep your eyes off my girl.*

"The entire unit for this floor is bad and will need to be replaced. The good news is it's under warranty so won't cost you a thing." He glanced again at Tess, who kept her eyes glued to her laptop. "The bad news is the unit's in Buffalo and with this weather it's going to take me several hours to get it."

"The snow's melting." I pointed out the window. "It's up to forty-two degrees already."

"A virtual heat wave," Tess mumbled under her breath.

"But like I said, the replacement unit is in Buffalo, and it's still snowing over there," he pointed out. "I can have it in by tonight so you'll have heat tomorrow. That's the best I can do."

"Fine. Thanks," I grumbled.

He handed me an invoice. "Do you really own this entire building?"

"Yes. Why?"

"My aunt works at that diner across the road." He pointed out the window at Shelly's Café, a diner I'd eaten at a few times. Lousy food. Lousy service. "She's seen you driving down the road in a beat-up piece of crap car and said you must not be a very good lawyer." He looked around. "I'm guessing you must have spent all your money on this building." He left with another sideways glance at Tess.

"See what I mean? That's three people in one week who've dissed my car," I said incredulously, adding, "Did you see him checking you out?"

Her lips pinched together and she grabbed the new purse Lilah had given her. "Should I take the laptop? I assume we're going to work at your place."

"Leave it. I have a better idea." I took her hand. "We never picked out your Christmas gift. Might as well do it now."

"My gun?" Her eyes lit up.

"Your gun." I locked the office. "But please tell me you're not going to get a pink one." Nikkolynn had a pink gun. She hadn't a clue how to use it, but she had one, nonetheless.

Tess pressed the button to the elevator instead of heading to the stairs. "I promise, no pink. Come on. I want to show you how long it takes to get downstairs." The thing rattled to life as it made its way to us. "See." She pointed to the doors as they creaked open ever so slowly. She glanced inside the elevator, making sure it was empty—or rather making sure Garen wasn't inside waiting to pounce. She pressed the main button, giving me an *I told you so* look as we made our creaky descent.

I reached over and pressed the large red emergency break button and we screeched to a stop. Her hands went to her hips. "The owner's not going to be pleased if you break his elevator. And what if it won't start back up? You'll be in big trouble, mister."

Her arms wrapped around my neck as she lectured. "Some things are worth the risks," I said before kissing her. Oh yeah, definitely worth it.

~*~

We drove directly to the gun store across from the mall, slowing as we passed a car dealership. Both Tess and I glanced out at the snow-covered cars. "You should get that." She pointed to a sporty black convertible. "One of my guilty pleasures is Jags. Jaguars," she clarified, as if that were necessary.

"Tess, I'm a guy. Every guy knows what a Jag is. It's embedded in our DNA."

"My brother had a black Jag Hot Wheel car that he loved. He carried it everywhere. You can blame him for my obsession." She turned to me. "Do you want to take a peek?"

"You do realize that if I get a Jaguar, as in, big cat, I'll never hear the end of it from Magpie," I pointed out. "I was thinking more along the lines of an Avalon. Or maybe a Lexus. That says Successful Lawyer, don't you think?"

"A Lexus?" Her eyes widened in disdain. "Okay, *Cole*, get a nice safe Lexus." Aside from being a klutz and a great guy, Cole's taste in cars leaned to the boring side and I often teased him about it.

I laughed heartily, mostly because it pleased me to see Tess get her spunk back. "I won't tell him you said that."

We parked in front of the gun shop. I loved the store. I loved the woodsy smell. I loved the displays, everything from camping to hunting to fishing gear. And I loved the guns—from pistols to rifles, they had it all.

"How can I help you today?" asked a burly man with long hair and beard. He reminded me of the guys on the reality show, Duck something or other. He even had a duck call on a tether around his neck.

"Are you one of those brother's from the duck TV show?" I had to ask, since the resemblance was so uncanny.

"No. My name's Nate, but I get that all the time. Must be the facial hair." He stroked his untamed beard. "Is Uncle Si crazy or what?"

I laughed. "I know, right? He makes the show, although I do like the older brother, too," I said, eyeing a nice bow hanging on the wall above him.

"Jase. He's a good ole boy," Nate agreed. "What can I help you with today?"

"Do you carry the Glock Nineteen Gen Four?" I loved how the words rolled off Tess's tongue like hot butter. The woman knew guns.

"I do." He pulled out a key, opened the display case, and grabbed the gun, setting it on a cloth on the counter. "This Gen Four is becoming more and more popular, probably because of its size."

Tess took the gun and bounced her hand up and down to test the weight of it. She laid it across her palm, no doubt testing the size against her hand. "Does it break down easily for cleaning?" Before Nate could answer her, Tess disassembled the gun and reassembled it in rapid succession. Nate gave me an impressed look. I beamed proudly.

She looked at several more guns but in the end decided on the first. "Here's the permit form." Nate handed her a twenty-six-page *book*, really. "You're going to want to take this home and fill it out. Bring it back with the proper ID." He opened the form and highlighted what she had to bring back with her. "It takes New York six to nine months to approve the paperwork."

She took the book. "Another reason to hate it here." She stuffed it into her bag. "First I'll have to get my real license replaced since I'm taking back my real name. Who knows how long that takes? How am I supposed to protect myself until then?"

"Tess, I'll protect you. And Seth will when you are at his house," I assured her.

She spun around and faced me, her eyes lit up like the fourth of July. "*You'll* protect me? What? Am I a poor defenseless female who needs a big strong man around?" She stormed out to the truck and continued her tirade. "This is the twenty-first century, buddy. I don't—"

"Whoa," I interrupted, cupping her face in my hands. "I'm sorry. I didn't mean to offend you. I'm just a stupid male so please have some pity on my pathetic species. We say dumb things all the time."

She fell into my arms. "I want my gun back. I feel vulnerable without it." She took a few jerky breaths. "I know that's stupid since I've never used it to protect myself, and it certainly didn't help me the last time Garen showed up, but it gives me peace of mind."

I stroked her hair. "Let's go over to my place. I think I can help your peace of mind."

We drove directly to my house. I led her to the den, where I kept my gun safe. Opening it, I said, "You can choose any one you feel comfortable with."

Her face lit up as she held the Derringer first. "My dad has this gun, only his has a pearl handle. I miss him already," she mumbled. She set it down and examined a few others. Picking up my Glock twenty-three, she nodded. "This one." She turned to me. "Are you sure about this? You know I don't have a concealed weapon permit."

I plugged my ears. "Lalalala, I didn't hear that." She smiled. I locked the gun safe. "They make that model in neon green, too. If you want we can get you that instead of the Gen Four."

"Tempting," she said. "But I like the Gen Four."

"I got my love of guns from my dad, too. Then Seth's dad after my father died." I slipped the twenty-three in a zipper case before adding several fully loaded magazines. No use having a gun without ammo. "Should we do some target practice so you feel comfortable with it?"

"Yes. And I'm sorry I got angry earlier."

"No apologies needed." I kissed her forehead. "Let's go."

At the range, I gave her a brief rundown of the gun, but she didn't need it. At first I held off telling her that despite the fact that the magazine held thirteen bullets, New York law dictated no more than seven bullets per magazine. When I did summon the courage, she only mumbled, "Great. More good news for whack-jobs like the ex."

We each put on our ear protection. "You go first," she insisted. I fired off the seven rounds in rapid succession, hitting the bull's-eye five out of seven times. The sixth and seventh shots were just outside the inner circle.

Tess fired next after reloading the magazine. She too fired off her rounds quickly. She outscored me, hitting the bull's-eye dead center each time. We slipped of the earmuffs as we looked over the target.

"Put down that gun and come here," I teased. "I think I'm in love."

Before she could, the door to the shooting range flew open, startling us. Instinctively, Tess turned and pointed the gun at the intruder, who stopped dead.

"Whoa." The kid that checked us in earlier threw his hands up. The gun wasn't loaded, but he didn't know that. "Just wanted to let you know we're closing in ten minutes." He darted out the door.

Tess set the gun down and sank onto a bench, dropped her head into her hands and broke down. "I'm trying so hard to put *him* out of my mind, but I can't. I'm tired of being terrified at every little noise."

I sat down next to her and wrapped my arm around her shoulders. "I know you are, Tess. I know you are."

Chapter 31
Tess

I tucked Booker's gun into the new purse Lilah gave me. While the purse wasn't one I would have picked with its bold orange color, it had a great side pocket, perfect for storing the Glock. I headed downstairs, not wanting to be late.

We had no news on Garen yet. I hated leaving the safety of Seth's house more and more each day, but I didn't want to become a hermit either. I still struggled to reclaim my life.

A heavenly scent filled the air before I reached the bottom step. Seth stood at the stove creating another masterpiece, if the smell were any indication. Living here had its perks.

"Perfect timing." Seth smiled and set an omelet garnished with a dollop of sour cream on the bar. I parked my hungry butt on the stool. He handed me a fork and stood next to me with a paper and pen, waiting for my review. "Remember, don't spare my feelings," he said.

"Seth, will you stop already?" Maggie came out of the laundry room with a couple of shirts in her hand and some socks. She still wore her pink flannel nightgown, along with a pair of fuzzy slippers. Quite the contrast to Seth with his black pants and white chef's jacket. "Tess, you don't have to evaluate everything you eat." Her eyes narrowed on Seth, who set the paper down. "She's not going to want to eat here anymore if you keep doing this."

Maggie shook her head and went upstairs. As soon as she was out of sight, Seth picked up the pad and pen again. "She's grumpy because she didn't get enough sleep last night. She used to just get loopy, but ever since she got pregnant she gets like that." He gestured upstairs.

"Is she not feeling well?" I asked, biting into the incredible omelet. I wondered if he ever made anything that wasn't delicious.

"Leg cramps. Doctor said it was normal. She and Lilah were out shopping for the nursery all day yesterday," he said, yawning.

"I'll bet you didn't get much sleep either." I took another bite. "Oh, and five on presentation." He liked me to grade the food not only on taste, but presentation also, five being the highest mark.

"I massaged her legs to help alleviate some of the pain," he explained, eagerly writing down the five. "I worked for the MET for a number of years. Lack of sleep doesn't faze me." He yawned again.

"I can see that." My voice weighed with sarcasm.

"I mean I don't get ornery like some people. I just get sleepy," he assured me. "How about the taste?" He pointed to my plate. "I think I went a little heavy on the Aged Gouda."

"Aged . . .?" I looked at him, completely lost

"Cheese. This has four different cheeses and crab meat." I had to swallow my grin. I found the seriousness he and Booker put into cooking hilarious. "Here." He handed me a slice of cheese. "Taste this and tell me if you think the same taste overpowers the omelet."

Again, I held back my laugh as I bit into the cheese and instantly knew what he meant. "You're right. The omelet is a little heavy with this."

As he feverishly wrote, Maggie came flying down the stairs. "You're not going to believe this. Look outside. Hurry." My first thought was of Garen. Somehow he'd found me. My heart pounded against my ribs. Then I noticed the huge grin on Maggie's face.

Seth rushed to the window and pulled back the curtains. "Is that a . . . It is. Booker got himself a Jag." Seth's face lit up like a Christmas tree as he turned to Maggie.

"Jag as in Jaguar?" she asked. Seth nodded.

"Go easy on him, Mags. Don't take your bad mood it out on him," Seth warned, heading for the door.

Maggie stomped her foot. "I. Am. Not. In…" She stopped, and exhaled loudly. "Okay, I'm a little ornery, sorry." She kissed Seth's cheek before turning to me. "But Book is so getting harassed for this. I mean, seriously. A Jaguar!" She waved me to follow and we both slipped on our boots and coats. Seth went out in his slippers and chef's hat, but no coat. Maggie grabbed it for him. "Men," she grumbled.

Seth and Booker circled the car like two hungry tigers waiting to pounce as we walked down the driveway. "Here." She tossed Seth's coat at him. He caught it, but didn't put it on.

Booker mouthed, *not enough sleep?* to Seth. Seth nodded and laughed, though he tried to cover it with a cough.

"I saw what you said, catman." Maggie shot him a nasty glare. He mocked fear by stepping back and blocking his face with crossed wrists.

"Nice car. Jaguar, right?" I asked with a wink.

"It most certainly is." He practically glowed. "Like the color? It's called Satellite Grey Metallic."

"I would have called it gun metal," I said.

"That's what I thought, too. In fact, that's why I picked it." He ran his hand along the hood.

"Don't touch the paint job." Seth took the edge of his chef's coat and wiped off Booker's fingerprints.

"I am not going to be ridiculous like you and my grandfather were over the silly Aston Martin." Booker leaned against the hood.

"Don't worry, sweetie. He didn't mean it. The Aston Martin is not a silly car." Maggie rubbed Seth's back dramatically. Seth rolled his eyes.

"Didn't you once say you were a simple man with simple tastes?" Maggie asked. "I hardly call this simple. This is a blatant display—" She stopped. "Okay, I'm going to go back inside and get some sleep before I alienate all my friends and family."

Seth gave her a quick hug. "If your legs bother you, let me know. I'll come massage them." She gave him the okay sign as she made her way inside.

"Six more months, my friend." Booker slapped Seth on the back. "We'd better get going. I have a phone conference at ten," he said to me.

"What? Wait. I want to take it for a spin," Seth said, his voice bordering on hysterical.

"I'll get my purse." I jogged inside and grabbed some workout clothes. I hadn't done yoga in forever and my stiff back protested when I woke this morning. I hoped to squeak out some time later today to go downstairs to the gym.

Seth came in as I left, his coat still in his hands. His lips were blue. *Mag's right. Men.* Booker held the car door open for me and I slid onto the warm seat.

"Seat warmers are standard in Jags in Upstate New York," he beamed. "Pretty sweet, huh?" He ran his hand over the dark gray dashboard.

"Very. And you're closer to me now." I leaned over and kissed him. "Convenient."

"Keep that up and I'll let you drive it later." He kissed me back. "Yup. You are definitely driving this later."

"I didn't know you were going car shopping after you dropped me off." I turned up my seat warmer.

"I wasn't, but on my way home I happened to drive by the car lot again. I stopped just to look and, well, they had this Jag with only seven thousand miles on it. It's practically brand new." He glanced at me. "The guy was a master salesman. He had me at hello." He chuckled and pressed a button on the dash. "He even gave me fifty dollars for the POC, sight unseen. I was in the truck when I bought the Jag, but when I brought the POC in an hour later to pick up the Jag, his face turned a little green."

"Fifty? Can't believe you got that," I snorted softly. "I thought you were getting a Lexus."

"Yeah, right, after your Cole comment?" he said drily.

"Didn't they have a convertible on the lot when we drove by yesterday?" My personal favorite.

"They did, but convertibles aren't very practical for Upstaters." He gestured to a snow bank to make his point.

"Oh, right. Yet another good reason to move to Cali."

As promised, they replaced the heater in our office. The place was toasty warm when we arrived. Between not having worked yesterday, and our trip to see my family, we were really behind. We worked at a fever's pitch all day. Booker ordered in lunch so we wouldn't have to stop. By five-thirty, I was spent.

"Hey, handsome." I slid his rolling chair back and slumped onto his lap. I wrapped my fingers up in his hair. He grinned lazily. "I was hoping to get some yoga in after work. Do you want to come downstairs with me?"

"I do enjoy your Downward Facing Dog." He nibbled on my neck. It didn't take long to get lost in a kiss.

I pulled back first. "You're never going to win that bet if you keep kissing me like that," I said, breathless.

"I've been thinking about that stupid bet," he grumbled. "If I lose, you win, so what's to stop you from doing whatever it takes to sabotage me? Seriously, those lips of yours are a secret weapon."

"Then by all means, we shouldn't kiss." I stepped away.

"Let's not get hasty." He pulled me back. "I have a better idea. If I win, I'll give you the prize money. You can use it to buy whatever you want. A new car, maybe."

"Are you serious?"

"Yes. You already know I only made the bet to keep from getting lost in a physical relationship with you right away," he reminded me. "And I'm a guy, so there's no way I *want* to lose, but I'm going to need your help."

"If you're sure, then I'm in." I snuggled in closer.

"I'm sure. Besides, if I don't have your help with the bet, I'm a dead man." I bounced on his shoulder as he laughed. "I love you, Tess." He stroked my cheek.

I kissed him softly. "And I you."

"Why do you need me to watch you do yoga anyway? You're carrying the gun in your purse, right?"

"Despite my stupid remark yesterday about not needing you to protect me," I said sheepishly, "I feel safer with you, if anything for an extra pair of eyes."

"I wish I could, but I have a dinner meeting at seven in Syracuse, remember?" He glanced at his watch. "In fact, I need to leave in half an hour."

"That's right. I forgot." I frowned.

"You can come with me if you want. I'll even let you drive the Jag," he tempted.

It took me all of a nanosecond to agree. "Yes!" I gave him a quick kiss and hurried out to straighten my desk.

Ten minutes later his cell phone rang. "Hey, Brent. Tell me you found him," I heard him say. Brent was one of Booker's buddies who'd been working on tracking Garen down. "You did?" I jumped up and ran into the office. Booker looked at me, all smiles. "Dead? Are you sure?" My heart leapt. Dead meant Garen was forever out of my life. I should've felt guilty for thinking that, yet I didn't, not even a little. Booker said yes and okay a few more times, and asked, "Are you sure?" before hanging up.

I broke down in tears. Booker pulled me into his arms. "It's over, babe. All over. Garen's dead."

I emptied my soul of all the fears I'd carried around with me for years. No more looking over my shoulder. No more worrying about opening the door and finding Garen there, waiting to kill me. Free. Finally free of the putrid sickness named Garen. I cried so hard my body shook. Booker held me tight, stroking my hair and reassuring me.

"What happened?" I asked wiping at my tears several minutes later.

"That phone call was from my buddy Brent from the Port Fare PD. Seems Garen was over in Buffalo. The clerk recognized him from the flyers." Book handed me another tissue. "The clerk, a nineteen year old sophomore at UB decided to be a hero and confront him. He told Garen he knew who he was and was calling the cops. The ballsy clerk produced a gun from under the counter, which is totally illegal, but we won't go there. Garen's seen on the tape begging the kid not to shoot him, claiming he's innocent and that you were some sort of psycho chick, bent on destroying his life. Thankfully, the clerk didn't buy it. Garen jumped him. They fought over the gun and it went off, killing Garen."

"How fitting he died committing an act of violence." I stood and paced across the room. "It's over. It's finally over. No more hiding. No more fearing every little sound." I turned to Booker as he came closer. "I'm free. It's as if this huge weight's been lifted off me." I jumped into his arms. "I'm completely free." Booker cinched his arms around my waist and spun me in a circle, then set me down. I wrapped my hands around his jaws and kissed him soundly. "I'm free."

"Yes, you are." He hugged me tight. I broke down on his shoulder again, still purging the pain, sorrow, and fear that consumed my life for far too long.

"Pull it together, Tess," I lectured myself.

"No. Let it out," Booker encouraged. "After all you've been through, you deserve this moment."

"Thanks." I bit the inside of my cheek to keep from bursting into tears yet again.

"We need to head to Syracuse," he said, grabbing his briefcase and putting a couple of files inside. "We can talk more about this on the drive over."

Syracuse. I completely forgot. I didn't want to be trapped in a car for over an hour each way. I wanted to run down the streets, shouting.

I needed to do some yoga. "Would you mind if I didn't go? Now that I no longer have anything to fear, I'd really like to do some yoga."

"How are you going to get to Seth's after? I won't be back until late, probably close to ten." He snapped his briefcase shut. "I don't have time to drop you off."

"That's right. We drove here together." I sat in a chair in front of his desk. He tugged the curtains closed and it sparked my memory.

"Wait. Lilah has to pick up some curtains around six-thirty at the shop just around the corner. I bet she'll give me a ride to Maggie's."

"I know she will. Check and make sure that's still a go." While he finished getting ready, I called Lilah from my desk. She was more than willing to pick me up, and since Cole had to work late, she offered to take me to dinner to celebrate my new freedom.

Booker rushed out of his office as I hung up. "I have to go. Are you coming?"

"Lilah's going to pick me up. Are you sure you're okay with me not going?" I slipped my arms around his neck.

"Yes. Go enjoy your sweaty yoga," he teased. "I'll stop by Seth's on the way back." He gave me a quick kiss and left.

I straightened the office and then made three phone calls, all extremely important. One to my mom and dad, and one to each of my siblings. After I hung up, promising to call them each again later, I grabbed my workout clothes and stepped into the bathroom to change.

When I came out, I wasn't alone.

Chapter 32

"You alone?"

Startled, I stepped back. "What are you doing here?" No answer. I moved cautiously to my desk and gathered my purse from the drawer. I slipped my clothes inside and repositioned Booker's gun on top. Ridiculous, really. It's not like Nikkolynn was a threat, but her demeanor bothered me. I glanced up at her again as she stepped closer to me. Her face was red and tearstained. She'd been crying.

"So w-where's Booker?" she stuttered. She hugged herself tightly, her purse wedged under her arms.

"He left for the day." The phone rang. I didn't answer it. The office was officially closed. The answering machine could get it. My yoga time dwindled fast.

"Is he at home?" she pressed.

"No. He has a meeting in Syracuse." I pushed my purse handle onto my shoulder and walked past her to the door.

"So, are you and Booker officially together?" she asked.

I angled back to her. I guess having run for the past four years, I'd grown weary of cowering. Or maybe I felt empowered because Garen was dead. Whatever the reason, I'd had enough of Nikkolynn. "Yes, we're together. I love him."

Her eyes narrowed slightly. "Has he asked you to marry him?" She snugged her purse tighter.

"No. We've not discussed marriage. When do you leave for New York?"

She ignored my question. "I still love him." Tears welled in her hazel eyes. "I keep hoping he'll change his mind and give me another chance, but I'm starting to give up." She wiped her nose with her hand.

My heart softened. "Nik, even if he doesn't marry me, he'll find someone eventually. You really should go to New York and start over."

"I came to the same conclusion earlier today. In fact, I bought my plane ticket to New York already. I decided it's best to leave town right away. Start over . . ." She burst into tears.

I patted her back and let her cry. "It's going to be alright. You'll find someone who will make you just as happy, you'll see." The poor thing continued to cry for several minutes.

She took a deep breath. "Loving him is like a disease, you know. And there's no cure," she said dramatically. I'd have laughed at the cliché if she didn't look so sad. "But you're right. It's time to move on."

I held open the door and she walked out and to the elevator. "I'll tell him you stopped by," I said as she pressed the button.

"No. It's probably better you don't. My flight leaves tomorrow. It's time."

I nodded as the doors groaned open. She stepped one foot inside and stopped. "I don't know if I can do this," she said, her eyes fluttering to keep back the tears.

"Once you get to New York, things will be much better, Nikkolynn. You'll see." She slipped inside the death trap and nodded weakly as the doors creaked to a close.

I hurried down the stairs to the basement. I only had fifteen minutes left. Bikram yoga was out. No way would the basement heat up before Lilah came. I'd have to do a hard and fast routine. Time for a little of my Lindsey Stirling addiction. I fished the CD from my bag.

"We meet again." I jumped back at the sound of a man's voice. I hadn't expected to find anyone in the gym. A tall, nice looking guy approached from the treadmills, a brown towel around his neck, his hand extended. "Judging from the look of confusion on your face, I'm guessing you don't remember me. My name's Devin. I'm the patent lawyer on the third floor." He shook my hand. "I dropped some forms off for Booker to look over back in October."

"I'm sorry. I'm terrible at remembering names." And apparently faces. I couldn't recall ever meeting him before, let alone seeing him in the office.

"No problem. You were pretty busy typing up some documents." He wiped his brow with the towel.

"It's nice to meet you, again." Still jittery, I took a deep breath and worked my way to the mats, setting my purse next to the weight rack. Devin came over and picked up his water bottle from the floor near my purse. *Garen's dead. It's over. Relax.* I turned and smiled.

"Book tells me you're the best secretary to walk the earth." He took a long pull from his bottle.

"He exaggerates," I assured him.

"Not so sure about that. The docs he's faxed me from his office are flawless. You do good work." He wiped his brow again. "I'd better get going. It was nice meeting you again."

"Same." I smiled as he headed for the door.

"Hey, if you ever get tired of working for Booker, the door's always open. The secretary I have now is a nightmare." He grimaced. "Thankfully she's temporary."

"Your regular secretary quit?" I did my best to make small talk, not wanting to come across as rude or snobby.

"Yes. And like I said, this one's . . .." He frowned.

"Why not hire another one if she's so bad?"

"She's my mom." He chuckled heartily. "She's filling in until I can find a new one. And trust me, I'm looking." He waved and left.

I rushed to the sound system and put in my CD, cranking up the volume since I was the only one in the gym. I ran through my short routine, finishing with a few minutes to spare. I'd arranged to meet Lilah here, and since she hadn't arrived yet, thanks to the latest snowstorm I'm sure, I went through a few dance moves. I felt free, for the first time in years. To celebrate, I attempted a triple pirouette, something I'd not done in years. I fell flat on my face at the sound of my name.

"Hello, Terese."

Chapter 33
BOOKER

"I'm gonna be late." It didn't help that it grew darker by the minute as snow clouds filled the sky. It began snowing about ten miles ago and steadily grew worse. I looked at the clock on the dash. "I'm supposed to be there in thirty minutes. Yup. Definitely gonna be late." Now would have been the perfect time to put the overpriced car to the test, but with the snow I didn't dare. I reached for what I thought was the windshield wipers, flipping the turn signal on instead. "Crap." Nothing was where I was used to it being and it drove me nuts. I flipped a few more levers before the wipers came on.

I relaxed into my seat. "Give it some time. You'll get used to it," I counseled myself. I thought back to Tess's face when she learned about Garen. The elation in her eyes, the ear-to-ear smile. It felt good knowing he'd never bother her again. Honestly, the scum wore on me, too. I'd had more than one nightmare of walking into work or in the gym and finding Tess dead, beaten to death by Garen.

"Stop torturing yourself, Gatto," I grumbled. The entire car filled with the ringing of my phone. The salesman set up the Bluetooth for me. I smiled and pressed the answer button on my steering wheel.

"Gatto, here."

"Booker, it's Brent. Just wanted to update you on the Garen Johnson case." Brent's voice sounded loud and clear over the car stereo. *Nice.*

"Go ahead."

"The information we got wasn't accurate."

"Meaning?" I immediately lightened up on the gas pedal.

"Meaning it was the clerk that was shot and killed. Johnson escaped in a stolen late model gray sedan with a dented front fender. I'm still working on getting a license plate number for the car."

I slammed my hand on the steering wheel. "Are you even sure it was Johnson?"

"I checked the surveillance tape myself not more than ten minutes ago. He looks a little rough around the edges, but it's him. We have him on tape admitting to the clerk he was Johnson. I'm sorry, Booker. We'll keep looking. The good news is that the weather in Buffalo is terrible, and it's heading to Port Fare. It's highly unlikely he left the area."

"It's snowing pretty badly here, too. Thanks for the heads up, Brent."

I debated calling Tess at the office. "She's probably in the basement doing her sweaty yoga," I mumbled to myself, fighting the uneasy feeling in my gut.

But I needed to call someone to go check on her, to let her know the truth, just to be safe. "Seth," I mumbled. I pushed what I thought was the call button and somehow ended up turning the flashers on. After trying a few more buttons, I pulled over and called Seth the old fashioned way. I punched his number in on my cell.

"Hi, Book. Are you out in this nastiness?" he asked.

"On my way to a meeting in Syracuse," I explained. "I need a favor. We got news that Garen's been caught."

"Awesome," he replied.

"No. It was a mistake. He's still out there somewhere and he's killed a clerk. But Tess thinks he's dead." I turned on what I hoped was the defroster. I hadn't noticed my short, shallow breaths until the windows clouded over. "I think she's downstairs working out," I said. "Would you mind running over there and making sure everything's okay?"

"Book, Mags and I are on our way back from Buffalo. The roads are a mess. I'm afraid it's going to be a while before we reach Port Fare, but we'll check on her when we get back. How is she getting to our place if you're in Syracuse?"

"Lilah. In about thirty minutes." I shoved my hand through my hair. "Don't worry about it. I'm overreacting, as usual."

"Maybe Lilah can go over early?" Seth suggested.

"Right. Thanks. Drive carefully," I said.

"You, too."

After he hung up, I called Lilah. It went straight to voice mail. I dropped my head against the headrest, willing my stomach to calm. "Call again in a few minutes. Maybe she's busy with Sofia," I counseled myself.

I pulled back onto the freeway and headed for my meeting. Five minutes later, my phone rang again. It was the client in Syracuse cancelling our appointment because of the weather. Worked for me. I got off at the next exit and got back on again, this time heading for my office, and to Tess.

Snow now packed the road, making it dangerous to go very fast. I should have gotten the stupid Lexus. The Jag was too light and slid everywhere in the snow. "Calm down, Gatto," I told myself for the hundredth time. Until today, no one had even seen Garen. Chances of his showing up in Port Fare today were pretty slim. And yet the hairs on my neck stood on end. I couldn't do it again. I couldn't live through another murder of someone I loved. I punched the gas pedal. I had to get to Tess.

When I started across the overpass, I hit a patch of ice. My car spun in three circles, hit the guardrail, and ricocheted into a snow bank.

"Great. You don't even know if she's in danger, you madman." I got out of the car and inspected the right rear fender. Ruined. That would cost me a pretty penny. I hadn't even owned the car for twenty-four hours.

A couple of teens in a suburban pulled up behind me. A blue and orange checked hat popped out the unrolled window, followed by a head covered in bushy blond hair. "Hey, man, need some help?"

"That'd be great. Thanks." The blond guy, who introduced himself simply as Fred, helped me push the car back onto the road.

"Dude, this is a nice car." He tugged his hat over his beet-red ears and circled the Jag, shaking his head. "Too bad about the fender, but it doesn't look too bad. The body seems to be intact."

"I hope it runs." I said, brushing the snow off my pants.

"I'll wait for you to try before I leave." He shook my hand and jogged back to his suburban.

"Thanks," I called after him. I got in and started the car without a hitch. I waved to Fred, and started back to Tess. *She's going to laugh when she sees what I did to my new car.*

I slowed my pace, not wanting a repeat of what just happened. I was close now, maybe ten minutes away. I called Lilah, this time she answered.

"Lilah, I'll pick up Tess."

"Good. I didn't want to take Sofia out in this storm. Arizona girls and snow don't get along," she said. "Perfect timing, too. I was just about to walk out the door."

As soon as I hung up, traffic came to a dead stop. I looked down the freeway and spotted red and blue flashing lights ahead. Now Tess would be waiting for who knows how long. I almost called Lilah back, but decided to give Brent a call instead. He'd probably be out in the storm anyway, dealing with emergencies.

"Hey, Brent. Booker again. I need a favor."

"Sure thing."

"Tess is at the office alone and I'm stuck behind an accident on the four-ninety. Can you swing by and make sure you don't see Garen or the gray sedan around? I know it's a long shot that he's in the area, but just want to be safe."

"I drove by your office not more than five minutes ago. The parking lot was completely empty except for a couple of vans for the satellite company. The parking lot hasn't even been plowed yet."

I released a long breath. The satellite vans were stored there at night. Tess was safe. "Thanks, that makes me feel much better."

"No prob. Got to go. We've had six accidents in town already. We're swamped. You'd think people would know how to drive in this stuff, having lived here their entire lives." He chuckled. "Take care."

"You too." I leaned back and scrubbed my jaw. "She's safe."

They cleared the accident quickly and I was on my way within ten minutes. I drove directly to the office.

Next to the satellite vans, a lone car sat in the parking lot.

A late model gray sedan with a dented front fender.

Chapter 34
Tess

"But . . . you're dead."

Completely stunned, I didn't stand. I didn't scream. Instead, I lay in the middle of the mat with my mouth open, looking up at Garen.

"Sorry to disappoint you," he sneered. "Don't know who you get your info from, but obviously they're about as brilliant as you."

I swallowed hard when I saw the small handgun he held. "You hate guns," I whispered.

"Yup, but sometimes a gun can do what a fist can't. You seem to need more than just a beating to die." He scratched at the straggly beard on his face. His greasy hair lay flat against his head. His clothes were wrinkled and filthy. He appeared as if he'd been living on the streets, so unlike the polished perfectionist I'd lived with for eighteen months.

"You're like that Energizer bunny. You keep going and going, Terese. Punishment after punishment, you keep right on living." His teeth clenched. "Well, not anymore."

I found the strength to stand. Not sure if it was fear or anger that permeated my soul, but it revitalized me. "I was told you got into a fight with a store clerk and he shot you." My hands hung fisted at my side.

"Other way around. In fact, that's where the gun came from." He looked down at the small gun, turning his wrist to get a better look.

Gun. I needed to get to my purse.

"Where's your boyfriend, whore?"

"We broke up," I lied.

He barked a laugh. "He got sick of the mannequin, too?"

"He's never called me that. In fact, I'm quite the opposite with him." My boldness took me by surprise. It enraged Garen. He charged me, his arm cocked, gun in hand, ready to punch. I cringed and turned away, circling my head with my arms.

"Drop it or I'll gladly put a hole in you."

Booker! I couldn't see him behind Garen, but I knew his voice, despite the fact that I'd never heard him use that menacing tone before.

"I said drop it or I'll kill you, roach. Your choice," Booker demanded.

Garen straightened and raised the gun in the air slowly. "You got me."

Right. I didn't buy his statement and I hoped Booker didn't either.

"Turn around slowly and drop the gun. Oh," he added, "and put *both* your arms up."

"Sure thing." Garen raised his left arm halfway, and in one fluid movement, scooped it around me and dragged me in front of him. He smelled strongly of sweat and greasy hair. I turned my face to the side to keep from gagging.

With his face safely behind my head, Garen laughed. "Look. Rambo's come to save you."

Booker had a gun in his hand and another larger gun strapped over his jacket, resting against his chest.

With the cold steel of Garen's gun pressed against my temple, and his other arm around my waist he said, "Looks like I'm in control now."

"Let her go." Booker's eyes burned bright with anger. "You've already killed one person today. If you let her go, maybe I can convince the DA to lower the charges to accidental manslaughter."

"Yeah, right. Accidental manslaughter will never fly." He tightened the arm around my waist. The gun never moved from my temple.

"I'm an ex-MET agent. My word carries a lot of weight." Booker stepped toward us. Garen pulled back the hammer of his gun. Booker's hands went up in the air and he removed his finger from the trigger. Garen slowly released the hammer. I heard each and every tick as he did.

"Let her go. You've tormented her enough," Booker demanded. "She's done nothing to deserve this."

"Nothing?" I could feel the anger in Garen as his breath quickened and the gun pressed deeper into my temple.

"She messed with my plan. I had everything mapped out for my life. Everything. Graduate Summa Cum Laude from high school. Check. Get a full ride scholarship to Harvard. Check. After college; *uncheck*," he hissed. "You see, the Life Plan called for me to get an internship with a DC politician to start my journey to the White House. Only this alleged trophy wife here," he tapped the gun on my head, "screwed it all up with that stupid picture."

"Picture? What picture?" I asked, utterly confused.

"Think, whore." He tightened his arm around my ribs and I winced. "Remember that picture you sent me in your swimsuit on the beach? Well, I caught my pervert roommate with it. We got into a huge fight. The school filed a report that went on my permanent record."

"That kept you from getting a job with a politician? Seems to me that would help your resume with the lowlifes in DC." Booker started to laugh, then stopped. "Wait. Just how badly did you beat this guy?"

"Enough to teach him a lesson. Anyway, with the incident on my record, I had a hard time finding a job with a decent politician. That's why I ended up having to work with Graft." Garen thumped the gun against my head. "All because of her."

"I see. Is that where your pattern of abuse started, then?" Booker asked flippantly.

"Put your guns down and slide them my way or I'll put a bullet through that smart mouth of yours," Garen demanded in a tone I knew all too well.

"Do it, Book," I pleaded. "He'll kill you."

Booker's jaw twitched twice before he slowly lowered his guns to the ground and straightened. He gave each gun a weak shove with his foot. They slid a few feet, stopping short of where Garen and I stood.

Enraged, Garen shoved me to the ground and squeezed off three rapid shots, hitting Booker once in the leg. I screamed as Booker dropped onto the mats. Stepping closer, Garen fired two more times before finally hitting Booker's other leg. Book slumped over his damaged body, groaning in pain.

I sprung to my feet and rushed Garen, my fists flying. Garen twisted to the side and side kicked me in the stomach, sending me backwards. I flew onto the weight rack as he scurried for Booker's guns. He scooped them up and tossed them over by the treadmills. One fired on impact. The bullet ricocheted near my head.

"I should tell you . . . I called the police. They're sending in . . . the SWAT team." Booker grimaced through his teeth, clearly in pain. He bent over his bleeding legs, pressing on the wounds. Blood ran everywhere. A pool of it grew beneath him. I looked away to keep from fainting.

"No one's getting out of here alive, Rambo, but me." Garen shook his gun at Booker. "I'm going to take care of her first because I want the pleasure of seeing you watch. Then I'm going to beat you senseless before I kill you, too."

I stiffened. Garen's words closely mirrored those of the two guys who killed Book's mom and sister. Never in the four years since I'd met Booker had I seen fear in his eyes, until now. He too must have caught the similarity, and clearly it terrified him.

My days of being a victim were done. I grabbed a ten-pound dumbbell off the weight rack and wrapped my hands around it. As Garen drew closer, I twisted toward him with all my strength. He pulled back just as I made contact, lessening the full impact I'd hoped for. Nevertheless, he slid sideways across the floor.

Booker forced himself up. Fury replaced the fear that seized him just moments ago. He held the Glock he kept in his calf holster confidently in his hand, and aimed it at Garen. Unfortunately, Booker's legs gave out. He stumbled just long enough for Garen to get off two deafening shots directly at Booker's chest. The force of the bullets knocked Booker back. The mirrored wall cracked, and he slid, lifeless, to the ground. Garen dropped the gun to his side and laughed.

No! I dropped down and grabbed my purse. My hand quickly found the gun. My thumb flipped off the safety as I spun, positioned on one knee. The gun barrel pointed directly at Garen's heart. He turned to me. His laughing ceased. Before I squeezed the trigger, two shots rang out in rapid succession. Blood gushed from the right side of Garen's chest and his left hip as the gun flew from his hand. His blood splattered my face. I willed myself not to faint. As he staggered and fell to the ground in front of me, a warm wetness trickled over my chest. Blood, all down my shirt. The room spun out of control and I fell over as everything went black.

Chapter 35
BOOKER

"Tess!" I dragged my way across the gym floor, my gun still in hand. I'd been a cop long enough to know to never put my gun down. I'd take no chances with Garen. Tess's blood soaked shirt about stopped my heart. *Did I hit her when I shot Garen?* I searched feverishly for a wound; relieved when I saw only a skimmed shoulder, probably when I shot the gun from Garen's hand. I pulled her to my chest. "Tess." I held her tight. "I can't do this anymore." I rocked her in my shaky arms.

Within seconds police rushed the room. "Freeze! Police!" I lifted one arm in the air, the gun still in my hand.

"Booker!" Brent rushed over to me. "What happened? You only called a few minutes ago."

I gave him a quick rundown as one of his men checked Garen, while another called for an ambulance. He took Tess from me so my wounds could be dressed. Garen groaned off to the side. Good thing the SWAT team arrived, otherwise I would have put another bullet in him. This time it would have been in his head.

"Any other injuries aside from the legs?" the medic asked as he applied a pressure bandage to my thigh. I about broke my teeth grinding them together to keep from screaming out. "Are those bullet holes in your coat?"

I didn't bother looking down. I nodded. "Johnson shot me twice in the chest, but I'm wearing a Kevlar vest." The impact blew me back against the mirrors, knocking the wind out of me, but the bullets didn't penetrate the vest. I could only imagine the bruises I'd have. I swore softly as the medic tightened the dressing around one of my legs.

"Sorry," he said, taping it into place.

"Are you sure it's only this shoulder wound on Tess, that she's only fainted?" Brent asked, laying Tess down carefully next to me.

"I couldn't find anything else. She doesn't do blood well. Faints every time." I reached out to wipe the blood splattered on her face as the memories of my mother and sister ate at me. "I can't do this anymore," I repeated softly as I lay back on the mat, pushing away the nightmares.

~*~

I sat in the dark, thinking. Not a good thing. The nurse left after giving me something to sleep. I don't know why they bothered. They'd be back in ten minutes to take vitals or draw blood, waking me again anyway.

All I did for three days was relive everything. I saw Tess's blood-soaked shirt, her blood-splattered face over and over. In my dreams. Wide wake. It haunted my every moment. And of course, thinking of her only reminded me of everyone else I'd lost. My nerves were fried. Cole tried to get me to see a shrink from the trauma team, but I refused. I wanted to be alone.

I convinced him to put me in an isolation room so I could drown in self-pity in peace. Mags and Seth came by, and when they saw the isolation sign in place, Seth knew it was my doing and not Cole's. He called me on his cell and we had a heated discussion through the windows of the room over the phone.

"This has you written all over it," he snapped.

I made a weak attempt to fight back. "Seth, I had surgery on both my legs. Why is it unreasonable to believe I have an infection?" The damage to my right leg was minimal, mostly muscle. Thankfully Garen was a lousy shot. The left leg had a small chip out of the bone and the most extensive damage. Cole said I'd have a couple months of physical therapy before I could walk without a cane. I hated the cane. It made me feel like an old man, but if I tried to walk without it, the pain about dropped me.

Magpie paced back and forth as Seth continued to lecture me. Her stomach poked out a bit now. To see any kind of a tummy on her thin frame looked funny. She never could gain weight, no matter how hard she tried. I blamed it on her mother. Cole said it might be genetics. Whatever. Her mother was a waste, and as sour as my mood had been over the past few days, I didn't want to hear it was genetics. I wanted to blame someone for everything.

I also didn't want to listen anymore to what Seth had to say. I knew he was right, but I continued to let everything churn and eat at me. I pretended my phone battery died, which he didn't believe either. He stormed out. Maggie, with her soulful blue eyes looked at me. She mouthed, *Love you, Garfield*, and left.

Lilah and Sofia came by a short time later. I waved at them through the window. Sofia brought a stuffed bear for me. She gave it to the nurse before they left. It broke my heart to see her sad little face as she waved her chubby fingers at me.

Tess's shoulder wound didn't require surgery. Turned out she was up on her knees when I shot Garen's hip out. The bullet grazed her shoulder after taking out his hip.

It took nine hours of surgery to rebuild Garen's hip socket. Both his hip and shoulder joints were completely destroyed and would have to be replaced after the bone healed. I don't miss when I aim my gun. I wrestled with putting a bullet in his head, but years of training to shoot to stop, not shoot to kill, were embedded deep within me. Besides, unlike Garen, I wasn't an animal, although I did hope that he'd live a long painful life of constant joint pain. Okay, so I wasn't a *complete* animal.

Tess didn't have to spend any time in the hospital. They cleaned her shoulder, dressed it, and sent her home. She'd come by a number of times the first couple of days to visit me. Each time I made an excuse not to see her, claiming I had an appointment with a specialist or that I was extremely tired and could she come back another time. She stopped coming after the third day.

Five days after my surgery I was discharged. Cole drove me home, and was given strict instructions, by me, to not let anyone know yet. I needed to get some rest because I certainly didn't get any at the hospital. I was tired of chaos. I needed some peace and quiet.

The next morning I rose early, unable to sleep. I let Daisy out. She took care of her business while I filled her food bowl. I let her back in and she ran straight to her food. "Slow down and enjoy it, girl." I ruffled the fur on her head. She kept inhaling her meal. I hobbled over to the couch and sank into one of the recliners. I fell back asleep until the doorbell rang two hours later.

I shuffled to the door, biting back several groans. I looked through the peephole and saw Tess standing there, looking beautiful in her green sweater. *I love that on her.*

I reached for the handle, not looking forward to what I had to do, but it was time. The least I could do was tell her. That I owed her.

"Hi. How are you feeling?" she asked. No hug, no kiss. She knew, or at least suspected, something was amiss.

"Good. Come on in." I waddled into the family room. The only sound was the click of my stupid cane on the wood floor. I dropped into the recliner with a grimace.

"Are you okay? Would you like something for pain?" She sat next to me and touched my arm. I pulled way and folded my arms across my chest. It was going to be hard enough without having her touch me.

"No. The pills don't help with the pain. They just make my head foggy, and put me to sleep," I explained as Daisy bounded into the room. She ran straight to Tess. No surprise. The dog loved Tess almost as much as I did. I stopped my hand from rubbing the ache in my heart.

"Garen's claiming it was self-defense." She stroked the dog's head. I could have sworn Daisy smiled. "He's claiming you walked in on us in a compromising situation, and in a jealous rage you shot him."

"Seriously?" Idiot. "What about the clerk he killed over in Buffalo?"

"An accident." She clenched her jaw. "He said he was scared the clerk was going to shoot him and was trying to wrestle the gun away when it went off. Vintage Garen. Everything bad that happens is always someone else's fault."

"He can't think that will fly in court," I pressed. She shrugged but said nothing else.

With the exception of the grandfather clock in the corner with its rhythmic ticking, deafening silence filled the room. Even Daisy seemed to sense the tension as she slinked away.

Finally, Tess cleared her throat. "I can't thank you enough for saving me. I can never repay you." She stared at her hands as she spoke instead of me. "And I'm guessing that you've had enough of my drama, and you want out." Her eyes met mine. They mirrored what I felt. Heartbreak.

"I can't do this anymore, Tess. I left the MET because I was sick of the drama, the heartache. I want . . . no, I *need* a simple life. It's why I chose real estate law over criminal or, heaven forbid, family law." What some dysfunctional families did to each other disgusted me.

"I see." She stood. "And I understand. Garen may be in jail, but he's hardly out of my life. Who knows how long the trial will last? And he may even get off. It wouldn't be the first time a guilty man walked free."

I struggled to get up and finally relented and used my cane. Tess's face etched with anguish at watching me struggle. "I hope we can still be friends." I wanted to kick myself the moment the words left my mouth. They were the kiss of death on any relationship.

To her credit, she only nodded and turned for the door. "I'll walk you to your car," I said. She bolted ahead of me, slamming the door long before I got there. I hobbled into the kitchen and took a pain pill. I didn't want to feel for a while.

Chapter 36
Tess

My heart hurt. No matter what, I thought I could count on Booker. "I suck when it comes to picking out men. Absolutely suck." I knew he was going to break up with me by the way he'd been acting. His ridiculous excuses for not seeing me at the hospital, the phony isolation stunt, were transparent. But to hear the actual words falling from his lips cut like a knife. If Booker had ripped my heart from my chest and stomped on it, it would hurt less. I wiped away the tears as they soaked my face.

Now I had to go to Lilah's and pretend nothing was wrong. She invited me over to help her plan a baby shower for Maggie. I thought it was a little early in the pregnancy to plan a shower, but Lilah was so excited about the baby, I didn't point it out, not wanting to rain on her parade. So not in the mood for party planning at the moment.

I sat in the car for a few minutes, reining in my emotions. I even applied some fresh mascara. After a few deep breaths, I headed for the door.

I played it well. I smiled, made suggestions for party games, and even agreed to host one, putting myself in the center of attention for the first time in a long time. She had no idea I wanted to break down and cry.

"Since both Cole and Seth will be working, I'll have to make sure they move the furniture around in the living room the night before to accommodate the guest seating." Lilah wrote herself a note in the margin of the yellow pad she'd been using to map out the shower. "I doubt Booker will be healthy enough yet to help. How's Booker doing anyway? Cole said he's in a lot of pain still."

"He . . . ah . . ." I took a deep breath as I forced myself not to cry.

"What's wrong? Is Book okay?" She wrapped a hand around my arm.

"It's not that. He . . . he broke up with me." I tightened my jaw before giving her a recap of what happened. I impressed myself. I didn't shed a single tear. In fact, my sorrow turned into anger the longer I talked.

"He said he was sick of the drama, and he needed a simple life?" she repeated, sounding as exasperated as I felt. "*Estúpido!*" She slapped the table and stood as she went into a tirade entirely in Spanish, flipping her hands repeatedly in the air. She must have forgotten that I grew up in San Diego, and while I didn't speak it well, I knew a lot of Spanish words. Thankfully, Sofia was in bed, otherwise she would have gotten a real education on how to cuss out a man in Spanish.

Cole entered the kitchen, a look of confusion on his arched brow. "Lilah, what's wrong?" He squeezed her shoulders.

"Booker!" was all she said.

Relief and a smile filled his face. "What did he do now?"

"Broke up with Tess." Lilah slapped her hand on her leg in frustration.

"He told me he was sick of the drama, and wanted a simple life," I explained to Cole.

"I see." Cole pulled out a chair for his wife, before sitting next to her. "I believe this can be blamed on his 'save the world' mentality. Booker's obsessed with protecting those of us he loves. I know for a fact he'd lay down his life for me, without a second thought. For any one of us. Me or Lilah, Seth, Maggie. And now you."

"In that crazy head of his, Booker feels he failed his sister and his mom, and he's afraid of failing us also," Lilah said. "It's an irrational thought. I mean, seriously, how can you defend your family against two punks with guns?"

"And he knows that, too, deep inside, but Booker can't let that thought go." Cole shook his head, clearly worried about his friend. "Tess, did you know that Maggie lived with Booker at one time? Not in the romantic sense, this was strictly platonic. A brother and sister relationship, if you will."

"No. I know he has her dog, Daisy May." I leaned back in the chair wondering what this had to do with me.

"Remember Mags telling you that she and Seth wanted to wait until they were married before they slept together?" Lilah asked, somewhat calmer now thanks to Cole's peaceful ways. I nodded. "Well, she moved in with Booker for a while, to make things easier on her and Seth. Anyway, everything started out okay."

"But about a year-and-a-half in, things fell apart." Cole leaned forward, placing his elbows on the table.

"It didn't help that he and Seth were in the middle of a drug sting operation that went bad," Lilah said, rubbing Cole's arm.

"Booker came staggering into my office one night at three in the morning," Cole explained. Pain for his friend weighed on his face. "Book stumbled into my office ghost-white and sweating profusely. The temperature outside was negative two."

I stared mindlessly at the table while Cole laid out what happened.

"Book insisted he was having a heart attack. He kept telling me his heart was pounding to the point of being painful. He collapsed onto the corner of my desk, not bothering to clear a spot, sending a file sideways onto the floor." Cole took a breath, clearly bothered.

"Was he?" I asked.

"No." Cole shook his head. "Panic attack. He and Seth were working undercover that night and were ensnared in a shootout. Seth went around to the front of the building without Booker knowing and he thought Seth had been shot. It threw Book into a panic."

"Panic attack. I had several of those over the past few years thanks to Garen," I said dryly. "They can be debilitating."

"Extremely. It wasn't until then that I noticed he'd lost weight, a good fifteen pounds, if I were to guess. Booker's face was drawn and his eyes had dark bags underneath." He sat silently for a minute, as if dwelling on the memory.

"What does all this have to do with Maggie living with him?" I pressed, knowing I didn't want to hear the rest of this. I didn't want to feel sorry for Booker at the moment. I was angry, and I *wanted* to be angry with him.

"I was pretty sure I knew what triggered the attack that night," Cole continued. "He'd been stressing about Maggie's safety for months, and it seemed to be escalating. The incident with Seth brought it all to a head."

"Stressing about Maggie?" I asked.

"Yes. He mentioned a few weeks earlier that he wasn't sleeping well. That he'd wake in the middle of the night and rush to see if his security system had been breached. Then he'd recheck each door and window in the house two or three times to make sure they were secure."

"Afraid that what happened to his family would happen to Maggie," I said, as sorrow touched my heart. How awful for him. It broke my heart to know how much he'd suffered, and still suffered with that memory.

Lilah set a glass of water in front of me, pulling me out of my thoughts. I thanked her and drained the glass, not realizing just how thirsty I was. Probably from all my crying.

"So, what happened?" I asked.

"We ran several tests, to be safe, but that's what it was. Maggie moved out and back in with Seth the next day, and that's when I moved in with them. Maggie hurt for Booker, and didn't want to leave him alone, but she knew it had to be. That's why he has Daisy. Maggie didn't want Book to be completely alone," Cole explained. "Booker slept for twenty-six hours straight that first night. I had him speak to a specialist, and she taught him some coping skills that helped tremendously. But in all honesty, Maggie's moving out was all it took."

I sat quietly for a moment, thinking about what Cole and Lilah had shared with me. "Do you believe that the incident with

Garen triggered the panic attacks again?" Feeling guilty, I fingered the glass instead of looking at them.

"No, at least he swears he's not had any," Cole said, taking my hand in his. "Honestly, I think he's scared that something horrible is going to happen to you, and he'll lose you, just like he's lost so many other people in his life. He needs time. That's my professional *and* personal opinion."

I pushed to my feet. "So I'm supposed to wait around until Booker decides to get his head together?" Frustrated, I paced to the window above the sink and looked out at the stupid snow. *Does it ever stop snowing here?*

"Tess, I didn't tell you all this so you'd feel obligated to wait around for him," Cole explained. "I just wanted you to have the full picture before you make a decision. You know me. I'm a fact kind of guy."

I smiled, remembering when Booker had said the exact same thing about him. After Cole learned he had cancer, he researched several different avenues of treatment. After deciding which one he believed to be the most promising, Cole presented his findings to the oncologist and told him that was the protocol they'd follow. Never once did Cole whine *Why me* or *This isn't fair*. He saw a problem and took control of his situation.

"I love Book, as much as I do my own brothers. He's kind, compassionate, giving, extremely sarcastic," Cole chuckled. "He's also been through some pretty horrific stuff, and is struggling right now. But then again, so have you."

Lilah stepped to my side. Cole came next to her and leaned against the sink, folding his arms across his chest. "Only you can decide how you want to handle this," she said. "Are you done with the guy? Or do you want to give *Estup* . . . Booker some time? The way I see it, it boils down to a couple of things. How much do you love him, and is he worth the headache?" She smiled softly. "I think I know what you'll say. But remember one thing, Tess. You're in charge of you. Not a man. Not any man, or woman, for that matter. Take control. Do what you have to do to reclaim your life, no matter what that is. We'll stand by you, one hundred percent." Cole nodded at his wife's words.

"Don't get me wrong, I love the guy." Lilah chuckled. "I mean, we've had our troubles, but we worked it out. He even tracked down Sofia for me. If he hadn't, I still wouldn't know she was alive. But he can be infuriating, and stupid, and—"

"Who's stupid, mommy?" Sofia padded into the kitchen, her curly hair a mess from her nap. She wrapped her arms around her mother's legs and plopped her thumb in her cherub mouth.

"Did I wake you?" Lilah asked, smoothing down her daughter's hair. Sofia nodded. "Sorry." Lilah scooped her up and kissed her cheek.

"Where's Uncle Book?" Sofia asked me around her thumb. It took me a second to interpret the muffled sounds.

"He's at home." I smiled.

"I miss him." She snuggled in closer to her mother.

I waved to Sofia. "I'll see you later, sweetie." She wiggled the fingers of her thumb sucking hand at me.

As I drove away, all feelings of sadness leeched from my body as I thought about not only what Cole shared, but about Lilah's words. For too long I'd let Garen overshadow who I was. For too long I pushed aside my needs to try to make a marriage with a violent creep work. I sacrificed my self-worth as he tore me down, little by little, every day, not even realizing it until the damage was done. What was I thinking?

I smacked the steering wheel. "Ouch." I pumped my hand a few times. "I'm done. I'm done being stepped on, walked over. I'm done cowering. I'm not going to live like this anymore. Enough! Fear will not rule me another day." I rolled down the window. "I'm taking my life back," I yelled out. A couple of teens getting into a red pickup turned and gave me a mitten-covered thumbs up. Time to rescue Terese Layla Selleck.

I flipped a U-turn right in the center of town, disrupting traffic, and I couldn't care less. My only focus now? Reclaiming. I drove straight to the county jail. The judge refused to set bail on Garen, citing him as a flight risk, so he sat in prison, rotting, as his injuries healed. The thought warmed my heart.

A detective led me to a sterile room after I filled out the visitor's paperwork and went through an x-ray scanner. I almost turned and left as my old friend fear tried to wiggle itself into my heart.

No. It ends here. Today.

Two armed guards escorted Garen into the room in a wheelchair. He wore a bright orange jumpsuit, definitely not his color. He looked small and insignificant to me for the first time ever. I laughed out loud when they shackled him to the metal table between us. Not wanting to be any closer to him than I needed to be, I remained standing.

"My, my. How the mighty have fallen," I chuckled.

"Hello, whore. Miss me already?" he laughed.

"I've come to let you know that I'm done with you. I'm done worrying and wondering if you are around the next corner waiting to attack me. I'm done hiding and letting your depravity dictate what I do, and how I feel. I'm done dealing with losers like you. Done. One hundred percent done." I planted my hands on the table and leaned in ever so slightly. "I'm taking charge of me. And I'm going to do everything in my power to make sure you die in this rat-infested hole. Capiche?"

He grabbed at me, but the table held him firmly in place. As did the guards who each placed a hand on his shoulders, punching him back down into the chair. Not going to lie, it was easier to be brave knowing he couldn't reach me. *One step at a time, Tess.*

"You're nothing but a bully. A cruel, depraved bully, who derives pleasure out of beating women. But never again will you hurt me. Never again will you control me. And the next man I give myself to will deserve me." I turned around and patted my butt. "And you can kiss this goodbye forever." One of the guards chuckled.

Garen went crazy, swearing, jerking on the cuffs trying to break free from his table, spittle flying everywhere with each word. I walked to the door. The goliath sized guard standing there that I hadn't seen before smiled wide and nodded.

I glanced back one last time at Garen as he wiped the spit off his mouth with his shoulder, his eyes still wild with rage. "P.S. You suck in bed." As if I had anything to compare him to since he was the only man I'd ever been with. I wanted to rub a little salt in his open wounds. Immature? Probably, but I just didn't care. "Of course, a pretty boy like you shouldn't have a problem finding a little love in here. Maybe you can learn a few things. I mean, any port in a storm, right?" I smiled and waved my fingers goodbye as he went ballistic again. The guard opened the door and offered me a subtle fist bump, while one of the two holding Garen pulled out a Taser. The last thing I heard walking out the door was Garen screaming in pain. What a sweet sound.

As I strutted across the parking lot of the prison, the words "This Girl is on Fire," from the Alicia Keys song popped into my head. That was exactly how I felt. On fire. In charge. Free! "And I'm not backing down." I didn't even care that it was snowing . . . again. A rush of empowerment surged through me. I never wanted it to end. I wanted to scream from the rooftops: 'I'm back!' I settled for singing the rest of *Girl on Fire* at the top of my lungs as I drove out of the lot.

Next on my list: Booker Gatto. I hadn't made up my mind completely about what to do about him after talking with Cole, but I had decided a few things. I went to the office building and straight to Devin, the patent attorney on the third floor's office. An older woman dressed in a pink floral shirt sat staring down at her laptop, while Devin, dressed in a full suit, leaned over her pointing at the keyboard.

"Mom," he said, his voice heavy with exasperation. "This key is the control key. Remember c-t-r-l is short for control."

"Yes, yes. That's right. Sorry, son." She reached up and patted his cheek.

"It's okay, Mom." He straightened and turned to me.

"Tess." He stepped forward. "I didn't hear you come in."

"Hello, Devin. I've come to ask you if your job offer was legit." I glanced at his mother to see if I'd spoken out of turn.

She jumped up first. "Yes. It is. I'm filling in until he can find a new girl." She took my hand. "My, you're a lovely thing. My name's Millie, by the way. Are you married?"

"Mom," Devin said, his face turning red.

"I'm curious is all, dear." She brushed her son's protest aside with a wave of her hand. "Well?" she pressed.

"I'm single." My answer received a large grin from her. Devin slapped his hand over his face.

"Let's go into my office and talk, Tess, shall we?" He took my elbow and guided me through a second door, which he promptly closed behind me.

He agreed to match the salary that Booker paid me, and if I would start tomorrow, he'd offer his mother as a temporary secretary for Booker until he could hire a new one. He also offered to pay me to work an hour's overtime each day for a couple weeks to train his mother. "Don't want to leave Booker in a lurch," he said. In my head I thought she'd need more than an hour a day training to function properly, but the idea of frustrating Booker helped me stay my tongue. He was about to get what he deserved

Chapter 37
BOOKER

After a week of wallowing in self-pity, I hobbled to work, hoping that business would phase out the memories. I walked into my office, cane and all, to find an older woman in a blue floral print shirt sitting at Tess's desk.

"Good morning, Mr. Gatto." She held out her hand and shook mine. "We've met before." My pinched brow encouraged her to explain more. "I'm Devin's mom. The patent attorney on the third floor."

"Yes. That's right." I smiled at the gray haired woman, still confused. "Where's Tess?" I asked.

"Oh, dear. I assumed she spoke to you." She wrung her age-spotted hands. "My son offered her a job and she took it. She asked me to fill in until you could hire a permanent replacement. She's showed me how to fill in many of your forms, and if I get confused I just call her and she walks me through it. She's an amazing girl."

"Yes. She is." I ground my teeth together. I so deserved this.

I hobbled into my office, closing the door behind me. I hadn't thought about Tess quitting. It was probably for the best.

Only it didn't feel that way. I sat on the corner of my desk, growing angrier by the minute, so much so, I now owed seventy-five cents to that stupid curse jar. I hobbled over and grabbed the jar. Instead of adding quarters, I threw the thing across the room, shattering it and a picture frame.

"Mature, Gatto, very mature."

Chapter 38
Tess

Devin handed me an envelope. "Your first paycheck. You'll note I've already given you a raise." He winked. Devin loved to flirt. Not an overbearing, *everyone thinks I'm sexy* kind of flirt, but more of the nerdy un-suave kind, who stumbled over his lines. He tucked his hand in the pocket of his vest.

"You didn't have to do that, Devin." I took the check and slipped it into my purse.

"Yes, I do. You've gotten this place running smoothly in under a week. And you've done a great job training my mother."

"She's very sweet," I said as Millie, his mom, walked in the door, laptop in hand, ready to go. She claimed to enjoy the lessons. I think what she enjoyed was expounding the qualities of her very available son to me.

"Sorry I'm a little late." She smiled brightly, and gave Devin a peck on the cheek. "I made chicken noodle soup for dinner, dear. Your favorite. It's in the crock pot on the counter, as usual." With pink cheeks, Devin disappeared into his office.

"How are things going with Booker? Is he treating you well?"

"I've only worked with him a few days. He doesn't say much, but he did break a jar that he keeps quarters in his first day back. He said he dropped it, but the picture frame on the wall was destroyed too, so I'm not sure what happened." She frowned and lowered her voice. "He's not a very happy camper. In fact, he's rather grumpy. I hope he finds a new secretary soon."

I pinched my lips together. *Good, serves him right.*

"He's not like Devin, that's for sure. My son is a good boy, don't you think?" She put her laptop next to mine and opened it. A letter taped to the keyboard addressed to me fluttered out. "Oh, yes. About this letter. Booker went home early. His leg was bothering him, and he told me to take a long lunch. I went for a stroll down by the Erie Canal. Have you ever been there in the winter?" I shook my head. Millie and her tangents. You'd ask her one question and somehow she twisted the conversation around to canning peaches. "It's lovely. You really should go for a walk. Devin loves the canal. I'll tell him to take you. Devin," she called out, straightening her purple paisley dress.

"Wait. What does that have to do with this envelope addressed to me?" I removed it and turned it over, wondering who it was from.

"Oh dear, lost my train of thought again." She tapped her forehead with her fingers softly, which she did every time she forgot something. "After my walk I came back to the office. Well, you know how I keep the door locked whenever Booker's not there. It's kind of scary being on the top floor all alone. I mean, I could scream for a week and no one would even hear me."

"Yes, very scary. Now, how did you get this?" I asked, trying yet again to put her back on track.

"It came flying under the door. Whoever it was didn't even knock. Of course maybe they assumed since it was after five we were already gone." She hit the power key and sat back, waiting for her computer to boot up. I'd told her several times she didn't have to power it all the way down each time she closed it, but she kept forgetting.

With time to kill as she tried remembering her password, I opened the letter, surprised to see who it was from. I reread it three times, trying to get past the uncomfortable feeling it gave me. I reached for my phone, then changed my mind. I may have moved past Garen, but it'd be a while before the paranoia ended. *The letter means nothing. I'm overreacting.*

"I have a question about one of the court documents Booker wanted me to file today," Millie said.

Crap. "Hold on a second." Unable to shake the feeling, I grabbed my new cell phone, another milestone to celebrate my breaking free from the past, and called Booker. I decided to tell him what the note said and he could do what he wanted with the information. The call went straight to voicemail.

I tucked the phone and the letter in my purse. Great. I'd have to drop it off on my way to Maggie's. I hadn't seen him since that horrible day at his house. Part of me was excited, just a little. A larger part hated the idea of seeing him again. Maybe I should just tape it to his door and ding-dong ditch him. I shook my head at the junior high prank. We were both adults. We could talk to each other without it being awkward. *Yeah, right.*

Millie babbled on about the court document she needed help with. It took her all of two minutes to swing the conversation around to Devin and his being a straight-A student all through college. I tried to concentrate, but my mind wouldn't let the weird, cryptic letter go. I vacillated between telling myself I'd read too much into it, to feeling the need to go and show it to Booker sooner than later.

Sooner won. "Millie, can we do this tomorrow? I forgot about an important appointment I have at the . . . dentist."

I grabbed my purse and coat, dashing out the door before she said a word. I jogged down the stairs, two at a time, and groaned when I saw the snow. "Why do I still live in this frozen wasteland?" I quickly scraped off my car while calling Booker one more time. Again, the call went straight to voicemail. Grumbling under my breath that I should let it go, I drove out of the parking lot toward Booker's. Nik may be crazy, and a major drama queen, but she had it right. Loving Booker was an incurable disease.

Chapter 39
BOOKER

I dragged myself out of bed, not an easy task with a mind full of painkillers. I grabbed the bottle and flushed the rest down the toilet. I'd live with the pain instead of a foggy brain. I made a cup of my favorite hot chocolate and drank it way too quickly in an effort to wake myself.

"Six p.m.," I complained, frowning at the clock. I'd slept the entire afternoon. Still needing to shake the foggy effects of the painkillers from my head, I dressed warmly and went outside to shovel today's layer of snow off for the millionth time this season.

It took me thirty minutes to shovel half the driveway that normally took me ten. Canes and shovels don't play well together. I knew I could call Seth or Cole. Either would have come in a heartbeat, but keeping busy meant no time to think about Tess. I planted the shovel in a snow bank next to my house near the front door and hobbled to the shed for the snow blower. I had no idea if I had the strength to handle it, but I was about to find out.

Just removing the machine from the shed turned into a joke. I huffed and puffed like an old man. I stopped to wipe the sweat from my face. *Swallow your pride and call Seth.*

"Hi, Bookie." Nik's voice startled me.

I reached out for the side of the shed to steady myself. I didn't want to see her right now. Or ever, really. Without looking up, I said, "I thought you were going to New York. I know you cashed the check." She cashed it the day I gave it to her. Same ol' Nik. Couldn't handle money.

"I made it all the way to New York, even stayed a few days before coming back." She sighed. "I've made a life changing decision."

"What are you talking about?" I turned to her. She stood ten feet from me, dressed in an expensive looking fur jacket and furry boats. Only her outfit didn't have my attention. The pink gun she pointed straight at me did. *Why is my life full of crazy people?*

"If I can't have you, nobody can." She lifted the gun higher. "Give me your gun. In case I miss the first time. I still remember how fast you can draw that thing."

"I didn't wear the gun to shovel my driveway, Nickel." I used my pet name for her, hoping to calm her down. The girl had irrational thinking down to a science.

She stomped her foot. "Now you call me Nickel? I've been asking you since I got out of jail to call me Nickel and you wait until I have a gun pointed on you to do it."

I decided to try charm next, even if it meant throwing my species under the bus and surrendering my man card. "Nickel, I'm a guy. Put us all in one room and we still only have half a brain between us." I smiled widely. "Come on. Let's go inside where it's warmer. I'll make you some of that hot chocolate you like."

"Give me your gun." She pulled back the hammer on hers to emphasize she meant business. She was the second person in less than a month to do that to me. Anger boiled inside as I unstrapped the gun. I kicked it into a snow bank.

Big mistake. Nik fired her gun. Luckily, she missed. However, in my rush to get away from her, I stepped back with my bad leg—well, the worse of the two since neither was in great shape—and fell into a snow bank, opposite my gun.

"I loved you, Bookie. I'm a changed woman. I would have been a good wife." She wiped away tears with her opposite hand. The gun stayed shakily on me.

"Nik, I'm sorry. Really I am. I didn't mean to hurt you, but you broke my trust. I'm having a hard time overlooking that, especially with a gun pointed at me." I worked my way to a sitting position.

"It doesn't matter now." She tugged her hat and scarf off and tossed them to the ground as she unbuttoned her coat.

"Why are you taking off your coat?" I asked as she shrugged the coat down each arm and tossed it next to the gloves, all the while keeping her eyes and the gun trained on me.

"My sister loves the coat. I don't want to get blood on it."

I slapped my hand over my face. "Are you kidding me? Nik, please. Let's go inside and talk about this. What do you say?"

Ignoring my question, she laid out her plan, just like the nut jobs in the movies always did before they killed someone. "I'll shoot you first, then I'll kill myself. We're going to die together. Star-crossed lovers. Just like Romeo and Juliet."

"Nik! That's crazy. We're not Romeo and Juliet. We're not star-crossed lovers." *I'm a dead man. I'm not going to see Tess ever again.*

"In my mind, we are." She raised the gun just as something silver flashed above her head. Nik fell to the ground. Her gun slid across the icy patio toward me. Behind her stood Tess with my now dented snow shovel in her hand.

"Tess, you do know that a concealed weapon permit doesn't cover shovels, right?"

She rolled her eyes at my comment and tossed the shovel aside. I scrambled, with considerable effort, first for my gun, then for my cane. Nik didn't move. She was out cold.

"She left this note at the office for me, apologizing for what she was about to do," Tess said, handing me an envelope addressed to her in Nik's writing. "She thought the office was closed for the night. Lucky for you Millie didn't leave on time."

"Very lucky. Thank you for saving my life." I picked up Nik's gun and tucked it into my calf holster.

"I guess that makes us even," she said, with palpable anger in her voice. "And not that I'm not grateful, but I never asked you to save my life. I had my gun pointed at Garen's heart and would have killed him if you hadn't gone all super hero on me and started firing your gun. FYI: If I'd shot him, he'd be six feet in the ground right now, not in prison causing everyone trouble."

She turned, pulled out a . . . *cell phone?* and called for the police and an ambulance as she walked down my half-shoveled driveway looking so freaking sexy in her black knee high boots, I almost called her back.

Instead, I opened the envelope, removed the letter, and read it while waiting for the police.

Tess,

I'm writing you this because you of all people know how I feel. Like I said when I dropped by the office a few weeks ago, loving Booker is like a disease, an incurable disease. And you're right, he'll never choose me. He's moved on.

I've tried to move on also, but I can't. He's in my every waking thought. He's even in my dreams. Booker's my Romeo, and I'm his Juliet. And I don't want to move on. I want him. I'm very sorry, and I hope you'll someday understand and maybe forgive me for what I have to do. You were so sweet to me the other night, I felt I owed you this note.

Best wishes,

Nik

"What did I ever see in this woman?" I stuffed the letter back in the envelope and looked at Nik. "Oh yeah, short skirts, smoldering eyes, and a great kisser." I shook my head. "Lesson learned. Find a woman with substance." I immediately thought of Tess. A woman with substance and so much more. "I'm an idiot."

~*~

Two weeks after the Nikkolynn incident, she was charged with attempted murder and admitted to a psychiatric hospital for evaluation, after getting twenty-seven stitches in her head. I could get around a little better with my cane, and for short walks I didn't need it at all.

I ached for Tess. Seth and Cole tried to distract me by taking me bowling and skeet shooting. I will admit, watching clumsy Cole try and shoot skeet made me laugh quite a bit—and fear for my life not a little.

Tonight we were going to a new action movie that neither Lilah nor Magpie wanted to see. "We're in the family room, Garfield," Maggie called as I came in. I set my cane on the counter and walked into the adjoining family room unassisted. I was met with applause. I bowed.

Sofia rushed me, grabbing my hand. "Hurray, Uncle Book. No more cane." I quickly sat in a nearby chair to keep from falling over. Still a work in progress.

"What are you girls up to while we're gone tonight?" I asked. Lilah signaled for Sofia to come change into her pink princess jammies.

"Tess's coming over and we're watching a bunch of chick flicks." Magpie pointed to a pile of DVD's on the mantel.

"Tess is coming over? When?" I asked coolly.

"Any minute." Lilah smoothed the static electricity out of Sofia's hair, or she tried to. "Tess is leaving for San Diego. We're having a little farewell party for her, just us girls."

My heart leapt. "Tess is leaving?

"Yup. I thought you should know," she said boldly. "Maybe now you'll pull your head out and beg her on bended knee to forgive you for being an idiot. Then you can beg her to marry you before she wises up. Maybe, if you're lucky, Tess will take you back."

"Lilah, it's complicated," I said.

"It's complicated? Cole forgave me for lying to everyone. That was complicated, Booker," she said, waving a hand in the air, something she did when she got excited, or angry, apparently. "What you have is a person, a really great person who, for some unknown reason, loves you. And you toss her aside because you want an uncomplicated life." She grabbed Sofia's hand. "If you want an uncomplicated life, join a monastery." Leave it to Lilah to not sugarcoat it. "Tell Uncle Book goodnight, sweetheart."

Sofia climbed on my lap. "I'll marry you, Uncle Book." She patted my cheeks.

"I'm too old for you, angel." I gave her a kiss on the head and a hug.

"When I get bigger we can get married. How about when I'm ten?"

"Yeah, that won't land me in jail," I muttered. Seth and Mags laughed.

"You won't be in jail," Cole said, scooping Sofia up onto his shoulders and heading up the stairs with Lilah. "Because I'd kill you first."

"When's Tess leaving?" I asked Magpie.

"Tuesday morning." Mags squeezed my hand. "She said there's nothing to keep her here now and she's sick of the snow."

Seth sat on the couch and Maggie joined him. "Did you hear the good news about Jack Mahoney?" he asked. I shook my head. Jack was the lone survivor in a shootout that killed three of my men this past summer in an undercover operation. Another reason I left the MET. "I had lunch with him yesterday. He got a job offer to be a deputy sheriff in Sugar Maple, West Virginia. That's where he's originally from. He still has a few months of rehab, but he's thinking about taking the job."

"Good for him. Take it and get out. Move to a nice, quiet little town. Away from all the death and decay around here," I grumbled.

"Come on, Booker. There's no such place anymore. Life's a crapshoot. Sometimes you win . . . other times, not so much." He sat back. "Tell me. What's really going on inside that head of yours?"

I drew in a long deep breath and began spilling my innermost thoughts like a schoolgirl at a pajama party. Yeah, real dignified of me. "I can't take it. I keep seeing her face splattered with blood and . . ."

"You're sixteen, watching your mother and sister all over again." Seth finished my sentence. "It's over, Booker. Not to sound heartless, but you need to bury them, emotionally, stop carrying them around. You know your mother would say I'm right if she were here, as would your father."

"You don't know what all happened to them," I said. "I can't forget."

"I do know. I overheard my dad talking about it with my mom right before they died," he said gently. "It made me sick to know you had to witness that."

"You never told me."

"I didn't think you wanted me to know," he said simply. "But now it's time to let it all go. Tess is a great girl. You'd be a fool to let her slip away." He laced his hands through Maggie's hair.

"I don't think I'm strong enough to risk losing her like that. It's better I let her go, safe and alive. I seem to be a magnet for horrific deaths." I rubbed at the ache in my leg.

"So you think if she's not here and she dies, you'll be okay?" Mags asked. "Or what about one of us? There are no guarantees something tragic won't happen to us. Are you going to cut us out of your life, too?"

I leaned back in the chair and rubbed my jaw. She just didn't get it.

"I know you think I don't understand, but you're wrong." She wrapped her hands around Seth's. "Remember, I spent my first eighteen years unloved, not knowing what it meant or how it felt. And I can tell you that if Seth were to die tomorrow, as devastated as I'd be, I wouldn't regret having loved him. Loving and being loved is worth the pain. Not being loved is the real tragedy, Booker." Seth squeezed her hand.

I dipped my head and wiped my eyes. Maggie came over next to me and gave me a hug. "You bark like a junkyard dog sometimes, but you're really just a big old pussycat."

I chuckled. "You're never going to stop with the cat jokes, are you?"

"Not as long as there's breath left in my body," she vowed, then added bluntly, "You're an idiot if you don't stop her. You of all people know how hard it is to find real love. Tess is worth the risk. Love is always worth the risk."

Seth stood and helped me out of the chair, embracing me as we stood. "Think about what we said." I nodded. "Okay, enough crying. Let's go watch people blow things up and boost our testosterone levels. What do you say?"

"Have fun," Mags said. "I love you," she added to Seth as he turned and winked at her.

"Wait for me." Cole charged down the stairs. For once he didn't stumble.

With a heavy heart, I walked out to Seth's car, lost in thought.

~*~

I spent the weekend fighting with myself. One minute I planned on begging Tess to forgive me, the next I fought nightmares. We all spent the day at Seth's Sunday—well, minus Tess. Being around Seth and Cole and their wives was like pouring acid on an open wound. The stolen lover's glances, the hand holding, watching Seth rub Magpie's aching legs made me miss Tess and what we could have if I'd just stop carrying the past with me everywhere I went.

By Monday I decided to take Seth and Mags advice and beg Tess for forgiveness. Knowing she was getting on the plane in the morning and I'd probably never see her again terrified me almost more than the thought of Garen getting out of prison and coming after her.

I got to my office, completely forgetting that I'd ordered a new elevator and lift system to be installed. Four times the creaky old thing had gotten stuck between floors last week. It was time to update it, though I'd miss its old charm.

Knowing that it was being replaced seemed to instill a sense of nostalgia in everyone and they all wanted to ride the antique thing one last time. I'd have taken the stairs, but with my legs I never would have made it. I piled on with a dozen other people, two being Tess and Devin. I stood in the front corner near the control panel and pressed the buttons for everyone, like some elevator doorman. The poor thing rumbled to life and creaked its way to the first floor. Two people got off. After the doors closed, I chanced a look at Tess. Devin stood next to her, much too close in my opinion, and they were talking. Tess giggled, she actually giggled at something he said. *She never giggles.* He then fingered a strand of her hair. I wanted to crush his hand. Which was stupid really because I'm the one that threw her out.

I faced the number panel again, rethinking my plan. Maybe I waited too long and she'd moved on. Maybe I'd lost her for good . . . Maybe it's for the best.

The elevator ground to a halt on the second floor and two more people got off. The third floor was next. Everyone but me would be getting off this time. That's when I was going to do it. I'd take Tess's arm and hold her inside with me. I'd ask her if I could talk to her for a moment, we would go up into my office, and I'd commence my begging.

As the elevator stopped on the third floor, panic took over. I turned and faced the number panel, and everyone got off but me. The doors slowly creaked shut. I rapped my head on the wall and spit out a string of curse words that would have my mother washing my mouth with soap for a week over.

"I do believe that's a dollar seventy-five for the curse jar, Gatto."

"Augh!" I wheeled around so fast I lost my balance and fell into the corner of the elevator. Tess walked toward me, looking way too sexy in a narrow skirt and black high heels. The outfit had Lilah written all over it. I made a mental note to yell at her for it.

"I thought you'd get off on the last floor," I said, righting myself.

"You thought wrong." Tess slammed her hand into the red emergency break button. The elevator shuddered to a halt. It did not sound good.

"The owner's going to be pretty upset with you if this thing breaks," I teased lightly as she planted her hands on either side of my head, trapping me in the corner.

"Some things are worth the risks. Isn't that what you once said?" she asked, leaning in. My words were coming back to haunt me once again. This time, I didn't mind so much.

"Okay, Gatto, I'm making this offer once and once only, and if you don't accept it, I'm out of here," she said. Her face was so close to me I could kiss her if I moved forward just the smallest amount. "I'm getting on a plane and leaving this God-forsaken, frozen wasteland and going home to warm beaches and constant sunshine."

Not going to lie, loved the new aggressive sassiness. A lot. I reached for her and she brushed my hands away. "Nope. I'm in charge. You keep your hands off until I say so."

I smiled wide. *Yeah, lovin' this.*

"Here's the deal. For some unexplainable reason, I'm still madly in love with you. Maybe Nik was right. Maybe loving you is a disease. But unlike her, I can and will move on. Never again will I allow a man to dictate how I feel. Never. I'll think, feel, and do what I want. Got it?" I nodded as my hands reached for her again. She looked down at them, then back into my eyes, glaring. I dropped them to the side again.

"As I was saying, I guarantee that we'll have tough times, but I also guarantee that if I don't ask you to be mine," her eyes softened, "I'll regret it for the rest of my life, because I know in my heart you're the only one for me."

"You guys watched *Runaway Bride* last night, didn't you?"

"Maybe," she said. Her mouth ticked up on one side as she fought a smile. "Wait, you know the lines from *Runaway Bride*?"

"Seriously? It's Maggie's favorite movie. Do you know how many times I watched that thing while she lived with me? I have half the movie memorized. I have nightmares about it. And you misquoted it, by the way. She says something like I guarantee that at one point one or both of us will want out."

"No, I didn't misquote it. You see, unlike . . . Hmm. I forgot the main character's name."

"Maggie Carpenter," I said. Tess's lip twitched. I shrugged.

"Unlike Maggie Carpenter, I'll never want out. I will spend the rest of my life working on this marriage. I'll fight tooth and nail to make it successful, and if it fails, it won't be because I gave up. I love you, Booker Gatto. I want to spend forever with you. Will you please let the past go and marry me?" She blinked back tears.

Suddenly, all my confidence evaporated. All my fears were clawing at me again. All the pain, choking me.

"Booker, if you don't say something, I'm giving up on us." She swallowed. "I can't take this anymore."

"I'm scared." I forced it out softly, surprised at my own raw emotion.

"Me, too," she replied. "You and me, we're a mess."

I nodded. "Big time."

"But who's better for each other than us? Who can understand the pain, the heartache we've suffered than us? Who better to help each other heal? To mend our broken hearts? No one," she wisely pointed out. "It's time to move on."

"You don't understand." I touched her cheek, pulling my hand back immediately, as if it'd been burned. Feeling her soft skin overwhelmed me, and I needed to stay strong. "Tess, I've never loved anyone like this before. It's consuming. The feelings I have for you are so overwhelming it frightens me. You're the air I breathe." I dropped my head back against the elevator wall. "Oh man, I sound like one of Magpie's cheesy movies. I'm messing this up." I couldn't put into words the overwhelming feelings I had for her.

"Let me try. When you go to sleep at night, I'm the last thing on your mind. I'm front and center again when you wake up. You hear a funny joke and can't wait to share it with me. When we're together, you lose track of time," she said, as if reading my mind. "I walk into a room and your heart quickens." She took a deep breath. "And you feel if anything were to happen to me, you have no idea how you'd go on. In fact, you're not even sure you could."

"Exactly, and more. You have no idea what it was like for me to see your face splattered in blood that day." I shivered at the memory.

"I imagine you felt the same way *I* felt watching the man I loved being shot, *several times*, by my ex, no less," Tess pointed out. "Booker, all those feelings I described are exactly how I feel about you. Why do you think I'm here giving you one last chance to pull it together before I walk away?" Of course she felt the same way. For a smart guy, I could be quite dense at times.

Tess put her hands on my chest. "I want to share forever with you. I love you, all of you. The good and the stupid." She thumped my chest.

I gazed into those beautiful Caribbean blue eyes of hers, so deep I could see into her soul. She was right. How did I think for one minute I could let her go? Impossible, even if something horrible . . . I refused to let my mind go there. Time to put the demons to rest. No, time to kick 'em out and lock the door.

"Okay, enough talk." She took a deep breath. "I'll give you to the count of three to answer or I'm starting the elevator, getting off at the next floor, and you will never see me again." She blinked back tears. "One—"

I buried my hands in her hair and kissed her. Actually, more like devoured her. As we kissed, I let all the doubt go. Let it drain from every pore. It felt like a huge burden had been lifted from my heart. She said it best. Time to move on. I turned my head and deepened the kiss as her arms locked around me. We stood there, two damaged souls, pouring everything we had into the kiss. A beautiful, mind-blowing kiss.

I also knew that the first bet I'd ever lose was going to be in an elevator. Unfortunately, Tess pulled away. I literally groaned. She laughed. *Yeah, not seeing anything funny here.*

"Slow down, tiger. We've waited this long. Besides, I plan on taking the bet money and opening a dance studio." She punched the stop button with her palm and the thing slowly started its ascent again.

I smacked the red button with the side of my fist and it stopped, followed by an eerie grinding sound. "I'll give you the money." I tried pulling her back into a kiss.

"Did you just proposition me?" she asked, her hand firmly planted on my chest.

"No! That's not what I meant at all, I swear."

"Relax, Gatto, I was just pulling your chain." She flashed me a wicked smile. "And since you haven't actually said yes to my question yet," she slapped her hand over my mouth before I could, "there are some things you should keep in mind, aside from the fact that I'm damaged goods."

"Go ahead, but they won't change my mind," I mumbled beneath her hand.

"I like your attitude, Gatto. Okay. First of all, there's a very good reason you haven't lost that bet of yours. I hate the whole intimacy thing. I flat out hate it. It's not a temptation for me. At all."

"Pshh. One night at the Fantasy Inn and I'll fix that." I waved my hand at her silly statement.

"You are such a guy," she said, her brow arched.

"Thank you."

"That wasn't a compliment."

"What else do you think is a deal breaker?" I said, wrapping my arms around her waist.

"This one just may be, Book. I don't know if you remember or not, but I can't have children. If you marry me, there'll be no little Gattos running around destroying the house." Her sober face made me sad.

"We can adopt, Tess. The ability to have a baby does not make you a parent. It simply means your reproductive system functions properly. Parenting is love, time, and commitment."

"Are you sure?"

"Two hundred percent," I promised. "Now, is there anything else you care to throw at me, because I'm telling you, there's very little I'd consider a deal breaker."

"You tell me, what would you consider a deal breaker?" she asked, her arms folded.

I thought for a minute. "Only one thing comes to mind. If you're really a dude, that would be a deal breaker for me. I mean, I consider myself open minded and all, but that's a deal breaker."

She smacked me on the chest. "You're obnoxious sometimes."

I gathered her to me as she laughed. "I love you, Tess. I'm sorry for hurting you."

"I love you, too." She kissed me.

It didn't take long for me to get lost in her kiss again. I pulled back, breathless again. "I do need you to promise me one thing. I need you to promise me this will be a very, very, *very* short engagement." A kiss smothered her answer. I sure hoped she said yes.

Chapter 40
BOOKER

Ten years and three days later

"Happy anniversary," I said, pulling my wife next to me and holding her tight.

"It's our anniversary?" she asked, her sea blue eyes wide. She hadn't forgotten for a second. We spent last week in Rome, New York, at the Fantasy Inn, trying out the new rooms and making beautiful memories. Besides, she'd been cooking all day today, or rather trying to cook. No promises that the food was edible. I had to give her credit. She never stopped trying to learn how to cook. I had a lifetime supply of Tums in the bathroom cabinet to prove it.

"I have a gift for you, little Ms. Tease." I reached in my back pocket and removed a long, slender, gray box. I laid it across my palm and presented it to her.

"Oh, Book. Thank you." Tess took the box and carefully removed the lid. Before pushing the tissue aside, she looked up at me. "I don't believe these are the new ballet shoes I asked for."

"Ballet shoes are not romantic, Tess." Her dance studio had taken off the past few years, and she now had a one-year waiting list to get in.

"But they are practical. The side of mine tore out this morning during one of my lessons." She frowned. "My favorite pair, too."

"Go buy some new ones. You deserve them," I said, sneaking in a kiss before she finished opening the gift.

She peeled back the paper and gasped—the exact reaction I'd hoped for. She removed the bracelet from the box and I helped her put it on.

"I don't think I've ever seen a tennis bracelet like this," she said, moving her wrist back and forth.

"I had it made," I said, taking her wrist in my hand. "The ten diamonds represent the ten years we've been married. And the ten ruby hearts are for the number of years you've held my heart." I ran a finger along the dangling red hearts. They caught the light just right and twinkled.

"I love it." She leaned in to kiss me, but I placed my index finger on her lips, stopping her. First time I ever stopped one of her kisses.

"What?" she said under my finger.

"I have another gift." I stepped to the back door and grabbed the handle of my surprise. "Close your eyes."

"What is it?" she asked, her eyes pinched shut. "It better not be a snake or anything slimy."

"Tess," I balked. "Would I do something like that?"

"Yes."

I placed the gift in both her hands. "Open your eyes." She peeked first, then tossed her head back and laughed. "And it's engraved with your name." I turned the shovel over to show her. "I was going to get you a gun, but then I thought, 'Tess doesn't need a gun to protect herself'. Saved myself four hundred bucks buying this instead." I tapped the shovel.

She set it down and flew back into my arms, just where she belonged. "I think your sense of humor is the best thing about you." She kissed me. "Well, maybe the second best thing." She bounced her eyebrows.

"You're wrong, my beautiful wife." I ran my hands over her long auburn hair. "The best thing about me is you." I pressed my lips to hers and was lost in everything Tess within seconds.

"Hold on, Gatto. We have company coming," she said without breaking the kiss.

"Don't answer the door," I replied, also not breaking the kiss.

"Yuck! Get a room," came the unmistakable voice of our oldest. I moved back. There stood our three children, the two boys pretending to gag, as my daughter smiled wistfully.

"I own this entire house. I'll kiss my wife anywhere I want." I pretended to be a monster with a claw and chased them back into the family room as screams mixed with giggles filled the air. The place looked like a cyclone hit it, books and toys peppering the floor. "You'd better pick all this up before mommy sees it." With long faces they began picking up their mess.

I got back in the kitchen as Tess quickly shoved a white envelope into a kitchen drawer and closed it. "What are you hiding?" I asked.

She slapped playfully at my hand as I tried to open the door. "Sorry. That gift's for later."

"I thought you already gave me my gift this morning." I slipped my arms around her waist. "Remember, before the kids woke up." I nibbled on her neck.

"That," she said with a quiet moan, "was part one."

"Part one? How many parts are there?"

"That all depends on you." She flashed me a seductive grin.

"I do believe I created a monster," I beamed proudly, remembering how apprehensive she was on our wedding night.

"Bragging or complaining, Gatto?" She looped her arms around my neck.

"Bragging all the way, baby. Bragging all the way."

"Incorrigible." She pushed on my chest. "I need to get the games set up before everyone arrives." She gave me a swat on the butt and made her way to the family room.

As I put the finishing touches on the Caesar salad, the only contribution I was allowed to make for our anniversary meal with our friends, I couldn't help but think about the changes our life had been through over the past ten years. We had three children, our oldest son adopted seven years ago. He was my fishing buddy. We couldn't love him more if we shared DNA. Two years later twins, a girl and a boy, expanded our family thanks to Tess's sister. She offered to be a surrogate for us. We even got to be in the delivery room to watch them being born. It was an experience I'd never forget, and a debt I'd never be able to repay her sister.

Garen was convicted of accidental manslaughter in the death of the store clerk and sentenced to three years in prison. However, he received the death penalty for killing Tess's lawyer in a brutal murder trial that tested the family's mettle thanks to the media circus Garen turned it into. In the end, his old boss, Senator Graft, was the one to put the nails in Garen's coffin. After being arrested for racketeering and embezzlement of campaign funds, Graft agreed to turn states evidence against Garen for a lighter sentence.

Garen hadn't stood trial for setting fire to the trailer in an attempt to murder Tess yet. With no Statute of Limitations on murder, the prosecutors decide to hold off on those charges in case Garen ever got out a jail, however unlikely with the death penalty looming over him. We were taking no chances. The guy was one slimy piece of scum so it didn't hurt to know there were backup charges waiting for him.

Nikkolynn, on the other hand, served only five years before being released for good behavior. Within a day of her release, she and one of the prison guards ran off together to Hawaii to sell painted coconuts to tourists from a roadside stand. Nice to know that trying to kill me was only worth five years in jail.

"I guess loving me isn't an incurable disease after all," I said to the shrimp as I tossed it into the salad.

The back door sprung open. Four little Colters came screaming into the house, followed by Cole and a pregnant Lilah.

"If it isn't Ducky and the gang." I gave Lilah a hug as Cole directed the kids into the family room. Tess came flying into the kitchen, and went straight to Lilah, scooping up her hands. "I've been dying all day. How did the ultrasound go?"

Lilah glanced at Cole as he sauntered into the kitchen. "Do you want to tell them or should I?"

"By all means," Cole waved his wife on.

"We're having all girls. Again."

"Girls?" Tess laughed. "Wait, did you say again? You're having triplets again?"

"Yup. Soon we'll be a family of seven girls," Lilah said, rubbing her tummy.

They tried for two years to get pregnant on their own before going on some drug that supposedly increased your odds of conceiving. It worked great; they had triplets. Sofia loved being the older sister and helped her mother quite a bit with the babies. We all did. No way could they have done it without help.

"Have you picked out names yet?" Tess asked, leading them into the living room so Lilah could sit.

"Caboose one, two, and three," Cole said emphatically.

"Maybe," Lilah said.

"Maybe? We'll have our seven," Cole replied.

"You said I could decide how many we're going to have since it's my body that has to go through the pregnancies. I'm just not sure I'm done yet," she said simply.

"I'm going to have to pick up extra shifts at the hospital." Cole sank into the couch.

"Knock, knock." Seth entered with a platter of appetizers from his restaurant. Three streaks raced in behind him. His kids.

"Here, let me take that." I grabbed the tray from him as he picked up the kids' coats and hung them in the closet. They'd already joined the other kids in the family room.

"Mags did teach them to pick up their coats, so you know." He slipped off his boots and set them by the door.

"Is it snowing again?" I asked quietly. Tess still hadn't acclimated to New York weather.

"Yeah, and it's that lousy slushy stuff," he complained, rearranging the appetizer.

"These scallions look really good. Tess made veggie lasagna." I smiled optimistically.

"Is that what that smell is?" He wrinkled his nose. "You have to give her credit for trying."

I popped one of the bacon-wrapped scallions into my mouth after setting the tray on the counter. "Heaven," I said quietly, trying not to groan.

"I have another platter out in the car, just in case."

"Knew I could count on you." I slapped him on the back. "How's the new restaurant going?"

He'd opened Prescott's Place, a fine dining restaurant in Port Fare, right after Tess and I married. It was an instant success. Last year he opened a second one in downtown Rochester.

"I wanted to talk to you about that. I've decided to sell the city one. The head chef is amazing, and he does most of the work there anyway," Seth said. "He wants to buy me out. I'll need you to draw up a contract."

"No problem. Why the change of mind? I thought it was doing well."

"It is. Very well, in fact. But after everything that's happened, I decided to step back and take stock in myself and what kind of father I want to be."

"Seth, you're an amazing dad. You're great with your kids," I assured him. Seth was just like his father. Amazing in every way.

"I'm never home. Trying to run two businesses is a time suck. I leave for work at six a.m. and don't get home till eleven or even midnight." He slumped onto a stool. "That's not the kind of father my kids need, especially not now, after the funeral and all. No business success in the world can compensate for failing at my most important job. My family. The funeral was a wakeup call for me, you know?" I nodded, looking into his eyes, still so full of pain. "One minute she's there, greeting me with her warm loving smile, the next minute she's gone."

The funeral shook us all. She went from having a simple cold to full blown pneumonia two days later. The next day she was gone.

"It's the right decision. I'll be there in the morning when they have breakfast, and I'll be home by seven each night. It's a good thing." He took the appetizers and set them down on the table in the living room. Everyone dug in. Couldn't blame them. Seth had an incredible gift with food.

I looked around at my friends, no, my family, laughing, enjoying one another's company, as did our kids in the next room. Despite some horrific heartaches, my life was pretty great. We had our challenges, but we were there for each other.

"Daddy," Seth's youngest, Eliza, tugged on her dad's jeans. He scooped her up and kissed her cheek.

"Daddy, where's mommy again?" She patted his cheeks with her chubby hands.

"The cemetery, remember?" he said softly.

Epilogue
Maggie

"Hi, Mom." I shifted the umbrella in my hand as I set a yellow rose next to her headstone. It was the first time I'd seen it in person. When she died, I didn't have the strength to pick it out. Seth selected one for me. He showed me pictures, but they didn't do it justice. Etched into the square stone were roses and a little girl walking hand in hand with her mother. Ironically, I couldn't remember a time when I walked hand in hand with my mother. But that didn't matter anymore.

"I brought some yellow roses for Katie. She's my daughter. She died six months ago." I blinked back tears. "I decided it's about time I came to see you. I'm sorry I haven't before now. To tell you the truth, I had too much anger inside." I toed a clump of snow next to her headstone as I spoke. "I couldn't understand why I wasn't good enough for you, not a good enough child, not a good enough student, not good enough period. And it hurt, Mom, it hurt a lot." I zipped my coat a little higher against the cold.

"After I got married—oh, I married Seth, by the way. Do you remember him? You didn't care for him when you first met him, but you were wrong. He's been an amazing blessing in my life. He helped me to heal, and move on. If not for him, I don't think I'd be here today visiting you.

"As I was saying, after I got married, my heart began to soften toward you. I realized that your addiction stole who you really were. I decided it was time for me to put the past behind me and finally come visit your grave. I was eight months pregnant at the time, and just that day my doctor put me on bed rest for high blood pressure. I thought: no big deal. I'll visit after the baby's born and bring him here for you to meet. Two weeks later, after a horrible labor and delivery I might add, they placed little Eric in my arms. I looked down at his splotchy pink face as he screamed at the top of his lungs and fell in love. I placed his ear next to my mouth and spoke soft tender *I love you's*, and *Mommy's here, you're safe,* in his ear. He immediately stopped crying. He just lay in my arms, and blinked his eyes as he drank in Seth's and my voice.

"In that instant, my anger for you ignited all over again, only stronger this time. My sweet Eric was scared, and all he wanted was to hear my voice reassuring him that he wasn't alone in the world. That he was loved. He wanted what I wanted. Only, unlike Eric, I never got that from you."

I closed my eyes. I had to do this, to forgive her, despite the pain that still haunted me, that still tore at me. I steadied myself and continued.

"Each new birth fanned the anger. Three years later Samuel Cole was born, and three years after that Eliza. And of course our little Katie. She would have turned one next week." I turned from my mothers' headstone, as if somehow she could see my tears. She hated it when I cried.

"Sorry. I get emotional over my family. It's just that I love them more than anything." I dried my face with my gloved hand as a flock of geese flew overhead, squawking noisily to each other through the falling snow. I smiled, remembering how much Eliza loved to chase the birds as we walked along the canal.

Collecting myself, I faced her again and continued. "It took me a while, but eventually I pushed past the anger, realizing I needed to forgive you so *I* could heal. I doubt I'll ever understand why you hurt me like you did, but it is what it is." I chuckled. "And I'm not even sure you care, but I do forgive you." As I said the words, my heart felt lighter. "I'm glad I came," I said, mostly to myself.

The snow finally stopped. I shook the wet mess off my umbrella and snapped it closed. "I have to go. Our friends are celebrating their tenth anniversary and his wife is surprising him with a Caribbean cruise. She's petrified of water, but she knows how badly he wants to go. I want to see his face when he opens the envelope."

The clouds were breaking apart and rays of sunshine began punching through, spotlighting the ground. "Looks like it's going to be a beautiful day after all." I brushed the slush from the top of her headstone. "I'll come by more often. I promise. I'll bring the kids by, too. They enjoy it when we visit Seth's parents. Eliza swears she can see them flying around us whenever we stop by."

I repositioned the rose before turning toward my car, stopping after a few steps. I angled back to my mother's grave, admiring the headstone again for just a moment.

"I love you, Mom."

Domestic Abuse Hotline 1-800-799-7233

Sherry Gammon

Other novels by Sherry:

Exciting news! Book one of the Port Fare Series, Unlovable, is being made into a movie! For all the latest news on the move, like my *Unlovable Movie Page!*

https://www.facebook.com/UnlovableTheMovie

Unlovable ~ Book One of the Port Fare Series*:* High school senior Maggie Brown is truly the poster child for Heroin Chic, complete with jutting bones and dark-ringed eyes. But drugs are not Maggie's problem... her mother is. Seth Prescott is an undercover cop assigned to Port Fare High, and despite his job, he's developed strong feelings for Maggie. Seth's working tirelessly to flush out the sadistic drug peddlers that have invaded the small town of Port Fare, New York, while Maggie fights to stay alive as the search turns deadly. Seth and Maggie's romantic journey is one of humor, heartbreak and self-discovery as their world is about to change forever.

Unbelievable (Book 2 of the Port Fare Series): Deliah Lopez Dreser's in town to take care of family business. They say the apple doesn't fall far from the tree, but there's more to Lilah than meets the eye. Cole's in danger of losing his heart when this firestorm throws sparks his way. However, is she simply playing him for the fool in order to exact revenge for her brother's murders? Maggie and Seth's reaction when the truth is revealed pushes friendship to the limit. And this time around it won't be a Dreser causing an uproar in Port Fare. It will be Cole's good friend Booker. But does Booker have it all wrong?

Not So Easy (Souls in Peril): Senior Max Sanchez has it all. He's the star pitcher for Port Fare High's baseball team. He's dating the head cheerleader, Emma McKay, and he has a great group of friends. Junior JD Miller's life is Not So Easy. Unlike Max, JD struggles with making friends. He's a social misfit, and he's being bullied at every turn. He's also barely surviving. A tragic accident changes everything, merging their lives together, and Max soon learns that life is not so easy for everyone. Max works to the point of exhaustion trying to help JD survive the chaos that is his life, and his eyes are opened to a world he had no idea even existed. Not so Easy is a story about hope, surviving, and never giving up.

Pete & Tink ~ A novella**:** Pete Pancerella loves two things in life: Video games and Spongy Crèmes. He's happy, content, and he's also a geek. All that is about to change when his mother wishes upon a star and Tink answers the call. But will it take more than a five-and-a-half inch faery to whip this manga-loving goofball into shape?

A Fantasy Christmas ~ Loving Marigold : Young Marigold Yarrow has a secret. She's also in love with Jack Mahoney. In the middle of her ninth grade year, Jack's family up and moves to Port Fare, New York, leaving the small town of Sugar Maple, West Virginia - and Marigold - far behind. Nine years later Jack and Marigold meet again. They join forces to weed out the shady Abbott boys. The unscrupulous brothers are illegally selling moonshine near her home on Sugar Maple Ridge. And they'll do anything to get Marigold to leave the ridge. Anything. But this time it could be magic that tears Jack and Marigold apart.

The Experiment: *Co-written by Jeffrey and Cindy C Bennett:* Time is running out for the Collaborative's oppressive rule of the remote world Senca One. The government attempts to suppress the escalating riots, even while seeking to further their experiments. When their parents are taken, triplets Juliet, Cilla, and Emiah Tripp set out to locate them, and soon discover they are at the center of a hunt to capture *them.*

ABOUT THE AUTHOR

Sherry Gammon's debut novel Unlovable quickly rose to the top seller list on Amazon. She has added several more novels to her body of work.

Sherry and her wonderfully supportive husband, currently call Upstate New York home, which is also the setting for her novels. It is where they are raising their family. Sherry has a degree in Legal Assisting, and served as a medical technician in the Air Force. She and her husband worked in foster care for a number of years, from which they adopted their youngest son. She has worked in the education system for a number of years, and is currently lucky enough to be teaching teenage girls, ages 12-18. She has lived in Michigan, California, Utah, Texas, Pennsylvania, and the beautiful, but over-taxed state of New York where she has spent the last eleven years, and now considers home. It is where she spends her nights writing instead of sleeping :}

Please drop by my webpage and say hi! I LOVE hearing from my readers!

~ Find me ~

WordpaintingsUnlimited.com

Twitter ~ Twitter.com/SherryGammon

Facebook~Facebook.com/sherrygammonauthor

Instagram ~ instagram.com/authorsherrygammon

Pinterest~ pinterest.com/sherrygammon/

Goodreads~Goodreads.com/author/show/4623294.**Sherry_Gammon**

www.ingramcontent.com/pod-product-compliance
Lightning Source LLC
Chambersburg PA
CBHW070845260626
47170CB00007B/2511